When Angels Fall

A NOVEL

IRENE LIEBENSFELD

Edited by Sheridan McCarthy
Cover art by Irene Liebensfeld
Text design by Diana Wade

Published 2021 by Field of Love Publishing
Manufactured in the United States of America.
ISBN 978-0-578-93743-4

To George,
each sunrise and sunset was made
beautiful by sharing it with you.

To our sons, Aaron and Alex,
the greatest need of the human spirit
is not to be loved, but to give love.
Loving you has given my life purpose.

CONTENTS

PROLOGUE

"Assignment: Memories. Due Friday." I read these words on a blackboard as I entered my senior English class back in 1974. I owe a lot to my dedicated and exceptional teacher, Mr. Williams. Still, I often struggled with his assignments. His instructions were intentionally ambiguous. When asked to give more direction, he'd respond, "Further parameters would only limit your creativity. After all, this is a creative writing class. Use your imagination."

It took me several attempts at his "Memories" assignment before I had something I felt I could turn in. On my first attempt, I tried writing about the origin of the word, starting with the Greek goddess of memories, Mnemosyne. I wrote,

> It is said she was born of earth and sky. She's the mother of the muses, making her the source of art, poetry, literature, dance, and even music. Memory is the soul of our creativity.

However, I could hear Mr. Williams's voice in my head. He'd say, "Miss Ward, you're regurgitating other writer's ideas. Where are yours?" So I threw that paper away.

Then I began writing about the nature of memories.

Memories are fickle, capricious, and mutable. Sometimes they're clear and sharp like a knife. Other times they're ghostly, phantasmagorical specters tauntingly sailing past our peripheral vision. I try to look back at my earliest memories, but all I see are brief, ephemeral vignettes. These have colors and textures, but many details elude capture. When I successfully pull back the gossamer veil of time, I can see a pair of milk-white arms reaching down to me in my crib. I've been crying but stop when I see these familiar arms. Frustratingly, I'm unable to make out my rescuer's face. I can see a shimmering cascade of red hair falling toward me as the light streaming through a window paints it copper. Even my skin recalls how the strands tickle my arms as I am lifted into a loving embrace. This memory is comforting. Why can I see so many details but not the face? These must have been my sister's arms, for she is the only one in our family with red hair. I haven't seen her since I was five.

Emma married at eighteen and moved to Washington State in June of '63. Nate, her husband, got a job in the timber industry out west. When my sister exited our house for the last time, Daddy said I clung to her as if my life depended on it. 'You screamed like your limbs were being torn clear off.' According to my brothers, I was inconsolable and wouldn't utter a word for weeks. My memories of Emma are fragmented and fleeting, and yet, there are times when I hear a particular lullaby or a tone of voice that makes me pause. These touch on something far back in the recesses of my mind that I can't pull forward into the light, but I know it has something to do with Emma. Is that a memory or just a feeling born from experience?"

Frustrated by the elusiveness of these memories, I abandoned them. I want to write about something more tangible. Diving in the ocean of memories, I found what I thought was my first complete memory. It made me wonder, *Why does the mind record one event but not another?* It's strange; I can't recall anything about that pivotal day when my sister left us, but I can remember a day a few months later with complete clarity. Trying to recall early memories, I pulled on a string and unraveled others, for no memory stands alone—each is entwined with others. I found a memorable day that I thought others would recall, so I wrote about it for the assignment. However, long after the assignment was turned in and graded, I kept swimming in memory's ocean, where I found my muse and a deep desire to write. Through writing I've discovered myself and illuminated the times and legacy that shaped me.

Legacy has more than one meaning. For the rich, it is the accumulated wealth left by parents and grandparents ensuring their privileged existence. For the poor, it's more than a few pieces of well-worn furniture. Like war, poverty leaves scars. A mother who survived bombings might show panic when she hears thunder, thereby instilling a fear of storms in her children. Many survivors of the Great Depression hoard and reuse things like aluminum foil. An inheritance is what we receive from our parents. A legacy is much deeper; it's generational.

Like every family, mine has a body: a head, a heart, and legs to propel it. Like any living organism, it's vulnerable to disease. Family secrets can be a cancer slowly eating away healthy tissue. My story tells about a family's struggle to overcome a legacy of poverty and the consequences of lies and hidden truths.

There are few roads out of poverty. Some men dream of a sports contract but only an elite few obtain it. Education offers the most reliable escape. Education is expensive, but the lack of it is costlier. If you don't see success in your family, it is hard to imagine it as a possibility. To succeed you need vision, ability, opportunity, and good teachers, but most importantly, you need tenacity. I am a determined young woman encouraged by changing ideals but struggling with the limits of my gender. My people were baptized in poverty. I am a daughter of the sixties: a turbulent time of war, protests, change, and hope. Like many others, there is no one event that defined me; rather it's a composite of experiences. My heroes are conflicted—they are both protagonists and antagonists. The hurdles have been many; each one crossed has strengthened my resolve. My dream is to grow wings to fly beyond the caste and character to which I was born.

Part One

1963

CHAPTER ONE

❦✣❧

MEMORY

*T*o understand one memory, you must know what occurred before it. This is because our state of mind colors our perceptions and selects what's imprinted into our brains. Ask five people to recall a distant event, and you'll get five different stories.

This is my memory of November 22, 1963. In the weeks before, I had been feeling abandoned, angry, and neglected. Five months prior my sister, Emma, moved to the West Coast. She'd been a second mother to me. Adding to my sense of desertion, my brother Buddy started first grade, leaving me alone during the day with Mamma. Buddy is fifteen months older. Until school took him, he was my constant companion, playground protector, and trusted confidant. For me, this day is the point from which time is measured, the way historians use Christ's birth to delineate calendars. This day's events are indelible and can be played back like an old movie.

It's a sunny, crisp fall day in the District of Columbia. After lunch, Mamma shoos me out of the house. It's Friday, and the Thanksgiving holiday begins soon. I'm looking forward to having my brother playmates home. Wearing my new pink sweater, knitted by my Aunt Martha, I lie down in the backyard of our row house and stare up at the sky. From my grassy bed, I breathe in the musty perfume of decaying autumn leaves. My imagination wanders across the sky; motionless clouds patiently wait for me to decipher their patterns.

It's taken awhile, but I've finally adjusted to the daily solitude caused by my brothers' and sister's absence. I've even learned to savor some of the quiet and calm. Today Daddy is working the day shift, leaving Mamma and me alone. The usual mayhem, discourse, and discord are on hold. All is still except for the muted sounds of the vacuum mixed with Mamma singing along with Miss Peggy Lee on the radio. They're singing "Fever." Blended voices softly filter out to the yard through an open window.

Mamma's singing is a good sign that she's returned from wherever she retreats to inside herself after a long battle with Daddy. As usual, it was she who raised the white flag and conceded defeat, followed by moving sluggishly around the house for days, silent like some vacant zombie or somnambulist. Singing means Mamma is coming back from her dark place. Listening to her, I'm content, nearly happy. The slightly damp grass cools the back of my shins as Miss Lee and Mamma harmonize. I hear, "Daddy, oh don't you dare. He gives me fever."

Abruptly, the music stops. A newscaster's voice comes on in a firm, steady drone. Soon after, the vacuum goes quiet; all I can hear is the incoherent buzz of the radio man's pronouncements. Suddenly, Mamma starts crying, "Oh God, oh dear God, dear, dear God, no." Her voice steadily rises with each plea to the Divine. Frightened, I run into the house. Mamma seems dazed; tears well up in her eyes. She's still holding the silent vacuum wand when I come over to her and tug at her skirt.

"What is it, Mamma? Why are you crying?" I beg, terrified by the sudden change and distress in my protector. The radio man's voice continues to drone on.

Mamma turns and seems surprised to see me. She releases the vacuum wand, letting it drop to the floor with a thud. Scooping me up in a firm hold, she hugs me a bit too tightly as she says, "Oh, Babydoll, oh my sweet girl, they shot the president!"

About an hour after Mamma's outcry, my brothers start streaming in. Their unspoken fears are confirmed; the president is dead. On the radio, "The Star Spangled Banner" plays as our neighbors return home from work earlier than usual. In disbelief, we gather with them in our courtyard. Many are crying, and I wonder why when they've never met this man, the president. Some speak about the bright promise the young vibrant, couple represented to our nation and the world. Before long Daddy joins us and holds Mamma in his arms as she weeps on his shoulder. I peer up at them, terrified by the sight of seeing the big people breaking down. I'm scared, but no one seems to notice me; they're too occupied with the news and with each other. At that moment, I think of Emma and ache for the safety of her protective arms.

Now, after the passage of years, I am grateful we didn't own a television back then and that Mamma sent me to my room before she, along with the rest of our family, headed next door to crowd around our neighbor's TV set. However, when she sent me to bed that night, I felt alienated: a grudge I held on to tightly for a long time. When I begged Mamma to take me with them, she told me, "You might be five years old, but that's still too young to be watching the news, Babydoll. Go on to bed. We'll be right next door."

Next door was just on the other side of a wall; even so, I felt abandoned once more. I couldn't understand that they were trying to protect me. I didn't begin to let go of that hurt until at thirteen I saw a film of Jackie Kennedy in her perfect pink pillbox hat trying to climb out the back of a moving convertible, seemingly to retrieve pieces of her husband's head. Then I understood why they'd left me behind.

However, being absent from the evening news wasn't why I ultimately felt betrayed.

Our neighbors, being better off than us, owned a telephone in addition to a television. Part of Mamma's payment for watching their two kids after school was emergency use of their phone. Emma must have thought it an emergency. She and her husband, Nate, called that night. Everyone, including Buddy, spoke with them and heard Emma's voice; everyone, that is, but me. Though I had tried to hang on in the five months since she'd left, I was losing my mental pictures of her. I couldn't fully recall the sound of her laughter or the turn of her lips as she smiled. The only distinct image I had of her face was the black-and-white photo of her high school graduation that I'd stolen from the living room and placed next to my bed. What I had of her was dissolving with time until she seemed more fictional than real. Later, when I was older and started corresponding with her, she became my "pen pal" and eventually my confidant and mentor. Yet back in November of 1963, she was far away and there was no one I wanted more than her.

During my earliest years, I had two mothers: my sister was the playful, comforting, and steady mother while Mamma was the all-business and sometimes emotionally distant one. Daddy told me that Emma used to carry me around on her hip, calling me her own little baby doll. "That's what got you your name," he informed me. After her departure, I missed her singing, laughter, and soapy-clean-smelling skin. I missed the morning light spilling through the window and falling upon her hair, making it shine like a brand-new penny as she dressed me. I ached for her easy way of explaining things. I yearned to hear her sing "Some Enchanted Evening" as I drifted off to sleep. I missed how she'd bring me to her bed when I woke frightened. Most of all, I missed how she made me feel safe.

So, when on the morning after Kennedy's assassination I rose to learn that everyone had spoken with Emma except me, a sense of betrayal overtook me, leaving me mistrustful and lonely. For Americans, the days of Camelot were over. On national television two days later, a man shot and killed Kennedy's accused assassin, thus silencing him forever. For many Americans, faith and trust in our government could not be restored by the Warren Commission's findings that there was no conspiracy. Such feelings mirrored my own: trust was not something I gave out easily after those days of loss and perceived betrayal.

Part Two

1964

CHAPTER TWO

❧ ✤ ❧

SWIMMING

Sometimes Daddy would take a few of us kids with him to work. Daddy told Mamma it was so she could get some work and the shopping done without us little ones slowing her down. Buddy had a different take on it; he said it was to make sure she didn't run off again. That scared me, the idea of Mamma running away and not taking me.

Since before I was born, Daddy had a second, part-time job at Rosedale Pool in Kingman Park. He maintained the pool and grounds. Sometimes he'd teach kids to swim. At the end of each summer, he and Mamma organized a swimming pageant for all the kids to participate, à la Esther Williams with a little Neptune on the side. Mamma organized the decorations, painting large pieces of cardboard adorning the back wall at the far end of the pool, opposite the diving boards. The pageants were held in the evening and everyone from the neighborhood came.

Each time we went to the pool, I'd take off almost as soon as the tires stopped turning. I'd stay out of Daddy's sight until it was time to go home, when I'd magically reappear, my timing aided by the neighborhood's communication network. Daddy never knew how far I wandered, nor did he ask. Sometimes, if I had a nickel in my pocket, I'd head to the DGS store up on the corner at Benning Road. Or I'd go with some of the local kids, and we'd search for lost change near the bus stop at Benning and 17th Street. If we were successful, we'd buy some penny candy or a soda or Popsicle and share our bounty.

We didn't live far from Fort Lincoln. In our neighborhood, we were the poorest kids. Our secondhand clothes gave us away. This was a fact the neighborhood kids delighted in pointing out. Mamma bought most of our clothes at the Goodwill Charity Store up on Bladensburg Road.

I always felt accepted in Kingman Park. Everyone there seemed happy to see me and never made fun of my clothes. One afternoon, I followed my friend Silky home to get some lunch. Her mama, Miss Althea, was widely known as the best cook in Kingman. I liked listening to her talk; like my daddy, she was from North Carolina, and they shared a similar accent and vernacular. Unlike Mamma, there were no rules to their speech. It wasn't merely the relaxed way of talking in Kingman that reminded me of Daddy and put me at ease; it was their friendly, welcoming, generous ways and their nearness to God. I loved going over to Miss Althea's house. Everything she cooked tasted better. Even plain rice with butter was ten times better than at home. Every grain was fluffy, slightly salty, and sweet. And there was always a plate for one more in Miss Althea's house.

After we ate, we stacked ourselves up on the front porch steps. The men stayed inside. The porch roof created shade that stretched down the steps and stopped at the sidewalk's edge. Miss Althea was at the top, Silky's older half-sister, Odella, was next, then Silky, then me. The one on top cornrowed the hair on the next one down, and so on, leaving my hands free at the bottom, which I suppose was planned because nobody would trust their hair to me. I loved that communal, sisterly activity while sharing news, gossip, opinions, all while Silky deftly moved her fingers through my hair.

It was so hot the air seemed to have waves in it, smelling stale and muggy. With the bright sun blazing in the bleached blue sky, Silky's uncle Isaac emerged from the white light. His whistling could be heard before his features came into full view. With the sun behind him, all we could see was the figure of a man approaching until he got very close, his face only becoming recognizable when he joined us in the shade. "Well hello, Isaac," said Odella.

He plopped down next to her mother. Pointing a long finger, he asked, "Now, who's that cracker and what she doin' here? You ain't start lookin' after no White folks' kids now, have you, Althea?"

"She's our guest," she countered.

"She's Mr. Jack's youngest," added Odella.

"Mr. Jack from the pool?" asked Isaac.

"How many Mr. Jacks you know, fool?" said Miss Althea. She didn't seem pleased to see him.

"Mr. Jack got another girl?"

"What I just tell you? You deaf as well as blind? She's Mr. Jack's."

"I ain't blind. She don't look much like his redheaded girl. But now you mentioned it, she look a bit like Mr. Jack hisself. If she's his, I guess she's okay. She can stay."

Offended, Miss Althea responded, "Did I ask for your permission? I don't need you tellin' me who can and who can't sit on my front stoop. What you doing here, anyway? Ain't you supposed to be washing dishes at the Grill?"

"I don't work there no more."

"You don't work there no more? What happened this time? You ain't been there more than three months."

"You know what that honky son of a bitch called me?"

"Isaac, you watch your mouth now."

"Althea, as I was headin' to work, the bus overheated, broke down. So I jumped off and ran eight blocks to get to work. Not likely Bob Hayes or Otis Davis could've run much faster. I ain't never been late once before. But 'fore I could catch my breath and explain, Mr. Triandos ups and calls me a lazy-assed mavro just 'cause I was ten minutes late. That God damn ..."

"Isaac! Don't you be usin' the good Lord's name in thataway! You hear me now?"

"Yeah, Althea, I hear ya. It's been a rough day, and the day's only half spent."

"So, you up and quit again. You got another job waitin' for ya?"

"Nah, and don't you be lecturin' me none. I'll get me another one."

"And you'll quit that one soon as some cracker says something you don't like."

"You gotta have respect for yourself 'fore anyone else do. They ain't gonna show us respect unless we demand it."

"Yeah, and I hope that respect fills your stomach and pays that electric bill."

"Ah, come on now, Althea, don't be thataway. I don't wanna be arguin' with my big sister right now. Hey, you got some cold beer in that fridge of yours? It's awful hot, Sis, and I sure am thirsty."

She flicked her head toward the front door while making a clicking sound with her tongue. "Next time you can bring some your own self."

"Next time I have a few bills in my pocket, you know I will." Before he rose he looked over at me, caught my eyes, and said, "Girl, your old man is all right. You tell him that Isaac Washington hasn't forgotten what he done for us."

After he got up and was swallowed by the dark shadows inside the house, joining Silky's dad and the other men, I asked, "Miss Althea, ma'am, what did my daddy do?"

"You don't know?"

"No, ma'am, I don't."

"Well, you know about segregated pools, don't you?"

I shook my head. "What's say-gray-gated mean?"

"It means only White folks got to use the swimming pools." "Why would that be, Miss Althea? That don't seem right."

"Well, I guess you's too young," she said and paused. "Guess that's a good thing too." She took a deep breath and then continued. "Not that long ago, it used to be all these pools were for Whites only. Come a scorcher like today, we could only watch them White kids whooping it up and having a good ol' time in the cool water while we wilted in the swampy, thick-as-grits air. The only swimmin' left us was in the Potomac and that's a dangerous, deceitful, two-faced river. It looks all calm and gentle on top, but don't you trust it. Below is a whole 'nother story. On a hot day it looks mighty inviting, like it's calling your name. But that river will snatch you up 'fore you know it and pin you down on its bottom and won't let you go until you're good and dead. You remember that! You hear me?" she said sternly and waited for my reply.

"Yes, ma'am, I'll remember."

"See you do. That river is a thief. Back when we didn't have no swimming pools to cool off in, child, sometimes it be so hot it be too tempting to stay out of it for some. Every summer we'd find some poor child drowned. Your daddy was the caretaker of two of them White swimmin' pools. On real hot nights, we could count on him showing up. He'd pull out his keys, remove them fence chains, and let us all go for a nighttime dip. Even after his work was done, he'd stick around a while so as we could have our fill. He'd have been fired, or worse, if he'd been caught."

"But I don't understand, Miss Althea, why'd they keep coloreds out?"

"You'll have to ask them White folks. Ain't no good account, I can promise you that."

"Why ain't any other Whites comin' now?"

"That's another question for them Whites. We ain't stoppin' 'em; you can be sure of that."

When I got back to the pool, Daddy was packing up to go. I told him that Isaac Washington said to say hello and that he remembered what Daddy did for them. "Isaac Washington? Haven't seen him in a coon's age. Shoot, he must be well into his twenties by now. How's he been doin'?"

"He seems okay I guess, 'cept he's out of work right now. His sister, Miss Althea, is none too happy about that."

"Really, do you know where he lives?"

"No, sir, but I know where he is right now. He's at Miss Althea's house."

"Do you know where that is?"

"Yes, sir, it's not far; it's over on Gales Street."

"Okay, show me. I've got somethin' that might interest him."
When we drove in front of Silky's house, Daddy parked the truck
and got out. I peeled myself off the vinyl seat and stepped out of
the hot truck to stand on the sidewalk under a tree as I waited. The
old muffler must have announced our arrival. Before Daddy was
halfway to the porch, Isaac came out to greet Daddy.

"Why, hello there, Mr. Ward. What can I do for ya, sir?"

"I've come to see what I might do for you. I just stopped by to
ask if you or someone ya know is lookin' for work."

"I might know of someone. What kinda work is it?"

"Down at the railway yard they're hiring a new porter. It's
just for a couple of months. One of the old-timers got hurt and is
gonna be out for a while. Would ya be interested?"

"Yes, sir, Mr. Ward, I surely would."

"Now, even though it's just for a few months, if they like ya
you'll have a good chance when a permanent position opens up.
Do ya know what it'll mean working for the union?"

"Yes, sir. It's the brotherhood, sir," Isaac responded as he
straightened up to stand a bit taller.

"That's right, Isaac. It's a good job, a union job, and I hope you
get it. You'll need to dress sharp when you meet the boss. Dress in
a suit if you've got one. If not, a starched white shirt will do, but use
extra starch. Wear dark slacks and put a sharp crease in 'em. Make
sure your shoes are shined so you can see yourself."

"Yes, Mr. Ward. I'll wear my Sunday suit. Just tell me when and where and I'll be there."

"Monday, I'll meet ya at the corner of Second and I streets at seven in the mornin'. Don't be late, Isaac—I won't have time to wait. I'll take ya to meet the boss." With that, Daddy headed back toward our old white truck.

Isaac called after him, "Thank you, Mr. Ward. I'll be waiting for ya. Don't worry, I won't be late."

I was jumping back into the truck when Daddy replied, "See ya Monday, then." Daddy got in, started the engine, and drove off toward 17th Street. As the truck's shock absorbers were long since shot, we bounced along the road. Daddy turned on the radio. A newscaster was talking about President Johnson signing something. "Thank the good Lord," Daddy said. "Jim Crow's dead." Then he changed the station. I didn't know about Jim Crow or why Daddy was glad the man was dead, but I didn't ask. Later, I'd ask Mamma or my oldest brother, Eugene. Daddy wasn't good at explaining certain things, and I sensed Mr. Crow was one of them. When Daddy heard Muddy Waters singing, "You Can't Lose What You Ain't Never Had," he stopped turning the dial and began singing along. When that ended, the Joy Boys, Willard Scott and Ed Walker, came on. Daddy laughed along with their humorous banter for the rest of the ride home.

My straight, yellow hair was a novelty in Kingman Park. Most of girls there wanted a turn at playing with it. I never came home without it being cornrowed or plaited. It drove Mamma crazy. That day was no different. As soon as I got in the door, she took out a comb, grabbed me, and started to pick out the rows impatiently. When she was finished, my hair stuck out in every direction. I'd look like some mad banshee until I got around to washing it. "Why do you let them braid your hair every time? Can't you say no just once?"

"But I like it, Mamma."

"You like your hair like that?" she asked while staring at me incredulously.

"No, Mamma, I like them messing with my hair."

"But sweetheart, the neighbors think we're bad enough without you coming home looking like Buckwheat."

Offended, I snapped, "I don't look nothin' like no Buckwheat."

"Please, Charlotte, you don't want to sound ignorant. You know better than to use a double negative. Say, 'I don't look anything like Buckwheat.'"

"I don't look anything like Buckwheat." I parroted her words, tone, and Philadelphia accent.

"Tell that to Mrs. Sawyer. She shakes her head and rolls her eyes each time you come home with your hair done up that way."

"What's it to her how I wear my hair? She ought to mind her own business and her own kids; that Larry is a lying, foul-mouthed cheat and Bobby is a pervert."

"Watch your mouth. You don't even know what a pervert is."

"I know it's nothing good, just like Bobby's no good."

She gave me a hard stare, and I knew it was time to shut up before I was banished to my room without supper. Instead, I went to set the table. After dinner, I asked Mamma the same question I asked Miss Althea: "Mamma, why did Whites keep coloreds out of the swimming pools?"

Mamma thought about it for a moment then answered, "Ignorance, Babydoll, plain old ignorance. The truth is people fear what they don't understand and hate what they fear. Now, go wash your hair. I've got the kitchen to clean." I wanted to ask Mamma about Jim Crow, but thought better of it. So I went in search of Eugene.

CHAPTER 3

℘❖ℛ

BOZO AND RONALD

When he got the chance, Daddy worked on cars for extra cash. He was a mechanic. It was something he learned growing up on a farm, working on tractors and trucks, and perfected while in the army in Europe during World War II. He said the skill saved his life; because he could fix things, he was too valuable a soldier to be put on the front lines. For most of the war, he stayed back with the brass. He still saw battles, and had to dodge mortar shells and bombs. Near the war's end, he was sent home when he got some shrapnel in his leg and arm. Between his job at the railroad, the pools, and fixing cars, Daddy seemed to be always working, especially in those earlier years.

One time, for payment for fixing a neighbor's car he got a used TV. The man had just bought a color set and didn't need his old black-and-white one anymore. We were all excited. The Ward children could finally keep up with the other kids at school and at the playground when they talked about TV shows. Back in February, we missed seeing the Beatles on the *Ed Sullivan Show*, and the kids at school talked of nothing else for a solid week. Our first TV was a 21-inch Philco console set with two knobs on the front. The base swiveled so you could turn it to face different directions.

That first TV night at the Wards', we watched *Lassie*. June Lockhart was playing little Timmy's mom. Right after Timmy found out that they might be moving to Australia, a commercial came on. In it, an announcer introduced the new spokesman for McDonald's restaurants, a clown named Ronald McDonald. The clown's voice sounded familiar. As I listened, I tried to recall where I'd heard that voice before. "Hey, kids, isn't watching TV fun?" said the clown. "Especially when you've got delicious McDonald's hamburgers! My magic tray here keeps me well supplied with McDonald's hamburgers, french fries, and milkshakes." His nose was a drink cup. On his head was a rectangle-shaped cardboard tray with a large drink to one side. In front of his striped costume at his waist was a tray with a drink, a hamburger, and some french fries. Each time he removed a hamburger, another one magically appeared, so he had an endless supply. "Watch for me on TV—we'll have lots of fun!" he chuckled. Then he shook his own hand, and it honked—that was the Ronald McDonald's handshake.

"He looks familiar, and his voice too," I said.

"Yeah, he does sound real familiar," agreed Buddy.

The clown's voice hit a switch, and a light went off in my head illuminating a memory once lost and forgotten. In the picture in my head, he was a different clown. Slowly, the memory became more and more focused. There were no stripes on his other costume. His hair and nose were red. It was the day Chip's Cub Scout troop was on the Bozo the Clown show. Eugene had just moved up to Boy Scouts, but he was going with Chip's troop too because it used to be his, so they were letting him come along. They were dressed in their uniforms. Eugene's was olive green and Chip's was navy blue. We were all excited. Daddy had worked the night shift and came down the stairs to say goodbye as we were heading out the door. "Don't forget to wave to me, boys. I'll be watching at the Panotowskis' house," he said. Because we didn't have a TV then, he'd planned to watch the program with Mr. Panotowski, whose son was in the same troop. The two men wanted to watch their boys on television rather than live in the studio.

We crossed town and eventually turned off Nebraska Avenue onto a circular driveway. There stood a long, imposing building with a tall flagpole. The building had a short brick tower toward one side with a sign that read WRC-TV in red letters. I gazed up; behind the building soared a large metal tower like a huge Erector Set.

We were late, so as soon as we pulled up the two boys jumped out of the car and ran off to join their troop, who were entering the building. After parking, Mamma grabbed my hand and rushed Buddy and me into the station. There in the lobby was a large sign saying NBC with a rainbow-colored peacock on it. Our local WRC was an affiliate of NBC. We were directed into a studio and climbed some bleachers to watch the program, grabbing the last seats on a bench. A woman moved over to make room for us, and Mamma and she got into a conversation. I had to sit on Mamma's lap. The lady's son was there too but from a different Scout troop in Virginia. When we saw Chip and Eugene come out, Buddy tried to yell to them, but Mamma stopped him with one of her looks. A Rocky and Bullwinkle cartoon was airing on several TV monitors that were scattered across the stage. The boys filed out from behind a large curtain and were instructed to take a seat on a big red circus ring with white stars painted around it. As they waited for Bozo, they chatted or looked around the stage.

Back in front of our new TV set, I interrupted my reminiscence and a Lux soap commercial and said, "I remember now—he's Bozo the Clown. I know that voice. It's him. I'm sure!" I nearly shouted.

"It's Willard Scott. He's on the radio, one of the Joy Boys," contradicted Eugene. "That's where you heard him."

"That's not what I am remembering. I've seen him before. I know it. He was the clown when you were on TV. You gotta remember Bozo!"

"That's right," chimed Buddy.

"Eugene already told you!" snapped Chip. "He's one of the Joy

Boys. Now forget about it, will you?"

"He may be on the radio, but he's Bozo too. I know that voice. You can't forget that voice. Don't you remember? You were all sitting on a big round bench when Bozo came over to you and introduced himself. He was really, really tall and you …"

"Forget it! Just forget it, will you!" Chip barked. "The show's about to come back on. Shut your fat trap and be quiet for once." Just then Timmy came back on the TV screen with Lassie. My feelings were hurt, and I sulked as we watched the remaining show. When Timmy learned that Lassie couldn't come with them to Australia, he got real upset too. His father patiently explained it wouldn't be fair to Lassie. "If we bring her, she'd be in quarantine for six months." He was asking Timmy to do what was right for the dog and not just think of himself. As the show played on, I was confused by Chip's harsh reaction. I couldn't understand why he snapped at me. But even more unusual was Eugene. Why hadn't he defended me? Eugene was always our protector and peacemaker.

The more I thought about it, the more pieces of memory fell into place, creating a clearer picture. When Bozo met each boy, he let them squeeze his nose, which honked. It was remembering the big red honking nose that pulled all the pieces together. When it was Chip's turn, instead of honking it he ripped the glued-on nose right off the poor clown's face. From his facial reaction, it must've hurt. Chip saw Bozo's look and took off running with the nose still in his hand. When the clown tried to chase his little brother, Eugene leapt into action and tried to tackle the six-foot-three-inch clown. He could only slow Bozo down by hanging onto his leg. Finally, Bozo caught Chip and snatched him up. With Chip under one arm and Eugene still wrapped around a leg, he exited the stage. That's when I heard Mamma say to the lady sitting next to us, "I feel so sorry for those boys' mothers." I tried to say something to her. How could she not know those were her boys? But when I tried to ask she gave me the same look she used on Buddy, and I knew to be quiet.

The cartoons were back on the monitors, followed by some commercials. When they finished, the big clown returned with his nose reattached, but my brothers were nowhere to be seen for the rest of the show.

The next thing I could remember was coming home. I was excited to see Daddy. "Daddy, Daddy, did you see the boys? Did you see Bozo?" I yelled as we entered the house.

His response offended me; he pushed me aside when I tried to hug him. Looking at Buddy and me as he removed his belt, he commanded, "You two, go to your rooms and stay put 'til I say so. I've got some talkin' to do with y'all's brothers."

From the sounds coming up from the living room and through my bedroom door, it seemed Daddy was letting his belt do most of the talking. It was when this memory floated into my head that I finally realized why Chip didn't want to reminisce about Bozo, especially with our parents only a few feet away over at the dining room table. Thankfully, they were oblivious to our conversation and absorbed in their own.

CHAPTER FOUR

❧✧☙

FREEDOM SUMMER

*I*t was a hot, muggy June day and school was out for the summer. Sweltering heat sent the temperature soaring to the upper 90s. A few house fans provided limited comfort. Searching for relief, we spent our days at crowded local pools, Sandy Point State Park beach, or playing with the neighborhood kids in someone's lawn sprinkler. When some boys managed to open up a fire hydrant, we gleefully played in its gushing fountain until the fire department arrived to shut it off. Despite the heat and humidity, I was enjoying the slower pace and having my brothers home.

One Thursday in June, Mamma, Buddy and I returned home after spending the day at the pool. Eugene and Chip had preferred to make money that day; they'd spent the day mowing lawns. After getting supper started, Mamma joined Buddy and me at the dining table. From the kitchen, she brought out a pitcher of chilled sweet tea and three glasses filled with ice. An electric fan whirred away, sending a breeze across the table. Daddy walked in while Buddy and I were making funny sounds by singing into the oncoming fan's current. He carried several newspapers under his arm. We never bought newspapers; Daddy got them for free. Daily rail passengers left newspapers, among other things, on railcars or in the station. He'd bring home the *Washington Post*, the *New York Times*, the *Philadelphia Inquirer*, or the *Baltimore Sun*. Mamma like the *Inquirer* because she could keep up with the news from her hometown. Daddy preferred the *Post*.

"I brought ya your paper, darlin'," he said as he joined us and dropped copies of the Inquirer and the Post on the table.

"Are you hungry?" Mamma asked.

"Nah, I'm fine. I can wait 'til supper. Sit and enjoy your paper."

Just then Chip and Eugene walked in. Their shirts were soaked through with sweat and their tennis shoes were stained green from the grass. "Whew, you boys look a sight," said Daddy.

"Take off those shoes where you stand and then go upstairs and wash up," Mamma instructed them. "Take those shoes to the laundry when you come back down."

After they went up, Mamma returned her attention to her newspaper and started to catch up on a story that had dominated the front page for the last several days. The FBI was searching for three missing young men who went to Mississippi to register voters. They were with a group called the Congress of Racial Equality. Other young civil rights volunteers had gone missing down south earlier in the summer. What put these three on the front page of newspapers nationwide was that, unlike the previously missing kids, two of the three were White. They had gone missing from a small town in Mississippi called Philadelphia. Since their disappearance, Mamma'd had us include them in our nightly prayers and ask God to help find them unharmed.

Staring at a photo on the front page, Mamma exclaimed, "Look, Jack, they found those missing young men's car down in Mississippi." She paused and then added, "Oh, dear God, the car looks burned. That doesn't bode well."

"Yeah, I read that story. You mark my words; they're dead for sure. They've gone and gotten themselves killed," responded Daddy.

"You make them sound guilty of a crime. How do you figure that, Jack? If they're dead, how could it be their fault? If anyone is a victim, it's those boys."

"That's not how a Southerner will see it, sweetie. You can bet your bottom dollar on that."

"Tell us, pray tell, how does a Southerner see it?"

"Well us Southerners, darlin', don't take none too kindly to a bunch of Yankee carpetbaggers coming south and telling us what's wrong with us."

"And for that they should die—is that what you're saying?"

"Nah, honey. What I'm sayin' is if you poke a nest full of rattlesnakes, don't be surprised if you get bit, is all. If the South is gonna change, it will have to be by Southerners themselves and not a bunch of Yankee do-gooders."

"I think Southerners have had their chance. A lot of people, especially young people, feel the coloreds shouldn't have to wait for another generation to be repressed before they have equality."

"Honey, from Philadelphia, Mississippi, to Philadelphia, Pennsylvania, coloreds are held down and get a raw deal. You Yankees think you're so much better. 'He who is without sin among you, let him be the first to throw a stone.' There's plenty of discrimination and prejudice above the Mason-Dixon Line. Before you Northerners come south and tell us what to do, read your Bible, for it says you should 'set your own house in order.' Maybe the North should fix their own problems before they come callin' and tellin' us we've gotta fix ours."

"Jack, I won't deny that the North has plenty of problems and guilt. That's not what I am saying here. What I am asking is how can you insinuate that those boys brought it on themselves? It's like saying if I choose to walk out of here wearing makeup and a short skirt, then I'm at fault if I get raped. That kind of thinking gets the rapists, the violent ones, off the hook and punishes the victim even more. It perpetuates the crime."

"I'm not sayin' that a rapist should get off the hook. Let me ask you somethin'. Would you get all made up, wear a miniskirt, and leave the Blue Mirror night club at closing time unescorted? Would you do that?"

"No, of course not."

"That's right, honey, 'cause you've got better sense. You know you'd be askin' for it. Folks gotta take responsibility for getting themselves in a defenseless situation. Yes, the rapist should be punished, but you shouldn't go around tempting fate neither."

"We live in a society of laws. If a young girl is molested walking across campus at University of Maryland, she shouldn't be made to feel that she brought it on herself just because she was out late at night. Yes, it's best to be careful, but if something happens we should have the full support of the law and our community. Jack, do you know that fewer than seven percent of coloreds in Mississippi are allowed to vote? When I say allowed, it is because they are not protected by the police when they try to register while White Southerners are allowed to prohibit them from registering. Yes, the North isn't without sin, I'll grant you that, but it's ahead of the South when it comes to civil rights."

"That's the story you Yankees like to tell. How come colored travelers need their Green Book to find a hotel where they can get a room for the night up north? Whites don't need one. You think coloreds can get served in a Howard Johnson in Delaware or get a room at the Astoria in New York? How many colored kids did you see up at your school in the 'City of Brotherly Love' when you was growin' up? Not one; ain't that right. Nothin's equal, honey, if education ain't."

"The only way they'll have equal education is if you have equal representation at the voting booths. If anything is going to change, laws must be the first and that includes the ones about schooling. That's what those boys were trying to accomplish. I think those young men are brave. They're heroes."

"Heroes? Is that what you think? It's a battle, that's true, but I thought you were a pacifist. Didn't you once tell me that wars were the fault of men's egos? You said that if mothers ruled the world, there wouldn't be no wars. Watch who you call heroes in front of our kids, Maggie. Do you want them in the trenches fighting the Klan face-to-face?"

"No, of course not. I am just saying I don't blame those boys for what they did. I blame those that kidnapped them, if that's what's happened to them."

"I wouldn't let whoever is responsible for this off the hook, but, Maggie, we gotta teach our kids to watch out where they poke around. There ain't no sense in courtin' trouble. Anyways, we don't know what happened to them boys yet. I understand their motivations and youthful passions; truly I do, Maggie, we all want a better world. But they ought to have known what they was gettin' themselves into 'fore they started putting their toes in that viper's pit. Those boys showed up at a knife fight with a bunch of pens. They didn't know who or what they was up against down there. But you can bet the organizers knew, and they didn't do enough to protect them. The organizers found a bunch of idealistic, naïve do-gooders to be the perfect patsies to become martyrs. Those

Yankee organizer carpetbaggers are just as much to blame as the Klan and other Southern bigots. They should have protected them. If they're dead, ignorance and stupidity is what got them killed."

"I will continue to pray and hope that they'll find them alive."

"You go on and do that if it makes you feel better, but their fates are sealed. That happened when they got on that bus and came south."

"Enough, we'll leave it with God," Mamma said as she pushed her chair from the table and prepared to stand. "Dinner will be ready soon. Buddy, Babydoll, set the table. Then get Chip and Eugene down for supper," she instructed as she headed into the kitchen. That was Daddy's cue to go and wash up before supper.

CHAPTER FIVE

❦

FOUR SQUARE

There are four incarnations of Mamma: Zombie, Manic, Playful, and the General. After a long siege in one of our parents' epic battles, Mamma inevitably surrenders. That is when Zombie Mamma is most likely to appear. It's more than submitting; she gives up—not just on her marriage but on life, the world, and everything in it, including her kids. When I was younger, I was frightened and watchful when Zombie Mamma appeared, even though this meant I was free from rules and policing. Us kids were left to run wild and could do as we pleased. Still today, when Zombie Mamma is around, it doesn't matter if I speak proper English, my bed is made, or my homework is complete. It's as if a door opens on a vacuous room and sucks her in, and then the door slams behind her, leaving her in darkness and unreachable. A shell of Mamma drifts through the days, making us breakfast, packing lunches, and doing laundry as needed. But I've always known this isn't our real mother. When Zombie Mamma looks at me, I can tell those aren't my real Mamma's eyes.

When I was little, I wasn't afraid of Zombie Mamma, but rather of the world she abandoned us to. Back then, with my guardian missing in action, everything became scarier. I felt unprotected against neighborhood villains, sibling squabbles, Daddy's tirades, and what lurked in the shadows. Now I am more afraid for her than for myself, but all I can do is bide my time, hold my breath, and wait for her to find her way back to us.

Back when I was small, after even a minor argument or a letter or phone call from her sister or some other discernible or indiscernible reason, Manic Mamma appeared. At first she would have lots of energy, like someone who just drank six cups of coffee. She'd move and talk fast, but you could tell she was struggling to keep a smile on her face. She was riding a roller-coaster. She'd start out like the Little Engine That Could struggling to make it up the hill. I'd silently chant, "I think she can, I think she can." You could tell she made it to the top of the roller-coaster when she became a bit too cheerful, a little too energetic. When a roller-coaster reaches the summit and begins its free-fall descent, the screams you hear are perplexing: Are these screams of glee or terror or both? It was the same with Manic Mamma's free fall. With Manic Mamma it was inevitable that she'd crash, and then she'd spend a few days mostly in bed and complain if you let any light into her room. When she emerged again from her room, we knew to anticipate the General along with all her strict rules and regulations, and swift punishments for any infractions.

In my childish fantasies, I would be her rescuer. Especially when Zombie Mamma appeared, I dreamed of having the wisdom to find the door that led to where she'd gone and the courage to enter it. In my waking dreams, I would have the unfaltering determination to find her, and no matter what evils awaited, I would have the strength and wisdom to lead us both into the light. Once outside of that vacuous, shadowy chamber, I would forge the lock to keep it closed forever. That was my childhood fantasy. Aren't we all the heroes of our own dreams? Aren't we all more imagined than real? Who we think we are is not the same as who we are. I imagined that I was terribly brave.

We were all very happy when Mamma started singing again. That was when Playful Mamma arrived. Even Daddy changed when Playful Mamma showed up. He'd bring her little gifts, tell her how beautiful and talented she was, or just sweep her up in his strong arms and start dancing with her as he sang some tune into her ear.

Daddy has a distinctive and soothing voice, somewhat like

Dean Martin's or more like Roger Miller's. But to tell you that Mamma can sing doesn't begin to describe her talent. Mamma has perfect pitch, and her voice is effortless, smooth, and strong. You can understand every word she sings clearly. Playful Mamma sings while she works. When the windows are open, her voice empties out into the yard. On the sidewalk in front of our house, I've often spied a passerby suspending his or her journey in order to listen to her serenade. "Your mother should make a record," said Mr. Thompson, a neighbor, more than once. "I could listen to her singing the Yellow Pages."

The morning that Buddy was to start school, I cried. School was swallowing up all of my brothers. Now I had no one to play with during the day. After we dropped him off at school, I started to cry again. Playful Mamma tried to cheer me up. We seldom had spending change to buy any treats except on very special occasions, but Mamma must have thought this was a special occasion, so she said, "Come on, Birdie, let's treat ourselves to a couple of scoops of ice cream."

"You did it again, Mamma; you called me Birdie."

"Did I? I didn't mean to. I meant Babydoll."

"Why do you call me that sometimes?"

"Do I? I didn't realize. I'm sorry." She stood for a moment as if she was undecided about something, but then reached down and stroked my cheek and smiled. She lifted me up, swung me around, and said, "Yes, you are my sweet baby doll. What flavor are you going to get? You best figure it out before we walk into High's!"

Playful Mamma would take me to the library on Wednesday mornings after the boys went off to school. There, she met her best friend, Mrs. Hoffberg. Mrs. Hoffberg was older than Mamma, and she volunteered at the library, where she read children's books. Us little kids would form a circle around her, and then she'd read and give each character their own distinguishable voice. When she read Beatrix Potter books, each character sounded British. Some had refined voices while others spoke in a Cockney brogue. Or she would speak in a Dutch accent, like when she read *The Silver Skates*. The Hoffbergs lived in Zurich before the war. It was after Mamma and she became friends that I realized her German accent was her own voice and not just one she used for story time.

The first time she invited me and Mamma into her home for tea was after we walked her home on an unusually mild February day. That's when we met Mr. Hoffberg. When we arrived he was sitting in an armchair in a corner of their living room. Tall floor-to-ceiling white bookshelves lined the walls in the corner of the room behind his chair. The upper sections were crammed with books, and the lower parts were filled with record albums. Mr. Hoffberg was listening to what I later learned was Mahler's Fifth Symphony. When we entered, he lowered the volume, stood up, and greeted us warmly. He joined us at the table for tea and cookies. After that day, we made frequent visits to the Hoffbergs' home. Often, Mrs. Hoffberg would paint, and Mamma would sit and chat. In spring and summer, sometimes the three of us would work in her garden, chatting as we pulled weeds. Every inch of Mrs. Hoffberg's yard was well organized yet wild, with a profusion of plants like an English garden. In their front yard, they had zoysia grass. I loved removing my shoes so I could feel its cushiony thick bed beneath my feet. When we finished our gardening chores, Mrs. Hoffberg would reward us with a bouquet of fresh flowers.

One beautiful spring day, we entered Mrs. Hoffberg's yard as she was capturing some newly blossomed irises with her paints and brushes and perfectly immortalizing their moment of glory. She made several studies of these same flowers, but each rendering was wildly different. They were the same flowers and same arrangement, but the movements and strokes of the brushes changed the energy and mood that were displayed on the canvas. It was a magical lesson in how an artist can interpret the world. I fell in love with painting because of those captured flowers.

Sometimes during our visits, I would sit with Mr. Hoffberg while Mamma and Mrs. Hoffberg were somewhere else. He would talk to me about his youth in Zurich or about working for NASA. We discussed the American goal of putting a man on the moon. But most of the time, he preferred to talk about music. He'd tell me about a composition, what inspired its creator, and about the composer's own history. Then he'd tell me to close my eyes as he lowered the needle to the record on the phonograph player. Occasionally he'd interject a comment before a new movement, but mostly we listened silently together, enjoying the sound of the music as it filled up the room.

One afternoon, Mamma walked in from the garden with Mrs. Hoffberg just as a record of Schubert's music was ending. Mamma started to sing "*Ave Maria! Jungfrau mild, Erhöre einer Jungfrau Flehen …*" I had never heard my mother sing in German, so I was a bit surprised. I watched Mr. Hoffberg's face light up in astonishment. Mamma stopped after the first verse and said, "It is such a beautiful song. It's one of my favorites."

"Do you know what it means?" he asked.

"Yes, it is a prayer to the Virgin Mary sung by the young maiden Ellen. It's from a poem by Walter Scott."

"Do you know the rest of it?" he asked. In response Mamma continued to sing the following two verses. When she finished, Mr. Hoffberg hugged her as he said, "You make a superb Ellen. You've given us a wonderful gift today: a private concert by a true artist. How special you've made me feel. You must have had some formal training, my dear. Is that so?"

"I studied opera for a little more than a year at the Peabody Institute in Baltimore. But long before that I sang in church while I was growing up. "Ave Maria" was a favorite at church. My mother was a music teacher. I grew up with music."

"May I ask why you didn't continue your studies?"

"Ah, you know, the usual story of responsibilities and the lack of money."

"You have a gift. I had no idea how talented you are. Thank you, thank you, my dear. I hope to hear you sing again."

"Gladly."

When we walked home that day, I felt proud that this surprising woman holding my hand was my mother.

CHAPTER SIX

❧✧☙

PLAYSKOOL

*B*efore I started going to school, it seemed to be a private club that my brothers disappeared to five days a week. During my early years, when Eugene and Chip went to school, Buddy stayed behind to play with me. When he headed for his first day, joining the "big kids' club" and leaving me alone, I was horribly jealous. I couldn't understand why I had to wait until I was six to join the club.

Each school day after Buddy started attending school, the house became a lonely, quiet place. With the boys out of the house, life seemed suspended as I waited for their return. Mamma was busy with housework and the endless ironing; to earn extra money, she took in other people's ironing. Strangers would come on their way to work with bags of clothes and empty hangers and return the next day after work to pick up their pressed wardrobe. She'd dilute the thick baby blue or pink liquid starch with water in a bowl, set it to the side of the ironing board, and dip a rounded looped brush in the bowl. With the wet brush, she'd shake droplets of the liquid over the stretched cloth of each shirt. Then she'd take the hot iron, drop it on the shirt with a thud, and move it back and forth until all the wrinkles were gone. Rows of starched shirts were strung across our living room on a portable wardrobe rack Daddy had built. While she cleaned, ironed, and cooked, I learned to occupy myself in the house or yard while waiting for my brothers to return from school and for life to begin again.

Until school took him too, Buddy had been my constant playmate. He was the leader in every game, the director of each story reenactment, the architect of our cardboard houses, and my protector from playground bullies.

Two weeks after he started school, a package mysteriously showed up on my bed. Behind a window of cellophane, there were three booklets, a box of crayons, some pencils, an eraser, a small chalkboard, and some writing paper, all spread out on a black piece of cardboard. Each of the booklets was on a subject from school: reading, writing, or arithmetic. I was so excited. I ripped the package open and flipped the pages of the first book. It ultimately opened onto a picture of a queen waiting to be colored in. She was robed, holding a staff, with a crown perched on her head. Next to her was a capital "Q" and a lower case "q"; these were followed by dotted lines to be traced to practice writing each letter. I scooped up the booklets and ran downstairs. "Thank you, Mamma; it's not even my birthday. Thank you, I love them. Will you help me get started?"

"What are you talking about?" I was surprised to find her perplexed by my statement and by what I held in my hands.

"These," I said while lifting the booklets so she could see them better.

Taking them, she responded, "I did not get these for you, Babydoll. Where did you find them?"

"They were on my bed in a packet."

"On your bed; how did they wind up there?"

"I thought you put them there," I said as I shrugged my shoulders.

"Such things do not just show up. Who gave these to you, Babydoll?"

"I don't know. Truly, I thought you did, Mamma. Maybe Santa came early."

Eugene had a job taking care of dogs and looking after a house while some folks were away. He'd stop off at their house after school. When Eugene finally came home, he played school with me using my new booklets. He showed me how to hold the pencil. With his direction, I carefully traced each letter. I asked him, Chip, and Buddy if they had gotten the package for me, but each said no. When Daddy came home, he learned about the mysterious package, and that's when the real interrogation began.

"Ya'll come down here right quick," he yelled up from the bottom of the stairs. You could tell by his tone that he was angry. One by one, we were sent into the kitchen to be questioned about the arrival of my Playskool set—still, no one confessed. After Daddy had interviewed each of us separately, he ordered us to line up in the living room for a group interrogation.

Daddy cleared his throat, "Since none of y'all is ownin' up, these must be ill-begotten goods. I won't tolerate thievin'. Whoever is responsible better come forward now. This is your last chance."

No one said a thing. "Okay, then, if that's the way y'all want it." Dad removed his belt, and we all knew what that meant. "I am going to start beating each one of y'all until someone starts talkin.'" Poor Chip was the closest to Daddy, who grabbed him and started wielding his belt across his back.

"Daddy, Daddy, I didn't do it. Please, sir." Chip let out a cry with each stroke and kept twisting, trying to get out of Daddy's grasp. Some of Daddy's blows missed as Chip twirled, trying to dodge the belt, but most hit their mark.

Eugene couldn't take any more and yelled, "Stop, Daddy! Please, sir, stop it. Beat me instead. I did it, I did it."

Daddy spun around and started to beat Eugene with his belt even harder than he'd been hitting Chip, the blows landing wildly. Mamma screamed, "No, Jack, no, stop it! For God's sake, stop it, Jack!" But Daddy just kept landing blows as Mamma cried.

"Why didn't you own up to it, boy, when I asked ya?" Daddy yelled between blows. "You a coward?" Eugene fell on his knees and put his hands over his head to protect it from the assault of blows. Daddy's rage showed no sign of abating. Finally Mamma fell to her knees next to Eugene and covered him with her own body, catching Daddy by surprise. He couldn't stop in mid-stroke and landed one blow on Mamma's back.

"Go ahead, protect your mama's boy—your precious lying, thieving Eugene."

Still kneeling, she looked up at Daddy. "No, Jack, it couldn't have been Eugene. It wasn't on her bed this morning after he left for school, but Babydoll found it before he got home. He got home late today. It couldn't have been Eugene."

Daddy lowered his arm. "Is that the truth, boy?"

Eugene nodded, "Yes, sir."

"Then why in Sam Hill did ya say you did it? I don't get it. Why, Eugene, if you're innocent?" he asked, bewildered.

"Because I don't want to see anyone get hurt."

"So you'd rather get whooped?"

"Yes, sir, it's easier than watching."

Daddy shook his head. "Eugene, don't ya see someone is a low-down thief in this house? It's a far sight better to get a whoopin' now than to keep on stealin'. Stealin' ways is the Devil's path and leads to nothin' but grief. There's not much lower than a common thief." He turned to the rest of us and continued. "Wards might be poor, but we're no criminals. Whoever's the thief, you best know I'm gonna get to the bottom of this. You mark my words. There's gonna be hell to pay. One of y'all's guilty." With the belt still dangling from his hand, he pointed at me. "Get on over here, Babydoll. You're next. Did ya make up this whole story about findin' the package on your bed?"

I started to cry, "No, sir, I swear. Please, pleeeease, Daddy, I didn't do nothing wrong, I swear on a stack of Bibles. Cross my heart and hope to die."

"Enough!" shouted Mamma. "You've made your point. For God's sake, let it be, Jack." Then in a pleading voice, she added, "Stop this for my sake, please."

"Maggie, you're always protecting your cubs. 'Spare the rod and spoil the child.' It's a hard world out there. They gotta be toughened up, but you're making 'em weak. You think you're protectin' 'em; but what you're really doin' is cripplin' 'em."

"I am begging you, Jack. It's not right to beat the innocent."

Daddy shook his head and said, "One of y'all is a low-down, good-for-nothin' crook. Worse than that, you're a coward who'd let others take the blame. All y'all go to your rooms. None of ya's gettin' no supper tonight. Whoever's the culprit, you think on that. You think about how ya got everyone to go to bed hungry tonight. If I ever catch any of y'all stealin', I swear to the good Lord almighty, I'll skin you to an inch of your life. You can bet I'll make you wish you weren't never born. Ya'll hear me? Now get on out of my sight."

Walking up the stairs, I knew that Eugene was not just kind but brave too. I also realized it had to have been Buddy who had pilfered the Playskool set. But how, I couldn't figure out. He didn't have any money, so he must have stolen it like Daddy said. I knew he felt bad about not owning up to it, but he was terrified by Daddy's rage. It made me realize that he truly felt bad about leaving me at home every school day. He understood how jealous I was and how much I missed him.

The next time I went to the Ben Franklin five-and-dime, I saw the same Playskool packet as the one that had mysteriously appeared on my bed. I asked Buddy again if it was him who had gotten it for me, but he knew better than to confess. If Daddy learned of it, he would blister his behind so badly he wouldn't be able to sit for weeks. I couldn't stop wondering how Buddy managed to steal the set. The packet was far too big to hide under a coat; besides, the weather wasn't cold enough for coats yet. How had he managed it? I was impressed by his cleverness, and I was touched by his thoughtfulness. Most of all, I was glad he was my big brother, and I forgave him for abandoning me each day when he went off to school.

CHAPTER SEVEN

❧ ❖ ☙

ELEMENTARY CHRISTENING

*F*rom deep within a dream, I felt a loving hand softly stroke my forehead and gently lift errant strands of hair from across my face. "Wake up, sleepyhead" came the supplication, penetrating sleep's haze. "Wakey, wakey, Babydoll." As my mind floated upward, I realized it was Buddy's voice beckoning me to consciousness. "You don't want to miss your first day of school, now do ya?"

School! The word sent a jolt inside my head, and suddenly I was alert. My eyes sprung open.

"There you are." Sitting beside me on my bed was Buddy, still in his pajamas. "You better hurry up and get dressed."

"Hey, Buddy," I said as I leapt up from my bed.

"Hey, yourself. Mamma said to tell you she'll fix your hair when you get downstairs. Come on, you don't want to be late your first day. Better get a move on." As he left my room he said, "Last one dressed and at the breakfast table is a rotten egg." Then he turned, exited, and shut the door. From across the hall, I could hear Eugene's radio playing and him singing along to the Beatles, "And it's worth it just to hear you say—you're going to give me everything."

"Eugene, Chip," Mamma yelled up the stairs, "you better hurry up or you'll miss your buses." With that, the radio went silent, followed by the sound of two pairs of feet running down the stairs.

Hanging on my closet doorknob was the navy blue jumper dress and white shirt Mamma had carefully starched and ironed the night before. A pair of polished black shoes sat on the floor next to them. Stuffed inside one of shoes was a pair of white socks with lacy trims. I dressed as fast as I could in the unfamiliar clothes and carried my shoes downstairs. When I got to the table, Buddy was pouring his milk into his cereal and smiling up at me. "Hey, slowpoke, what took you so long? You lose." "I'll beat you tomorrow," I promised.

"You can try," came his quick retort.

The only sign of Eugene was his empty cereal bowl. Chip came out of the bathroom, grabbed his lunch bag, and headed toward the front door, then paused. "Good luck, Babydoll. I'll see you when you get home, and you can tell me all about your first day. 'Bye, Mamma," he yelled to her in the kitchen. "You too, Buddy," he added.

As the front door was closing, Mamma came out of the kitchen and said, "'Bye, Chip." Then she turned to me. "Before you sit down, follow me to the living room, and let me fix your hair."

As soon as I caught up with her, she spun me around. Standing behind me, she started brushing my hair, yanking the brush roughly through my many tangles.

"Ouch!"

"Stay still," she commanded. "I don't have time to mess around."

I stood stoically as she battled my hair into submission. Once it was free of tangles, she took a comb from her apron pocket and made a part across my head with the comb's edge. With her fingers she divided each half into three parts and made two long braids. She finished the ends with strands of white ribbon. She spun me back around and said, "You'll do. Now go eat your breakfast."

Waiting for me was half a grapefruit with each segment neatly sliced and separated so that I could easily eat each piece with a spoon. Sprinkled sugar glistened on top just the way I like it, and a slice of buttered toast waited by its side. Buddy was nearly finished with his breakfast when I sat down. "You ready for your big day, Babydoll?"

"Yeah, I'm ready."

"You nervous?"

"Nah, but do you think the teacher will like me?" I asked anxiously.

"Sure, why not? If you want, you can take her an apple. That'll let her know you want to start off on the right foot."

In a panic I asked, "Mamma, do we have an apple for my teacher?"

As she cleared the breakfast dishes from the table, she responded, "Yes, I'll put it in a bag for you to carry. You better hurry up. We have to get going."

"I'm done," I said as I pushed my untouched toast toward Mamma. "The grapefruit was enough. I'm not that hungry."

"It's a big day. You'll need a bit of something in your stomach."

"I can't eat any more. I'm fine. I'll be all right."

"Okay, you two. Let me rinse these, and we'll go."

Buddy stood up and said, "Look for me when you go out to the playground for morning recess. I will be next to the seesaws, okay?"

"I'll find you," I said confidently.

"At lunchtime, I'll wait for you at the side exit, the one we will enter through this morning. Don't dillydally now. We don't have a lot time if we want to get back for any of the afternoon recess."

"I'll be sure to hurry."

At long last, I was going to find out what went on inside the red brick buildings that stole my brothers away from me five days a week from September to mid-June. Mamma returned from the kitchen with a reused brown paper bag containing my apple offering for my teacher. Printed on the bag were ice cream cones, sundaes, and the Giant Food store logo. After we left the house, Buddy and Mamma walked while I skipped all the way to school.

When we entered the building, there were two sets of double doors at the end of a long hall. My classroom was the first one on the right-hand side. By the door was a sign that read MISS FALLON, GRADE ONE. "This is it. This is your classroom, Babydoll."

Before Buddy continued down the hallway to go to the second-grade classrooms, he said, "Remember, the playground will be crowded at recess, so look for me by the seesaws. I'll be waiting for you." I nodded that I would. I saw him walk down the hall, pause at a bulletin board, then enter a room midway down.

"You ready?" Mamma asked, and before I could answer she put her hand in mine and led me into my classroom. We stood next to the door for a minute before she turned me around and said, "Are you okay? Are you nervous?"

"I'm fine, Mamma. I'm not a bit nervous." But Mamma was experienced in the first day jitters and knew I was lying.

"It's okay to be nervous, but you'll soon be an old hand. Remember, your brother isn't far away, and he'll be waiting for you in just a couple of hours to take you home for lunch." Mamma pointed at a woman standing behind a large desk. She was a short and stocky and was neatly dressed. Her dark hair was in a French twist with every strand neatly placed. "There's your teacher. Now, you be good and mind her." Then she bent down and gave me a quick kiss. "Just wait here against the wall with the other children until the teacher tells you what to do. I have to get back home. You sure you're okay?"

"I'm fine."

"That's my good girl. Okay, I will be waiting to hear about

your first morning at school when you come home for lunch. Remember to wait for Buddy. See you in a couple of hours then," she said as she playfully tugged one of my braids. With that she turned to leave.

I stood for a couple of seconds but then stepped back into the hall and watched as she walked toward the double doors. Just as she was pushing them open, she turned and saw me watching her. She smiled and gave me a hand signal to go into the classroom. I went in, but quickly turned back to peek out into the hall again. She was gone. Only the swinging doors gave evidence of her exit.

Alone, I turned back around and walked into the classroom. I gazed around the room and studied the other kids. Some seemed to have friends already; others were obviously frightened. A few kids were crying. Some were desperately trying to keep their moms with them. I was nervous but not afraid. The sun poured in through the bank of windows. The panes of glass tilted inward. Two fans mounted on the wall above the blackboard rotated from side to side and blew the smell of chalk and freshly washed blackboards across the room.

"Will the remaining mothers give a final hug to your children and kindly leave the room so we may begin?" pronounced the teacher.

Some mothers acted quickly and gave their child one last kiss before exiting the room. Others had more difficulty leaving. One scrawny boy screamed when his mother, who was struggling with her own emotional pain of separation, tried to peel her son's arms off her legs. Each time she removed one arm, his other one would wrap around a leg. The teacher came over and asked, "Now what's your name?"

"It's okay, honey, you can tell her." Still, he didn't answer. He only stared up at his mother pleadingly as he continued to cry. "Sweetheart, this is your teacher. She will look after you in class." The teacher smiled at him. He stopped shrieking and slowly let go of his mother's legs while sniffling. "Go on, honey, tell the nice lady your name."

"B-B-B-Bruce."

"Well, it is nice to meet you Bruce. My name is Miss Fallon. Now, there is no need to worry. We are going to have fun. We will learn some new things, meet some new friends, and when we finish today, your mother will be waiting for you. Isn't that right?" she asked, looking up at the boy's mother. His mother nodded in affirmation. Then the teacher signaled for her to leave. The woman's tear-streaked face was nearly as red as her son's. When she reached the door, she turned to look back one last time before finally exiting.

The teacher led Bruce over to the wall and announced to all of us, "Now everyone, my name is Miss Fallon. I will be your teacher this year. All of you, I want you to come over here and line up against this wall behind Bruce."

Once we formed a line along the wall, she said, "I will call each of your names. When you hear your name, raise your hand, and I will come over to you and hand you a card with your name printed on it. I will then direct you to your desk. You will place the card on top of your desk by the front edge. Then you will take a seat. This will be your desk each morning. When you come into class each day, you are to be seated and sit quietly and await instruction. Does everyone understand? If you understand say, 'Yes, Miss Fallon.'"

"Yes, Miss Fallon," most of us replied.

"Okay, now let's begin," she said.

She went alphabetically. "Theodore Albritton," we heard her say, and a tall skinny boy raised his hand. The teacher summoned him and showed him his desk and placed the nameplate on top of it.

"Theodore, this is your desk. Each morning you are to come into the classroom, hang up your coat if you have one with you, come to this desk, and sit quietly. Do you understand?"

"Yes."

"You are to respond, 'Yes, ma'am' or 'Yes, Miss Fallon.' Do you understand, Theodore?"

"Mm, yes, yes, ma'am, Miss Fallon, ma'am." A few kids giggled.

Miss Fallon turned and looked at them, and they stopped. Next she called, "Cathleen Campbell." A pretty, well-dressed girl quickly walked up to the teacher.

"I am Cathy Campbell, ma'am," she said confidently as she took her nameplate and followed Miss Fallon to her desk. She placed it in front of her and sat down. Miss Fallon called several more before she called Bruce Showalter, who was the small boy who had held fast to his mother's legs, pleading not to be abandoned. His tears were mostly dried, but his sniffling continued. After he was settled in his seat, there were only three of us left.

I heard her call "Charlotte Ward." I looked around the room. Someone else had my last name. Charlotte was a family name too; I had an Aunt Charlotte who lived somewhere in Georgia. She called the name again, but no one answered. I was curious.

"Will Charlotte Ward please raise her hand?" Miss Fallon called out again, with a bit less sweetness to her voice. No one responded. She addressed the girl standing in front of me: "What is your name?"

The girl replied, "Karen Wilson, ma'am."

Then she asked me. "And what is your name?"

"My name is Babydoll," I replied. "Babydoll Ward, ma'am." Everyone turned to stare at me.

"Excuse me. In this classroom you will be called by your Christian name. Your name is Charlotte Ward, and that is how I will address you."

Some of the kids started snickering. "Quiet!" she commanded.

"But, ma'am, that's not my name. I'm Babydoll," I said, assured of myself. "I always have been."

"That may be what they call you at home, but it is certainly not your Christian name." The whole class burst out laughing, and I grew angry at them and my teacher for making me look foolish.

My face must have shown it. She looked down at me sternly and said, "Now you go take the desk directly in front of mine. I don't want any more trouble from you. Do you understand, Charlotte?"

I wasn't going to argue anymore. I went to my seat and sulked. When I went home for lunch, I told Mamma that she had to straighten the teacher out.

"What do you mean, Babydoll?" she asked.

"She keeps insisting that my name is Charlotte. I tried to explain, but she wouldn't listen. Everyone laughed at me, and now she's got me sitting in the desk in front of hers. I got in trouble my very first day. You have to tell her that she's made a big mistake."

"But Charlotte is your name."

"What! No it ain't. No one's ever called me that. I don't understand, Mamma. What are you saying?"

"Sweetheart, I've told you before, there is no such word as ain't. You should say, 'It is not,' and Babydoll is your nickname, just like Chip's real name is Jackson just like Daddy's. Buddy's real name is Clyde."

"I knew Chip is really Jackson junior, but I thought that was so he wouldn't get confused with Daddy. But Buddy is really Clyde! I didn't know that. Why, Mamma, why'd you give us those names if you weren't going to use them? It's like we're all living secret lives or something. Is Eugene really Eugene?"

"Yes, we never gave Eugene a nickname."

"Why's he different? What makes him so special?"

"It's not that he's special. It's just no other name seemed to stick to him. Emma never got a nickname either. Sweetheart, your given name is Charlotte. You were named after Daddy's cousin Charlotte. Babydoll is a term of endearment."

"Cousin! What cousin!" I shouted, "Holly cow, I thought she was my aunt. We've always call her Aunt Charlotte. Is our whole family built on lies?"

"No one is trying to lie to you. Daddy and Aunt Charlotte grew up like brother and sister. Aunt is a term of endearment and respect. That's why we call her Aunt Charlotte. Honey, Charlotte is your real name. Babydoll is your nickname. I thought you knew."

"How was I supposed to know that? You never told me. Do Eugene, Chip, and Buddy know my real name?"

"Why, yes, but it's not some kind of conspiracy, Babydoll."

"Don't call me that. It's not my name. You just said so. How could you have allowed me to go off to school and make a fool of myself? Everyone must think I am a real idiot for not knowing my own name. How dumb is that? How could you, Mamma? How could you?"

"Please, Babydoll ..."

I cut her off. "Don't ever, ever call me that again. My name is Charlotte!" I shrieked.

Part Three

1965

CHAPTER EIGHT

⚜

LEAP YEAR

*A*t the end of Buddy's first year in school, his teacher met with Mamma and recommended that he repeat first grade. Reading and writing weren't coming easy to him. He pleaded to be allowed to go to second grade along with his friends. Mamma promised his teacher that she'd spend the summer helping him catch up, so Mamma and Eugene took turns trying to teach Buddy how to read and write while I looked on. I was a sponge and absorbed each new lesson. Buddy was still having trouble and would bang his head in frustration when he couldn't grasp a concept. We went to the library frequently and brought home piles of books. In a library, I felt rich. It held a bounty of books, each one offering me a new adventure. After each trip, I returned home with a pile full of treasure.

Despite all their efforts, Buddy had even more trouble in second grade, so Mamma and Daddy had him repeat it. Despite my rocky first day, I loved going to school those first few months. The best part was walking with my big brother. On our way home from school, Buddy would lead the way as we'd cut through the woods to explore or stop at the playground to climb the jungle gym.

Still, I grew impatient for the other kids in my class to catch up. I read *Heidi* and *Charlotte's Web* while they read "See spot run" in the Dick and Jane books. When I finished all the books in our classroom, Miss Fallon brought me more. Sitting in a corner of the room, I'd read on my own while she taught the class. In December, Mamma had a conference with Miss Fallon, who recommended that after Christmas break I take reading, writing, and arithmetic with the second-graders while still officially in first grade. Mamma had concerns about this: not for me but for Buddy. Miss Fallon pushed, and Mamma finally consented. After that, I started each day in Miss Fallon's class but joined the second-graders for the primary subjects. I returned to first grade for art, music, and physical education as well as the end-of-the-day announcements. There were two classrooms for each grade. It was disappointing to me that I wasn't in the same room as Buddy, but in my second-grade class, I was happy, proud, and no longer bored. I didn't know then that it would set me apart from the other kids and create a gulf between Buddy and me.

What Buddy excelled at was being popular. He was often the first picked in a round of kickball. Those first few months, he'd make sure I was picked for his team at recess, but once I crossed the hall to the second grade, he began to ignore me. Soon, I was one of the last kids chosen. After school, he no longer waited for me at the side exit. Now I walked alone. Toward the end of my first year in school, Mamma was called in to school again. Miss Fallon, with the support of our principal, strongly recommended that I skip second grade and go straight into the third next year. I listened through their bedroom door as my parents argued about it.

"I don't know, Jack. I think it will hurt Charlotte less if we keep her in second grade than it will hurt Buddy if we let her skip ahead. His confidence is so poor. He doesn't think he can learn, which makes it even harder for him."

"You can't keep protecting that boy forever, Maggie. He has to toughen up and learn that if it's twice as hard for him, then he best work three times as hard as everyone else. Holding Charlotte back ain't gonna fix that. You'd just be delaying the inevitable."

"It's not as simple as just working harder, Jack."

"It ain't? Course it is. Did he learn to ride a bike, swim, tie his shoes? The boy can learn, Maggie. He just gotta want it bad enough. It's a sink or swim world out there, sugar. A little competition might be what the boy needs."

"He *is* trying."

"Well, he best get to tryin' harder. It ain't right punishin' Charlotte just 'cause her brother has sensitive feelin's."

"Oh, come on, Jack. This is not just about his sensibilities. You have to believe you can do something to succeed at it."

"Didn't you say the teacher thought Charlotte would get bored at school if we didn't let her go on to third grade? You gotta choose, Maggie—are we gonna punish Charlotte 'cause her older brother has trouble learnin'? That ain't fair. What's that gonna teach 'em? The next time Buddy has a problem, he's gonna think that all he's gotta do his bang his head on a table and cry to get his mommy to come and fix it for him? What if we keep her back and he's still got problems? How ya gonna make it up to Charlotte? I say the girl's earned it, and we shouldn't stand in her way. That ain't right. It certainly ain't how the real world works, and that's something they both need to know."

"Okay, Jack. We won't stand in her way, but we have to find more help for him."

"That's on you, darlin'. The kids are your responsibility. I'm the breadwinner."

In June, it was officially announced that I'd skip second grade. Again, Mamma spent the summer trying to teach Buddy. In third grade, he went from ignoring me to being hostile. He was the ringleader when I was taunted and the master of name calling. I didn't yet understand that I was a constant reminder of his failure. He was supposed to be ahead of me. In fourth grade, they put him in a separate, "special" school where Buddy gained a new title:

dyslexic. For years, I had anxiously anticipated my membership into the school club, wanting to be with my Buddy. I didn't know then that school would be what would drive us apart. I lost my mentor and best friend. In time, I realized he lost a whole lot more.

CHAPTER NINE

❧ ✦ ☙

VIRGINIA GENTLEMEN

*M*amma and Daddy were at it again. When it came to arguing, Daddy was a marathon man. Daddy could grab hold of a perceived insult quicker than quick, and Mamma couldn't help from showing him up. One thing he couldn't abide was a wife disagreeing with him in front of others—that was mutiny. To him, a good wife was honor bound while in public to support her man, no matter what came out of his mouth.

What started this fight was when Mamma picked him up at work. I went with her. Daddy and some men were in the parking lot talking about President Johnson sending more troops to Vietnam. Mamma joined in the conversation. Daddy thought we had to stop communism from spreading and some dominos from falling by taking a stand in Southeast Asia. "We stopped Mussolini's fascists and Hitler's goons; we should be able to stop a bunch of Vietnamese communists," he said.

But Mamma thought we had no business getting involved in a country most of us couldn't find on a map. "The Vietnamese haven't attacked us," she pointed out. "Why are we even over there?" But the worst offense was when she corrected Daddy's statistics in front of his workmates. Apparently, he was misinformed as to the current level of US troops in Vietnam. As soon as they got into the truck, the battle began.

When he called in to work the next day, saying there was a crisis at home and he couldn't come to the rail yard, we knew it was going to be a long siege. Their argument grew and expanded on all the unfinished topics they had between them. After he'd been ranting for the better part of two days and a night, Mother threw up the white flag, confessing she was to blame for everything and anything. She promised to try harder to be a "good" wife. But he wasn't ready to take prisoners or accept a cease-fire; he hadn't emptied his reservoir of resentment yet. From the rants and carrying-on coming from our house during these battles, the neighbors branded him a drunk. He was a big man to be feared when he got worked up. Daddy didn't drink hard liquor, though, or at least not often. He'd drink a few beers from time to time, but never when they were quarreling. He didn't need it to get uncorked. He could do that all by himself.

The final siege of this campaign began when Mamma barricaded herself in the bathroom early in the day. The bathroom was her refuge because it had the only door in the house that locked from the inside. For hours, Daddy yelled insults toward the locked door. At first, Mamma yelled back, but she had gone quiet since late afternoon. As night fell, she pulled the towels off the holder, made a pillow, and lay down in front of the door in preparation for the long battle ahead. Daddy must have finally gotten tired of yelling at a closed door and dozed off on the couch. From the sound of his loud snoring, Mamma could tell he'd fallen off to sleep. She seized her moment, her purse, three kids, and not much else. Chip was not home that night; I forget why.

It must have been about two or three in the morning when Eugene woke me. He placed a gentle hand on my shoulder and shook it. "Shuuush," he whispered with a firm finger over his lips. "Be silent as a mouse, Birdie."

"Who's Birdie?" I asked—a little too loud because he clamped his hand quickly over my mouth and spoke softly,

"We don't want Daddy waking." It was at that moment I realized it was quiet in the house. He released his hand from over my mouth. I started to form a question, but Eugene headed me off. He whispered, "You can talk all you want once we get on the road. Here's a bag. Grab some clothes, your toothbrush, and your blanket, and tiptoe." I never got to ask my question; I fell back to sleep soon after Mamma coasted our blue '49 pickup truck down the street and then started its engine halfway down the hill.

I didn't wake up until we stopped for breakfast at Lowery's Restaurant in Tappahannock, Virginia. Mamma's sister, Martha, wasn't a bit surprised when Mamma called her from a pay phone at Lowery's. After that, Mamma gave the keys to Eugene. "I can hardly see straight; I am so tired. You better take over." Eugene had just gotten his driver's license the week before. Buddy and I didn't want to squeeze back into the cab, so we rode the rest of the way in the back of the pickup with our dog, General Patton.

When we arrived in Norfolk, Aunt Martha was late for work. Her husband, Ben, was a US Navy ship's captain and was out at sea somewhere. Each sister had what the other wanted: Martha had a nice house, a job, independence, stability, and money. Mamma had kids in abundance. Aunt Martha worked for the town of Chesapeake, the next town over from where she lived. She had to get to work and didn't have much time. She unlocked the front door and gave Mamma a hug, a key, and some quick instructions before she took off in her Buick Riviera. While pulling out of the driveway, she said, "We'll talk when I get back, Margaret. I get home around six."

Apparently, we made it just in time before the truck gave out. Mamma was heading to the store to buy toothbrushes (I had forgotten mine) and some groceries when, two blocks from Aunt Martha's house, it stalled and wouldn't restart. She came back to the house and got Eugene. We all had to go with them because Mamma wouldn't leave us alone in the house without either herself or Eugene to make sure we behaved.

"It's the starter motor again," he informed us. "It has been giving us trouble for a while now. I can try to get it going. I'll tap it from underneath, Mamma, while you turn the ignition. Wait for my signal." Eugene and Mamma tried to get it going several times, but the truck wouldn't start. "Do you hear that clicking sound, Mamma, when we try to start it? That sounds like the starter solenoid is going too. I can pop a new starter and solenoid in. I just need to find out where I can get the parts."

"Is that expensive?" asked Mamma.

"Shouldn't be too much," Eugene answered. "But what worries me is the carburetor. I noticed after we got off the highway and into town, it was idling fast. Something is going on with the choke and that can be tricky. The engine was still hot, so I don't think the carburetor is the issue with it starting, but the choke still needs work." That's when we all started missing Chip. Like Daddy, he was a genius when it came to fixing engines.

Buddy and I raced each other as we ran back to the house ahead of Eugene and Mamma. But when we got to Aunt Martha's front yard, he tried to push me to stop me from overtaking him and we got into a big fight. When Mamma rounded the corner with Eugene, she saw us in full swing of a really good hand-to-hand combat. I had just landed my best blow with my foot straight into his chest, knocking Buddy to the ground. "Stop it!" she yelled. "I can't believe this. I let you two out of my sight for two minutes and you're at it again. Babydoll, you are acting like a barbarian."

"He started it," I yelled indignantly.

"She's a liar," lied Buddy.

"I don't care who started it. It stops here and now!" Mamma snapped. To separate us, Mamma made me go with her to the store. We had to take public transportation. As we were walking up to Chesapeake Boulevard to catch the city bus, I suddenly remembered what Eugene had called me that morning before we left. "Mamma, why do folks sometimes call me Birdie?"

Mamma stopped in mid-stride, turned, took me by the shoulders, and asked, "Who calls you that?"

From the sound of her voice, I wasn't sure if she was still angry at me for fighting Buddy or at someone for calling me Birdie. I didn't want to get Eugene in any trouble, so I said, "Well, sometimes you do." Which was true, though she hadn't in a very long time. I only remembered her calling me Birdie as well when Eugene called me by that name. Because she looked at me skeptically, I added, "Daddy did once, but he said it wasn't my name, that it was a slip of the tongue. If it's a slip of the tongue, why did you call me it too? Who is Birdie, Mamma, and why won't anyone tell me?"

"I will tell you someday but not today."

"So, she does exist. But why do people confuse me with her?"

"When you are older, I will tell you."

"When will that be?" I asked, frustrated.

"I'll let you know."

"I hate secrets," I announced.

"I know, Charlotte, but you're just too young right now. You'll have to be patient and wait. Now come on. I'm really knackered.

Let's get the shopping over and done with so we can get back to the house." With that we continued in silence. I sulked all the way to the grocery store and all the way back.

When the bus stopped for us, Mamma asked the driver, "Where is the best place to go for grocery shopping that's easy to get to?" and he answered, "Wards Corner. That's the best in all of Norfolk. You're in luck—this bus goes by it."

After we found our seats, I asked, "Hey, Mamma, did he say 'Wards Corner?' That's our name. Do you think we're related?"

"I doubt it; least not close enough to go calling on them," came her reply. When the bus left us off, we crossed a big parking lot. In front of the grocery store was a large arch. On the top of it, there was a huge sign that read GIANT and under the arch it read OPEN AIR MARKET, though it wasn't really open air. But there wasn't a front door either. When we walked in and over a metal grate, a big gush of air greeted us. It was a huge two-story, red brick building. I'd never been in a single store as large before. At first, I felt overwhelmed, and I think Mamma was too, at least a bit. We stood in the entrance, not sure of which direction we should head first. Signs overhead throughout the store read CHEESE CAVES, FISH WHARF, SOUTHERN MANOR PANCAKES, LAUNDROMAT, BAR-B-QUE, HOUSE OF FLOWERS, and more.

My eyes didn't know where to stop. They sold normal groceries, but a lot of odd stuff too like pickled eel, barbecued frog legs, and chocolate-covered ants. It became a contest between Mamma and me to find unusual items and point them out as we wandered the aisles. A sense of adventure and fits of laughter overtook us. There was even a restaurant inside where we stopped for some ice cream. The signs said they were open 24 hours every day but Christmas. "Who would need chocolate-covered ants at three o'clock in the morning?" I wondered out loud.

We left the grocery store laden with bags. Three-quarters of the way through the parking lot, we saw the bus arriving at the stop. We both took off as best we could—half running, half walking fast—rushing with all of our bags. We made it just in time.

When Mamma stepped onboard she was out of breath. A young man helped her with her bags and offered her his seat. While thanking him, she sat down, settled herself, and then took my bags. A gray-haired gentleman got up to give me his seat and said, "Here you go, miss." My feet were sore and I was tired from the long trip and interrupted sleep. The man's kind offer made me smile and think that it was true about the fine manners of Virginian gentlemen. Yet before I could claim the offered gift, Mamma snatched my arm, pulling me away from the seat and from my momentary fantasy.

In a stern, low voice she instructed, "Children stand; their elders sit." In a more audible voice, she addressed the older gentleman. "Thank you, sir, that is very kind, but she prefers to stand." When I started to try to explain that she was in error, she squeezed my arm tighter, turning it red. "You'll stand," she grumbled in a low voice while staring directly into my eyes. Our shopping camaraderie was over, and her expression, grip, and tone dispelled any notion of further protest.

The driver looked up into the rear view mirror and began to pull over. "What's going on back there?" he demanded. "Why doesn't that girl have a seat?"

"You know kids; they can't sit still. This one has ants in her pants. She wants to stand and hang onto the grab-pole," Mamma offered while keeping her death grip on my arm. I could feel my hand going numb, and my fingers started tingling.

"It don't matter, missus; she can have my seat," said the old man. In a conspirator's voice meant just for my mother, he whispered, "No need to make a fuss now, missus."

"She's fine," she said softly to the gentleman. Speaking in a louder tone, she added, "Tell the driver, Charlotte, that you want to stand." I didn't think that grip could get any tighter but just then it did. Her eyes said, *"Don't you think of disobeying."*

"No thank you, sir," I nearly shouted at the driver. "My dear mother here has been promising me all morning that if I behaved really well I could stand and hold the pole on the ride home. Please sir, I've been very good," I said mimicking Mamma's Philadelphia accent. My accent and tone were perhaps a bit too sarcastic; I felt Mamma tug my arm firmly as she stared into my eyes. To mollify her, I offered in my own voice and in a softer, more pleading tone, "Really, sir, I'm tired of sitting. I want to stand! Please, pleeease, don't make me sit, sir." In a brief silence, I hoped for my sake he believed me. Satisfied or mollified, he pulled off into traffic again. Mamma loosened her grip, and I hugged the pole and fought back the tears that wanted to erupt in my eyes. The driver glanced back a few times and shook his head, hinting that he wasn't totally convinced by my performance. As the bus moved along, I stood hugging the pole. Gradually, I looked around the bus and explored the faces of the other passengers. A middle-aged woman shook her head and looked unhappy with me. I was confused. What had I done wrong? A man two seats away seemed to be snarling. Other disapproving faces glanced my way and at Mamma too. Even when a seat became available by a departing passenger, I remained standing, quiet and glued to the pole. I grew increasingly frightened. When the bus finally came to our stop, I raced off it as fast as I could and didn't even stop to help Mamma with her bags. The young man who had helped Mamma before helped her again. When she exited the bus, she thanked the man and handed me two bags to carry.

It wasn't until I was much older that I figured out what happened on that bus. Jim Crow was alive and well in 1965. The gentleman who offered me his seat and the one who gave up his for my mother were Black. The White "gentlemen" on that bus never offered us their seats or their help. The only things they offered us were their cold looks and whispered invectives.

It didn't take too long before Daddy figured out where we had gone, and the phone starting ringing nonstop. When it finally did stop ringing, Mamma knew he was on his way. Aunt Martha warned that her husband, Ben, would be home in ten days. One way or the other, this had better be resolved before he got home, she seemed to imply. Daddy and Uncle Ben didn't get along.

Daddy showed up that night with Chip in a rented car. In front of Aunt Martha, he was on his best behavior, all sweet and full of apologies, promises, and Southern charm. He took Chip with him to pick up a new starter for the truck. He, Chip, and Eugene spent the rest of the day working on it. It took a second trip for more parts before they got it running right.

It wasn't until after Aunt Martha left for work that Daddy started in on Mamma. "If I don't get back quick, I'll lose my job and that'll be your fault."

"Then go back to work, Jack. I didn't ask you come down here."

"I can't just sit by and let you tear this family apart. Darlin', where will we be if I lose my job? This ain't your home. We gotta get back now. We may have problems, but this isn't the place to work them out. Let's get on back. Renting that car is gonna throw us back months. The kids are missin' school. If they miss much more, the authorities are likely to start askin' questions. This game you're playing has gotta stop, Maggie. This family needs to get home. Maggie, I am no quitter. You know that, and I won't let you break up our family. This little escapade of yours has to end before it ruins us. You've had your fun and adventure—now it's time to come home."

"Adventure? Fun! Mother of God, is that what you think this is? You think any of this has been fun for me? I want a divorce, Jack. This is no joke."

"You'd leave me after everything I've done for you? Where would you be if I hadn't married you? Divorce? I thought Catholics don't believe in no divorce. Ain't divorce a sin?"

"What's one more sin? I'm already in hell."

"What in the Sam Hill are you saying, Maggie? God forgives those that repent."

"That's your Baptist God, Jack."

"If not God, Maggie, what about your daddy? What would he think about a divorce?"

"Jack, it's not working. Not for me and not for you too. I can't do it anymore. It's destroying both of us. Can't you see that? I know you have sacrificed a lot for me and the kids. I know you work harder than any man I know. You've tried your best. For the love of Jesus, we've both tried. I am grateful, Jack; really, I am. But I just can't go on like this. I can't stop from setting you off. It's too hard. I am not strong enough. I can't be what you want, what you need, what you deserve."

"Maggie, you are exactly what I want and need. I love you, and you know I've tried to be what you need. Don't say it's ain't workin' for me. I love you and the kids, each one of them. Why do you think I'm here? You can count on me, just like I promised."

"Yes, you've kept your promise. But I think we'd be better off apart, Jack."

"Apart, apart—and how are you going to support everyone on your own? Four kids, Maggie, that's a lot of mouths to feed. How you gonna do that and take care of 'em too? I can't afford to pay for two homes. The kids would be better off with me. Are you willin' to walk away from them too?"

"I'll find work. Eugene is nearly grown, and Chip is not far behind. We'll manage."

"What about Buddy and Charlotte? Soon Eugene will be off, or do you think he'll stick around and be the man of the house? You want to shackle him like that? Don't be selfish. Don't be an idiot. How you gonna work and take care of these kids? You ain't worked in years. What do ya know how to do 'cept diaper changin' and laundry? Do you think you can support them by singin' in some dive? That don't pay neither. Some low-paying hospital job cleaning people's slop is what you'll find. You won't find the same jobs waitin' for you as there were during the war. They're askin' for more learnin' nowadays. You didn't finish nursin' school. It don't matter how much experience you got, ya don't have that piece of paper. You can't type. You can't earn enough to feed, house, and dress them kids. If you walk out on this marriage, don't expect me to be supportin' you. What would be the point of me slavin' away if I ain't got my family? I work hard. I work extra jobs to keep us all goin'. It ain't easy, Maggie." Mamma slumped onto the couch and started to cry. Daddy looked down on her for a moment. Then he sat next to her and picked up her hand.

"Maggie, sweetheart, I am beggin' you—don't tear this family apart. Even if you're lucky enough to find some lousy job, who'd take care of them kids while you're out of the house? You can't afford no hired help. Who's gonna care for them? Maggie, face it, you need me. I need you, and the kids need us both. I know it's hard. It's damn hard. But it'd be a whole lot harder if we weren't together. Deep down you know that's true." He paused, took a breath, and said, "Come home, Maggie. Please come home."

Mamma's crying turned into occasional sniffling while Daddy stroked her hand. They were sitting in Martha's living room on her newly reupholstered cream-colored Victorian camelback sofa. A copy of a Homer painting hung on the wall above. In the painting was a man in a small, rudderless fishing boat struggling against a stormy sea. It made me think of Daddy. Martha's polished coffee table sat in front of them. On top of it was a long white doily and a crystal bowl resting on its center. Mamma's crying had stopped as she sat staring into the bowl. Daddy broke the silence in a softer tone.

"Come home now, Maggie. You know I love you. No one loves you like I do. Ain't I out there every single lousy day bustin' my back to take care of y'all? I'm no quitter. Who else ya gonna count on? It ain't your sister, I can tell you that. Yeah, she loves her little sister all right, but not how I do. She's not goin' to sacrifice for you: not her nice house, and darn tootin' not her marriage. She needs to keep that husband of hers happy. Ben's not used to kids and scarcely tolerates 'em. He don't like messy, and the good Lord knows kids are messy. You stay here, it won't be long before things get ugly. Sure as a cat's got climbing gear, your daddy ain't taking you in."

Mamma just sat there staring into the bowl. She was surrendering, but Daddy didn't know it yet. They both sat for a while silently, Daddy waiting and Mamma thinking.

But Daddy got frustrated by the silence, and again he was the one to break it. "You hesitate any longer, Maggie, and it might be too late. If I don't get back tomorra' I might lose my job. I already missed too much damn work over these shenanigans. If I lose my job, where will we be? Don't quit on me. Don't quit on this family. Think what you'd be doing to the kids."

Her shoulders slumped down while she took a long, tired breath. He waited a moment and then said, "You better make up your mind soon if you want to have a house to come home to. It does me no good to pay rent on an empty house. I'll let it all go down the crapper. Don't you think I won't," he warned.

"Okay, Jack, we'll go back," Mamma said in a barely audible voice. This time, Daddy accepted the white flag of surrender. By the time Aunt Martha got home, we'd finished packing and were ready to get going. A light drizzle of rain had started. Mamma hugged her sister a long time, and Aunt Martha seemed reluctant to let go too. The two whispered to each other. I didn't believe what Daddy said about Aunt Martha; I could tell she loved her little sister deeply and would do just about anything for her. I doubted what he said about Uncle Ben too.

After Chip climbed into the truck and onto the passenger's seat, Eugene backed it down the driveway. The rest of us piled into the rental car. Daddy drove, and Mamma barely said a word the whole ride home. Her mind was off somewhere else. In the passing glow of headlights, I watched her blank eyes reflected in the side mirror as she stared out onto the passing wet pavement. We had just crossed over the York River when I leaned over in between the two front bucket seats to give her a kiss, but she didn't seem to notice my touch. I knew then that the Zombie had returned. As I was about to plop back into my seat, I turned my head and caught sight of her hand. It held a tight grip on the door handle, as if she were ready to open the door of the swiftly moving car. From the middle rear seat, I didn't take my eyes off her for the rest of the long drive home in fear that she might jump. I stayed alert, ready to grab her in case she made a sudden move.

Part Four

1966

CHAPTER TEN

8)❖(3

THE BLIZZARD OF '66

*T*he winter had been mild overall, but that changed toward the end of January when the temperatures took a nosedive. On the last Saturday of the month, it began to snow heavily, and it didn't stop until the next day. Winds picked up, creating whiteout conditions. Accidents and tragedy surrounded the city. But children, isolated by impassable roads, rejoiced and thanked the snow gods for delivering a weeklong surprise vacation from school. Highways, airports, and the federal government were closed for days, bringing an eerie silence to the city and the imprisoned families in their homes.

When we thought the last flake had fallen, we tried to escape from our house, but the wind had piled the snow up against both the front and back storm doors, barring our release. Chip climbed out a window and trudged through the snow to retrieve the shovels from the shed. First, he had to dig out the shed door armed only with a dustpan and his gloved hands. Once in possession of the shovels, he returned to clear the front door. After he carved out our escape, the rest of us joined him and helped clear our back door, sidewalk, and, eventually, our cars. Our German shepherd, Labrador retriever, and who-knows-what dog, Patton, had anxiously waited for a sufficient path to be created so he could get outside to relieve himself. He pranced and barked, encouraging us to speedily release him from the confines of the house. Once freed, he ran to the edge of our first cleared path and tried jumping into the snow, but it was too deep. Normally, Patton didn't like doing his business in his own yard. Surrendering to his fate, he lifted a leg and peed on the pure white snow, staining a patch yellow as steam rose from the warm liquid and up into the cold, frigid air.

After we finished liberating our home turf and dog, we set out to find gainful employment. We hired ourselves out as a team throughout the neighborhood, working hard for a day and a half, and made what was for us a fortune. At first, Buddy suggested that I should be paid less because "as a girl" I couldn't possibly shovel as much snow as he could. "Not true," I countered. But before I could add more in my defense, our perennial peacemaker, Eugene, jumped in and quickly headed off our disagreement before it could escalate into an argument. He pointed out to Buddy that he and Chip could shovel more than Buddy. He cautioned that each should work hard and be rewarded equally. In the end, his logic won out, and we shared alike without further debate or conflict.

Once all the cars, driveways, and sidewalks were cleared, we set out to play. We created a series of igloos with connecting tunnels. As epic neighborhood snow wars erupted, we fortified the Ward encampment with ramparts. So we could rise unexpectedly, we made holes in the tops of our igloos and tunnels. With Eugene as our commander, we were organized. Buddy and I were given the task of mass-producing snowballs. I supplied ammunition to Chip, who had the best throwing arm in our troop. From our fortified defenses, we rained snow missiles at the neighborhood mongrel forces, averting invasion and triumphantly retaining possession of our yard.

Back in the house, Mamma kept a steady stream of hot chocolate coming and towels by the front door, so that when we came in red faced, frozen, and dripping, she was prepared. Except for the snow battles, which were all in fun, we didn't have a fight or real argument among ourselves despite having been trapped together for days. The snow battles were mostly us Wards unified against the other neighborhood kids. Camaraderie was high. We were winners, and our union made us strong. It felt great to be a Ward.

But then the weather changed; it got unseasonably warm. Our igloos, tunnel networks, and ramparts all melted away in record time, leaving behind a sea of mud. Schools, businesses, and the federal government reopened. Life returned to "normal." Soon, the snow and our solidarity were but a memory.

CHAPTER ELEVEN

൫ ❖ ൙

A DOLL'S HOUSE

*A*unt Charlotte, who was not really my aunt but Daddy's cousin, visited us every couple of years or so. It was the day before my seventh birthday when she brought the big crate, and it's the first time I remember meeting her. Her husband, Garrett, worked for the Atlantic Coast Line Railroad down in Jacksonville, Florida. Uncle Garrett was the reason Daddy got the job at the Baltimore and Ohio Railroad. In '63 it became the Chesapeake and Ohio. One of the benefits of working for the railroad was that you got to ride for free.

From their visits, my brothers knew well Aunt Charlotte, Uncle Garrett, and their sons: Earle and Garrett Jr., also called Chip. This time, Aunt Charlotte came alone. Daddy and Eugene went to fetch her from the station. I was curious about my namesake. I waited patiently, huddled beneath the overhang that covered the front porch, trying to stay in the shade where it was cooler. The day had been hotter and more humid than was normal for early June, with temperatures reaching ninety. Finally, they pulled up in front of our house. Aunt Charlotte didn't look exactly like Daddy, but you could tell they were family. When she emerged from the truck and walked around the back, there was something familiar in the way she moved; they may have had different parts, but they were put together the same way. Daddy got out next and stopped at the back of the truck to help Eugene with the cargo. There was one suitcase, a burlap bag, and a large crate. I ran over to the truck to greet her.

"Why hello there, young Charlotte. How about ya give me some sugar?" she said as she bent down to kiss me. "The last time I saw ya, you weren't much bigger than your Kissy doll. You still have her?" Her voice and speech sounded like an exaggerated version of Daddy's.

I smiled up at her. "Yes'm, still do."

"Do you remember when you got her?"

"For Christmas, I think, when I was four and a half."

"That's right, sugar. Do you know who got that pretty little doll for you?"

"No, ma'am, I don't recall."

"We did—that's me and your Uncle Garrett. That was the last time we was up here. Phew, it's been a while."

"You gave it to me? Thank you—she's my favorite doll."

"Why, you're welcome, darlin'. Now, ain't you a sweet little thing. Your mama's been teaching you some fine manners." Then she chuckled. "Do you recall the first thing you went off and did when you got that Kissy doll?

"No, ma'am, I don't."

"Well, you went into your room to play with her; so you said anyway. Next thing we seen, your old tabby cat comes out wearing a red and white dress, shakin' and dancin' clear across the livin' room, trying to do whatever he could to get that outfit off. I neared pissed my pants laughin' so hard. Bet it was glad that doll didn't come with no bonnet, or you'd have had that on it too, I am sure. You was just a wee thing. How you managed to get that dress on a full-grown cat, I'll never know."

"I don't remember that."

"You still have that cat?"

"No, ma'am, he died a ways back."

"Whoo, child, it's hotter than a billy goat's ass in a pepper patch out here. You'd think I'd be used to it, coming up from Florida. I forgot how humid this city gets. It's thick as grits. You think your mama has some nice cold iced tea in that house?"

"Probably. She usually has some."

"Then let's get ourselves inside, why don't we? We'll sit a while and have us a fine chat." I took her hand and led her inside. "Lordy, you've sprouted up since last I set eyes on you, child. What they been feeding ya?"

Daddy and Eugene brought her suitcase and burlap bag into the house. Mamma greeted Aunt Charlotte with a warm hug and told Eugene to take her bag up to my room. Mamma had made a pallet on the floor next to her and Daddy's bed for me. I was to sleep in with them while Aunt Charlotte was visiting. When Eugene came back down, he went out to help Daddy with the crate.

"What's in that?" I asked when they set it down in the living room.

"Well, wouldn't you like to know, little missy," Aunt Charlotte said.

"Is it a surprise?" My curiosity had been aroused.

"It's a surprise, all right. It's for your birthday tomorrow."

"That big thing is for me?" I asked excitedly.

"Yes, darlin', it sure is. Don't ya know I came up special just to give it to ya? It's somethin' I'd hoped to give to a daughter of my own, but the good Lord saw fit to only give me sons, which I am eternally grateful for, but what's inside is meant for a girl. Anyways, you're my namesake, so I got to thinkin' it should belong to you. I've been waitin' for your birthday to give it to ya. You'll have to wait 'til tomorra, though, to find out what's inside."

"You brought that big thing all the way from Florida for me? Wow." I felt excited and special. Having to sleep on the floor next to my parents' bed and hearing my daddy's snoring weren't the only reasons I had a hard time getting to sleep that night. I couldn't wait to find out what was inside the mysterious wooden box. I was more excited about it than the birthday party Mamma and I had spent weeks planning.

The next morning, I was woken up by the smell of bacon frying. Sunlight filled the room. When I came downstairs, I saw Aunt Charlotte and Mamma working in the kitchen side by side. They moved around our small kitchen as if they had been working together for years. Charlotte was wearing one of Mamma's aprons. It was obvious that Mamma enjoyed Aunt Charlotte's company, though she didn't always approve of some of the colorful things she'd say.

"Well, hello there, sleepyhead," greeted Mamma. "So you finally decided to get out of bed and join us," she added as she grabbed some dishes from the cabinet. "Here, take these and set the table."

"I had a hard time falling asleep last night. My mind wouldn't shut up," I said as I took the dishes from her outstretched hands.

With a spatula in her hand, Aunt Charlotte turned and looked at me. "Well, gooood mornin' there, birthday girl. Y'all ready for some hotcakes, grits, and bacon?" she asked.

"Yes, please," I said and hurried to set the table. Afterward, I went into the living room. It had been decorated with a happy birthday sign and some of the smaller pieces of furniture had been removed to make room for my guests.

When I returned to the kitchen, Mamma said, "Charlotte, call your brothers and Daddy to breakfast. Chip and Daddy are in the basement and the other two are upstairs."

"Where's the crate?"

"Your daddy took it to the basement," Aunt Charlotte answered.

"Can I open the crate after breakfast?" I asked the two women.

Mamma replied, "No, dear, I think we should wait a bit. We have too much to do to get ready for your guests." She turned to my namesake. "Charlotte, when do you think would be a good time for little Charlotte to open your gift? Should we wait until just after cake and ice cream or should we wait until after dinner when it's just the family in the house?"

I jumped at that and started to hop up and down. "Dinner! What? No way. Mamma, no, please. I don't think I can wait that long," I exclaimed as my voice grew higher in pitch with each word I spoke.

Aunt Charlotte said, "Lordy be, child, you're shaking like a dog passin' peach seeds. Simmer down, child."

Mamma sighed and rolled her eyes at that but said nothing.

"Pleeeease, Mamma. I'll die if I have to wait that long."

"I doubt that, but in any case, it's not up to me; it's up to your aunt."

I turned to Aunt Charlotte, but before I could get another word out, she warned, "Whoa there. Now, take a breath, sweetie, 'fore you bust a gasket. Why don't ya open it after the cake when all your friends are here?"

I breathed a sigh of relief. "Thank you, thank you, Aunt

Charlotte," I said as I ran over and hugged her around her waist.

"You're mighty welcome," she replied, and after I released her, she returned to the work of finishing up breakfast.

As soon as all the bacon and the last pancake had been eaten, we cleared the plates. Mamma told the boys to bring the dining chairs into the living room so we could play musical chairs. Soon my guests started to arrive. First to show up were two of the three girls from next door, Carolyn and Laurie. Pamela had said she was too old to come to a seven-year-old's party. She told me this after she learned Eugene wouldn't be at home during the party. She was sweet on him and was always bringing over cookies she baked, telling me to make sure he got them. She was constantly interrogating me about what foods he liked, what movies he went to see, or who was his favorite singer. I liked her cookies, so I didn't bother telling her that Eugene didn't seem all that interested. Most of the time he seemed oblivious to her flirtations.

Next were Jennie and her little sister, Sarah. Recently, Mamma had started looking after them whenever their mama was out looking for work. She didn't charge for it. Their daddy had moved out and didn't leave a forwarding address, as Mamma put it. Next to arrive was Colleen Sullivan, followed by Karen Wilson from school. Last, Cathy Drummond from across the street walked in.

Mamma and Aunt Charlotte had planned games. There was a tailless donkey printed on a poster that was taped to the wall. The first game was pin the tail on the donkey. Karen swore she wasn't cheating, but it was obvious that she was. She tilted her head up and looked beneath her blindfold. Even so, she wasn't the closest to the donkey's backside. That was Laurie and she got to pick a candy from a bag of prizes. Next, we played clothespin drop, followed by a relay with spoons and hard cooked eggs, which was my favorite game. We finished with musical chairs. Karen won that one, mostly because she was bigger than everyone else except me and pushed her way onto the last seat, knocking little Sarah to the floor with a thud. Jennie got mad at that, but Aunt Charlotte saved the day by yelling, "Time to blow out some candles. Who wants cake?" Mamma came out of the kitchen with a cake with vanilla butter cream icing and seven candles, and started singing, "Happy birthday to you ..."

I barely touched my cake because I was so excited about opening my presents, especially what was in the crate. But Mamma said I had to open Charlotte's gift last. As the girls sat around, I started opening the boxes. Mamma always made me open the presents carefully. After I opened each present, she took the wrapping paper, pressed out the wrinkles with her hands, and folded it so it could be reused at another time.

The first present I opened was from Colleen. She gave me a couple of Dr. Seuss books. One was his latest book, titled *I Had Trouble in Getting to Solla Sollew*, and the other was *If I Ran a Zoo*. I'd already read the second one, but I liked it a lot. The girls next door brought me a Tressy doll. Tressy's hair got longer or shorter so that you could style it in many ways. To make her hair grow, you pulled on the ponytail on top of her head. Later you could roll it back up to make it short again by turning a button in her back with a key. From Karen I got the Beatles Flip Your Wig board game. Jennie and Sarah gave me a paint-by-numbers picture of a horse. Cathy's present was a Skipper doll with bendable, posable legs. Last, Mamma handed me a present from Eugene. "Should I wait to open it until he gets home?" I asked.

"No," said Mamma, "he wanted you to open it in front of your friends." Breaking her rule about wrapping paper, I ripped it open. Underneath the reused paper was the new *Mary Poppins* soundtrack album. With it was a note from Eugene promising to take me to see the movie too.

At long last it was time to open the big box. Daddy and Aunt Charlotte brought it back upstairs and detached the lid, but left the lid sitting on top. With Aunt Charlotte's help, I slid the top off, then peeked inside. Mamma came over to help us lift it out of its container. Out emerged a large doll's house. Next to come out of the crate were two shoeboxes filled with miniature furniture. Each piece was carefully wrapped in old newspaper. "Your great-grand-daddy built that for me. It's an exact copy of the Ward family home down in Ahoskie, North Carolina, the one your daddy and me grew up in," Aunt Charlotte informed me.

For the rest of the afternoon, my party guests and I played with the doll's house, arranging and rearranging all its furnishings.

When the last guest left and we finished cleaning up all the plates and glasses, I asked Aunt Charlotte to tell me more about the present.

"My granddaddy made it for me, and Grandma Rose decorated it. See here in the dining room, we had wallpaper just like this. Grandma Rose painted it to look just the same only smaller. She did a real fine job, I can tell ya that. See the pink dogwood flowers here, don't they look like they're growin' on a vine instead of a tree like they do in nature? We had lace curtains same as these. I spent hours and hours playing with this doll house. Growin' up, it was my most prized possession, and now it's yours. Grandma Rose would've liked that. Looky here, this is just like our kitchen. This table goes smack dab in the middle of the room. We did a lot of bakin', cookin', laughin', and cryin' around that table. This room up here in the front, that's where your great-grandparents slept 'fore Granddaddy Jackson died. After that Grandma Rose moved down to this room here next to the kitchen. Your daddy and Raymond slept in the blue room upstairs in the back of the house. This little bitty room was mine."

"Wow, it looks like a stately house. I like the big front porch. Was it a plantation?"

"Nah, it was just a good-sized farm is all."

"What's the difference?"

"Land, mostly. A plantation, I'd guess, would have at least five hundred acres and usually plenty more. Back before the War

Between the States, they'd have a lot more slaves than a regular old farm. A big farm probably had no more than five or six slaves workin' it—at the most, ten.

"I thought you all were poor?" I queried.

"Your daddy and me, we growed up poorer than church mice, but our people didn't always wear patches on their britches. Back when we was young, lots of folks were poorer than us. Seemed like everyone was poor. But us Wards, we always had a roof over our heads, and, 'cause we had the farm, we had food to eat. Share-croppers had it a whole lot worse. They didn't have a pot to piss in or a winda' to throw it out of neither. Compared to them, we were livin' the good life. Back 'fore the flood, the Wards were prosperous farmers, that is 'til the First World War came along—that's before your daddy and me got born. But Grandma Rose, she was the one that came from real gentry. Her daddy lived in high cotton and her half-brothers too. Her stepbrother James was a lawyer and her stepbrother Jessie was the town's doctor. All the men in that family were educated."

"How come only the men?"

"'Cause her daddy, like most men back then, believed education was wasted on a girl. All they could do when they grew up was raise children and run a house. They didn't need to go off to some fancy school to learn that."

"What happened? It's such a grand house. From the looks of it, you'd think the people who lived in it were doing well."

"Well, our folks had been doin' pretty darn good once upon a time. But then hard times come along. Lots of things happened. There was a big drop in tobacca prices. Farmin' is hard, and it's risky. We had soil erosion, white mold, blue mold, gray mold, brown spots, black rot, hornworms, and potato beetles. Finally, the soil just plain got wore out. You name it, we had it. Us kids had to go out and pick off all them dang hornworms from every single blessed leaf on every plant. That took days. Then a few weeks later we'd be at it again. Nowadays, they got chemicals for hornworms, aphids, and the like. Because of them worms, I swore I'd never marry me no farmer. When Garrett walked into church and I heard he worked for the railroad, I knew he was the man for me. After the First Great War, the Wards were barely hangin' on. When the Depression come along, it just up and finished us off."

"And what about Great-Grandma Rose's family? Did they lose everything too?"

"Nah, them and their close kin kept their houses up real nice while we were too poor to paint and too proud to whitewash. Their women were always dressed stylish, and their hands were soft. They had colored help to do the hard work. You didn't see any of 'em pickin' no worms, that's for sure. We used to see old Dr. Marshall driving all around the county in his shiny Ford Model A when I was young. Later he got a Model T. He drove around makin' house calls 'til he got too old. Doctor Marshall had three daughters; all of 'em went to college too. One became a teacher at our school. I don't remember his brother too good. He died when I was but small. Hey, did you know Grandma Rose's daddy was a colonel in the Confederate Army?"

"No, I never heard that. So he fought to keep slavery. Did he own slaves?"

"Well, yes, of course he did."

"Ooh, that's embarrassing."

"It's no such thing. All over this country back 'fore the Civil War come, almost anyone with a bit of money owned a slave or two. It was just the way things were. Yes, it was more common in the South, but a good many Yankees owned slaves too. In the South, if you scratch at a family tree you won't have to get under the bark very far 'til you find yourself a slave owner. That's just a fact.

"Did the Wards own slaves?"

"They had a few, not near as many as the Marshalls, though. Before the War, the Civil War that is, the Marshalls had close to sixty slaves, I heard tell. Wards never owned no more than five or six at most that I know of."

"So, did we get the farm from the Marshall side of the family?"

"Nah, that homestead had long been in the Ward family since 'fore the War of Independence. Grandma didn't get hardly nothin' from her daddy 'cept maybe her temper and a stubborn streak a mile long. She used to say he was meaner than a skillet full of snakes. I heard others say 'bout the same, just in different ways.

I heard tell that he once beat a colored girl to death. Grandma never confirmed it, but she didn't deny it neither. I 'spect it's true, or something close to it anyway. He was well known throughout the county and then some. A lot of interesting tales got told about him."

"Like what?"

"Well, he outlived three wives and two of 'em were sisters. Grandma's mama, Nancy Lewis, was his third wife, and she come along when he was already old. When he died, he didn't leave nothin' to Rose. He was still angry that she run off with Grand-daddy Ward and got married without his say-so. But I don't think they ever saw eye to eye on much of nothin'. He didn't think women should have opinions of their own, and that's one thing Grandma Rose had plenty of—opinions, that is. She didn't keep 'em to herself none too often neither. According to her pa, the only thing a girl was fit to speak of was the weather and family. But he weren't alone in that. He did pay for her piana lessons, though, back when she was young. A woman with genteel talents was fine, but she shouldn't think or speak unless spoken to.

"When the old colonel died, he left everything to his two sons, who each had different mamas. The oldest, James, his mama was Iona McLaughlin. When she died great-granddaddy George Marshall, that was his name, married Iona's younger sister, Riona. Just like them Israelites in the Bible."

"What do you mean by that? What did the Israelites do?"

"Well, back in Bible times, if a bride up and died on a man, he could go back to her father and ask for another one, seeing how the first one didn't work out.

"You mean kinda like a warranty on a new car."

Aunt Charlotte chuckled a bit. "I guess you could say it like that, though I never heard it told thataway."

"Is that what great-grandpa Marshall did, went to his father-in-law and asked for a new model?"

"Don't know how it worked out—but when his first wife died, he ended up with the younger sister, Riona. I guess you could say he got a newer model. Anyway, Riona, the second wife, had a son too, and she named him Jessie. By and by, that younger son 'came a doctor and was always helpin' folks. I never heard an unkind word spoke of Dr. Marshall. However, I can't say the same 'bout his brother. The brother was more like their pa. Ornery."

"Was Rose close to her half-brother Jessie then?"

"They kept in touch and were kind to one another, but I wouldn't say they was close. After Granddad Marshall died, and they laid the old coot to rest, his will got read. Uncle Jessie felt bad about how his pa had treated Rose. Jessie gave her the family silverware, some fine dishes, the piana, an old paintin' she liked, and twenty-four acres just outside of Winton on the Chowan River, all from his own inheritance. That was a pretty piece of land. The Ward men and boys would go out there to turkey hunt or fish. Aunt Sarah's people would join us out there. They built a sleeping shed that the boys used when they went huntin'. On hot summer days, we'd head out there to go swimmin'. Oh, it was a glorious spot. After church, we'd go there for a picnic. The air was cooler by the river. Grandma Rose had to sell it eventually to try and keep the farm goin'. We used to see Great-uncle Jessie every Sunday at the First Baptist Church and say hello. But we never broke bread together; that is, he never came to our house and we never got an invite, far as I know, to supper at his."

"Tell me more about Grandma Rose."

"Well, she was small, like her mama, but tougher than a pine knot. She could be cantankerous, but quick as a whip. Don't get me wrong, she could be sweet as a peach if'n you behaved and she liked ya. Uncle Wyatt, your granddaddy, may have been running the farm, but everyone knew she ran the house and that means the family too."

"What about my daddy's mama? What was she like? Where she come from?"

"Aunt Sarah? She was real tall. She was more than a head taller than Grandma Rose. But she was a whole lot skinnier than anyone else in the family. She was thin as a killdeer."

"What's a killdeer?"

"That's a little bitty bird with long stick legs. The point is, there weren't an ounce of fat on her. Her hair was thick and real dark. That's where Eugene gets his thick dark hair from. Aunt Sarah's kin had a farm over north of Winton. She was a Butler 'fore she

116

got married. The Butlers were havin' hard times too, even harder than us Wards. A lot of your daddy's cousins started movin' over to Elizabeth City. We lost track of 'em after that. They had Meherrin Indian blood in 'em, but you never spoke of it."

"Why'd didn't you speak of it? I'd have thought it would be something to be proud of?"

"Proud of? Nah, still ain't nothin' you go crowin' about, though it's a lot better than it were. Back in them days, it was like tellin' folks you was part colored. Course, there's no such thing as being part colored. You can be part German, part Italian, even part Indian. But if you're any part colored, you're just plain colored."

"Why's that?"

"Just is. Why's the grass green?"

"Was Grandma Sarah nice?"

"Yeah, she was sweet, but she didn't talk all that much. She had big, dark watchful eyes and had real quiet ways. The cows, when we had some, and the goats too, gave out more milk for her than anyone else. She was gentle and patient. If babies was cryin' at church, folks knew to hand them over to Aunt Sarah. She'd get 'em quiet faster than their own mamas could. She didn't chatter much. When she spoke, it was 'cause she had somethin' to say. Grandma Rose did enough talkin' for the pair of 'em anyway. If you saw one, you could be sure the other wasn't far off. Those two could have a whole conversation without ever sayin' a word. Grandma Rose would grunt, and Aunt Sarah'd know just what she'd wanted."

"What happened to her? Daddy has told me very little about her. He gets upset when I ask how she died. Why is that?"

"Shoot, that's enough storytellin' for now. I sure can ramble on, can't I? It's gettin' late, and there still a bunch to cleanin' up to do. I best be helpin' your mama fix dinner, and you best be after the cleanin'."

"But why won't he talk about his own mother?"

"Sweet pea, I reckon he's got his reasons. You best respect that and leave it be. You try 'n open that box, somethin' likely to jump out and bite ya. You go on now, help clean up. You can start with takin' out the trash and sweepin'. When you're finished with that, you come set the table. Okay now."

"But—"

"You best leave it be, missy, just leave it be. You hear me now? We've had enough storytellin' for one day."

CHAPTER TWELVE

☙ ❖ ❧

SURPRISE CATCH

I t was a Sunday, cloudy, and a cool day for August. I'd never seen Eugene so agitated. He and his best friend, Scott, had tickets to hear the Beatles at D.C. Stadium the next evening. But Mamma said she didn't want him to go. She'd heard rumors that the Ku Klux Klan was going to show up. Apparently, the Klan was upset about what John Lennon said about the Beatles: "We're more popular than Jesus now." Daddy said the Klan wasn't all wrong this one time. However, after a lot of desperate pleading and politicking, Daddy relented and gave permission for Eugene to go despite Mamma's reservations. After hugging Daddy, Eugene shrieked for joy. Throughout the house you could hear Eugene singing, "I want to be your man" or "Baby's in black and I'm feeling blue." I had begged and begged for him to take me along too. Tickets were still available, but Mamma said no emphatically, and this time, Daddy wouldn't override her decision.

The day before, the boys had gotten up at the crack of dawn to go fishing. I wanted to come along with them and jumped out of bed when I heard them in the hall. "Wait for me," I called. I'm coming too."

Buddy didn't want me around, though. "You can't come 'cause you're a girrrl," he said, as if being a girl was like having a disease.

"Yeah, you best stay home, kiddo," agreed Chip. "You'll just get tired and bored." What I was tired of was either being too young or being a girl, so I decided to follow them. Because it was still early, it was a bit chilly and I grabbed my sweater and took off to follow them. They were walking fast. At first, I tried to stay back far enough so they wouldn't see me, but that proved impossible to do and keep up without losing them, especially when they entered the woods. Eventually Eugene took pity on me. He said something to the others, then came back to walk with me. Chip called over to us: "Don't start whining to be carried if you get tired," he warned.

But Eugene gently took my hand and said, "Don't worry, sweetie. You'll do fine." While we walked together he pointed out things like young sassafras saplings. He told me that's what you use for root beer. He pointed out curled heads of tiny fern plants erupting from the ground and moss growing on trees. "If you ever get lost in the woods," he said, "moss can show you the way. It usually grows on the north side of trees, because that gets less light." There didn't seem to be a limit to Eugene's knowledge. He saw everything. "Looks like the ranger has been by here. Some trees must have fallen across the path. See how they're cut and the logs are piled up."

Our journey seemed to take forever, but we finally came out of the woods in front of a large pond. The boys opened a Maxwell instant coffee jar filled with squirming worms. That morning, they'd searched through the soil around the compost pile in our yard for fat worms. It hadn't taken long. Now each of them grabbed one out of the can, put it on their hook, and went to the water's edge to cast out their lines. Then they just stood there. Nothing seemed to be happening. I didn't want to admit that Chip had been right—I was bored and wished I had stayed home. I picked up a few stones and started to throw them in the water, but Chip yelled at me: "Quit it; you'll scare all the fish away."

"I told you it was a bad idea to let her follow us," said Buddy.

"I want to fish too," I cried.

"Then you should have brought a fishing rod," retorted Buddy.

"You can make yourself useful," said Chip. "Go in the backpack. There's a half loaf of bread, a butter knife, and a jar of peanut butter. Make everyone some sandwiches for breakfast," he commanded.

After our meal, I went off and started picking some wild blue indigo plants that were close to the pond. Once I had a full bouquet, I was bored again and moped around. The sun had burned the morning mist off the pond and the temperature had risen. I took off my sweater and tied it around my waist. Just then, Eugene's line started to tug, and he reeled it in. When the hook exited the water,

.

there was nothing on it, not even the worm.

Eugene looked over at me. "Come here, Charlotte, we can share," he offered. "But you'll have to bait your own hook," he warned. I was determined to be brave. I reached in, felt the slimy worms, and grabbed one. Eugene handed me the hook. I took it with my left hand and tried to impale the tiny creature on its sharp spike, but I froze.

"I can't, Eugene; I just can't spear it." I whispered to him, hoping he'd keep my shameful secret from Buddy and Chip.

So the others couldn't see, he turned his back. "It's okay, honey. It was a good first try." With the hook still in my left hand, he deftly took the doomed worm from my right and skewered it onto the hook. Then in a louder voice he said, "Attagirl." Transfixed, I watched the worm struggle on the hook. The others looked over at us. "Now cast it out," Eugene commanded, but I hesitated.

"I don't know how," I told him.

"That's okay. I'll show you," he said as he moved behind me. He placed his hand over mine. "It takes a bit of practice, but you'll get it, honey. Make sure the bail lever—that's the spool—is flipped upright, and you have a bit more than a foot of line between your rod and the hook. See? Hold your rod and place your index finger against it, pressing the line to the shaft. This is how you control the line. Now we're going to cast," said Eugene as he placed his hand over mine. "When I say let go, take your finger off the line." He brought my arm back, flicked it forward, and said, "Let go!"

I did as he commanded. Together, we watched as the hook and worm soared out over the lake and disappeared into the murky water. Pointing out into the lake, he asked, "Do you see the orange bobber floating on the water?"

"Yeah," I answered.

"Keep an eye on it. That's what's going to tell you if a fish is nibbling on your worm; it will tug on the line to get at the bait, and the ball will bounce a bit. When you feel something tug at the end of your line, your first instinct will be to jerk the line. But you might lose him that way. Try and visualize what's happening below the water. See, your fish is swimming around when he sees the bait. He starts to nibble on the outer edges, testing it. But you can't catch him yet. You must entice him to bite. So wait a little bit. After you first see the ball bobbing, when you think he's taking that bite, pull up so that the tip of the pole goes up. This will hopefully hook your fish. The trick is to know when to reel it in. If you're too fast, you'll scare him off. If you're too slow, he'll get your worm but you won't get him. If you see the bobber start bouncing up and down or if you feel something pulling, you let me know, and I'll help you."

I waited and waited but nothing happened. Eugene went off into the woods to pee. I was about to give up when finally, I saw the bobber move and felt a tug. I started yelling, "I think I got something, I think I got something!" I started reeling in fast, but when my line came out of the water there was no fish and my worm was missing.

I was content to return the rod to Eugene when he got back. He went over and picked up the coffee jar and was about to put another worm on his hook when Chip yelled, "I have something!" We could see his bobber dancing up and down, and his line went taut. When his line came out of the water, there was a small shimmering fish flapping back and forth. He reeled it nearly all the way in, reached over, grabbed the fish by its jaws, and unhooked it. He then found a twig and slipped it through and under one of the fish's gills, straight through its mouth. I went over to look at it. It had a sad, painful, and panicked look in its eye.

"Let it go, Chip," I begged. "You're hurting it." When he didn't respond, I went on. "Please, Chip, please, don't let it die."

"I told you she'd only start whining," complained Buddy.

"It's too small to eat anyway. Just throw it back," commanded Eugene.

"I don't want to go home empty-handed," said Chip.

"Yeah, and what are you going to do with it? It's too small to make a meal out of. You know what Daddy will say: 'If you're not going to eat it, don't kill it.' It'd be a waste to let it die for nothing when it could grow big enough one day for a good catch. Daddy says, 'Wasting's a sin.' Just let it go. Let's try and catch some bigger ones, something we can take home."

Chip looked down at me. "If I let this one go, you'll have to be quiet if I catch a bigger one. Do you promise?" I nodded my head affirmatively. To my surprise and relief, Chip reached down, removed the stick, and gently returned the poor, wounded creature back into the water. They kept fishing for a bit but grew bored too when nothing tugged on their hooks. The weather had warmed even more, so I removed my shoes, moved my sweater from around my waist, and tied it around my neck, and then waded into the water. I felt the soft, silky soil ooze between my toes.

"This spot is no good. We need to try somewhere else," suggested Eugene.

"I wish we had a boat. I bet it's better in the middle where the water is deep," said Buddy. "That's where the big fish are."

"We could hike over to the peninsula," offered Chip.

"We tried that last time," responded Buddy. "Hey, Chip, did you bring that rope for the swing?"

"Yes, it's in the backpack."

"Let's build a raft," Buddy offered. "I got the Swiss knife. Did you see those cut logs on the walk in? They weren't that far back. If we tied them together we'd have a raft."

"I don't know." Chip was skeptical.

"Let's give it a try at least," begged Buddy.

"I brought it so we could make a rope swing out over the water," Chip said.

"We'll need to find a tree that hangs out over the water in a deep section. Do you see one like that?" asked Eugene. We all glanced around, but there wasn't a specimen answering to that description.

"I think I know where there's one. It's on the other side, down a ways toward the dam. I think I can find it."

"Ah, come on, Chip," said Buddy. "Give up the rope and let's build a raft."

"Okay, okay, we'll do it." It took us about a half hour to gather the logs together by the shore and another half hour to tie them together. We set the raft in the shallow water and prepared to launch.

"Does she have to come?" complained Buddy.

"We can't leave her behind," Eugene reasoned.

In preparation, I took my sweater and looped one sleeve through my belt and tied it off, so I wouldn't lose it. Eugene told me to get on first, then Buddy. He and Chip took the raft out deeper. "Go on Chip, hop on," Eugene instructed before giving our vessel one final shove and jumping on himself. We were all crowded together on our tiny raft as we started drifting further out. We hadn't thought about oars, but it didn't matter. It didn't take long before we started to sink. One by one, the boys jumped off, leaving me hanging to the last of the timbers. But once they were off, the raft started to float again. I began to drift further out.

"Jump," cried Buddy, followed by Eugene and Chip in a chorus: "Jump, Jump!" Finally, I took the plunge and leapt off and began swimming toward shore. When I had nearly made it, I felt something tugging me back into the water.

"Help!" I screamed, "Something's got me." I tried to stand up and could barely feel the bottom as I bobbed, trying to keep my head above water. The silt on the pond's bottom felt like quicksand, pulling me deeper down into the sludge as I tried to pull myself forward. I was starting to panic. Chip and Eugene waded out and grabbed me and began to haul me in. As I started to emerge from the water, Chip noticed that my sweater was dragging behind. He reached in and started pulling. On the other end of my sweater was the largest snapping turtle any of us had ever seen.

"Looks like you win the prize for the biggest catch today," said Chip. The turtle didn't want to let go. I had to untie the sweater from my belt. Buddy and I wanted to keep it as a pet and convinced the others to help us bring it home. We took turns holding it on its sides as we carried it all the way home, careful to avoid getting bitten. Most of the time, it kept its head hidden inside its shell. Occasionally, just the tip of its head protruded.

By the time we reached our yard, we were all hungry, stinking, dead tired, and thirsty. Unfortunately, Mamma was in the yard taking down the laundry when we got inside the hedges.

"Ah, sweet Jesus, Mary, and Joseph, what in the world do you have now?"

"Charlotte caught it. Can we keep it?" pleaded Buddy.

"Absolutely not. You can all turn right around and take that poor thing back to exactly where you found it."

"But Mamma, we're famished and tired, and it's a long walk."

"That's too bad. You should have thought of that before you hauled that poor creature home. You don't know how to keep it alive, and when it dies, it'll stink to high heaven. You're going to take it back to its home right this instant."

"But—"

"No buts, just be gone with you now." We hesitated. Then she added while pointing, "Go!"

"Can't it wait 'til we clean up a bit and get something to eat? We're starved," Chip begged.

"It's getting late, and I said go. I mean this instant. Don't make me say it again."

With that we all turned around and headed back toward the pond. By the time we returned home, it was heading toward evening. "Dinner will be on the table when you've all cleaned up," Mamma informed us. After such a long hike in wet, stinking clothes, my skin felt raw and I wanted desperately to take a bath. However, with only one bath in the house, there was a hierarchy in who got in first. As the youngest, I went last. By the time I got a bath, the water was cold. As soon as I was clean, I went to bed, forgetting entirely about supper.

CHAPTER THIRTEEN

℘ ❖ ℭ

NUN ENCOUNTER

Colleen Sullivan lived in a row house around the corner from ours. There were eleven kids and counting in the Sullivan family; her mama was pregnant with another Sullivan. All of them looked like variations on the same theme. They had light eyes: blue to pale green. Each had straight blonde hair: from light strawberry blond to almost white. All had freckles and pale, milk-white skin, and they were all slender and mostly average to a bit below average height. They were all athletic and excelled at competition. Her daddy was a mortician. It was the only job he could find that paid enough to feed and clothe all his kids, Colleen once told me. It must have paid well; the Sullivan kids went to private Catholic schools. During that summer, Colleen and I had become best friends. She went to Saint Anthony's school.

Catholic school students were going back to class a week before us public school kids. Colleen and I were unwilling to let our school schedules separate us just yet. We got it into our heads that I would go with Colleen to school and dress in one of her uniforms to pretend that I was a new student. Colleen reasoned that they would just think that my paperwork got misplaced, and I could go through the first day with her. I was curious about the differences between Catholic schools versus public. I'd just seen the movie *The Trouble with Angels* with Hayley Mills. It took place in an all-girls Catholic school, which made our idea seem romantic and adventurous. Adding to my curiosity, I knew if it wasn't for the money, Mamma would send me to Saint Anthony's. She talked about it often with Daddy, but I think it was more than just money that kept Daddy saying no.

Mamma and Daddy didn't see eye to eye on religion. Rather than argue anymore about it, they decided to let us choose our own church. The boys chose to worship God by keeping his commandment to rest on Sundays and would sleep late on the Sabbath. I was curious about my Catholic and Baptist roots. Going to school with Colleen was a chance to peek inside my mother's world.

So, on the last Monday in August, I got dressed in one of Colleen's uniforms, snuck out of the house, and met Colleen just outside her home. To avoid walking with a bunch of her siblings and dealing with the obvious questions that would follow, we took off early. To kill time, we went past the school and headed up to Fort Bunker Hill Park and meandered around a bit until it was time to head back toward the school. We walked up to St. Anthony's and entered through a side door.

I was in the school for less than a minute when I was already in trouble. Although Colleen and I wore the same size, I was a good three inches taller. Her skirts hit below the knee on her, but on me, they were apparently too high. But I didn't know that yet.

We had just entered the building and my eyes were still getting used to the darkness in the hallway when a nun dressed head to toe in a full black robe, except for a bit of white around her head, came storming toward me. At first, I looked to see what was behind me, but when she reached me, she grabbed me by my ear and started dragging me down the hall. Colleen just froze and wasn't any kind of help. I tried to pull away, but the nun was strong and quick. She pulled me into a classroom, grabbed a ruler, and put it against my skirt.

"What is the meaning of this? Your skirt is a good three inches too short."

"I am sorry, ma'am, I must have grown more than I thought this summer."

"'Ma'am'? Since when do you call me 'ma'am?' I am Sister to you, Sister Burk. I don't remember you. Where do you come from?"

"Excuse me, Sister, I went to Our Sister of Perpetual Sorrow last year." I recited the lie that I had practiced with Colleen.

"Really, did you now." She sounded skeptical. "And this is what your mother allowed you to wear to school today?"

"Ah, no, Sister Burk, she didn't see me wearing it. I was so excited about my first day in a new school that I left the house before she got up."

"So your mother was off sleeping when you got yourself ready for school?"

"Yes, Sister."

"I might have known. Hold out your hand."

"What?" I asked, confused.

"Now don't make me tell you again. You heard what I said." Over her shoulder and just outside the classroom door, I saw Colleen gesturing. She was holding her hand out in front of her with her palms up. I quickly mirrored her gesture. Before I knew what was happening, Sister Burk struck me hard on my palms with her ruler.

"Ouch," I cried.

"Perhaps now you'll remember to dress decently. Now go back home, get your lazy mother out of bed, and don't come back until you've lengthened that skirt."

With my hand still stinging, I turned and left the building without saying a word to Colleen. That was the beginning and the end of my Catholic school education.

CHAPTER FOURTEEN

❧ ❖ ❧

À LA LUCY

*M*amma took in laundry from other people. Mostly she just ironed their already cleaned shirts; however, she had a few wifeless customers who had her washing their clothes as well as ironing them. In mid-September our washing machine broke. We couldn't afford a new one right away. Daddy found an old hand-crank laundry wringer that he mounted on the wall over the laundry sink in the basement. When one of her clients, Mr. Saunders, came by to drop off his laundry one day, Mamma was at the convenience store picking up a few things. Mamma had to go to the local mom-and-pop store because large stores like supermarkets were closed on Sundays because of the blue laws. I was in the house alone; Daddy and Chip were out front working on a car. When Mamma returned from shopping, I was in the living room dancing and singing to the Supremes' song "You Keep Me Hanging On." Mamma grinned when she saw me pantomiming some of the lyrics, but she quickly lost her smile when she caught sight of the oversized laundry bag that stood next to the sofa.

"What's that?"

"Oh, Mr. Saunders dropped his laundry off. He said he'd swing by Tuesday after work to pick it up," I informed her as my song was ending.

She let out a groan, but then started to chuckle.

"What's so funny?"

"I'll let you know after I put the groceries away. Where's Buddy?"

"He's up the street at Carl Weber's house. He said they invited him to Sunday dinner. Daddy said it was okay with him if it was okay with you."

"Sunday is family night. He should be home."

"But the Webers are Orioles fans, and they have a color TV set. Come on, Mamma, it's a big game today. It's game two of the World Series, after all, and Jim Palmer is pitching for the O's. Sandy Koufax is pitching for the Dodgers. It doesn't get much bigger than that. Buddy said, 'It's a historic matchup!' Really, Mamma, you gotta let him stay."

"There is no such word as 'gotta,' and I don't have to do anything of the sort."

"Please, Mamma, it's important to Buddy—real, real important. He'll just die if he can't watch the game, and he'll be the only boy at school tomorrow who didn't if you don't let him stay. Do you know what kind of freak that would make him?"

"He can watch it here."

"But it won't be in color, and it's more fun to watch it with a friend."

"Okay, okay, he can stay at the Webers." With that she headed to the kitchen. When she returned to the living room, she said, "Charlotte, do you remember that *I Love Lucy* episode where Lucy stomps the grapes?"

"Yeah, I think so, why?"

"Because I have an idea. Give me five minutes and then come up to the bathroom."

"What's up?"

"You'll see."

So I grabbed a quick snack and then went upstairs to the bathroom. As I climbed the stairs, I heard music playing. When I opened the bathroom door, I saw Mamma kneeling and stirring soap in a half-full bathtub. The radio sat on the toilet lid and was plugged into the wall. Beside her on the floor were two piles of clothes. "Are your feet reasonably clean?" she asked.

"Yeah, I guess so—why you want to know?"

"You'll soon find out," she said, keeping the mystery going.

She then turned on the radio, turned the knob, and started searching for a station. She paused on 1390. The fast-talking Terry Knight was announcing, "The WEAM Team brings you the Wonderful Washington sound with the Monkees singing, 'Take the Last Train to Clarksville.'" Then we heard Micky Dolenz's voice come over the radio.

"You like them, don't you?" Mamma asked.

"The Monkees? Yeah, I guess so."

"Can you dance to it?"

"Ah, yeah, of course. Who can't?"

She turned the volume up a bit and put one of the clothes piles in the tub.

"Okay, Charlotte, get in and start dancing."

"What?"

"You can dance like a washing machine with your feet or you can scrub them with your hands. Which would you prefer?"

"Dancing!"

"All right, then. Get to it. Climb in the tub and start dancing."

So I got in the water and started moving my feet to the beat of the music. Mamma sorted through the remainder of the clothes. She hand scrubbed the ones that had spots or looked soiled, especially along the cuffs and collars. When she finished one she added it to the tub. When all the clothes were finally in the tub, Mamma left the bathroom while I was mashing and twisting the clothes below my feet. She returned two songs later. It was my job to rinse each load twice by dancing to one or two songs as needed. When I was done, she took the clothes to the basement to wring them out well before hanging them outside to dry. After that, we started washing the laundry together every Saturday. We learned the lyrics to all the current hits playing on the radio. Sometimes Mamma would sing along. We had a routine that we did together for the song "Reach Out, I'll Be There" by the Four Tops and one for the Supremes hit "Stop! In the Name of Love." Together, we synchronized our moves while Mamma sang and I harmonized. We laughed a lot during our laundry sessions, as we called them. This ended when, for Christmas, Daddy bought Mamma a "new" used machine.

Part Five

1967

CHAPTER FIFTEEN

ဆ ❖ ख

PREDATORS IN THE PARK

*P*edophiles are like other predators: they seek out the easy prey. Like the lion and the wolf, they look for the young that are some distance from the herd, the ones with distracted mothers. We'd been living in Colmar Manor for about three or four months. It's a neighborhood just over the D.C. line in Maryland. My new best friend was Stacey Diamond. She lived down the block from us. Like me, she was tall, blond, scrawny, and good at games. We were playing with some other kids at the playground in the neighborhood park. Close to lunchtime, the other kids headed back to their homes. Neither Stacey nor I was hungry enough to want to go home.

Daddy had worked the night shift and was sleeping in, and I was avoiding him. The day before, Daddy had been in a real sour mood. Two car repair customers' checks had bounced at the same time, causing some checks Daddy had written to bounce because he thought he had enough money in the bank. I had run into the house on my way to the kitchen and tripped over the telephone cord, ripping it out of Daddy's hand and onto the floor with a clang. Daddy had brought the phone to the table with its cord stretched across the room to make a few phone calls about the bounced checks. Unbeknownst to me, Buddy had done the same thing ten minutes earlier. Before I knew it, Daddy had pulled off his belt and started to whale away at me viciously. I was shocked by his ferocity and fell to the floor. I used my hands to cover my neck and head as he landed blow after blow across my back. Usually at such times, Mamma would come to my rescue, but Zombie Mamma was currently in residence and had settled in. This Mamma was silent and sat mute as Daddy beat me. The advantage of having Zombie Mamma was that she wasn't likely to notice how long I was out of the house, but she didn't rise to come to my aid either. My hands and back still bore the welts and bruises from my beating. Stacey didn't ask about my injuries, nor did she say why she didn't want to go home either. Honoring our code, I didn't ask her why, though I thought it had something to do with her new stepfather and the empty liquor bottles filling their trash can.

I discovered a row of honeysuckle along the fence by the edge of the woods and called to Stacey, who was still over on the blacktop. "Stacey," I cried, but she didn't respond right away. So I yelled louder, "Hey, Stacey, come over here. Come smell the honeysuckle."

When she joined me at the fence, I picked some and held them out for her. She took a deep breath, then asked, "Smells all right, but what's the big deal?"

"You ever taste honeysuckle nectar?"

"Naw. Where is it?" I showed her how to get to the nectar. I picked a single flower, broke its delicate funneled base with my fingernail, and gently pulled its filament out. Along its thread came a tiny bead of sweet nectar that I licked off with my tongue. Then I picked another flower and extracted a bead for Stacey. She took it with her tongue and savored the sweet, fragrant honey. Stacey quickly learned how to procure her own honey. We were both picking flowers and enjoying our harvest when we heard a man calling Stacey's name. We turned and saw an old, grizzled, gray-haired man approaching us.

"Hey there, Stacey. My name is Robert. I'm a friend of your parents. What are you doing here?"

Nodding toward me, Stacey responded, "She showed me how to get the nectar from the honeysuckle,"

"Oh, I'd love to try one. Would you teach me how?" he asked. Happy to show off her newfound skill, Stacey picked a flower, broke the base, and carefully pulled the filament down, exposing two small beads of nectar. She bent her hands so he could see the liquid. But instead of just looking at it, he took her hand with the flower in it and brought it toward his mouth. He extended his tongue and licked the nectar, and a few of Stacey's fingers too.

"That was real nice," he said. Immediately, I hadn't liked him, but now I knew not to trust him either, though I wasn't exactly sure why. It was instinct. While looking at me, he said, "You're a pretty thing. What's your name? Will you get some honey for me too?"

"None of your business, and no I won't," I snapped.

Ignoring my rude words and tone, he responded, "No? That's too bad. Do you want to play something else? I know lots of games. We could play hide-and-go-seek or have a treasure hunt in the woods. Would you like to play pony? I will be the pony and give you a ride."

"I'd like to play pony," said Stacey eagerly.

"No!" I barked. "We were doing just fine on our own. We don't know him. We don't need anyone else," I said, hoping he would get the message and leave. When he made no motion to go, I put both my hands on my hips and added, "So you say you're friends with Stacey's parents. Which one?"

"Why, both of them."

"Really, then what's their names?"

"Aren't you the suspicion one? I'm just here to look after you two. Come, I'll give you a pony ride, Stacey. Your friend doesn't want to play with us."

"No, Stacey, no! I am going home right now, and if you don't come too I am going to tell your mother," I added harshly as I started to leave the playground. I had expected Stacey to follow me, but when I turned, he was bent down and she was getting up on his back. He stood up quickly and started galloping toward the woods. I began shrieking as loud as I could, "Stacey, Stacey, no, no! Stacey, get down—no, don't go! I'm gonna tell your mama!" I kept screaming as loud as I could as I followed them into the woods.

When I got in among the trees, it was darker than it was out on the brightly sun-drenched field. My eyes took a moment to adjust as I decided which way to go. There were several paths. Just then I heard the rustle of some branches off to my right and took off in the sound's direction. I kept yelling Stacey's name, but she didn't respond. The sounds of their retreat through the woods grew faint, then ceased. I wandered about for a while, and was about to give up when I came to a small clearing. In the middle of it, Stacey sat on a log. Standing in front of her was the old man with his pants down around his ankles. He turned to look at me.

I was in shock at first and briefly stood frozen. Even with a house full of boys, I'd never seen a man's penis. It looked ugly and gross hanging between the old man's withered thighs. I took a deep breath, squared my shoulders, and walked past him over to Stacey. He merely smiled down at me and said, "You want to join us?"

Just then we heard sirens in the distance, rapidly approaching. The sound jolted all of us into action. The man bent to pull up his pants as I grabbed Stacey firmly by the arm.

"Come on," I said and yanked on her arm. Stacey stood up and willingly took off, running with me toward the playground. When we emerged from the woods, there was a police car pulling up and another one behind it. Two policemen jumped out of their vehicle and ran past us into the woods. A neighbor whose house stood directly across the street from the playground had seen the old man talking to us. She told me this as we stood next to the police cars waiting for the officers to return.

"I saw that man watching you both and thought he might be up to no good. I didn't know if either of you knew him. I had just gone into the kitchen to put a kettle on for tea when I heard you scream, dear," she said while looking at me. "Thank goodness you did. I saw you follow them into the woods. Right away, I called the police." Just then the two policemen returned but without the old man. He had gotten away.

Our parents were called to the police station. Stacey and I were each questioned. After they learned that nothing had happened to me—I never mentioned seeing the man's penis—they let me go. Stacey had to stay longer. What happened to Stacey, both in the woods or later at the police station, I don't know. My parents made it very clear to me that I should never mention the incident to anyone. They said it would give Stacey a bad reputation, and I would even be hurt if this got out. I tried to tell them that we hadn't done anything wrong, but they made me promise to never speak of it again.

"Trust us, sweetheart, it's for the best," Mamma said.

"We should all just pretend it never happened," added Daddy.

When I saw Stacey the next time, it was obvious that she had been told the same or, in any case, she didn't want to talk about it. The two of us went on and did as we were told: we pretended it never happened.

CHAPTER SIXTEEN

℘ ❖ ℭ

MANIC MAMMA AND THE GENERAL

We knew Manic Mamma had arrived when she started cleaning everything in sight. She'd start with the kitchen. Once the higher surfaces were scoured and scrubbed, she'd drop to her knees on the floor like a holy penitent, equipped with a bucket of warm, soapy water at her side. She'd glide across the kitchen's cold linoleum floor, moving rhythmically from side to side. With steady determination, she'd reach into the pail, and with each twist of her rag, she'd wring out her disappointments and sorrows, gaining strength with each newly gleaming surface while banishing, at least for a while, her demons and regrets as well as our dirt.

Mamma's manic cleaning episodes were a good sign, even though they happened when she was demanding, volatile, and most likely to inflict punishment. Manic Mamma would scrub, scour, and bleach, sterilizing anything she could find until no dirt or stain remained.

After Manic Mamma had been in residence for a while and there were no more uncleaned surfaces left in the house, she'd start in on us. That's when the General inevitably appeared. With the General, we knew to have our chores and homework done before she could ask. All of us would arrive at the dinner table with freshly scrubbed hands ready for inspection. Soiled clothes were removed and replaced with clean ones before we took our places at the dinner table. Even Daddy gave way to Manic Mamma and the General, wisely keeping his distance, and his hands clean.

These versions of Mamma firmly ruled the house and all its objects. No one, not even Daddy, dared to enter the house with dirty shoes. On the covered back porch, there were a bench and a box containing a wire brush and other instruments for cleaning mud-caked shoes. Only when this task was complete could we gain admission into our home. Once inside the house, Daddy would then go to the sink. He'd use copious amounts of Lava soap and a stiff brush while working up a lather. He'd scrub and scrub until all that remained of the auto grease were the indelible stains left in the crevices of his large, rough, work-worn hands. Cleanliness and order were the one area where Mamma was the commander. No one dared questioned her authority. Perhaps that was why cleaning helped her escape from the Zombie's clutches and from what demons lurked in the shadowy chambers of her mind. This, she could control. This, she could conquer.

We all knew to stay clear of the General and avoid breaking

any of her rules. She had radar that anticipated every infraction. Once, Chip left some grease on the front doorknob and ended up having to scrub the entire door and adjacent walls. One evening, despite an earlier warning to wash my feet before I went to bed, I forgot to wash them. This was a greater crime than you might expect because I spent my summers barefoot, running around in the dirt, and our washing machine had broken down again two weeks before. Daddy had spent a day off from the rail yard taking it apart. He'd diagnosed the problem but was waiting for another paycheck to buy some parts to get it up and running again. I had wiped my feet carefully but failed to remember to wash them before dipping them between Mamma's clean, hand-washed sheets. After I had fallen into a deep slumber, Mamma's voice and firm hand woke me.

"Charlotte, wake up," she said in an even tone, more tired than angry.

"What is it?" I asked groggily. "What's wrong?"

"You didn't wash your feet."

"Huh?"

"You heard me, sweetheart. Now get up."

"What? But, Mamma, it's the middle of the night."

"That's right, and you didn't wash your feet as you were told before you put them on the clean sheets. *Get up, now.*" Her waning patience became more evident in her tone.

"But I wiped them real good, Ma," I begged.

"Charlotte, you know that 'well' is an adverb and 'good' is an adjective. The correct way to say that is '*I wiped them really well*,' and that's not the same as clean, Charlotte. You know better. I warned you, and now there are consequences. I want you to get up and strip your bed." After a couple of additional prods, I surrendered to the inevitable and got up. Groggily, I stripped the bed and started to throw the sheets in the hamper before Mamma stopped me. "Oh no, you don't get off that easily. Grab the sheets and follow me."

"Why, where are we going?"

"To the laundry room to wash the sheets, of course."

"Of course, what? Mamma, it's after midnight. Everyone else is asleep," I cried. "Can't this wait until morning?"

"We'd both be sleeping right now if you had done as you were told. Do you think this is pleasant for me? Do you think this is how I want to spend my night? I have had a long day and would rather be resting in my own bed. However, I have a responsibility to teach you that there are consequences to your actions and inactions. This is one lesson I am sure you won't forget."

"But the washing machine is busted. How am I going to clean them?"

"How do you think?" she asked.

"By dancing on them?"

"No, dear, this is just one set of sheets, and I am not going to be the one wringing and finishing them off." Then it dawned on me what the task was that awaited me, dashing all hope for an early return to my warm, comfortable bed. I offered up a few more panicked protests, finally submitted to my fate, and followed her clumsily down the stairs. There, at one in the morning with everyone else off to sleep, my mother taught me the art of hand-washing laundry.

"Grab some fabric in each hand. Okay, now leave a few inches of fabric between each hand," she instructed. "That's right. Now, vigorously move your hands back and forth over each section, working the fabric. You'll have to put a lot more energy into it if you hope to get them clean before the sun comes up, Charlotte," she admonished. "Come on, now, put some real effort into it."

I started attacking the sheets, working furiously. Calling up all my anger and frustration, I channeled my feelings into my hands. Forcefully, I moved my hands back and forth across the sheet fabric. "Very good—now you've got it," Mamma said proudly. "Now, slide your hands to the next section, working across the fabric. That's good. Now you've got the hang of it. You're doing it well."

And so I worked my way back and forth, across and down so I didn't miss a single section of each sheet. Then she taught me how to wring all the liquid out of the fabric by twisting it repeatedly until it knotted up, squeezing all the soapy water out of its fibers. It took all my strength to get the last drops out. Then I rinsed each sheet twice, each time squeezing the water out before hanging them up in the backyard. I grabbed the clothespins and hung the sheets on the clothesline in the dark, with only a three-quarter moon piercing through the cloudy night and illuminating my way.

That tasked finished, I ran back toward my bedroom, but Mamma stopped me once more. "Excuse me. Unless you want to wash more sheets, shouldn't you wash your feet before you climb back into bed?"

I sighed, slumped my shoulders, and said, "Yes, ma'am."

Patiently, she watched as I sat on the side of the tub and scrubbed my feet clean. "Grab the pumice stone. Rub hard to remove any old skin. Now dry them well," she added before exiting and leaving me alone at last. Quickly, I redressed my bed in a set of fresh sheets. It was well after three in the morning when I finally climbed back into bed. Mamma was right. I never forgot that lesson. Until this day and even with Mamma thousands of miles away, I cannot get into bed without first washing my feet.

CHAPTER SEVENTEEN

೮ ❖ ೧

DUCK FEATHERS

*F*rom time to time, Daddy used to go to night clubs and play his blues harp or sing. He wasn't a regular member of any band, but a lot of the musicians knew him around town and welcomed him onstage for a set or two. Daddy played blues on the mouth organ, but he sang jazz and blues. One evening, he took Mamma along to the Showboat Lounge over in Adams Morgan, an area south of Beach Drive and the National Zoo. Eugene was old enough by then to watch us. They didn't get back until the next morning. We drilled them with questions when they came through the door. Though sleepy, Mamma was animated and happily told us about their adventures. She had ended up on stage with Charlie Byrd and Stan Getz. Daddy added to her story, proudly telling us how the crowd had erupted into enthusiastic and prolonged applause. "When your Mamma finished singing, 'You Came a Long Way from Saint Louis,' the folks kept on cheering long after she'd returned to her seat. She was the hit of the evening," Daddy crowed while Mamma blushed.

Mr. Byrd invited Mamma and Daddy to hang out with them after the club closed, to jam some more in a back room of the theater. Mamma said that Charlie was the finest guitarist she'd ever heard. By the time they left, they were hungry and decided to wait for a bakery restaurant called Avignone Frères to open to have breakfast. It was the cheeriest and most animated I'd seen Mamma in a long time.

"Here, we brought y'all somethin' special," offered Daddy as he placed a white cardboard box on the table.

"Souvenirs from our big night out," added Mamma. "Go ahead, open it. We picked them up at the bakery." Never shy, Buddy untied the string and carefully opened the box as the rest of us watched. Nested inside were two slices of chocolate brandy layer cake, a variety of cookies, and some treats that looked like peapods, carrots, and tiny ears of corn. "Aren't the marzipan pieces like little pieces of art? Try the cake; it's ridiculously rich and delicious. Go ahead, cut them in half. You'll have to share."

After that night, they started to go out together maybe once a month or every other month as fortunes allowed. Sometimes one of them would end up onstage; other times they'd simply dance and have a good time. They'd go to other hot spots too. They liked the Bohemian Caverns, which was at 11th and U Street Northwest near Howard University. After these nights out, they'd sleep late the following day, sometimes not coming out of their room until after 1:00 or even 2:00 in the afternoon.

It was the same this particular Saturday. I had gone down the street to play Double Dutch jump rope with Stacey Diamond and another friend, Debbie Cartwright, and her older sister, Karen. The Cartwrights lived directly behind the Diamonds. We had ended up playing in Debbie's yard. After a while, I decided to head home. So I climbed over the fence, crossing the Diamonds' yard as a shortcut home. As I approached the Diamonds' front yard, I was assaulted by a cacophony of strange quacking noises. When I turned the corner of their house and entered their front yard, I saw a bunch of white feathers littering the lawn. Stacey's younger stepbrother, Bobbie, Jr., had a duck clutched in his hands. He had a temper and a mean streak a mile long. The bird was clearly wounded, and Bobbie was torturing it by swinging it around in a circle by one wing as the bird squawked in pain and protest.

"What are you doing?" I demanded.

"Mind your own damn business," came his quick retort.

"Where'd you get it?"

"I found it on the side of the road." I wasn't sure if I believed him. Bobbie was known to lie.

"Well, you can't torture it. It's not right."

"I can if I want. It's mine."

"Even if it is yours, that doesn't give you the right to torture the poor thing. It's not only wrong to hurt it just for kicks, it's downright sick."

"Go to hell."

"You first," I said as I charged at him, taking him by surprise
and shoving him over. When he tried to get up and lunge at me,
I slugged him hard as I could in the throat. I got him good. My
lessons with Chip were serving me well; he had taught me how to
fight. I could see tears welling up in Bobbie's eyes as he started to
yell for his mommy. I knew that Bobbie, like most bullies, was a
coward. Seizing the opportunity, I grabbed the duck and ran home.

When I got in my house with the duck under my arms, I didn't
know what to do. Mamma and Daddy were still in bed, so I couldn't
ask them. The boys were nowhere to be seen. Suddenly I thought
of the bathtub. *Ducks like water, don't they?* I reasoned to myself.
I took the poor bird to the bathtub and put in a little bit of water.
After placing the bird in the water, I left the bathroom, closing the
door behind me, and headed for the kitchen to find some food.
When I returned, the poor creature hadn't moved an inch. No
matter how hard I tried to coax it, it wouldn't eat. I decided it just
needed some peace and quiet after such a traumatic day.

After shutting the door securely behind me, I went out onto
the couch and started watching a Lone Ranger cartoon. I thought
it ironic that today's episode, called "Hunter and Hunted," had
Tonto teaching some hunters a lesson about killing for no reason.
Halfway through the program, I heard Mamma come out of their
bedroom. By then I was engrossed in the cartoon; the sound of her
movements only partially registered in my mind. When I heard

her scream, the image of the duck suddenly exploded into my head. Realizing I was too late to warn her about my newly acquired waterfowl, I leapt from the couch and ran to the bathroom. "Oh, Mamma, I meant to tell you about him."

"Charlotte, what in the world is a duck doing in our bathtub?"

Just then, Daddy bolted out into the hallway while zipping up his pants. Apparently, he was responding to Mamma's cry as well. "What in the blue blazes is going on here?" he demanded.

"Stick your head in there and see for yourself," Mamma said while pointing at the bathroom door. "Be sure to look in the bathtub." As he entered the bathroom, Mamma stood with her hands placed firmly on her hips. While waiting for Daddy's return, she kept her eyes fixed on me, nailing me to the floor as I held my breath in anticipation. When Daddy reemerged into the hall, he was laughing, to my great relief.

"Is that our supper, Charlotte?"

With panic in my voice because I didn't know if he was kidding or not, I pleaded, "No, Daddy, no way, we can't eat the poor thing. For Pete's sake, I rescued him. He's suffered enough."

Still chuckling, he told Mamma, "I'll let you handle this one, Maggie."

"Gee whiz, thanks, Jack." Turning to me, she said, "So, Charlotte, I am waiting. Are you going to tell me why a duck is in our bathtub?"

Still afraid of Daddy's suggestion of our dinner options, I started talking quickly and desperately. "Bobbie Diamond had it and was torturing the poor bird. Bobbie's really mean-crazy, Mamma. The boy's heart is a thumpin' gizzard. His cruel streak is a mile long. I found him swinging that pitiful creature by its wounded wing. The poor thing was losing feathers all over the place. The duck was making a terrible racket, crying for help. I couldn't let Bobbie keep on torturing it, Mamma, I just couldn't." The words wouldn't come out of my mouth fast enough. I stammered on. "It wouldn't have been right not to rescue the poor animal, and besides ..."

"Okay, okay, okay. Calm down. I get it. But Charlotte, sweetheart, why is it in my bathtub?"

"I didn't know what else to do with it."

"Charlotte, we can't have a duck living in our bathroom."

"No, I realize that, but where can I put it where it'll be safe?" Just then Chip came stomping down the stairs to see what the commotion was about. You could always tell it was Chip walking. He had heavy footsteps and wore boots nearly the whole year round.

"What's going on? What's all the racket about?" After Mamma explained the situation, he thankfully offered a solution.

"I can build it a coop. It won't be any big deal. We've got plenty of old lumber out back and some chicken wire too. Come on, Charlie. You can be my assistant."

"Good," said Mamma, "I am glad that's sorted out. Make it quick. I'd like to take a bath at some point today."

"Yes, ma'am," I said as Chip and I headed out back. Despite Chip's suggestion of my assisting him, I mostly watched while he worked. The only help I provided was getting tools and supplies as he requested them, making him a sandwich, and cleaning up afterward. Of course, I named the duck Donald even though Daddy said I should have named her Donna. Daddy had to force-feed her at first, but eventually she ate on her own. He set her broken wing too. While she wore a splint, we kept her in the cage. Later, we found an old frame from an above-ground swimming pool that someone was tossing out. With that, we created a fenced pen where Donald could roam around while one of us was in the yard to protect her from roving cats. Eventually she started taking short flights around the pen and later throughout the yard.

It took nearly a year before she could fly well enough to be released. We had seen other white ducks out at Greenbelt Lake, so we decided to drive out there for a picnic and to say farewell to Donald. Eugene planned, scripted, and emceed a formal ceremony for her release back into the wild. Yet Donald didn't perform on cue. She lingered beside us, unsure of what to do. Other ducks landed and floated on the lake. As the afternoon wore on, I was both fearful and hopeful that she wouldn't fly away. But inside her, Donald was growing silently braver. Suddenly and unceremoniously, she took off, without a glance or a honk goodbye. I cried all the way home, but I was proud of what I'd done in saving her and then in setting her free.

CHAPTER EIGHTEEN

∞❖∝

HOT PEPPERS

*M*amma, the boys, and I took the station wagon to the railroad yard to pick up Daddy. He had to go in to fix something, but only worked a half day. Often, Daddy would bring something home that was left unclaimed on a train. There were always plenty of umbrellas, hats, and jackets to be had, but sometimes the things left on the trains were peculiar. When we pulled up to the employees' trailer, Daddy came out carrying a huge, restaurant-sized jar of banana peppers. I tried to imagine what kind of person would be carrying such a jar, and then the moment when they realized they'd forgotten it after getting off at their destination.

Mamma moved over on the front bench seat so Daddy could get in and drive. He placed the large jar between them. As we were pulling out of the parking lot, Daddy said, "Boys, whoever eats the most peppers from this here jar on the way home gets two bucks from yours truly."

Anxious for the money, I complained, "Hey, why only boys?"

Daddy chuckled. "You think you can beat the boys, little girl?"

"I can try. Can't I, Daddy?"

"Well, I reckon you can try," he said skeptically. "Okay, you can join in, but don't start hollering when your mouth and throat start to burn like they was lit on fire." Daddy laid down the rules. We were to have rounds. In order of age, we would each eat one whole pepper, seeds and all. Eugene was the first to try and the first to quit, saying there were easier ways to earn a couple of bucks. For him, as a seventeen- almost eighteen-year-old boy, that was true. I, on the other hand, had few opportunities to earn cash. Chip and I were the last two, once Buddy gave up after the fourth round. By then, it wasn't just the money for Chip; it was his ego. Daddy kept asking if they were too hot. Chip and I kept saying no while tears streamed down our faces. After the eighth round, Chip got sick and looked as though he might throw up. Mamma encouraged him to surrender. Daddy berated the boys: "You buncha sissies; you let a little girl whoop you." After he parked in our driveway, Daddy pulled out two crumpled dollar bills and said, "Here, baby, you've earned these fair and square. You are a whole lot tougher than I thought." I smiled at him, cheered by his newfound respect for me.

I took the two bills and was ready to make my escape and seek out something to wash out the burn in my throat and stomach. I was closest to the side door and jumped out with the intention of running for some water. I was barely out the door when Chip knocked me hard to get past me and made me stumble. Obviously on purpose, Buddy did the same as I was trying to get back up. When I got to the kitchen sink, Chip wouldn't let me put a glass under the faucet, and Buddy wouldn't let me get by him to reach the refrigerator.

"Why are you being so mean?"

"If you want to play boys' games, you better be able to take it like a boy," quipped Chip.

"I can take it. I just proved it. It's you that can't take it without crying or being spiteful about it, you bunch of wimps."

Just then, Daddy walked in and eyed Chip. We all moved out of the way to let Daddy pass to the refrigerator. He grabbed a cold Pabst and turned toward the back door. "Looks like you stirred up a hornet's nest there, my girl. Some victories come at a price," he said while looking down at me. "Remember that." Then he looked over at Chip and Buddy. "Boys, go easy. She won fair and square. Be men enough to own up to it," he said as he headed out the back door to the yard.

Mamma didn't like Daddy drinking beer in the house. She said it was a bad example for the boys. I never understood why just the boys and how drinking it outside made any difference. It seemed funny that Daddy, a Baptist, was the one drinking and Mamma, an Irish Catholic, had objected to it. So much for stereotypes.

Despite Daddy's proclamations, Chip maintained his guard of

the kitchen sink and Buddy still leaned on the refrigerator. Both glared at me while blocking my access to any liquids.

"Why is eating peppers a boy's game anyway? You are all a bunch of sissy losers. Oh, look, I have two bucks," I said as I pulled the two notes out of my back pocket and waved them in front of each of their faces. "Maybe I'll go buy myself an ice-cold Pepsi, and maybe an ice cream too," I taunted as I headed out the back door.

I ran outside and down the steps, and grabbed the garden hose. I turned it on and tried to drain the hose. When I could drink no more, I shut it off, turned around, and looked at my father from the back. He was sitting in the shade made by the house as the sun waned over it. He sat on a folding chair, the kind with nylon plaid ribbons woven on an aluminum frame, creating a seat and a backrest. A few of the ribbons were beginning to fray.

"Did you turn the spigot real tight?" he asked. "If you don't, that hose will drip. I ain't gotten around to puttin' a new washer in yet."

"Yes, sir. I tightened it real good," I said. With Mamma out of earshot so she couldn't enforce her language rules, I dropped into Daddy's relaxed way of speaking as easy as slipping into an old pair of slippers. I walked over to Daddy and asked, "Why they gotta act thataway, Daddy?"

"Who, your brothers?"

"Yes, sir. Who else? They're being mean to me just 'cause I beat 'em."

"If ya don't want to hunt with them big dogs, Charlotte, honey, best you stay on the porch."

"I can run with them, but they don't have to be such poor sports."

"You hurt their pride, is all. It'll mend by and by. Don't worry about it none. You just give it a rest."

I walked over and grabbed another folding chair that was leaning against the house. I returned to where Daddy was and plopped it open next to him. This chair was a little wobblier than his. It was rusty, and some of the long screws needed tightening, but I managed to get it steady and settle in next to him.

In front of us was our fenced vegetable garden. Silently, I looked out at it, examining its plants. We moved several times while I was young. This was the third home I could remember. But no matter where we lived, one of the first things our father would do, while Mamma unpacked, was to put in a garden. Daddy didn't bother buying seeds too often. He'd save seeds from vegetables or fruit. Using a couple of old windows he found on the side of the road, he made a garden box to germinate his seeds in small pots.

At each house, we had a compost pile. He had us asking neighbors with fireplaces for their wood ash. Daddy didn't believe in wasting anything. There was an old retaining wall on the north side of our yard made of a double row of cinder blocks spaced a couple of feet apart. Inside the cinder blocks skeleton, there was soil. Daddy planted a long row of strawberries there that just took off. They loved that spot. Daddy always knew what plants liked.

It was great when you went to harvest the strawberries; you didn't even have to bend down to pick them because on the lower side, the retaining wall was at waist level and the plants draped over it. Inside the fenced garden, the tomato plants were loaded with ripe red fruit. The plants grew up between a latticework of old twigs and sticks that Daddy created and laid over the plants. Laden green branches stretched out of their cages and sagged with their heavy fruit. Green beans grew neatly up strings that were tied to a stake and fanned out like a teepee. Well-ordered rows of onion heads, carrot greens, lettuce, and cabbage traversed the garden's floor. Bushes of herbs such as basil, sage, and rosemary edged the side closest to us. Zucchini and yellow squash seemed to grow four inches a day, and the okra was just starting to pop.

Piercing the silence, Mamma's voice came down from on top of the high porch as she yelled through the rear screen door. "Charlotte, come up here and take this basket and garden tools." As I walked up the steps, she said, "I want you to pick all the ripe tomatoes. Get a couple of onions, and garlic. Oh, and pick some basil and oregano too. We'll make a batch of Italian sauce."

I took the basket and tools and headed back to the yard. When I reached the bottom of the stairs, she stopped me. "Oh, and one more thing, pick a couple of red hot peppers too. You know your father likes a little spice in his sauces."

"Ain't the only thing I like spicy," Daddy yelled as he pivoted in the chair so he could look up at Mamma on the back porch.

"Jack, you mind your manners in front of your daughter," she reprimanded.

Daddy smiled and rolled his eyes at me as he shrugged his shoulders and turned back around.

Forgetting her rules for a moment, I called up, "Mamma, ain't we got a bunch of peppers in that jar? I am sure we didn't eat 'em all."

"Please, Charlotte, don't say ain't. It sounds uneducated. And, no, you didn't eat them all. There are plenty in the jar, but I prefer the red garden ones for the sauces."

"Do you need them right away or can I sit a spell?"

"No rush. I've got laundry to do." Then over her shoulder she said, "But pick and wash them within an hour, okay, honey?"

As the door was closing behind her, I said, "Okay, will do, Mamma." I went back over to Daddy and set the basket on the ground and resettled on the rickety chair. The two of us sat quietly for a few minutes looking out at the garden. Daddy pulled a pack of Pall Malls from his shirt breast pocket, tapped one out, placed the liberated cigarette between his lips, and lit it. I scanned his garden once again, marveling at its abundance. For the first time, I realized how brilliant my father was at gardening. In between puffs, he took a swig from the beer can as I gazed out at his creation. I've seen other gardens before and since, but his were always well ordered, weed free, and prolific. My father had a talent for making things grow out of dirt. Finally, I broke our silent revelry.

"This is the best garden I can remember you ever having. It's beautiful."

"The soil is good and rich here. I knew it the first time I walked this lot."

Perhaps it was because of my newfound confidence after the hot pepper–eating contest, or it was the comradery the contest had established with my father, but that afternoon was the first time I asked Daddy about his childhood when he actually answered me at any length. "How'd you know that?" I asked.

"Anyone's growed up on a farm can tell you that. Lots of things farmers know without knowin' exactly how they know it. A lot of stuff affects the soil. What you put into it, the topography, drainage, and more. The soil here is dark and rich with good drainage."

"What was your farm like?"

"It was home, is all."

"But how big was it? What did you grow? Were there many animals on the place? Did you have a horse you could ride? What chores did you do? What was everyday life like?"

"Whew, slow down there, Champ. You sure got a lot of questions. You fixin' to write a book?"

"I don't know, perhaps. Maybe one day I will. But today, I just love this garden, is all. It's beautiful. I want to know how you learned to be such a good gardener. I'd like to know more about my family. For instance, what was your mother, my grandmother, like?"

"Well, my ma wasn't all that talkative like you, but you two sure look a lot alike, 'cept you have light hair and blue eyes. The shape of your face and nose is like hers. You have her body: tall and skinny. Her name was Sarah, like in the Bible. Eugene has her dark hair. Buddy looks a lot like my grandmother Rose. Shoot, he looks more like her son than mine. I favor my pa."

"But what was your mama like?"

"She had big brown eyes that looked like a deer caught in a headlight. She always had a look of wonder on her face. When she set her eyes on you, it was like she was peerin' into your very soul. Even though she and Grandma Rose weren't blood kin, they were close as two peas in a pod. Lordy, they was inseparable. Those two couldn't have been more different, and yet they got along like mother and daughter. Ma was tall and real, real thin, and Grandma Rose was short and stout. Grandma's people were all educated. No one in Ma's family ever made it past the eighth grade. She quit after the sixth. The two of 'em liked Aunt Gladys, my uncle's wife, well enough. They used to get a big kick out of Aunt Gladys's antics and colorful conversations. But she knew she'd always be the outsider in that house. Those two were so tight, there was no gettin' between 'em. Everybody knew that.

"My ma didn't talk much, and when she did her voice was real quiet like. She didn't need to talk; Grandma Rose did it for her. She was happy to stay in Grandma Rose's shadow. I don't know if my daddy picked the perfect wife for himself, but he sure did pick the perfect daughter-in-law for his ma."

"Did they have a good marriage, your daddy and mama?"

"A good marriage? Well, I reckon so. I never gave it much thought. I guess they did. I never saw 'em hug much, kiss or flirt—nothin' like that. Back in them days, folks didn't show much physical affection in public."

"But what about at home? Did they show affection then?"

"Not in front of any of us. Folks didn't go on how they do nowadays. You didn't even hold hands in public 'less you was engaged. From what I could tell, my ma and pa got along good. When one spoke, the other listened. I never heard 'em have a cross word betwixt the two. Oh, they'd might have a difference of opinion and such, but I never heard 'em speak crossly or raise their voices 'gainst one another—leastwise, not so as I recall."

"Gee, it sounds as if they respected each other."

"Respect? Well, I guess they did. Yes, they surely did."

"What else can you tell me about the farm? Did you have horses?"

"We had mules. They're a whole lot better at farm work than a horse."

"What did you grow?"

"Tobacca mostly. That was our main cash crop, just like everyone else in that part of North Carolina. The closest town to us was Ahoskie, but we had family up in Winton and other parts too. The train came through Ahoskie, because of the tobacca. But we grew corn and goober peas too for the market."

"What are goober peas?"

"Peanuts, sweetie pie, that's what we called 'em, especially when you're pullin' 'em out of the ground. The colored sharecroppers we sometimes hired made a real fine stew from the fresh peanuts. Fill you up too. They used it in their greens. Tasted real good too. The women—Ma, Grandma, and, when she was around, Aunt Gladys—always put up a big kitchen garden. Come fall, they'd be canning away for days. The women folk made our clothes, soap, and candles too. Poverty makes you resourceful. We ate fresh whatever was comin' up in the garden. In the winter, we ate what they'd canned. We didn't buy much more than salt, flour, sugar, and cloth from the grocer.

"We had some fruit and nut trees on the place. We grew some of the sweetest peaches you ever ate. We had apple and pear trees planted by my grandfather, or maybe it was his father—I ain't sure which. We had a couple of old walnut and pecan trees too. There was a few real old pecan trees out by the dryin' barns. I don't know who planted those; could've been my great-great grandfather. I sure miss fresh pecans. They ain't the same unless they's fresh. They don't grow so good this far north.

"There was Ward sweat and blood in every corner of that farmstead. It was a Ward who cleared the land, dug the well, built the barns and houses, and planted them trees. Us Wards had been farmin' that land since long 'fore the Revolution."

"The American Revolution?"

"Was there another one?"

"What was daily life like for you on the farm?"

"It was a lot of hard work, but it was good times too. I grew up in the Depression. Before it, we was poor but didn't know it yet. After the Depression started, we was dirt poor and felt every bit of it. Long 'fore the Great Depression hit the rest of this country, a lot of us Carolinians already were having hard times. For Carolina, it began right after World War I. For the Wards, it started a bit later. My daddy said it started after his oldest brother, Clyde, died."

"How'd he die?"

"He got mustard gas in his lungs and a bullet in his leg over in France."

"What's mustard gas?"

"It's a poison the Krauts used as a weapon. It leaves your lungs all scarred up. He was a soldier in the American First Army. He made it back home after the war. You know those two brass missile shells we have in the living room on the bookcase, the ones with Verdun embossed on them?"

"Those are missile shells? I never noticed."

"Yeah, they're shell casings, all right. Uncle Clyde picked 'em up right off the battlefield near a town called Verdun. There was a big battle fought there. Uncle Clyde had someone back in France emboss the name 'Verdun' along with those leaves and acorns. He came home basically in one piece, but he was never the same—not in his body or his head according to my grandma. It was 'fore I was born. The mustard gas messed up his lungs real good. That part I remember. His lungs rattled sometimes when he worked hard. The bullet wound he had in his leg gave him some trouble too. He walked with a bit of a limp for as long as I knew him. But it was his head that was the most scarred. Folks all said he wasn't the same person when he come home. Long as I knew him, he was real quiet. He never married or even courted, kept to himself mostly, and drank when he could afford it. Eventually, he started making some pretty good moonshine himself, it being Prohibition and all. Made a steady livin' sellin' it. Anyways, he weren't much more than forty-eight, if that, when he died. Had a heart attack or somethin'. Went ta bed and never got up. That was Grandma Rose's and Grandpa Jackson's firstborn child. They both took it hard, but Grandpa Jackson showed it most."

"So you're named after your grandpa?"

"That's right." Daddy took another sip on his Pabst, then went on. "Soon after Uncle Clyde died, the price of tobacca dropped from nearly ninety cents a pound to barely nine. To make it worse, just a couple of years 'fore it fell, my granddaddy took out a loan from the bank. A neighbor on a farm next ta ours put theirs up for sale. They'd already sold off most of it and only had another fifty-eight acres of reasonably good farming land left. Grandpa bought it, hoping he'd have enough land for his sons to each have their own productive farms. When prices dropped, we prayed and prayed they'd go back up. But I guess God was too busy to answer those prayers. With the drop in tobacca prices, we couldn't hold on to the extra land. Grandpa sold it for less than half of what he paid for it. We got saddled with other debts too—new farm equipment, seeds, and supplies. Tobacca prices fell so much, it hardly paid to farm. You still had to buy seeds and equipment and such. Some years we lost more money farmin' than we earned.

"Granny had inherited a small lot when her daddy, Colonel Marshall, died. She never liked her daddy. I heard tales about him. He could be a real nasty old coot. I barely remember him at all, but I remember fearing him. Grandma Rose may not of cared much for her pa, but she liked that land she got from her Marshall kin. Eventually things got so bad, we had to sell that off too, which was a sorrowful pity. That was about one of the prettiest pieces of land along the Chowan River you'll ever see. As nice as it was, we didn't fetch much for it. Weren't a lot of folks buyin' land, so land got sold real cheap back in 'em days."

He looked out at the garden once more and then glanced at me. "Anyway, we still had a sizeable farm. It was a beautiful spread. We had each other. We had it better than a lot of folks and a whole lot better than them colored sharecroppers who had it 'bout as bad as anyone can and still be livin', that's for sure." He paused a bit but then continued. "There was this one colored family we hired regular-like during harvest times to help out with the reapin' and the curin'. These were the ones who made the peanut soup I told you about. Anyways, they'd stay in one of the cabins on our place when they was workin' for us. It was a family of all girls, but they could work as hard as any man." Daddy took out another cigarette and lit it. He blew out a long stream of smoke before he continued, "Each of 'em colored girls was named after a precious stone. Pearl was their mama. Then there was Opal, Ruby, Sapphire, and Amber. Amber was as thin as her Mamma was portly and stood near six foot. Amber didn't look like the rest of her family. If you weren't right up close to her, you'd think she was White. They all could sing, but especially Pearl and Amber. After the crops were brought to market, the women from our farm and several others around would put up a feast. Everyone would pull out their music instruments, and we'd be whooping it up 'til the wee hours. Pearl and her girls were popular at any harvest party count of their voices and all the songs they knew. We'd be singin', dancin', and playin' music for days. Plenty of moonshine got passed around."

"Wait a second. I thought Baptists didn't believe in drinking?"

"Honey, you know the difference between a Methodist and a Baptist?"

"No, sir; what is it?"

"A Methodist will say 'howdy' to you in the liquor store."

"What's that supposed to mean?"

"It means that a lot of Baptists drink, but they do it secretively. Ain't no real law in the Good Book against it. Some preachers say goin' to the movies is a sin, but the Good Book surely don't mention movies. Just like I can't find nothin' against dancin' in the

Bible, but some congregations say it's courtin' the Devil to dance. Honey, it's gluttony that the scriptures says is a sin. Nothin' wrong with lettin' off some steam and havin' a good time long as you don't get out of control and make an everyday habit of it or let it get in the way of what you're supposed to be doin'. Even Grandma Rose liked her lemonade spiked come harvest time. My ma liked it too, and I never met a better Christian woman than her. Harvest time was always my favorite time of year, even more than Christmas. Don't tell the good Lord I said that, will you?"

"I won't," I said. Soon I was afraid I had broken Daddy's train of thought and his willingness to talk of the past because he sat silently for several minutes, lost in his own thoughts. He shifted in his seat and looked down at the burnt, unsmoked cigarette he held between his outstretched fingers. An ashy, ghostly stem balanced in the air. He flicked the ash and dropped what remained to the ground, and then he smothered the burning ember with his shoe. He took another long swallow from his now warm Pabst while he stared out across our yard.

Patiently, I waited, hoping he'd continue. Eventually, he reached in his pocket for the pack of cigarettes. He tapped one out from its casement, put it between his lips, and reached in his pocket again for his matchbook. Deftly with one hand, he opened the matchbook, bent a match forward with his thumb, and closed the cover over the other matches. With the matchbook nested in the cup of his hand, he moved the match swiftly across the rough surface, lighting it. Protecting the flame from the mild breeze with his hand, he inhaled deeply, lighting his cigarette, and then blew out the flame. He took another long drag and blew the smoke upward in a slow, steady stream. At last, he began to speak again, rewarding my patience.

"Our farm had two good houses, not counting the sharecropper cabins. The older house, the one that Grandma Rose and us lived in, we called the big house. The other one sat facing it. We had a barn, drying sheds, a tool barn and some other buildin's. We had chickens, a couple of milkin' cows until they gave out, pigs, goats, and some geese. Ahoskie Creek ran back of the place. There was a spot where it was just deep and wide enough for a bit of swimmin' and some fishin' too. Sometimes we'd ride over to Grandma Rose's property on the Chowan. Come Thanksgiving time, we'd go huntin' out on Grandma's land. We'd get a turkey or two every year. The huntin', fishin', and swimmin' was real good there. Mamma, your grandma, was one of the best cooks in Hertford County. She could take turnip greens and some salt pork and turn 'em into a feast. But we didn't always get much meat on our plates. Some days, we was lucky to get grits, eggs, and pork fat for our supper."

"Charlie, girl, even when times are good, tobacca farmin' ain't easy. The chores never stop; there's work to be done year round. You go from January to November. In December, you mend all the farm tools and fences. We'd work out in the fields from sunrise to sunset 'cept when we was in school. After a long day in the fields, if

Mamma put out enough food for all of us to fill our stomachs, we thought it a feast day.

"Farmin' is in our blood, honey. My pa's family farmed that same four hundred acres since 'fore there was a United States. My grandma's pa and her brothers—half-brothers, that is—had a lot of schoolin' and even went to college. They were town people. But no one in my pa's family ever finished high school 'fore my sister Ida did. She was the first girl to finish high school in both families. Grandma Rose's pa thought education was wasted on a girl; so did a lot of folks back then. Both my folks were real proud when Ida and then my brother, Raymond, graduated high school. Raymond never liked school all that much, least not the way Ida did. He tried to drop out. When he was in the tenth grade, he came home one day and announced he was quittin' school. Said he had enough education to be a farmer. When Pa said he could use the extra help, Ma had a hissy fit. I guess that was the biggest disagreement I seen them two have. Ma couldn't change either of their minds until Grandma Rose stepped in. Even big old Raymond and my Pa couldn't stand up to all four-foot-ten of her, so Raymond stayed in school and graduated, by some miracle. By the time I reached the tenth grade, though, Grandpa Jackson and Uncle Eugene had joined Uncle Clyde in heaven. Pa announced at dinner one day that I was done with school. Grandma Rose didn't say a word. She knew it had to be. It turned out it didn't matter all that much; we slowly lost the farm piece by piece anyway. We had to keep sellin' parts off to pay the bank note and pay for other things like seed. The bank won in the end. Someone else is farmin' that land now. By the time I left for the army, we only had about seventy-eight acres left and not all of it good for farmin'. The remainin' share-croppers' cabins were teardowns by then. One of the roofs caved in and rot got to it. Uncle Eugene's old house sat empty for years. Seemed we had more ghosts than crops by then."

I thought how strange it was that Daddy was so close to his cousin Charlotte but only spoke to his sister once a year at Christmas time when she'd phone, and they'd talk for maybe half an hour. I never heard about any communication with his brother. Though I was curious, I sensed that there would be too many land mines for Daddy to want to reminisce over that landscape of memories, so I didn't ask. Daddy finished his beer and said, "Go on up ta the kitchen and fetch me another beer." I started to jump up when he added, "But if your mama sees you, just bring me some iced tea."

The kitchen was empty, so, I grabbed an iced tea for me and another Pabst for Daddy and ran out to the backyard. Before the screen door slammed, I was halfway down the steps.

"Tell me about your Uncle Eugene," I entreated as I pulled up next to Daddy and handed him his beer.

Once I resettled in my rickety chair, he continued. "Uncle Eugene had a face like nine days of bad weather and a personality to match. But he was a good hunter and a first-rate farmer. He was tall and real strong. Everyone was surprised when he took up with Gladys Stokes; at least that's what my ma told me. What I remember is that Uncle Eugene didn't talk much, but Aunt Gladys hardly stopped. She was the prettiest girl in three counties. I used to think that Gladys was the prettiest gal that ever lived, 'til I met your mother, that is."

Daddy took a deep breath, then continued, "Boy, when I first laid eyes on your mama, my heart stopped beating. She was the finest thing I'd ever seen. She wasn't just beautiful—everything about her was flawless and fine. Starting with that heavenly voice of hers. She sang around town at a few venues. The crowd were mostly G.I.s. We were all mesmerized by her. She moved graceful like a swan, and her figure was perfect—still is. She wore her thick hair up in a neat bun, and her clothes were stylish. You know she was a nurse at Walter Reed, and I was one of her patients?" I nodded that I did. "She was perfect. Her uniform was always clean and crisply starched, her nails smooth and tapered, and every hair in place. At the end of each of her shifts, she'd change into her street clothes before popping by our ward to say goodnight. Sometimes she'd sing us a goodnight tune. I think she knew what that meant to us, including seeing her out of uniform. It reminded us what we were fightin' for.

"Your mama could have been in one of those fashion magazines. She didn't just move; she floated. All of us guys in the ward were under her spell. Just lookin' at her was all the R and

R we needed. First time I met her, I was sleeping and heard this angel's voice calling to me. I woke up and saw her face looking down at me. I thought I'd died and gone to heaven. She was sitting next to me on my cot and placed a soft, warm hand on my arm. I can still feel that touch. It was electric. I guess you could say I fell hard. I would have sold my soul to the Devil to win her. Believe me, there was a long line of would-be suiters. When we hooked up, boy, those boys were jealous."

Daddy shifted in his chair and took a long swig from his beer before he went on. "Shoot, I sure got off track. Let's get back to Aunt Gladys—she was a looker too. Not as fine as your mama, mind you, but beautiful nonetheless. Folks used to say she looked a lot like Myrna Loy. Her eyes did look like Myrna's, but I thought Gladys was a whole lot prettier.

"Who's Myrna Loy, Daddy?"

"Oh, she was a famous Hollywood movie star way back when. Gladys loved going ta the picture shows. She'd read them movie magazines from cover to cover anytime she could get a hold of one. Ma told me that no one could figure out why she married Uncle Eugene until soon after the weddin' when she started gettin' thick around the middle. Six months later, little Rudy got born. Course that were 'fore I was born."

"You have a cousin named Rudy? You've never mentioned him. Where's he living at?"

"He ain't."

"What do you mean, he ain't? Is he dead?"

"Yeah, long-time dead."

"How'd he die?"

"He's dead, is all. Girl, it's gettin' late now, and you'd best get ta pickin' them vegetables 'fore your Mamma comes lookin' for 'em." With that, Daddy abruptly stood up, stretched his long frame, emptied his beer, bent to grab the other empty can, and threw the evidence in the trash can that sat next to the house before he went back inside. After he'd gone, I continued to sit for a while, staring out at the garden and pondering all that he had shared with me. But the shade, now stretching across the garden, reminded me that time was moving on. So I got up, opened the garden fence, and started picking Daddy's tomatoes.

Part Six

1968

CHAPTER NINETEEN

❦

NETTLES

After our trip to Virginia, when we stayed with Aunt Martha, Daddy went into overdrive trying to make Mamma happy, at least for a while. Soon after we got back, he bought a 1958 Ford Country Squire station wagon that needed some work. It was black with wood panels along its exterior sides. Inside, it was mostly red with some white trim. Best of all, we could all fit inside. When we first got it, we made several trips to the junkyard down in Brandywine for parts. It took about a month or so before Daddy and the boys got it through Maryland state inspection, tagged, and on the road for Mamma. Now that she had her own car, she took us to the beach or pool several times a week when it got up into the 90s, which is a lot of the time in D.C. in July and August.

For the Wards, it had been a good start to the summer of '68. Daddy had landed a better-paying job at the railway yard. School had just let out, and the lazy days of summer spread out before us.

Daddy and Mamma were getting along well and were frequently going out on dates. On Saturday nights they came home laughing and singing, and their cheerful mood spilled over into the following few days. On the first Monday of our summer holiday, I awoke to a voice singing, "Good morning, sleepy head." I kept my eyes closed until I could figure out if it was Buddy or Chip. Buddy's voice was sounding more and more like Chip's these days. "Am I going to have to tickle you?" *It's Chip, for sure,* I thought, and bolted up in my bed to show him I was only pretending to be asleep.

"What's up? Why are you waking me? There's no school today."

"We're going to the beach!"

"The beach! Really?"

"Yep. Now come on, get ready quick. We're heading to Sandy Point."

I jumped up, scrambled to find my bathing suit, and dressed. I grabbed a towel and ran down the stairs to join the others. The whole house was in a scramble. Legs were running everywhere while Mamma and Eugene, Mamma's second in command, barked orders. "Don't forget a change of clothes or you'll be wishing you had one on the ride home," advised Eugene. "Buddy, go grab the raft from the shed," Eugene instructed.

I rode up front with Mamma and Eugene while the rest of the tribe, along with the ice chest, beach gear, and Patton, rode in the back. I slept on and off with my head on Eugene's lap until he gently shook me and said, "We're here." Sandy Point State Park is on a promontory with a wide beach that gradually slopes into the Chesapeake at the base of the Bay Bridge, a suspension bridge made of steel that extends over four miles. It's a shadowy giant looming across the wide bay. An endless stream of behemoth seafaring cargo ships trudge up the bay's center on their way to and from the Port of Baltimore. Sandy Point has a bathhouse and playground. Ice cream vendors park their trucks and run down to the beach ringing their summoning bells. The place is heaven for little kids until the nettles arrive in July. There is a nettle net to keep the jellyfish out of the swimming area, but some, especially the smaller nettles, always make it through.

The previous year, before I learned about nettles, we went to Sandy Point in late July. I had an old donut floating tube with a slow leak. Eventually, it would get so deflated that periodically I had to blow it back up. I was scooping its deflated body out of the water when my hand caught the tentacles of a nettle, and it wrapped around and tangled up with my fingers, searing them. I started screaming. Chip was the first to arrive, but it was Eugene who lifted me out of the water and dumped me on the sand. He removed the stinging tendrils with his bare hands, never wincing or complaining. Then he washed my arm with bay water until the stinging subsided a bit and I calmed down. My hand looked like it had been burned. So did Eugene's fingers.

The next time we went to Sandy Point Beach that summer, no one could coax me into the water. I whined and pouted until

Eugene talked Chip and Buddy into surrendering the raft. He brought it near the shore and said, "Hop on, Charlotte." Then he took me for a ride in the water before letting me go. I floated, staring up at the blue sky, carefully splashing myself when I got too hot. Being the youngest and only girl in a pack of boys had its advantages. Gradually, with Eugene's help, I got over my fear of swimming in the Chesapeake, but only before mid-July when the nettles weren't yet plentiful.

Mamma worshipped the water and took us swimming every chance she could. She liked her water natural, preferring an ocean, bay, lake, pond, or river, in that order, over a swimming pool. It was a three-hour drive to the ocean, so we didn't go often. But Sandy Point was only a little more than a half hour by car. Between Mamma and Daddy, we learned to swim about the time we learned to walk.

At the end of August, while we were having dinner, Mamma started talking about the pending changes facing our family. The summer was coming to an end, and all of us would be heading back to school in a few days except Eugene, who had graduated from high school back in June. "The day after next is Chip's birthday. We should do something special. Jack, I want to take the kids to Ocean City on Thursday. We can celebrate Chip's birthday, and I can have at least one last day at the beach with all of my boys and Charlotte together."

"Why not Sandy Point or a pool? It's a whole lot closer. Ocean City is a far piece off just for a day's bit of fun. It's at least three hours down and another three back. Maggie, you'll be plum worn out after runnin' after a pack of kids in the sun and heat all day long. Think about it."

"I know, Jack, but who knows how much longer Eugene will be with us? He'll be nineteen soon and there's the draft."

"Honey, you'd have to leave 'fore the crack of dawn ta make it worth your while. You sure you want ta be doin' that, Maggie?"

"Eugene can drive back. Who knows if we'll ever have a day at the beach all together again? Sandy Point is not so nice this late in the season, and it is certainly not the ocean. I want us to have a memorable day. We can't afford a vacation, but we can have a special day." Just then she looked over at me and Buddy. "Charlotte, Buddy, can you remember our last trip to the ocean?"

Buddy answered, "Yeah, I remember. There's a boardwalk. A little train goes up and down it. The waves are big. You made Eugene go in the water with me."

"What about you, Charlotte? You couldn't have been but four or five the last time we went to Ocean City. Do you remember it?" I shook my head no. "Well, that settles it then. Pack your bags tonight, kids; we're leaving before the sun comes up." The boys and I all let out a cheer in unison.

"There's nothing like it," Chip said excitedly to me. "You'll love the waves." He chatted away about it until it was time for bed. "It tumbles you around like you're in a washing machine if you let the waves take you. If you catch a good wave, you can ride it all the way to shore. To get out beyond the waves, you must dive under them to get past the breakers. But once you do, you'll find smoother water," he advised. "Don't worry. I'll show you," he promised.

"But what about the nettles?" I asked.

"That's one of the best parts, Charlotte. There aren't any jellyfish," he said, knowing that would be the clincher. No one had to wake me for this trip; I was up before the sun and sitting on my bag ready to go when the boys stumbled down the stairs.

Mamma was the queen of S&H Green Stamps collecting. She traded for them with the other women in the neighborhood. Some better-off women who couldn't be bothered with collecting them just gave theirs to her. With each shopping trip to the grocery store, she would get a sheet of stamps and paste them in a booklet. The day before our trip to the ocean, she took her booklets of stamps to the trading store. We had breakfast long before the sun rose up in the sky. While we were eating our cereal, Mamma brought out a big box wrapped in brown paper. The paper was a patchwork of brown shopping bags turned inside out. Mamma had decorated the paper. On it, she had drawn a boy sitting in a boat with a fishing rod in his hands and a big fish dangling on the end of the line. "Happy Birthday" was written in colorful, bold letters. We were all curious and anxiously waited for Chip to open his present. To taunt us, he began to unwrap the package slowly, carefully pulling the tape from the paper.

"For Pete's sake, will you hurry up and open the darn thing

already?" admonished Buddy, "We don't have all day."

Finally, Chip ripped the paper, revealing the box's contents. Lettering on the box read two person inflatable boat. From the pictures on the outside, you could see it came with oars and oarlocks. Mamma explained that this was too big a gift for just one person—after today he would have to share it with everyone equally. However, today he was the captain. Today, it was all Chip's boat.

Just outside Berlin, Maryland, we stopped at a gas station to inflate the boat. The rest of the way to Ocean City, the boys took turns lying in the inflated boat in the back of the station wagon. As soon as Mamma stopped the car at the beach, we all piled out and ran to the water, except Eugene, who stayed behind to help unload. Before they could drag out the blankets, towels, and cooler, we had hit the waves. As Chip was about to launch the boat with the help of Buddy, I begged to go along. "I want to come too," I cried.

"There's no room. It's a two-man boat," Buddy emphatically stated.

"I don't take much room, and you ain't men yet," I retorted.

"We're going way out. We don't need you whining to get back," he said.

"I won't," I promised.

"Not this time," said Chip.

"Why does Buddy get to go?" I cried.

"This is a pirate ship," announced Buddy. "There's no girls allowed."

"That's not fair."

"Who told you that life is fair?" asked Chip. "Buddy's right. I am the captain, and there's no girls allowed. Girls are bad luck on a boat anyway." With that, they took off, fighting the waves to get past the breakers. It took them several attempts, and they looked as if they were tiring. I hoped they wouldn't make it, but they finally did.

With the surf breaking around my ankles, I blew up my donut tube and jumped into the water. It took me several attempts to get past the breakers, but I made it by diving under each wave. Once past the breakers, I threaded my body up through the donut and caught my breath. I floated along until it was time to reinflate the tube. I slid out of it and dog-paddled while I blew it back up. When I remounted, I turned to look at the shore and realized that I was much farther from shore than I had ever been before. I felt free, untethered, and I imagined being a dolphin. I fell in love with the ocean. I could see Mamma and Eugene waving to me, so I waved back. Then I turned to swim farther out. I wanted to make the people on the shore look like ants. I was still angry with my brothers. When I finally achieved my goal of shrinking everyone in sight, I floated for a time, looking skyward. It was peaceful. But my silent reverie was eventually interrupted when a Coast Guard boat came up alongside of me. A nice-looking young man—I later learned his name was Dennis—leaned over and threw me an orange life buoy and told me to grab hold so he could pull me aboard.

"I'm okay. I don't need any help," I informed him. That was when I learned that Mamma and Eugene hadn't been cheerfully waving to me. They were trying to signal to me to come back toward shore.

"You'd better come on board. Your mother is very worried about you." I reached for the orange life buoy, and Dennis pulled me toward the boat. Once I was on the deck, he asked, "So, where were you heading?"

"Away," was my only reply.

"Do you know about ocean currents, young lady?" I shook my head in the negative. "If you get caught in one, you can be taken out to sea. You'll be miles away in no time. In the future, you'd better stick closer to shore."

As the boat motored on, I sat silently and pondered my fate. The boat passed the southern tip of Ocean City and rounded into an inlet. I realized that if my mother thought she had to contact the Coast Guard to retrieve me, I was probably in a lot of trouble. The boat ride, unfortunately for me, only took a few minutes. I watched as the boat rounded the end of the island, and there on the leeward side was the Coast Guard pier. Standing at its end was Mamma with her hands on her hips. My fears were justified.

When I got off the boat, Mamma started in on me. "Jesus, Mary, and Joseph, Charlotte, what in the world were you thinking? Are you nuts? Don't you have any better sense?" she said as she slapped me upside my head. Mamma rarely hit us—that was Daddy's job.

It was a sign that she was especially upset.

"Are you trying to give me a heart attack? What's the matter, has the cat suddenly got ahold of your tongue? I'm asking you a question." I could only shrug my shoulders in response. "Truly, I don't know whether to beat you or hug you. If I start beating you, I might not stop—you scared me so bad. If I hug you, I might crush every bone in your body. I am so relieved to see you alive. Of course, you're grounded indefinitely."

For the rest of the day I was not allowed back in the water and had to sit in the hot sun as my brothers played in the surf. After that, Mamma wouldn't take me back to Ocean City for another two years.

CHAPTER TWENTY

80✝03

SPOCK AND SCOTTIE

I don't remember who first started calling me Charlie, and I
don't remember exactly when. But I know it was sometime
before Eugene finally got his own nickname. One Christmas
Eugene asked for a slide rule as a present. The year before that it,
was a chemistry set, which Daddy took away after Eugene dropped
a vial and burnt a hole clear through the upstairs bathroom floor
to the kitchen below. One summer he took a math class for fun. He
dreamed of working for NASA. He didn't want to fly spaceships;
he wanted to build them.

Eugene loved movies, musicals, live theater, and exercising
with Jack LaLanne. He also loved all things to do with outer space
and watched every NASA launch that was televised. His favorite
writers were Herbert, Heinlein, Bradbury, and Asimov. Most after-
noons after school, Eugene got to join two of his favorite passions:
science and theater. His best friend, Scott, came over and together

they'd watch *Star Trek* reruns.

Scott and Eugene knew each episode by title and would reenact them. Scott was a little taller than average but not as tall as Eugene. Scott had light, thin, straight hair. Eugene was skinnier with dark, thick hair. In their games, Scott would be Captain Kirk or, of course, Scottie. Eugene would play Spock or Dr. McCoy. Sometimes they'd let me play, but they'd insist I had to be the nurse, Christine Chapel, which limited the episodes we could play together; Christine's character wasn't in as many as the other main characters. I didn't like playing her, and especially in the "Naked Time" episode when she got all gaga over Spock. I would have preferred playing Uhura, or better yet, a Klingon. It seemed that even in space, "the final frontier," women were still relegated to being nurses or communications operators.

Even when we weren't pretending, Eugene would walk around the house holding his hand up with his fingers in a "V" shape and say, "Live long and prosper." I think it was Buddy who started calling Eugene "Spock," even when he wasn't trying to imitate the Vulcan. The name stuck for the most part. Mamma never called him by that name; Daddy did sometimes, but not often. But his friends and siblings called him Spock as much as we called him Eugene. To me, my oldest brother had finally proven himself human like the rest of us when he earned his very own nickname.

We were calling him Spock for more than a year when one evening, Daddy told me to head out to the shed to get his bar clamps. He was regluing some dining room chair legs that had gotten loose. The bar clamps were hanging right inside the shed door. I took a flashlight and headed out back. When I walk into the shed, I pointed the flashlight to my left and saw the clamps. As I reached for them, I heard a strange noise toward the back of the shed that startled me. When I swung the light in that direction, I saw Eugene getting up from his knees and Scott was—I thought but wasn't a hundred percent sure—zipping his pants. His face was flushed. They looked panicked and surprised.

"What are you doing here?" barked Eugene. Which surprised me, as Eugene rarely yelled at me.

"I could ask the same of you two."

"Nothing. We weren't doing anything."

"You were doing something."

"It's none of your business. Don't worry about it."

"Worry about what?"

"What are you doing out here, Charlie?"

"Daddy sent me to get the bar clamps."

"Then you'd better go on and do it. You don't want to keep him waiting." I turned to grab the clamps.

Then in a softer tone, Eugene said, "Charlie."

"What?"

"Don't tell anyone what you saw here. Will you do that for me?"

"I don't know. What did I see, Spock?"

"Just don't tell anyone that you saw us out here, okay?"

"I'll think about it."

"Please, Charlie, I'm serious. It's important."

"Why is that?"

"It just is."

"I don't know, Spock. Something doesn't feel right. I'm confused."

"Honey, nothing bad is going on here. Seriously, Charlie, I am asking you."

"Why is it important? What were you two doing?"

"Charlie, please. I'm begging you, please, let it go. Don't tell anyone, okay?"

"No, Spock, I won't tell. But I don't know what it is I am not telling."

Eugene had never been unkind to me, but after that, he and Scott were extra nice for quite some time. I could play Uhura anytime I wanted. I even got to play Scottie, on account of I was the best at mimicking accents.

Right around Spock's, aka Eugene's nineteenth birthday, he went to a meeting with a navy recruiter that Uncle Ben had arranged at Mamma's request. More and more boys were going to Vietnam and many returned in boxes. There was talk that a draft lottery would be coming soon. Eugene wanted to join up before he got drafted. We didn't want him to end up in the army and fighting in the rice paddies of Vietnam. The navy didn't guarantee that you would miss out on Vietnam, but your chances of survival were better. Our parents couldn't afford to send him to college, which would have given him the golden 2-S military service deferment ticket. Without college, poor boys were draft bait as soon as they turned nineteen.

When he came into the house after meeting with the recruiter, he saw Mamma's anxious face and announced, "Looks like I'll be wearing navy blues."

Mamma let out a sigh of relief, and I joked, "Good, blue is more your color. You definitely don't look good in olive green."

"It's not definite," he cautioned. "I still have to go up to Fort Holabird, the processing center in Dundalk outside Baltimore. They'll give me physical and mental exams, but if I pass I will be heading to the navy's Great Lakes station for basic training."

"Where's that?" Buddy asked.

"The recruiter said it's somewhere near Chicago. Everyone in the navy goes through there. The recruiter said that with my 'excellent grades and apparent good health,' I shouldn't have any trouble getting in. I'm hoping to get into the engineman training program up there."

"Well thank Jesus, Mary, and Holy Saint Joseph that's been settled," said Mamma. "My prayers have been answered."

"And may they keep you safe," I added.

"Amen to that," agreed Mamma.

CHAPTER TWENTY-ONE

80 ❖ ଅ

PEN PALS

Mrs. Saunders, our sixth-grade English teacher, spent a week of class teaching us how to write a formal letter. "There are five parts to a friendly letter," she informed us. "Heading, greeting, body, closing, and signature," she announced as she wrote each word on the blackboard. *How many parts are in an unfriendly letter*, I wondered but didn't ask. Next to each of the five words she wrote an example. Then she went over a sample letter.

"Your homework for tonight is to pick someone to write. You will need their address. This week in class you will write a letter with a minimum of four paragraphs. Tomorrow we will work on the introductory paragraph, and on Wednesday each of you will write about our field trip last week to the Wonder Bread factory. In the third paragraph you can write about anything you like. So you should think about what you'd like to tell the recipient of your letter. The final paragraph will be your closing. Be prepared to start writing tomorrow in class." This is how my sister became my pen pal—because of a class assignment.

Miss Charlotte Ward

1528 Allison Street

Brentwood, Maryland

March 11, 1968

Mrs. Emma Cranston

2570 Georges Street

Springfield, Oregon

Dear Emma,

How are you, the kids, and Nate getting along? How do you like living in Oregon? Do you miss Washington State? Which do you prefer? Our teacher has given us an assignment to write a letter to someone we know. So I picked you.

Last week we went to the Wonder Bread factory. It is down near Rhode Island and Georgia avenues, adjacent Howard University and where Griffith Stadium used to be. Did you ever have a school trip to tour the factory? Did you ever go to a game at Griffith Stadium? The stadium is gone now. They tore most of it down a couple of years ago. But you can still make out where the buildings were, and part of the fence is still standing. I can see it from a window I look out of when I go to the orthodontist at Howard University's dental school.

Did Mamma tell you that I got braces? The university now owns the property.

Mamma and I have gone to the Wonder Bread store next to the factory many times after my dental appointments, to buy discounted bread, but this was my first time inside the factory. It always smells so good on that block. On the tour, they took us across a catwalk over the area where they mix the bread and let it rise. It smelled of yeast, which is a bit funny, kind of sour smelling, and not so nice. But when we went to the rooms with the ovens, oh, that smelled really fine. Afterward, we each got a bag filled with goodies. We got a miniature loaf of bread, a Twinkie, some coupons, and a ruler with Wonder Bread written on it. Almost everyone couldn't wait and ate their treats on the bus going back to school, even though we're not supposed to eat on the bus. I didn't. I wanted to share mine with Mamma, especially the little miniature loaf of bread.

I have some sad news. Old Patton died. Do you remember him? Of course, you must. Who could forget such a good dog, though he was still not much more than a puppy when you left? He has been showing signs of old age for some time now. It took him longer and longer to get up off the floor, and he'd groan when he did. Sometimes he even needed a bit of help getting up. He's been a bit hard of hearing too. Well anyway, about two weeks ago, Chip was backing out of the driveway on his way to work. He was late and in a rush. Patton had been taking to lying on the asphalt so he could bake his old bones, as Daddy puts it. Chip forgot to look and didn't see him. He backed the truck right over him. Patton was too old and slow to get up out of the way in time. We all heard Patton's yelp and Chip's cry. It was terrifying. When I got out to the yard, Chip had Patton in his arms. The poor dog just looked up at him as if to ask why. He twitched a few times and died right there. No one asked Chip why he didn't look behind the truck. Everyone knew that Patton had taken to lying on that pavement in the driveway. Chip should have looked, but he knows that and feels horrible. Who could ask such a thing of the person who felt as bad as Chip? He's still pretty broken up about it.

Mamma told Eugene about it in a letter. I'm sure you know he's in boot camp up near the Great Lakes outside Chicago. It hasn't been a month since he left, but we all miss him a lot, especially Mamma. I think Eugene wasn't just her son but her best friend too.

Well, that's all the news I have for now. If you write me back, I promise to write again. If you write, tell me about your life out west, about your kids, are you happy being a mom, how's Nate doing, or anything else that you would like to share.

Sincerely,
Charlotte Ward
P.S. Don't tell Chip I told you about Patton.

CHAPTER TWENTY-TWO

࿔ ❖ ࿓

THE EVENING NEWS

*J*ust after 6:00 p.m. on the fourth of April, a preacher and father of four young children was fatally shot as he stood on a balcony outside his hotel room. Dr. Martin Luther King, Jr. was thirty-nine years old. Just the day before, he told a crowd, "We've got some difficult days ahead. … I've been to the mountaintop … I've seen the Promised Land. I may not get there with you. But I want you to know tonight that we, as a people, will get to the Promised Land."

Clouds threatened rain that evening as we tuned in to the CBS eight o'clock evening news. Walter Cronkite came on. He went straight into the headline without preamble: "Good Evening. Dr. Martin Luther King, the apostle of nonviolent protest in the civil rights movement, has been shot to death in Memphis, Tennessee. Police have issued an all-points bulletin for a well-dressed young White man seen running from the scene."

By 1968 Daddy got to calling the television the "idiot box"

or the "boob tube." It drove him crazy to see us sitting around with our eyes glued to the set when there was daylight outside. During summers when school was out, he'd take one of the small vacuum tubes out of the back of the set so it wouldn't work. He'd tell us it was broken so we'd go out to play. Once we were back in school in September, he'd put the tube back in and announce that he'd fixed it. It took us two summers before we figured out what he was doing. We convinced him to leave the television alone by promising to watch less and play outside more. During our campaign to convince him, we would turn it off when we heard his truck pulling up in the driveway. If there was daylight, we'd run out back; if not, we'd run upstairs. Finally he left the tubes and the set alone while we continued our subterfuge until it became habit.

For Christmas Daddy picked up a used Motorola black-and-white television console, replacing our old Philco, which had lost its picture six months back. We got by for a few months by using a dual set of televisions. We listened to the Philco while watching an old Zenith a guy at work gave Daddy. The Zenith had no sound, but the picture was good. Daddy placed the Zenith on top of the Philco, and we tuned both sets to the same station. There was a slight delay between the picture and sound. We were all happy to find the big Motorola in the living room on Christmas morning. On its top were two lids: under the right lid were the dials, under the left was a turntable, and in between was the TV. In January we watched the debut of *Laugh-In* with Rowan and Martin. We listened to Walter Cronkite tell us about the Tet Offensive. In February we saw Peggy Fleming take gold at the Winter Olympics in Grenoble, France, and we heard ex-Vice President Nixon announce that he was running for the office of the Presidency. In March LBJ shocked us all by announcing he wouldn't seek reelection. Soon after, Mamma's favorite, and fellow Roman Catholic, Robert Kennedy, announced his candidacy for the presidency. In April we watched the District of Columbia burn.

Throughout that month, the news was all we watched. Riveted to the Motorola, we saw Black mobs react to Dr. King's murder. News reports had little information about catching his killer. Whites huddled together, awash in the glow of their TV screens, as they witnessed Blacks setting fire in cities near and far. Young Blacks claimed the spoils of war and looted everything they could carry. Fury, anarchy, and chaos ruled the streets. Centuries of pent-up frustration, rage, and pain erupted before our eyes on the evening news. The smell of smoke flowed through our windows and doors, emphasizing the closeness of the fires and feeding our fears. From our second-floor windows, we watched clouds of smoke rise over our city. Mamma and Daddy wouldn't let us go beyond the front yard to play. Whites stayed close to home; Daddy didn't go to work for over a week.

The acrid smell from the fires lingered for months. Entire blocks lay in wreckage, reminding us of war's wrath. When the anger and sorrow were spent, neighborhoods lay in ruin. Familiar stores were now rubble and ash, putting an end to shopping downtown.

Mamma started on a new campaign: she wanted to move to the suburbs. She and Daddy no longer went to clubs in D.C. The Showboat had already moved to Silver Spring, Maryland, and others, like the Bohemian Caverns, closed soon after the fires got cold. Daddy quit his seasonal job at the swimming pool; he no longer felt safe going there after dark. The newer generation didn't remember him unlocking the gates on segregated pools. He had become just another White man.

CHAPTER TWENTY-THREE

৪০❖৪

CLOSED DOOR

May 25, 1968

Dear Spock,

I know Mamma already wrote to you about the riots, and I guess you watched some on the news or read about it in the papers. When I was watching it on the news, it all seemed unreal and far away. That's until one of us opened a door or window, and then you could smell how close it was. It's calmed down now, but folks are still on edge. From upstairs, we saw the smoke rising over the rooftops. Though it's been weeks since they stopped burning stuff, when the wind picks up you can still smell it. The National Guard left, but D.C. will never be the same. At least, that's what everyone is saying. Daddy told us that Morton's Department Store, the Savoy Theatre (you liked the Savoy), Miles Shoes, Peoples Drug Store, and a bunch of others are burnt down. All that's left are the buildings' skeletons, ashes, and soot. I've seen pictures in the *Post*. The stores not touched by fire were looted. The H Street shopping district is gone. All the big stores have abandoned the city. They say they'll relocate out in the suburbs.

Mamma wants to join the diaspora. She's on the warpath to move to Bowie or Laurel or someplace like it. She's not the only one. Every day there's a new "For Sale" sign going up. Downtown D.C. is dead. No one goes there anymore, not Whites anyway. Without their money, downtown businesses are going out of business. Daddy calls it the great White exodus. Daddy says that not all the fires were lit because of rage. He said some were bonfires lit by folks looking for a party and an excuse to steal. He said the looters dishonored Dr. King by using his assassination as an excuse to steal. Maybe he's right. Tell me, Spock, how is looting showing respect? I understand rage against injustice, and I understand frustration, and protest, but those fires, more than anything, destroyed Black homes, Black jobs, and Black communities. Mamma says it will be decades before the scars can be healed and not all scars were caused by the fires. Whites are afraid of Blacks; Blacks don't trust Whites. I guess it's always been that way; the fires just put a bright light on it for all to see. You can feel the unease everywhere, Spock. I knew the divide was there; I just didn't know how deep the hate went.

Mamma and Daddy have been having some big fights these last couple of months. It's like the tension outside came in with the smoke. Maybe six weeks ago, just before the riots, Daddy was driving the car with Mamma in the front seat beside him and Buddy and I were in the back. We were on the B.W. Parkway near the Pepsi-Cola building that's up on a hill when a guy in a black Camaro cut us off and made Daddy swerve to avoid hitting him. Something just snapped in Daddy. He got so mad he hit the gas and started to weave in and out of traffic, trying to catch up to the Camaro. Mamma started screaming for Daddy to stop, but that just got Daddy angrier, and he kept going even faster.

Buddy and I were so frightened that I clutched his hand and he let me. The Camaro turned off the Parkway at East-West Highway. At the end of the exit ramp, the Camaro barely made it through a yellow light. I thought for a moment that the chase was finally over. But Daddy acted like the light was a stop sign and ran through it when he had an opening in the traffic. Daddy finally caught up to the guy at Kenilworth Avenue and blocked traffic. He swerved our car in front of the Camaro at an intersection, stopped, and got out. He started pounding on the guy's door while screaming at the top of his lungs. The man looked scared to death. People were staring at us. Buddy and I slinked down in our seats, hoping no one we knew saw us. Mamma yelled at Daddy, "Jack, if a policeman comes, it will be *you* he'll arrest. You're acting like a bloody lunatic. You've made your point. For God's sake, get back in the car."

Daddy yelled back to her, "This idiot could've killed us."

"Him? What about you, Jack? You're the one who put us in the greater danger. You drove like a maniac. You've terrified the kids and me too." She was right about that. "Please, Jack, you're far too upset to drive. Give me the keys." I could see Daddy through the open driver's side door. You could tell that really pissed him off, but at least he got back in the car.

"I'm driving. Get back in the damn car, Maggie!" he shouted, and she did as commanded. The silence in the car was suffocating as Daddy drove home. Buddy and I were afraid to make a sound or breathe. Once we got back in the house, the arguing started up again, and they've been going at it ever since, with only a few lulls in their battles.

After weeks of quarreling, Mamma was exhausted and got real depressed again. She's been sulking around the house for a couple of weeks. I wasn't home when the latest argument started. When I was coming home, I could hear them going at it from three doors up the street. I was afraid the neighbors would call the police again, it got so loud. They were arguing about moving out to the suburbs. Daddy's not wild about the idea. They were still going at it when I went to bed. It was after two in the morning when Daddy woke me. He said he had to lie down for a bit and that Mamma had locked herself in the bathroom again. Between work and fighting, he hadn't slept in days. "Go sit by the bathroom door and keep her talkin'. Make sure she don't do nothin' crazy," he instructed.

"Crazy, like what?" I asked him.

"Don't let her hurt herself. There's no tellin' what she might do. I gotta lay down for a bit. You do your best and come get me if she opens that door." The thought of her doing something drastic really scared me. I waited for Daddy to leave the hallway. I stood until I could hear him breathing heavier as he settled down on the couch. Quietly, I slid down against the wall next to the bathroom's closed door and whispered, "Mamma, it's me. I love you. Please, tell me what to do." But the only sound I heard from the other side of the door was her softly crying. Spock, if you were still at home, it would've been you sitting there. I don't know how to fill your shoes.

When I heard Daddy snoring, I felt so alone and inadequate. There in the dark, I kept offering ideas just to break the silence. "Mamma, Daddy's sleeping soundly," I told her. "Do you want me to pack some bags? We can go see Aunt Martha." But she made no reply.

"What about going to see Emma? You've been aching to see her. We can figure out some way to get you out there. Martha will loan you the money, and I've got some saved. You can have it."

I rambled on, pleading with her to open the door. She wouldn't.

"Please, Mamma, I'm begging you—let me help you," I said and started crying.

She finally spoke then. "You can't help me. No one can. You should be in bed. Go," she said softly through the closed door.

That was all I could get her to say. I placed my ear to the door, but it was silent on the other side for a long time after that—no words, no crying, and no movement. In the morning, Daddy found me sleeping slumped on the floor by the bathroom door and shook me awake. I was ashamed. I'd failed at my post. As soon as I awoke, I got real anxious for her. First thing I did when I sat up was to call out to her in an anxious voice, "Mamma, are you okay?"

That's when Daddy leaned on the wall and started talking through the closed door. He had the Sunday *Washington Post* in his hand. While I slept, he must've run up to the store to buy a copy. "Maggie, I promise you, we'll move. We can start lookin' today if that's what ya want. I got the ads right here. Listen to this one. It's in Beltsville. 'Cozy Cape Cod, four bedrooms, two full baths, and eat-in kitchen.' You want me to call the number in the paper? We can go see it today."

Despite his efforts, it remained dead quiet on the other side of the door. I strained to listen for any hopeful sound. He cleared his throat and went on reading another advertisement about a home in Bowie. Still, no sound escaped from behind the bathroom door. With each second, fear grew inside of me.

"Maggie, please, honey, just open up the door," he begged, his voice a bit wearier than before. "We all need ya. Nothin' works without ya. Here, you wanna look at the house ads? You pick one. Honey, I'm beggin' ya. Darlin'. I'm tryin'. You know, I truly want ta make ya happy."

A faint sound came from behind the door, and I took a deep breath. I didn't realize until then that I'd been holding it. When I heard Mamma unlock the door, I started crying. I was so relieved and grateful to hear the lock click open and to know that she was alive. Spock, I was so scared.

We all miss you a lot, but especially Mamma. Do you miss us too? I don't just miss your friendship but your guidance too. Eugene, I failed miserably trying to fill your shoes. I don't have your skills. Aunt Martha is far away, and now so are you. In the last couple of days, things have been better with her and Daddy. Still, it's not like he's her confidant the way you are. Right now she's okay, but I get so scared when she gets all withdrawn. I want to be the one she can rely on, but I don't know how. I feel clumsy trying to talk to her. You know how to be her ally. You did it so well. What's the secret? Please, I need your help.

Back in March when Mamma got back from visiting you in Philadelphia, she was in a much better mood. Since their last fight, Mamma and Daddy have been out a lot looking at houses. She's been better for the most part. However, she hasn't liked any of the rental homes they've seen. Mamma called her sister and asked to borrow some money for a down payment on a house. Mamma wants to buy a home and not rent anymore. She and Daddy don't agree about this. He refused to borrow from her sister no matter how she begged. Then Mamma got a call from her dad. I was real surprised by that. I picked up the phone when he called. I've never heard his voice before. I sometimes forget Mamma has a living father. Mamma won't say why they stopped talking. She just said they had a disagreement. But that was years ago. After so long of not speaking to each other except when she was in Philly with you, I'd have thought they'd have talked for hours. But they weren't on the phone for more than twenty minutes. It turns out her daddy is giving us the money for the down payment—not a loan but a gift.

You'd think that would make Daddy happy, but it only hurt his pride. Daddy thinks it's charity, and you know how he feels about accepting handouts. (Remember how he forbade Mamma to apply for food stamps. Mamma did it behind his back and got food stamps and reduced lunches for us at school too. She swore us all to secrecy.) When Mamma told Daddy about Granddad's gift, Daddy said, "Don't I keep a roof over our heads and food on the table? A man takes care of his own without taking charity from others." But Mamma countered, "Jack, it's what families are supposed to do—help each other. My father would rather see me have my own home before he dies. He can't take it with him, Jack." Still, Daddy wouldn't bend, but Mamma wouldn't give up neither. "If we don't take the money now, I will just inherit it later when it will be too late for my father to see me in my own home. What's the sense in that?" When that didn't persuade him, she threatened, "Jack, I swear, if we don't use my dad's money to buy a home, I'll use it to leave you!" That got him. He finally surrendered. That was a surprise. Since then, they've been going out with a real estate lady every day after Daddy gets home from work. Mamma is determined.

They're still "discussing" which house to buy. Daddy likes a property they saw in Landover. It has a big garage. The boys and I haven't seen it yet. Daddy says it used to be a gas station a long time ago. It has a house behind it and a big yard (over an acre). Mamma is worried about that one because it needs a lot of work, but he promised Mamma to get it done quickly. She wants to look farther out and wants something that doesn't need so much work. She saw one she likes in Laurel, but Daddy hated it. Daddy doesn't want to move beyond the Beltway and dreams of having his own business. He's in love with the place with the big garage. He says it would give him the chance to do what he's always dreamed of, and that is work for himself. He says he could set the boys up in the auto repair business. He'll call it "Ward and Sons Auto Repair."

Chip isn't crazy about moving again. He's been playing baseball and just got moved from third base to catcher, which is what he's been wanting. Buddy and I are tired of moving, starting new schools, and making new friends. Dad says we can get a new dog after we move. Mamma just says we will have to see about that. Whichever house they buy, they promised this will be the last move for a long time. At least that part sounds good.

Mamma says there's a chance that you might attend the Naval Academy in Annapolis. I know she's been writing letters and making phone calls about it. That's exciting news. I'll keep my fingers crossed for you. I'd love to have you just down the road in Annapolis for four whole years. We could visit. Plus, I hope the war in Vietnam is over before you graduate.

Write when you can. I miss you A LOT.

Love you,

Charlie

June 9, 1968

Dear Charlie,

I've some good news; I've been accepted to the US Naval Academy. Soon I will be only a half hour's drive from you all. Today I wrote Mamma and Daddy in a separate letter. So if you read your letter first, don't let on that you know my news. I want to tell them. I have Captain Snyder to thank. While we were in Philadelphia overhauling our ship, the USS *New Jersey*, I frequently got to work near the captain. He's a great leader. He takes the time to know his crew and knows how to instill loyalty. I admire him greatly. After several conversations, he asked if I ever considered applying to the Naval Academy. He coached me on what I would have to do to get in and sent a letter of endorsement along with my application for admission. I have Mom to thank too. She went to our congressman's office to ask for a congressional letter of recommendation, which helped. She was persistent. I got my official acceptance letter just after our ship left Norfolk. I will be studying engineering. I am thrilled. If I give the navy an additional five years after graduation, they'll give me a college education. Not bad.

Since I started this process, everything seemed to be moving frustratingly slow until I got accepted. Now it feels like it's coming too quickly. The reality of it has set in, and I have mixed feelings about my Permanent Change of Station orders. I don't know if I'll have the opportunity to serve beneath a better commander than Captain Snyder. I know it's an incredible opportunity, but I feel guilty about leaving my fellow seamen on this ship too. I am heading to college, and they're heading to war. Yes, I agree with you: I hope this war is over soon, but it doesn't look like it from here.

After we left port in Philadelphia on May 4, we called in at Norfolk before heading south toward Panama. While in Virginia, I got to see Aunt Martha for just an hour, but it was great. Uncle Ben was there too. It felt strange having to salute him. Today our ship went through the Panama Canal. When we started to enter the first lock, I said to one of my shipmates that we could use a couple of tons of grease to slick her down. It was an incredibly tight squeeze. Sure enough, we got stuck in one of the locks. The captain brilliantly turned the propellers two rotations a minute and got it out of the lock (and I thought passing the parallel parking portion of the driver's test in Dad's old temperamental Ford truck was tough). I hope you can see this canal one day, Sis. It's an engineering marvel. The crew watched from the deck. We were all in awe of not only the canal but of the captain and the deck crew navigating our ship through the locks.

I hope to see you in August. There's a family weekend for the plebes then. Your last letter has been on my mind. I hope things are on a more even keel now. Dr. King's assassination and the riots shook us all up. But there is hope. Not all the major cities in the US had riots after King's assassination. Did you hear what happened in Indianapolis? Despite fears of riots and concerns for his safety, Robert Kennedy went to a scheduled rally in the city's Black ghetto and addressed a large crowd. He told the crowd what happened to Dr. King and then gave a short but impassioned speech for peace. Indianapolis is the only major city that didn't riot. If there is hope for Blacks and Whites to heal, I think it rests on Robert Kennedy's shoulders. If anyone can bring us together, it's him. I wish I was twenty-one already so I could vote for him. I hope he wins next November.

Yes, I know Mamma has been talking to Granddad and

that's great. Back when I had a couple of days of shore leave and she came up to Philadelphia, she stayed with Granddad. I'm a bit surprised she didn't mention it to you. The three of us had lunch together. It felt good. He made it obvious that he was proud of me. The rapprochement will hopefully heal some of their wounds. I don't know for sure what caused the divide between them. It's obvious that they love each other deeply, even if there are still some unresolved issues between them.

Finally, and most importantly, the answer to your last question is: I don't. I don't talk when Mamma gets down, or at least very little. What I try to do is listen. One of the best things you can learn to be is a good listener. As a daughter, sister, friend, student, or writer, learn the art of listening. Mamma is not looking for anyone to solve her problems. In any case, we can't. Only she can do that. What she needs is someone to listen, acknowledge her concerns and sorrows, help when asked, and show you care. The trick is simply to get her to talk. Just ask enough questions to get her going, and then shut up. If she won't respond, just let her know that you are there for her when she is ready to talk. Most importantly, don't try to be me or anyone else. That never works. Believe me. I've tried. Just be you; be honest. That's the best advice I can give. Needless to say, don't share this letter. It's just between the two of us.

I love you, kiddo, and yes, I miss you too. Daddy, Chip, and Buddy aren't much on writing, so I depend on you and

Mamma to keep me up to date. Keep the letters coming; they mean a lot to this lonely sailor.

Love always,

Your big brother, Eugene, aka Spock

CHAPTER TWENTY-FOUR

εΟ❖ʚ

TRAIN TRACKS AND THE MAGIC 8-BALL

*M*amma always made sure we had a cake with candles and a present to open on our birthdays. She didn't often have much to put in those packages, but by hook or crook, she'd get us something. Most often our gifts came from the Goodwill or Salvation Army store. The year I turned nine, I got a Magic 8-Ball. It was sitting wrapped in its reused wrapping paper on my dresser when I woke up for school that morning. I ripped off the wrapper and found my prize in its original packaging. Cartoons of a smiling man and woman framed the words "Tell Fortunes with Magic '8-BALL' FORTUNE TELLER" on a red background. I was thrilled, not because I was longing to become a prognosticator but because it was new: no one had played with it before or asked it a question. I was its first supplicant. This was a gift I could show to others without being mocked, or, worse pitied. When I was asked, "What did you get for your birthday?" I didn't have to lie because I had something others might desire. I threw it in my lunch bag and went proudly off to school.

Early in the school day, we began to hear rumors. It was not until just before lunch that our fears were confirmed. While we were cleaning up after our art projects, the class intercom started to crackle. Principal Lynch's voice began to break through the static: "Teachers and students, excuse this interruption. I have an important announcement to make. Senator Robert F. Kennedy, brother of our late president, was shot last night and is in serious condition at a hospital in California. Our thoughts and prayers are with the senator and his family at this tragic time."

When the bell rang for recess, we hurried down the hall toward the exit to the playground. I saw our beloved janitor, Mr. Henderson, and asked him if he had heard anything new about Bobby Kennedy. "No, miss, I haven't. All we can do is pray. He's in the Lord's hands now."

At recess, everyone wanted to ask the Magic 8-Ball a question: "Will Bobby Kennedy be okay?" a fellow fifth-grader, Sally, asked it when it was her turn. The die floated up through the blue liquid, pressing against the small window that opened into its dark interior. The words slowly appeared:

"My reply is no."

Not liking that response, Sally asked another question. "Will he die?"

Again, the response floated up to the ball's window. "Reply

hazy, try again." Sally, like everyone before and after her, kept asking it again and again until it gave them the answer they were seeking before passing the ball on to the next person in line. That night we listened to the radio for updates, and watched the news when it came on. It wasn't until the following morning when we finally learned that Robert, the youngest brother and perhaps best of the mystical Kennedy clan, had died.

I don't know who said it first, but we all knew that on Saturday we would wait for his funeral train to pass by. Chip, Buddy, and I left the house early and headed toward the railroad tracks. I'd never been to the tracks before, but my brothers knew the way. It was a long hike, but even so, we were among the first to arrive.

Time's march often obscures images once thought indelible. The passage of years has altered many visions, as river water does to rocks. However, my memories of that day from the time we arrived at the tracks are absolute and ineffaceable. They are tattooed images. My synapses stopped taking the occasional snapshots in black and white and began taking full audio and Technicolor recordings as soon as we emerged from the woods. My mental film of that day hasn't altered, no matter how many times I've replayed it.

We followed a path between a pair of houses to a small wood, where we emerged from the cluster of trees. The ground was honey-colored clay and packed hard from years of folks tramping through the woods to cross the tracks. Large chunks of gray gravel densely populated the railbeds. To kill time, we picked up stones and competed on who could throw the farthest until there were too many people along the tracks to keep up this diversion. Weeds grew along the tracks. I occupied myself for a long time by picking all the dandelions, oxeye daisies, and Queen Anne's lace I could find and then stringing them into the longest flower chain I ever made, before or since.

Chip pulled a penny from his pocket and placed it on the tracks, promising me a souvenir when the funeral train passed by. However, an earlier train came creeping through, slowed by the many people along the tracks. Once it passed, he recovered the piece of copper. The heavy engine had flattened it like a piece of butter between warm hands. You could no longer make out Lincoln's image on its shiny oval surface. Chip looked through his pockets and found a few coins, but he didn't have a second penny to place on the tracks for Kennedy's train to flatten, and he wasn't going to give up a dime or quarter. So I contented myself with my single memento.

As the crowd filed in, I began to realize that everyone coming from our side of the tracks was White, and everyone on the other side was Black. All were solemn, joined together in our sorrow. Yet as the day's events transpired, it seemed that those on the Black side owned the grief and despair in a far deeper and more measurable way. Throughout the day, some crossed the tracks, mingling with those on the other side. Anguish and loss had brought us together.

At least for today, we were united.

On the opposite side, a high hill jutted out overlooking the tracks. From a perch on top of the hill, a woman's voice descended on us. Her rich, deep, suffering tone weighed upon the air and moved through each of us. She vocalized all that we were feeling, giving it tangible sharp edges. Her large form was seated on a portable chair. I hadn't notice her arrival, or her entourage's. A middle-aged man and a much younger woman tended her.

At first I could only make out a few phrases here and there. "Oh, sweet Lord, what shall I do?" Beckoned by her voice, I crossed the tracks, wound my way through a thicket, and climbed the hill to be closer to her. As I reached the summit, I heard her trill, "Trouble done bore me down!" It was as though she was revving up. Gradually, other voices joined in, as if answering her call. She sang, "O-o-o Lordy," and a knowing chorus responded, "Ain't going to tarry here." I don't know if they knew each other or were responding from some heavy need to lift their voices, to find strength in their union.

At times her voice was sweet and dripping like honey off a spoon, like when she sang, "O mother, don't you weep when I am gone for I'm going to heaven above; going to the God I love." But when she gathered her forces and sang with all her welled-up pain, "About this time another year, I may be gone within some lonely graveyard. O Lord, how long!" I found myself crying, moved by her grief. Her voice, more than her words, touched pain I didn't know I possessed. I was not alone. Others were crying. It was as if she had gathered our souls into her own. Her songs pulled us together and made us one voice.

Someone down the hill shouted up, "Tell it, sister."

Then she stopped singing and started sermonizing. "They shot John, killed Malcolm and Martin. Now they took that sweet boy, Bobby. They're trying to kill hope." Raising her voice, she shouted with all her might, "Don't you let them!" She paused a moment and then continued in a slower, more deliberate and deeper voice. "God, I am weary. O' Lord, they've worn me down. It's time for the young ones to pick up this burden. Lord Almighty, give them strength."

The crowd answered, "Amen."

Then she started singing again, "Oh, walk together, children. Don't you get weary."

The crowd on her side of the tracks joined her in singing, "Walk together, children. Don't you get weary. There's a great camp meeting in the Promised Land."

Some people from the White side of the tracks joined in. A few seemed to be familiar with the lyrics. But most others, like me, stumbled through the verses, trying to pick up the lyrics as the song went along. "Oh, talk together, children. Don't you get weary." Voices multiplied as the chorus grew in strength and more people gathered along the tracks. "Oh, get ready, children. Jesus is a-coming." Verse after verse they sang, "Mourn and never tire.

Pray and never tire. Shout and never tire," until we came to the last verse: "There's a great camp meeting in the Promised Land." In that moment, I realized what the difference was between those who lived on either side of the tracks. We were all working poor, or at best on the lowest rung of middle class, but on the White side there seemed to be more hope for this life, and on the Black side their hope was greater for the next.

After that song, our leader was quiet for a while. But soon the spirit took her again. She sang her soulful songs and sermonized off and on throughout the day. For a while, I sat on a log at the far edge of the clearing where she sat. I was too shy to move closer and join the group surrounding her. I wanted to sit at her feet and be comforted by her strength and wisdom. I wanted to know what it was like to hold her hand and feel its warmth. I wished I knew the songs so I could confidently add my voice to the choir. But the words were unfamiliar. I feared if I tried to join them, I would be nothing more than a voyeur in a foreign land.

The train was many hours late, yet no one left the tracks. The sun moved behind the trees, and shadows lengthened. After many hours and at long last, a murmur went up the track: "It's coming." Weaving through the crowd as only a child can do, I made my way to the track's edge as the blackened funeral train inched down the tracks toward us. On the side of a few cars, white letters named it the Penn Central. It crept along until the last car was in view. Inside the car, dark silhouettes stood around the flag-draped casket that held

Bobby Kennedy. He was on his final journey to lie next to his fallen brother. In the shadowy car, I thought I saw one female silhouette with a veil standing at the head of the coffin. I imagined that those silhouettes were Ethel and her children standing stoically, perhaps all the way from New York City. I imagined that while we fidgeted through the hours, tossing rocks and weaving flowers, they stood steadfast, keeping their final watch over their fallen father. As the last car, number 120, passed, we saw the rear of the train. Standing on the back overlooking a garland-strewn railing, a man in a dark suit waved to us as we saluted back. We stood at attention until he and that train fully receded from sight.

The crowd was quiet then, each lost in their own thoughts. Many seemed unwilling to move, as if our inaction could reverse events. But the darkening sky told us it was time to head back. Eventually, reluctantly, we gathered ourselves and our feelings and began returning to our own sides of the tracks. Whites headed east and Blacks, west. Searching through the crowd, I spotted Buddy and Chip. Chip caught my glance and nodded toward the path behind him, signaling me to follow. Reunited, but lost in our own thoughts, my brothers and I silently began our journey home.

CHAPTER TWENTY-FIVE

৪০ ❖ ৪৪

THE GREASER GARAGE MONKEY

Growing up, Chip loved cars. He loved motors and getting greasy with Daddy. When he was a kid, his favorite place to go was a huge junkyard in Brandywine in the southern part of Prince George's County. He and Daddy would spend hours fixing up old cars and then selling them for some extra cash. If Eugene was Mamma's right-hand man, then Chip was Daddy's best buddy. Since he was small, Chip imitated Daddy's walk, Southern talk, and mannerisms. Listening to Chip, you'd think he grew up in Carolina and not D.C. Eugene was the tallest, but Chip was the sturdiest looking of us.

Sometimes Eugene or even Buddy would join in on a project with Daddy and Chip, but they were only visitors. When Daddy and Chip worked together, they hardly had to speak. Daddy would grunt, and Chip would hand him a torque wrench with just the right fitting. Or Daddy would clear his throat and Chip would jump into action, grabbing whatever was needed. You felt like you were interrupting their ebb and flow if you tried to help.

One day, Chip came home with Daddy all excited. Attached to the back end of our truck was a badly beaten up 1955 T-Bird convertible that Chip wanted to resurrect for himself. When they pulled up, Mamma stormed out of the house and the screen door slammed behind her. She greeted them with her hands on her hips and an exasperated expression. Before she could speak, Daddy said, "Man gave it to us free just to haul it off his property."

"I bet he did," came her reply. "By the looks of it, you should've charged him for hauling it away. Jack, honestly, the neighbors have had it with all your automobile rubbish. They're complaining all the time."

"They don't complain when I fix their cars for cheap, do they?"

"But what are they going to say about this hunk of junk sitting out front for God knows how long?"

"It won't be a hunk of junk for long," pleaded Chip. Mamma walked around the car examining it. The car's yellow paint was chipping, and the black and yellow seats were torn in places. Rust was growing out of the wheel wells. The front hood was damaged, giving it a crooked smile. The hood's hinges were up front above the bumper rather than in front of the windshield like most cars. One of the hinges was twisted and nearly busted through. The rear right fender had a huge dent along its side.

After her examination, she said, "I have strong doubts. I don't know if this one can be saved, even by you, Jack."

Chip desperately started begging Mamma. "Please Mamma, Daddy gave it to me. It's my first car. We're gonna fix it up together. It'll be great. Won't it help to have another car in the family? I promise, I'll run errands for ya when it's up and runnin'. Please, Mamma, you gotta let me keep it. I'll do anythin' ya want." Her only response was to throw up her hands and walk back into the house, signaling that Chip had won.

Working mostly on weekends, it took them close to ten months and numerous trips to the junkyard to get it on the road. It was ready just in time for Chip's sixteenth birthday. He passed the driver's licensing test on his first try. Along with a six-pack of beer, Chip took the T-Bird to a friend's garage in Hyattsville to get it through state inspection. He loved that ride, and I loved it when he'd take me and a friend or two cruising with the top down. He'd slip in an eight-track cassette of Link Wray, Roy Buchanan, or Danny Gatton, and we'd roll down the highway with the volume turned up loud. Sometimes we'd cruise up the Baltimore-Washington Parkway and he'd open her up on a straight section just to give us a thrill and to hear the engine purr. Other times he'd take me to the Hot Shoppes drive-in at Capital Plaza. Chip would order a Mighty Mo, and I'd get an Orange Freeze. I think it was the first time I felt "cool."

With his new car, he picked up a new group of friends, and gradually he started to change. When other boys were letting their hair grow long and natural, Chip began putting Brylcreem in his. When most kids started wearing bellbottom jeans, including me, he wore them straight-legged and rolled up. In the mornings, when we were trying to get ready for school, he'd hog the bathroom while using Brylcreem to straighten his curly hair. I'd be on the outside, knocking on the door and dancing with a full bladder, telling him to hurry up. It seemed he never paid attention to Brylcreem's jingle, "A little dab'll do ya." He'd come out of the bathroom with his hair all shiny, reflecting the hallway light. "Don't get too close to a heat source," warned Daddy, "With all that grease in your hair, you're liable to catch fire."

One Saturday Chip spent hours carefully painting the name *The Hornet* in black lettering along the right rear fender. He'd meet up with other teenagers who drove cars that had names out at places like Route 3 near Bowie, for road racing and to show off his ride. Over time, his wardrobe changed even more. He cut the sleeves off his T-shirts and wore a motorcycle wallet with a big chain attached to it at one end and to his belt loop at the other. His socks were silky with ribbing, and he wore a pair of black hard-toed boots. He was a genius with motors, but his school grades started to plummet, upsetting Mamma. One day he came home with a self-inflicted tattoo of a cross on his thumb, and Mamma hit the roof.

"If I ever see you with another tattoo, I promise I'll find a way to send you to military boarding school!" I don't know if he believed her threat, and I don't know where she thought we'd find the money, but he never came home with another self-made tattoo.

One Friday afternoon in mid-October, my friend Stacey was over at our house. As always, she had to stop our games, or anything else she was doing, to watch *Dark Shadows* at 4:00 p.m. But on this Friday, Chip was hanging around the house. Stacey had a major crush on him. She wanted to see her soap, but she also wanted to stick around to flirt with Chip. He liked the attention. Thinking she was my age, he said to me out loud as if she wasn't there, "Your friend's cute, but a bit too young."

Stacey responded in turn by speaking to him through me. "Charlie, you can tell your brother that I might be in the same grade as you, but I'm almost two years older."

"Tell him your own self," I responded. But she didn't have to. He heard, loud and clear.

Stacey begged to watch her soap at our house, so I said she could. I hated soap operas and largely ignored what was going on with the Collins family of vampires, though most of the girls at school were always talking about them, especially Barnabas. Mamma was mending some clothes and was sitting with us in the living room. As I was changing the stations searching for *Dark Shadows* on ABC, I momentarily stumbled across CBS.

"Wait," said Mamma, causing me to pause on the CBS channel. "Is that Joan Crawford?"

"Sure looks like her," I responded.

"What is she doing on a soap opera?"

Stacey chirped in, "That's *The Secret Storm*," showing off her soap opera knowledge. "Christine Crawford is on it. She's Joan Crawford's daughter."

"Let's watch this for a bit," instructed Mamma. "I'm curious." To my surprise, Stacey stayed and watched the show with us. It was probably because Chip was sitting not far from us in the dining area off the living room eating a snack. Mamma was a fan of the screen legend Joan Crawford. There on our television set was an obviously sixty-something woman playing the part of Joan Borman Kane, a part her twenty-something daughter, Christina, usually played.

"I think she's drunk," said Chip as she stumbled over some of her lines.

"Yes, she does look a bit tipsy," agreed Mamma.

"That's more than just a bit," suggested Chip. All of us spent the half hour laughing, joking, and somewhat stunned watching the once mighty Joan.

Daddy got home close to 5:30, and Chip was waiting for him to get permission to go to a Teen Club dance out at Bowie High School. He wasn't driving *The Hornet*. Some friends were coming over and they were all heading out together. Daddy said it was okay, but he had to be home by eleven.

"I'll be up waiting for you, so I'll know if you're late," he warned. Chip made it home on time; it was during the evening news. Walter Cronkite had just finished telling us about a possible, but not yet agreed to, presidential debate between Nixon and Humphrey. A commercial about the benefits of Aqua Velva after-shave was on the air when Chip came through the door. His upper lip was busted open. Above his eye was a gash, and he had a lot of blood on his shirt and pants.

"Good God, what in the hell happened to you?" demanded Daddy as Mamma leapt up from the couch and ran over to inspect Chip's wounds.

"We got jumped by some thugs, but I'm okay," he said to answer both of their spoken and unspoken questions.

"Why was that? What were you boys up to?" demanded Daddy.

"Nothing. We were just looking for our friend, Big John."

"Nothing, what?" Daddy asked while he got up off the couch.

"Nothing, sir. We were supposed to meet up with Big John. But we didn't see him anywhere, so, we went up to a group of guys to ask if they'd seen him or knew him. That's when they went crazy on us. It wasn't our fault."

"What do you mean they went crazy on you?"

"We just asked them if they knew Big John, and before we knew it they were throwin' punches."

Mom turned to Daddy. "Jack, we should call the police."

"No!" came Chip's obviously panicked voice. More calmly he added, "Don't do that."

Daddy smelled a rat. "Why's that, Chip? Why don't ya want to get no police involved? Were you boys up to somethin' no good?"

"No, sir, I told you. We weren't doin' nothin' wrong. These guys just started attacking us for no good reason. We had to defend ourselves."

"In that case, you should have nothin' to fear by callin' the police."

"Please, Daddy, no. We gave it back to them pretty good. Some of them got real hurt. Cops are probably already there. I left to stay out of trouble."

"Watch who you hang out with there, boy, or you'll end up in a whole lot more trouble than you can handle. I best never catch you hangin' out with a bunch of hoodlums."

"Nah, sir. You ain't got nothin' to worry about, Daddy. My guys are cool. They're good. Just don't you worry none."

At school the next week, Buddy and I heard rumors and reports about how a group of Bowie guys got beaten up. According to the Bowie teens, they were standing outside their high school after attending the Teen Club dance and were waiting for rides when a group of boys from our Lanham neighborhood pulled up. The Lanham guys asked the Bowie teens if they knew where Big John was. When they said they didn't know who or where Big John was, the boys in the car got out with baseball bats, brass knuckles, and chains and started wailing away. The boys in the car were prepared for a fight and apparently didn't like the responses from the kids on the curb. Two of the Bowie kids ended up unconscious and in the hospital. We were told that the police were looking for the Lanham kids. Buddy and I kept silent. The Lanham kids were never identified.

After that, things started to change between Chip and Daddy. A few weeks later, Daddy heard about a White gang beating up some Black kids over in Hyattsville and worried that Chip might have been involved. When Daddy asked Chip about it, it started a big argument that ended with Mamma crying and Chip storming off. "I better never hear of you in some racist feud against some coloreds. You best hear me, boy," warned Daddy.

"I ain't the one lookin' for trouble. But if any of them are, I'll be ready to give it right back. It ain't the same out on the streets no more, Daddy. You just look at some young Black punk these days, and he's ready to stick a knife between your ribs. If I want to go to a club, I am not going to have one of them standing in my way."

"Oh, Chip, they're not looking for trouble any more than you are," said Mamma.

"You don't know what it's like. You're not out there; you don't even go downtown anymore. Admit it, Ma, you're afraid, and for good reason. The Blacks are at war. We're just defending our turf."

"War? If it is a war, you have a choice. You can stay out of it," Mamma advised. "In any case, what are you doing at a club? You're too young."

"It's not just clubs, but restaurants, ball fields, malls, shopping centers. It's all sorts of places. This is our town. I'm not going to hide, but I will defend my territory."

"It ain't just your town—it's their town too. We gotta coexist. Sounds ta me like you're the ones lookin' for trouble," said Daddy.

"No, sir, we're not the ones lookin' for trouble, but if it starts we'll be the ones finishing it."

"What do you mean by that?" asked Daddy.

"I mean if some nigger …" Chip didn't get a chance to finish his sentence. Mamma dashed across the room and slapped him hard across his face." She looked at him and said, "I love you, Chip. You're my son. But no one who uses that hateful term, not even my own child, is welcome in my home." We were all shocked just as much as Chip. Mamma rarely hit any of us. "I didn't raise you to disrespect an entire race of people," she added.

"If I ever hear that you're involved in some racist bullshit, I'll kick your sorry ass to the curb," warned Daddy. "You hear me, boy?" Then he changed his tone and tried to reason with Chip. "Sure, plenty of Blacks are real angry; they've got plenty to be angry about. They buy a car, they get charged twice and the interest rate is double too. Even if they could afford it, no one will sell them a house in a good neighborhood. The law's in on it too. It's an 'old boys' network in the county government. They can't get a contractor's license in P.G. There's no laws against it, just no one in the licensing department is gonna give a license to a colored man. You can't run a legitimate business without a license. Son, if you'd been held down that long and everything is stacked against you, you'd have a chip on your shoulder too."

"I didn't hold them down. I am not the one responsible for their lousy life and attitude. I don't have to put up with their shit."

"You watch your mouth, young man," said Mamma. "You were not raised that way. You've changed since you started hanging out with this group of ruffians. You were never in trouble before, and you certainly weren't a foul-mouthed bigot. You keep hanging out with them and you'll be either in jail or worse. This ends here, today. I want you to stop hanging out with that crowd."

"They're my crowd. They have my back, and I've got theirs. There's nothing wrong with them. You're the ones who are prejudiced against my friends."

"You just better mind our warning," said Daddy. "You better stay out of trouble. You don't like our rules, there's the door. You're free to go through it. Just don't let it hit your butt on the way out."

That's when Mamma started to cry. "Dear Lord, what has this family come to?"

But Daddy went on. "My house, my rules. You understand me, boy?"

"Yeah, I understand you," he scowled.

"You see that you do."

With that, Chip headed upstairs.

Chip got a job over in Hyattsville at Sonny Routt's Garage

for a while. He'd sneak out a lot or lie about where he was going. Sometimes I'd overhear him talking on the phone with his buddies, Denny and Tommy, about looking for some action at clubs like the Pig's Foot at Bailey's Crossroads in Virginia, the Silver Dollar in D.C., or, more likely, the Town Hall over in College Park. Before heading out for an evening, they'd swing by the Tick Tock on University Boulevard near Riggs Road. Denny was over twenty-one and would pick up a couple of six-packs of beer for the ride. Sometimes on weekends, they'd head down to North Beach and hang out. I knew he'd frequently skipped school to hang out with his friends, but I never told Mamma or Daddy. I didn't like his group of friends, but I wasn't going to be a snitch.

I couldn't believe it when Chip told us he wanted to sell his sleek, classic yellow T-Bird. "Why, Chip, why? It's beautiful, and you and Daddy worked so long on it to get it just perfect. Why would you sell it?" I asked.

"I want a motorcycle and need the money. I can't afford two rides. Don't worry, kiddo, I'll give ya a turn on my new sled when I get it." Despite his promise of a ride on the back of his motorcycle, I was sad to see him let the convertible go. I'd had a lot of fun riding in it, and so had my girlfriends, which didn't hurt my brief popularity.

After Mamma saw a copy of his report card, she made him quit his job over at Sonny's garage. "You'd better start bringing your grades up quick if you want to graduate high school," she warned.

Our house sat on the slope of a hill. Chip and Buddy's bedroom was on the high end of the house. Their windows looked out onto the back and side yards and were two stories off the ground. My bedroom was on the other side of the house and in front. One of my windows looked out on an addition. In front of the house beside the addition was a beautiful, old, majestic flowering cherry tree; its knotty limbs stretched out over the addition's roof. It was easy to climb through my side window and onto the addition's gently sloping roof. On warm days and evenings, I loved to sit beneath the cherry tree's branches surrounded by its pink splendor. It was my favorite reading spot. It was also Chip's escape route. After the kids were sent to bed and the house quieted down, Chip would come into my bedroom and use my window to escape. He would walk his motorcycle down the driveway and half a block down the street before he started the motor.

One night, Daddy got up around two in the morning to use the bathroom and heard someone coming through the front door. He grabbed a baseball bat. Before he swung at the intruder, fortunately, he switched on the light.

Terrified, Chip screamed, waking everyone: "Stop, Dad. Don't hit. It's me, Chip." Mamma came bursting into the living room. Buddy and I ran to the top of the stairs and stopped when we realized it was Chip. We stayed there frozen as we listened to the argument.

"What in the hell! What do you mean by sneakin' out of this

house?" When Chip didn't answer, Daddy continued. "What's the matter, boy, cat got your tongue? Where in blue blazes have you been?"

"Out."

"Don't try and play me for no fool. I can see you've been out. What do you mean by sneakin' out of the house? You've no business bein' out in the streets at this hour. Who were you out with?"

"Nobody."

"Don't you lie to me, boy, or there'll be hell to pay."

"I wasn't out with anybody. I couldn't sleep. I just took my bike out for a quick spin to clear out my head."

That's when Daddy called us down. "Buddy, Charlie, get down here."

Both of us looked at each other, shrugged our shoulders, came down the stairs, and stood next to our brother.

"What time did your brother slip out of the house?"

"I don't know," I lied. "I was asleep."

"Has Chip been usin' your winda to sneak out of this house?"

I was in a panic. I didn't want to deepen my lie with another lie, but I couldn't betray Chip. I heard myself say, "Daddy, I don't know." Guilty, I couldn't look him in the eyes when I said it, which told him all he needed to know.

"What about you, Buddy? You share a room with your brother. Are you just as deaf and dumb as your sister? When did he leave the house tonight?"

"I was sleeping too, same as Charlie."

"Yeah, I thought so. You're both just as dumb as a bag of hammers. You're both grounded. I'll think of some extra chores for the two of you too. Maybe that will make you smarter." Just then, Daddy turned and leaned in toward Chip. The bat was still in his hand, which made Chip flinch. Daddy took a couple of sniffs. "Yeah, you took a ride all right. Who bought you the beer? Sellin' to a minor is against the law. Where'd you get the beer?"

"I don't know his name."

"You don't know? Well, I know you are one sorry-assed sneak." The more Daddy cursed, the angrier you knew he was. "Damn it, boy, I'm gonna cut your tail right here and now. Hand over your keys."

"What? You can't do that. They're my keys."

"Yeah, well, you're my son. Now hand them over."

"I bought that bike. It's my money that paid for the gas in it."

"Don't let me ask again," Daddy threatened. "I said, hand the damn keys over. It's that or I'll take an ax to it." We all knew Daddy didn't make idle threats. He'd do it.

Before Chip could respond, Mamma interjected, "Go on, son. Do as your father tells you."

Finally, and to my relief, Chip pulled the keys out of his pocket. As he placed them in Daddy's outreached hand, he complained, "You've got no right. It's my bike."

"I got no right? Hell, I've got every right. This is my house you live in. It's my food you stuff down your gullet. Your bike is on my property. You don't like my rules, you know where the door is. No one is keeping you here. You think you're a man, then go on, get off my dime and go support yourself." Chip looked for a moment as if he was thinking about leaving and even took a step toward the door.

Daddy's deep, warning voice made him pause. "Boy, if you walk out that door, you won't be welcomed back. You better think 'fore you do somethin' you'll regret. You hear me?" Chip hesitated a second more before he spun around and went up to his bedroom, slamming the door behind him.

"Maggie, you better hope he gets drafted," Daddy advised. "The army might be the only thing that will straighten that boy out."

"Do you want him to go to Vietnam and get killed, Jack?" she snapped. "Is that what you want?"

"Darlin', if he keeps goin' the way he is, he can do that right here."

The next day, Daddy chopped the cherry tree down, leaving the front of the house looking barren. A few days after that, when Chip came home from school, Mamma and I were at the dining room table. I was doing my homework and Mamma was having a cup of tea. When Chip passed us on his way toward the stairs, Mamma noticed on the back of Chip's jeans jacket two large new patches. The upper one had blue embroidered letters that read

PAGANS on a white background. A second one was below it, and it had a monster with a sword surrounded by fire.

"'Pagans,' what's that mean?" she asked him.

"It means I am a member of the Pagans. It's the name of my gang."

"Gang? Sweet Mother of Jesus, Chip. You'll be the death of me. Now you're a gangster?"

"Gangster! Don't be so melodramatic, Mamma. I'm not a gangster. You're watching too many old movies."

"You're a member of a gang. What's that make you? You've no business running around with that kind of crowd. Why are you in a gang? I want you out of it before something terrible happens to you."

"You don't understand, Ma. I am safer with them. They're protection. A gang is the brothers you choose."

"What kind of notion is that? Chip, you have a family."

"Yeah, well if somethin' goes down, my Pagan brothers are the ones who'll protect me, and I'll stand up for any of them. With the Pagans at my side, no one dares mess with me."

"Chip, this is foolishness. It's not the right way. Eugene made it through school without joining some gang. He didn't need a gang to protect him. I want you to quit."

"I ain't your precious Eugene."

"That's enough. You're precious to me too. Why do you think I care about this? If something happens to you, my heart will be broken. This, this gang thing will lead to nothing but trouble. Please, Chip, it has to stop before something awful happens."

"You just don't understand, Mamma. I need them."

Just then, Buddy walked in. Chip was standing with his back toward the front door. Buddy noticed the new patches straight away. "Cool, Chip, where'd you get those patches?"

Before he could turn around and answer Buddy's question, Mamma snapped, "Chip, I don't want to see you wearing that jacket in this house ever again! Do you understand me?"

"Yeah, I understand you, but you don't understand me." With that he went to his room.

"Dear Mother of Jesus, protect that child," she yelled up the stairs. "Saint Jude, will you help him find his way?" Mamma pleaded before picking up a basket of laundry and heading to the basement.

"Wow, what's with that?" Buddy asked me.

"Chip's in a gang and Mamma's not happy about it," I informed him.

When Daddy got home, I heard Mamma tell him, "Jack, I hate to say this, but you are probably right. The army might be what Chip needs to straighten out. I think he'd be safer in the army than with the group he's running around with now. Let's pray he lives long enough for the army to get ahold of him. I know one thing—he's on a dangerous path. Sweet Jesus, I am awfully afraid for that one."

CHAPTER TWENTY-SIX

࿇❖࿇

GENESIS

*F*rom the start, 1968 was a tumultuous year across the nation. In winter, the papers were full of news about the Tet Offensive, followed by photos of flag-draped coffins arriving from Vietnam at Dover Air Force Base. Mamma cried out in horror when she saw on NBC news a Vietnamese general's gruesome execution of a Vietcong operative. Then Walter Cronkite uttered his prophetic words, "It seems now more certain than ever that the bloody experience of Vietnam is to end in a stalemate."

In spring, we saw our and other cities burn following Dr. King's murder. In June, we stood along the railroad tracks as Bobby Kennedy's funeral train passed us by. Antiwar protests spread across college campuses like a virus. That summer, Daddy blamed Jerry Ruben, Abbie Hoffman, and their Yippies for inciting riots in Chicago that led to police sending a hundred people to area hospitals, caused the deployment of the National Guard, and disrupted the Democratic National Convention. Mamma said Chicago Mayor Daley's heavy use of police force was at least partially to blame for the violence.

It wasn't spring that brought us hope; it was autumn. Hope, we discovered, is an ineradicable thing fueled by promises. In October, President Johnson promised to halt the bombing of North Vietnam. President-elect Richard Nixon promised to end the chaos and destruction and to restore law and order throughout the nation. The South Vietnamese government finally promised to join in the Paris peace talks. The year ended with *Apollo 8*'s historic journey.

For the Wards, we had even greater reason to hope for a better tomorrow. Mamma and Daddy submitted an offer to purchase a house. At the Thanksgiving dinner table, they announced that their offer had been accepted. "By the New Year, we will be living in our own home at long last," Mamma promised. "We'll have the keys in ten days. When we do, it will be time for everyone to roll up their sleeves and pitch in. We've got a ton of work to do before we can move in. I want to start 1969 off right and in our own home."

Daddy was especially excited. It was on an acre and three-quarters, and it had a big garage. Mamma was enthusiastic but nervous because they had bought it "as-is." "It's going to take a lot of elbow grease to get it livable," she warned.

We worked hard and managed to get moved in by the third week of December. Even so, a lot of work remained. Much of the cleanup and initial repairs were done during Christmas break. Still, we took time to enjoy the season. There were woods behind our new property, and Chip and Buddy went off into them with an ax to find our Christmas tree. They came home with an almost six-foot-tall pine. It was the nicest tree I could remember us having. To me it was a good sign. Mamma opened the box filled with our decorations. Together we draped the tree's limbs with silvery tinsel and familiar ornaments. We wrapped the base of the tree with a white fleece skirt to create a snowy landscape for miniature houses along with our old train set. On the mantel, I put together the nativity set and hung our stockings. It was our first fireplace, and I wanted to make the most of it. It was too late for any of us to believe in Santa arriving down the chimney, but I placed cookies on the table beside it anyway. All was ready for our first Christmas in our own home. After dinner, and with the tree's colorful lights casting a warm glow, we gathered in our living room to watch the news on Christmas Eve.

The networks were broadcasting news of *Apollo 8* as it circled the moon. We listened as the spacecraft's crew took turns reading from the Book of Genesis. "In the beginning, God created the heaven and the earth," quoted Bill Anders. The reading seemed right, and it seemed good. And there it was for all to see on our television screen: man's first view of our beautiful blue planet rising over the moon, giving witness to creation itself.

Frank Borman ended the broadcast by saying, "And from the

crew of *Apollo 8*, we close with good night, good luck, a Merry Christmas—and God bless all of you, all of you on the good Earth." After a tumultuous year, there seemed no greater unifying symbol of world peace and hope than a godly view from that vessel.

Part Seven

1969

CHAPTER TWENTY-SEVEN

ဆာ❖ର

HOME BURIAL

*I*t was a new beginning for all of us, and we were each determined to make the most of it. We spent our Christmas break
and all of January getting the house livable. The realtor said the
price was low because it was sold in as-is condition. That included
a whole lot of junk and debris left by previous inhabitants. A few
items were usable, or at least could be repaired, but most of it was
just plain trash, even for us salvaging, resourceful Wards. Nearly
every day during those first few weeks, we took a truckload to the
dump. As we picked through the debris of other people's lives, I
felt like an archaeologist on a historic dig. In my bedroom, there
was a blanket with a large burnt hole in its middle. I imagined
a previous occupant falling off to sleep with a cigarette burning
between his lips—he wakes up smelling smoke and finds his
blanket smoldering. Chip, like Daddy, smoked. I showed him the
blanket as a warning against nighttime cigarettes.

There was an old hair dryer attached to a chair, the type that looked like an enormous space helmet and was used at beauty parlors. Mamma asked if it could be repaired, but I said it looked like an electric chair. After that she asked Chip to put it in the garbage heap. In the living room there was an old rusted metal baby's crib, the kind used by hospitals. It was filled with discarded air conditioning parts. Here and there we found a few tattered black-and-white photos. One was of a man sitting in a rowboat and wearing a hat that shaded his face. He held a fishing rod in one hand. The name SMITH'S MARINA was painted on the side of the boat. There was a box filled with moth-eaten baby clothes, and at the bottom of the box there was a blue cat collar that still had a few rhinestones on it. Mamma discovered a musical jewelry box that had a ballerina missing a leg. The tiny dancer still spun on her remaining leg to a music box tune when you opened the box's lid. Buddy found a pair of bowling pins with most of the paint chipped off them. There were a collection of milk jugs, several insulated milk coolers, and wooden milk crates with THOMPSON'S DAIRY written on the sides. There were a burgundy-red vinyl truck bench and three headless dolls. But the creepiest thing of all was an urn filled with ashes that we found on a shelf in the basement next to rusting paint and turpentine cans.

On the bottom of the urn was a worn label with a black cross on it. We could make out a few letters here and there, but no complete names or words. Years of moisture and decay had left the print illegible. Mamma called the realtor about it, who said she couldn't find anyone to claim it.

After that, it felt like the house was haunted. Chip kept trying to scare Buddy and me with every ghostly sound the house made— and old houses groan a lot. Each time we heard a floorboard creak or a pipe rattle, or saw a light flicker, we blamed the urn's ghost. Though he tried to act otherwise, even Chip seemed spooked at times. Several nights after Christmas, the wind picked up and really started blowing, making the house howl and moan. Mamma started muttering prayers and crossing herself.

"Jack," she told Daddy, "if we don't do something soon, I'll jump clear out of my skin. We must dispose of those ashes, but we can't just throw her out with the garbage. I know it's crazy, but I keep thinking the poor woman is telling us she wants to be put to rest. It's only right that we give this pitiable, unfortunate soul a proper burial."

"How do you know our ghost is a woman?" Daddy asked.

"I don't. It's just a feeling I have."

"What do you think we should do?" he asked. "The only thing we know for sure is that she or he is a Christian, 'cause of the cross on the bottom of the urn. That's not much. We don't know what kind of Christian. Even if we did, we can't be payin' for no burial, honey. I don't think it's a good idea to be sneakin' into no graveyard to do some middle-of-the-night grave digging. How'd ya feel about buryin' her in unsanctified ground?"

"One thing I can tell you, she wasn't a Catholic, or at least whoever had her cremated wasn't."

"What makes you say that?"

"We Catholics believe in the resurrection of the whole body after death, so cremation is out. But that doesn't help us. I think we should just put her in the ground someplace that won't be disturbed for a long time to come. It's not the same as a churchyard burial, but it's better than sitting down in our basement."

"How do you feel about burying her in the woods out back? Would that be too close?"

"No, I think that'd be fine. We know so little about her, but we know she's connected to this house somehow. Burying her in the woods will be the best we can do, and doing our best for the poor soul is what's important."

So on New Year's Day we bundled ourselves up, Chip grabbed a shovel and a pickax, Buddy carried a bucket with cokes and beers in it, Daddy carried the urn inside one of the metal insulated milk crates we found on the property, and Mamma carried a cross that Buddy had fashioned from some old timber and a couple of nails. He had carefully carved on the cross the words "Rest in Peace." I followed behind them empty-handed as we wound our way through the woods behind the house. The ground was dry and frozen, so Daddy started to break up the topsoil with the pickax and finished with a shovel. When the hole was deep enough for the urn's milk-crate coffin, Daddy lowered it into the hole along with the base of the cross just behind the box. Then he filled the hole in with dirt, tamping it down with his boot until the cross was firmly in the ground and all that remained was a small mound. While he dug, Buddy and I went through the woods gathering stones. We placed these over the mound and around the base of the cross. When that was done, we stood around the small grave.

"We ought ta say somethin' nice, don't ya think?" Daddy asked. "Maggie, you're a whole lot better at knowin' the proper things to say at this kind of occasion. Ya got any fine words fit for a backyard funeral?"

"Let's bow our heads," she commanded. "Dear departed soul, we didn't know you, but we wish you peace and eternal rest. In return, we ask that you haunt our home no more. May joy and peace surround you, contentment latch your door, and happiness be with you now and bless you ever more." She paused for a bit and concluded. "May you find comfort in heaven, and may God enfold you in the mantle of His love. In nomine Patris et Filii et Spiritus Sancti," she said while crossing herself, then added while looking at us, "in the name of the Father, the Son, and the Holy Spirit, Amen."

We all responded, "Amen."

With that Daddy opened two bottles of beer and three cokes and passed them around. "Wouldn't be an Irish funeral without a drink or two," he commented.

"No, I suppose not," said Mamma as she took an opened beer

from him. She raised the bottle to her lips, tilted her head back, and swallowed. "Wouldn't be a proper Irish funeral without a song or two either," she added as she lowered her beer bottle and then started to sing.

"Of all the money that e'er I had I spent it in good company. And all the harm I've ever done—alas, it was to none but me. And all I've done for want of wit—to memory now I can't recall." She raised her beer as she continued, "So fill to me the parting glass—good night and joy be to you all."

As I listened to the lyrics, they sounded more like a drinking ballad than a funeral song at first. But the tone of Mamma's voice gave it dignity and solemnity. I found myself shedding a few quiet tears for the nameless and forgotten soul who lay in the cold ground at our feet. I wiped my tears with the back of my gloved hand when Mamma sang the final verse. "But since it fell into my lot—That I should rise, and you should not—I'll gently rise and softly call—Good night and joy be to you all."

"Well done," said Daddy. "Sing us another one, Maggie."

By the time Mamma finished a second song, the shadows had grown longer and the air was noticeably colder. We filled the bucket with the empty bottles, gathered the gear, and headed back toward the house. Buddy led the way and Chip was next. The ghost's exorcism felt complete. Mamma and Daddy walked slowly, and I was once again in the rear. I saw Daddy reach out his hand and watched as Mamma took it. Together, they strolled out of the darkening woods and into the last of the afternoon light that blanketed our yard. Though it was someone else's ending, it seemed a good and fitting beginning to a new year and to our new lives in our own home.

CHAPTER TWENTY-EIGHT

ఴ ❖ ಜ

GATHERED AROUND THE FIRE

*D*addy got called into work for the second shift because someone didn't show up. He wasn't happy about it. My parents rarely went to clubs anymore, but the night before they'd gone to the Showboat Lounge out in Silver Spring, Maryland. Apparently, they had a good time listening to the music and dancing because they stayed until the club closed. At the new Showboat, they no longer got up onstage. This nightclub was a cavernous place seating over two hundred people. The larger venue had changed more than its seating capacity; it had changed its atmosphere. Even on his own, Daddy no longer went to any of the places that stayed downtown, like the Silver Dollar or the Bayou, because the music as well as the crowd had changed.

When he left for work that afternoon, he forgot to take the dinner that Mamma had hurriedly packed in a brown paper bag for him. When Mamma discovered it still standing on the dining room table, she said to me, "Oh dear, Daddy forgot his dinner. Let's you and me surprise him, shall we? He'll get hungry and want his supper. Get on your boots, coat, and hat; it's cold out. We're going for a drive."

We climbed into the old Ford station wagon and drove into D.C. as the last of the sun's rays disappeared over the horizon. From Rhode Island Avenue, we turned onto Brentwood Avenue toward the Ivy City railroad maintenance yard. When we entered the gate, we turned right and went under 9th Street toward the area where Mamma thought Daddy was working that night. The paved parking lot turned into gravel and Mamma stopped the car. Outside a red brick building, three men were trying to ward off the cold by standing close together around an old oil barrel that had a blazing fire in it. I recognized two of them. It was mid-January and the temperature hadn't made it above freezing all day. Mamma and I got out of the car. As we walked up to them, I greeted the two men I knew. "Hey there, Isaac, Roy. How are you doing?"

Mamma yanked my arm and spun me around right in front of them, embarrassing me. "Excuse me, missy. Since when do you address adults by their first name?"

"But, Mamma, I know them. We're friends."

"Obviously you know them, but that doesn't explain your poor manners, now does it?"

"No, ma'am."

"Sooo," she said with raised, expectant eyebrows, "what do you say?"

266

"I am sorry. Good evening, Mr. Washington, and, oh shoot, Roy, sir, I never caught your family name."

He smiled at me and Mamma and said, "It is Baylor, miss."

"Good evening, Mr. Baylor." I turned to their companion and said, "Hello, my name is Charlotte Ward. I don't believe we've met."

"Good evening, miss. I am Mr. Rustin. I am pleased to meet you. And this must be your mother, Mrs. Ward," he said as he looked over to Mamma.

"Yes," she said as she extended her hand. "It is nice to meet you, Mr. Rustin." They shook hands briefly.

"Do you work for the railroad, Mr. Rustin?" Mamma asked, making conversation.

"No, I am just visiting. Is there something we can do for you, Mrs. Ward?"

"We are looking for my husband. Do any of you know where I might find him tonight?"

Just then I heard my Daddy's voice calling to us. "Maggie, Charlie, I thought that was our car I saw pulling up. What are you doing here?" I turned to see Daddy approaching from across some tracks. He came over and gave both of us a hug. "What's going on? Is everything okay?"

Mamma answered, "Nothing is wrong except you forgot to take your dinner, Jack. Charlie and I didn't want you to go hungry. I'll be right back—it's in the car."

As we waited, Daddy said, "You remember Isaac, don't

you, Charlie?"

"Yes, Daddy. How are Miss Althea and Silky these days, Mr. Washington?

"Oh, they're doin' just fine. I'll tell 'em you was askin' about 'em, miss." Just then Mamma returned and handed Daddy the brown paper bag.

"Thank you, sweetheart. Hey, did you know that Isaac and Roy both worked on the train carrying Senator Kennedy's coffin from New York to D.C. last June?"

"No, we didn't," said Mamma, and I echoed her response excitedly. "That must have been quite an experience. Would you tell us about it?"

"Yes, it was. If you was on that train, it's somethin' you're never likely to forget. Ain't that right, Roy?"

"Yes, sir, you tellin' the truth. It sure was somethin' that stays with ya."

"Did you meet Mrs. Kennedy?" I asked.

"Nah, miss, we didn't. The Kennedy family stayed in the last two cars mostly. We were more in the middle ones. But young Joe Kennedy came through our car introducin' hisself to folks. That was somethin' to see."

"The air conditionin' gave out early," Roy added. "It got real hot in there. Folks got mighty thirsty. We ran out of most anythin' to drink long before we made it to D.C. We met mostly congressman, senators, and reporters in our car."

"I'd seen Mrs. King when she got off at Union Station, but I didn't speak with her none. We all just found out during the ride down that they caught the man they think killed her husband. We heard they caught him in London. Mrs. King was wearin' a veil, so you couldn't see much of her face, but you could tell she was still doin' a lot of grievin' of her own. There were a lot of famous folks on that train, but what I'll take with me 'til the day I die are the faces of all those folks outside the train along the tracks all the way from New York to D.C."

Mamma encouraged them to continue. "What about them?"

"At first, I didn't notice the crowds so much. At that time, the train was running close to regular speed, I'd guess. We was busy doing our jobs, so's we didn't have time to look around. Ain't that right, Roy?"

"That's right."

Isaac continued. "You had to bend a bit to look outta them windows. You can't do that when you're servin' folks. Near Elizabeth City in New Jersey there was an accident. I 'spect you heard about that. A couple of folks that were waitin' on the tracks got hit by another train. Very sad. I sure am glad I didn't see that. Anyway, after the accident our train slowed down about half speed the rest of the way to Union Station. Going at that speed, you could make out the faces then—they weren't just a blur whizzin' by. When I could, I peeked out. I saw every kind of person come to say goodbye to the senator. There were gray-haired men stuffed into their old military uniforms, salutin'. There were nuns prayin', brides with weddin' parties throwin' flowers, girls in bathin' suits, people wearin' their Sunday-go-to-church clothes, people with signs, people with flags, people on top of buildin's. There were thousands of folks come to give their respects. That's when you knew you was a part of history."

"I waved to the train as it passed, Mr. Washington," I said. "My brothers and I waited all day by the tracks for the train to go by. We were there."

"Oh, yeah, I remember that. Didn't you see me wavin' at you?" he joked.

Playing along, I said, "Yeah, I saw you." Then, being more serious, I said, "It was the same along the tracks that day, Mr. Washington. It is something you'll never forget if you were there. None of us will. Not if we live to be a hundred."

Mamma said, "God bless you, sirs. Thank you for sharing your story with us. It was an honor to hear it. Well, the fire and conversation are nice, but it's cold. We better let you gentlemen get back to work."

"Oh, we finished work for the day, Mrs. Ward," said Roy. "We're just chewin' the fat now."

"But I have to go," said Daddy. "I'm on the clock." He hugged us both, but he hugged Mamma a lot longer and whispered something in her ear that made her smile.

After he started crossing the parking lot, Mamma turned

around and thanked the three men again and wished them a good night. Then we got back in the truck, leaving the men to continue their conversation around the fire.

CHAPTER TWENTY-NINE

ℰ❖ℛ

THE MAN ON THE MOON

When I was very young, Mamma didn't mention her father much. At first I presumed that he was dead like my other three grandparents. I am not sure when I realized he wasn't in heaven but living in Philadelphia. Mamma hadn't given any clues as to why there was a rift between them. Though living, he was no more real to me than the man on the moon. The first time I met him, I was eleven years old. Mamma took Buddy and me up to Philly for a couple of weeks in July. Because Daddy worked for the railroad, we got to ride for free. The porters on the train knew Daddy and treated us well, adding to the enjoyment of our adventure. We each knew Mr. Baylor, who was working in the center dining car. He gave Buddy and me free ice cream and root beers as he entertained us with humorous stories.

As we approached Philadelphia, Mamma began to point out landmarks. We had a brief view of a winding river. "That's the

Schuylkill River," she informed us. "Philadelphia is like a peninsula dipping down between two rivers." Across the river, tall buildings began to come in and out of view between trees and other structures; their images seemed to flicker. "See that tall tower peaking above the buildings way over there? That's the top of City Hall. It looks small from here but it's massive up close. That area is Center City." Mamma was speaking rapidly. You could tell she was excited, or perhaps anxious about seeing her father and being back in the city where she grew up. "Look, see that tall, white art deco-looking building just to the right of City Hall? That's the Lincoln-Liberty Building. Your Aunt Martha got her first job in there." Then she pointed to the opposite car window, "Oh, look! That red brick stadium is Franklin Field. It's where the Eagles play. It used to host the Army-Navy game. The only thing my dad is more passionate about than the Eagles is the Phillies."

"Do the Phillies play there too?" asked Buddy.

"No, they play in Connie Mack Stadium in North Philly, though they won't be playing there much longer. It's old and seen better days. They're building a new stadium down in South Philly. I don't know when it will be ready—not this year, though."

The train seemed to sink as the tracks gradually went lower into the earth, obstructing our view. Then darkness enveloped us. "Ah, here we are. We're pulling into the station now," announced Mamma. "Get ready, and remember—I expect you to be on your best behavior around your grandfather."

When the train's brakes engaged, friction from the locking wheels squealed as they skidded along the tracks, gradually bringing the train to a halt. Mamma went into action. We gathered our bags and exited the train. Buddy and I had to scramble to keep up with Mamma. We climbed the stairs up from the tracks and entered a huge, light-filled central hall with soaring ceilings. I stared up at the intricate inset square patterns in the ceiling. Hanging from its soaring heights were straight, elongated art deco chandeliers. My eyes followed down the high stone walls to the colossal rectangular windows, each divided by oblong panels creating long stripes in the glass, allowing the bright afternoon sunlight to pour into the hall and flood across the marble floors. Every component of the imposing hall was rigid: it was all straight lines and right angles without a single curve to interrupt its design. It seemed masculine to me, especially when compared to Union Station in D.C. It too had recessed patterns in its elevated ceilings, but Union Station's ceilings are curved. There, the main hall is adorned with arched alcoves that lead to majestic, round-topped windows. The design is curvaceous and feminine in its beauty. This hall too was impressive but felt more intimidating to me.

My musing was abruptly interrupted when a large man rushed past me. His suitcase, trailing behind him, struck me hard and nearly sent me sprawling. I stumbled but recovered my stance. The man never paused, unaware of the near injury he had caused. It was then I realized I was alone. I looked all around seeking my mother, but my view was obscured by a blizzard of rushing travelers, their arms, legs, and luggage swaying as they passed. Realizing I had lost sight of Mamma and Buddy, I panicked.

"Mamma!" I cried, louder than I intended. People began to look at me. A man started to move toward me but hesitated when I yelled again, "Mamma, Buddy!" Still there was no reply. "Mamma, where are you?" Finally, I heard her voice.

"Charlie, Charlie! where are you?" Parting the crowd with her determined movements, Mamma appeared with Buddy not far behind. "Charlie! Don't dawdle. You could get lost," she warned. "Pay attention and keep up." She wasted no time, turned, threaded the crowd, and led us straight out a pair of large doors. Once outside, we crossed a driveway covered by a high portico. Imposing Corinthian columns divided this driveway from another one. As we passed the columns, bright, glaring sunlight momentarily impaired our vision. Mamma placed a hand over her brow and scanned the driveway and the road beyond, looking for her father.

I noticed, to our right and down a ways, a tall, slim, gray-haired man standing next to a light-blue Oldsmobile Starfire. The polish on its hood glistened in the afternoon sun. I heard him call out, "Margaret, over here." As we approached, he popped the trunk open. After he got our luggage stowed, he gave Mamma a quick hug. "Climb in—I'm doubled-parked. We'd best get going and save the introductions until later." Once we were on our way and had crossed a bridge, he asked, "How was your trip, Margaret?"

"It was good—uneventful," answered Mamma. "The children didn't give me any trouble."

"So, which ones are these?" he asked.

"That's Charlotte, but we call her Charlie. And this one is Clyde, though he goes by Buddy."

"Nice to meet you both." Not much more was said until we pulled up in front of a red brick house and Granddad said, "Welcome to Frankford."

"I thought we were in Philadelphia," questioned Buddy.

"We are," offered Mamma. "Frankford is just a section of the city."

Granddad's house was a duplex with a garage in the rear on the left side. When we entered, there was a closet to the right and the living room was to the left. A wooden staircase was directly ahead. All the door and window frames were of natural wood, and the ceilings seemed higher than at home. The furniture was old fashioned but in good condition. There were closed curtains or blinds on every window. On the left side of the room, a window air conditioning unit hummed. The living room walls had dark green wallpaper with large pink flowers, adding to the darkness. A stream of red, yellow, and green light washed over the hardwood floors in the foyer. I turned to see where the light came from. There above the front door was a stained-glass window I had missed seeing when we entered. It took a moment for our eyes to adjust to the dimness. Buddy and I hesitated in the front foyer, but Granddad beckoned us. "Come on in. The place isn't haunted."

Still, we hesitated. "Where should we put our things?" I asked, reluctant to drop my stuff on his clean floors.

"Okay, let's get to it, then. Margaret, take them up to your old room, would you, please? Once you've unpacked and settled in, you can clean the travel dust off you. The bathroom is at the end of the hall, kids. Come down when you're ready."

"Yes, Da, and where will I be sleeping?" When Mamma said Da to her father, it sounded more like *daaa*: the "a" was soft and long. I'd never heard her say it that way before.

"You're sleeping in my den. There's a bed made up for you. What would the children like for tea?"

"I don't drink tea," Buddy informed.

"He means something to eat," responded Mamma. "Just something simple. I will come down to help."

"Do you want some cha first?"

"Yes, that'd be grand. Thanks, Da."

"Right, I'll get the kettle on. You take your time."

Mamma led us to a room with two twin beds. "Was this your room when you were little?" I asked.

"We moved here when I was fifteen," she said. "So I wasn't so little. Mostly, Martha and I grew up in Fishtown. But the furniture is the same. The curtains too—our mother made those. Nothing has changed in here since I left. The same books are on the bookshelf, the same glass turtle on my dresser, same lamp, same braided rug. Goodness, it's like stepping back in time.

"Fishtown?" Buddy asked. "Isn't that a funny name for a town?"

"Well, yes, I guess it is, though we didn't know it at the time. To us it was just home. It's really a part of the Kensington area of Philadelphia if you're looking it up on a map. Fishtown is the part of Kensington that's closest to the Delaware River. Here, in Frankford, we are still next to the Delaware, just a bit farther north."

"Did Granddaddy grow up in Fishtown too?" I asked.

"No, he grew up down in Grey's Ferry. It's on the southwest side of Center City, which we passed by today. We're on the northeast side. Grey's Ferry was all Irish back then. We used to visit his family down there. My mother's family lived in Fishtown. She had lots of relatives living there too. Most of them have moved on to other parts of Pennsylvania and other states. After his wife died, Uncle Aiden retired and moved back to Ireland. Fishtown was a good place to live when we were little. It had a strong Irish community. We felt loved and protected."

"I thought Granddaddy is German. Why'd they live in an Irish area?" Buddy asked.

"His father was of German descent, but his mother was all Irish. He grew up in his mother's family."

"Did you know many of his German family?" I asked.

"It was very unusual and brave back then to marry someone who came from outside your own culture and community. His German side didn't keep in touch all that much when I was young. They didn't approve of my grandfather marrying a Catholic, especially an Irish one. They were Lutherans. I saw a few of them from time to time but nothing very consistent. Your grandfather may have a German last name, and he may even look German, but he's all Irish just like me."

"Tell us about your Mamma's family," I pleaded.

"Well, they came over much later. Da's Irish family came here during the first potato famine. That was around 1844 or so. The famine killed a million or more Irish and caused another million to flee the island. My ma's family came to America in 1906. She was born in Ireland but came over here when she was a young girl. She never fully lost her Irish brogue, though. Her father and uncles pulled their monies together and after a time opened a tavern for the folks working nearby and at the shipyards. Ma's family were hardworking folks. They came to this country with nothing but their hands, a drive to succeed, and strong family bonds. They did pretty well for themselves, and quickly too.

"Daideo—that's what we called my ma's daddy—he paid a man to come to the tavern after school to teach Ma how to play the piano. Their only piano was in the bar. She used to practice every day in front of the clientele. After a while, she got pretty good and customers would come in and make song requests. If she knew the song, they'd give her a coin or two. Eventually, one day a man came in and heard her playing the piano. Right then and there, he offered her a job playing along with the silent picture shows at a movie theater. You have to be pretty good and know a lot of music to do that. While you're playing you have to watch the movie and change the music and tempo depending on the scene playing out on the big screen. You play softly and sweetly if it's a romantic scene or fast and pounding if it's a chase scene. She must have liked that job. She spoke fondly of it. That was long before I was born. Once they had talking pictures, that was the end of that career."

"Do you get your musical talent from your ma, then?" I asked.

"Yes, she gave me her passion for music. I fell in love with music listening to her play. That's her piano downstairs. No one plays it anymore, but Da can't part with it. When I was small, I used to sit on the floor with my back to the piano so I could feel the vibration as she played. It's one of my earliest memories."

Mamma was quiet for a bit, lost in her thoughts. But then Buddy broke the silence and her reverie by asking, "You said there's a shipyard in Fishtown. Is that where Eugene's ship was when he was here?"

"No, that was docked at the navy shipyard in South Philly. It's on the other side of the city from here. But it's not hard to get to. It's where the Schuylkill River comes off the Delaware.

"What was it like in your granddaddy's tavern?" Buddy asked next.

"Well, I remember it as being very dark inside. The smell of beer and whatever was cooking in the kitchen would hit you when you entered. They had daily specials. Thursday was corned beef, potatoes, and cabbage, and Friday was always some sort of fish. The bar and the shelves were all made of the same dark rich, well-worn wood. The walls were painted a dark emerald green. It was a popular neighborhood gathering place. Folks would come for beer and a home-cooked meal, to catch up on the latest news, and to hear neighborhood gossip. It was called O'Brien's Tavern. O'Brien—that's my ma's maiden name. It got especially busy on paydays or when something big took place.

"Our ma said her daddy and uncles were wise—although they served liquor when it was legal, they didn't make a habit of drinking it. My grandfather used to say it would be drinking up the profits. But it was more than that. Ma would tell us, 'They'd have a pint or two now and again, but you'd never see them falling down drunk nor anything like that.' The same can't be said for a lot of the other men around Fishtown. Our family was industrious, and Daideo and his siblings made sure all the kids got a good education, even the girls. Daideo used to say, 'Things don't always go according to plan. Things can happen, and a woman may need to go out and support her family.' My ma went to two years of teachers' college. Like I said, he was wise."

"If Fishtown was so great, why did you guys move here?"

"Daddy said he wanted a bigger house and a garage or at least a driveway. He always liked having a nice car. In Fishtown, you weren't guaranteed a parking spot near your own house. There weren't any houses in Fishtown with a garage or driveway—at least not one we could afford."

"I don't blame him for moving then," commented Buddy.

"It wasn't really about keeping a nice car, even if that's what he told us. Ma was getting sick by then. Having a garage was for Ma. It was easier to have a car parked right next to the house. She had to go to lots of medical appointments. Eventually, we turned the dining room into a bedroom so she didn't have to climb the stairs or Daddy didn't have to carry her up all the time. Da had a toilet put in just off the back door. It's fine right now to use it, but in the winter you won't tarry out there too long. The room isn't heated that well. Even though this house is bigger than our other one, we all still missed the old neighborhood—no one more than Ma.

"Well, that's enough reminiscing for now. You two finish putting your clothes in the dresser and then wash up. Come down to the kitchen when you're ready." With that she kissed us both and then left the room. After a few minutes, I heard her walk down the stairs.

While we were at the house in Frankford, Buddy and I entertained ourselves by going out and exploring. At first we tried to stay out as long as we could, coming home only when the street lights came on, which was our cue to come home as it was for kids all over. We were uncomfortable in Grandad's house. It was like walking around in a library; we were afraid of making noises or breaking something. We were constantly on our best behavior, and that was tiresome. Mamma and Granddad drank a lot of tea at the kitchen table. Not all of their conversations seemed cordial, though they never raised their voices. Even at dinner, Mamma seemed anxious and tense when talking to her father.

Buddy and I found a park with a playground not too far away. Buddy quickly made friends, as he always did. This time he included me in the games. It felt good to be reunited with him, especially in this strange place.

On the first Wednesday we were at Grandad's house, we all got up early to watch the ABC special news broadcast of the Saturn V rocket launch and the start of the *Apollo 11* mission. The news started with an old black-and-white video from 1962 showing President Kennedy speaking to a crowd and saying, "We choose to go to the moon in this decade and do the other things, not because they are easy, but because they are hard."

After the deceased president's speech, there was a break for commercials and station identification. During the break, I announced to everyone in the room, "If George Mueller hadn't taken over the space program from Wernher von Braun when he did, we wouldn't be watching this launch to the moon in this decade as Kennedy predicted."

"Why do you say that?" asked Granddad.

"Because von Braun was a very cautious man, according to Eugene. He insisted that every part be tested separately. If we'd kept going using his methods, we'd still be testing stuff. We had the first Saturn V test two years ago, which actually was three tests in one."

"How do you know so much?" asked Granddad.

"Eugene is crazy about rockets and NASA and talks about it a lot. Plus I read the *Washington Post* pretty regularly," I replied.

"You read the newspaper at your age?"

"Yes, sir, why not? I like knowing what's going on."

"So what have you learned recently?"

I was anxious to impress my grandfather, so I added, "Well, there was an article about what happens during a launch. For instance, back when the Saturn V was launched, the force of it shook nearby buildings so much it broke windows. It took NASA's employees by surprise, and they've since moved the launch farther away from the buildings."

"Is that so?" asked Granddad.

Encouraged, I went on. "Yes, it is. Did you know that the Saturn V rocket's first stage consumes four and a half million pounds of liquid oxygen and kerosene? If anything goes wrong, poof, that's one humongous firebomb."

"How old did you say she is, Margaret? You have quite the scholar here. You must do very well in school, young lady."

"I do all right, I guess."

"She's being modest, Da. Charlotte does more than okay. She skipped a grade, and still she's at the top of her class," Mamma said proudly.

"Yeah, everyone knows she's a freak of nature, or a dork, more like it," interjected Buddy.

"Now that's enough out of you, young man. If you can't say something nice, have the good sense to say nothing at all," scolded Mamma.

"Ah, Mamma, go easy on him," I offered. "He can't help it if he's an idiot." Just like that, Buddy and I returned to our old familiar roles despite our recent camaraderie.

"Now that's enough!" snapped Mamma. "Look, the program is coming back on—let's watch it in peace. If you know what's best for you, you'd better both behave and be respectful to one another."

With Mamma's attention returned to the television, I snuck a scowling glance at Buddy, who responded by sticking out his tongue. But our attention was soon lured back to the news report as well, and our rancor forgotten. Anchorman Frank Reynolds informed us he was broadcasting from New York City, and he introduced ABC's science editor, Jules Bergman. Mr. Bergman was at Cape Canaveral in Florida and said, "We are T minus two hours and twenty-eight minutes from the scheduled launch of *Apollo 11* at nine thirty-two a.m." The four of us stayed glued to the television throughout the day, unwilling to miss a minute of what Frank Reynolds referred to as an epic journey.

Frank mentioned and then Jules reported in detail what they referred to as a "minor difficulty" at the Kennedy Space Center, which kept us on the edge of our seats and Mamma saying a prayer for the astronauts' safety. We all remembered what happened to the Apollo 1 crew just a few years earlier. An electrical fire in the cabin had spread quickly in the pure oxygen atmosphere, incinerating all three men. At that moment, I regretted my earlier comment about the combustibility of the Saturn V rocket.

As viewers waited for the launch, the television station aired videos from earlier in the day showing the astronauts having breakfast and walking in their space suits to the transport van. Across our screen came images of President and Lady Bird Johnson taking their seats in the viewing stands at Cape Kennedy. President Johnson had recently renamed the area Cape Kennedy in honor of our deceased president, but the name hadn't stuck. Most people were still calling it Cape Canaveral.

Mr. Bergman came back on and held up a model of the lunar module as he explained how it worked. Finally, and right on schedule, an unidentified NASA employee's voice came over the loudspeaker. "... twelve, eleven, ten, nine, ignition sequence start, six, five, four, three, two, one, zero, all engines running. Liftoff. We have liftoff at thirty-two minutes past the hour." There in Granddad's living room, we all jumped up, cheered in unison, clapped, and then hugged each other.

While still standing, Granddad gave the longest speech I had yet heard him give. "We live in exciting times, Margaret, my dear. Kids, there isn't anything you can't achieve if you just have imagination and drive. That's what President Kennedy knew when he said we'd put a man on the moon in this decade. Incredible! When I was your age, kids, there were more horses and buggies than there were automobiles on the streets. Folks didn't have telephones yet. We got our news from the radio and newspapers. Today, right here in my own home, I got to watch with my grandchildren a rocket take off and leave the Earth's orbit. Dream big, and who knows what you might achieve? Today we're sending men to the moon. What's next? Yes indeed, these are exciting times."

For the rest of that day, we all stayed riveted to the TV set as the Saturn V rose above the clouds with a smoke trail following it. We watched until Apollo separated from the launch rocket and became just a tiny speck on the screen. Still we were mesmerized by the screen's images as ABC switched to animation. Until it was time for bed, we listened in as Commander Armstrong communicated with NASA's command control center in Houston, Texas.

The next day as we were finishing breakfast, Granddad announced that he was heading to the garage to fix a table lamp. Buddy jumped up and asked if he could go with him. "I'd be glad to have the company," Granddad responded. By the time they came back in with the repaired lamp, they were best friends. After that, whenever we watched television, Buddy sat on the sofa snuggled next to Granddad.

That night before we went to bed, he asked Buddy if he wanted to watch the Phillies play the Cubs at Connie Mack Stadium. The next morning, I asked Mamma why he hadn't asked me as well.

"Probably he thought you wouldn't be interested."

"Why wouldn't I be interested?"

"Because you're a girl."

"Well, he's wrong. I am interested. Can you tell him?"

"Let's let it be. Let the boys have their outing. You and I can do something special, just the two of us. Would you like that?"

"That depends on what that something might be."

"Well, we could explore Center City, and after that I'll take you to Fishtown. We can eat some of the best pizza in the entire country at a place called Tacconelli's. Or you can try a Polish kielbasa at Czerw. I don't believe you've ever had a kielbasa before. Philadelphia has some exceptional sites. Did you know it was once the capital of the United States? There's a lot of history here. You haven't seen Philadelphia yet. How does that sound to you?"

"That sounds all right."

After she cleaned up the breakfast dishes and put them away, we left to explore the city of her youth. Mamma showed me her old house and where her grandfather's pub once stood. We had pizza and visited Independence Hall. We examined the crack in the Liberty Bell and its inscription. But of everything we saw, the most impressive to me was the organ at the Wanamaker Building.

"There is something extraordinary in here that I want to show you," Mamma told me, though I was dubious of her promise. We walked into the Wanamaker department store. In its center you could look up four stories. Straight ahead was a massive golden organ. Its pipes stretched all the way up to the top floor. There on the second level sat a man at a multi-tiered keyboard. As we came to the center of the atrium, and seemingly right on cue, the man began playing the organ. The sound resonated throughout the building and all the way up my spine. It was surprising to find this colossal instrument inside a place of business. "You're listening to the world's largest pipe organ. Isn't it wonderful?" Mamma exclaimed.

"Wow," was all I could manage to say in reply.

By the time we got back home, our feet were sore but we were happy. We came up the subway steps and out onto Frankford Avenue. Walking the seven blocks to home arm in arm, we hummed one of the tunes we had heard at Wanamaker's. It was the first time I felt like a companion to my mother and not simply a dependent child. Buddy and Granddad were already home. As soon as we walked in the house, Buddy launched into an oration about their day, describing the trip, players, crowd, food, game, and the stadium itself. They were especially happy because the Phillies had beaten the Cubs 5 to 3. He didn't ask, and I never told Buddy about my day with Mamma. I wanted to keep it for myself.

That evening and each one that followed, we returned to the television set to check on the progress of *Apollo 11*'s journey. Conversation with Grandad was easier by then. When we gathered in his living room, he taught us how to play some card games. First he taught us casino, then canasta and pinochle. We played while the news broadcasters kept us up to date with the mission. If we had teams, it was always the girls against the boys. In the beginning, Granddad would let us win, but once we learned the games, that changed. "Competition will make you get better as a player. You'll have to compete throughout your lives, and you can't always win," he lectured after we suffered a loss. We didn't need a lesson in winning and losing—Buddy and I were always competitive against each other, a fact that made us good at games and sports, and it wasn't long before I began to beat Granddad at least as often as he beat me. Mamma seemed more relaxed too. She and Granddad laughed more and more. Sometimes they'd share a private joke, but other times they'd share their humor with Buddy and me, recounting stories from Fishtown and their family.

As the lunar module, the Eagle, descended toward the moon's surface, we gathered again to watch the news. We heard Neil Armstrong speak to us from across the miles of space, and clapped when he informed us, "The *Eagle* has landed." We felt united with viewers from not just across the country but around the globe. As we cheered, we knew people were cheering everywhere for mankind's astonishing achievement. Walter Cronkite spoke for us and to us as the lunar module landed in the moon's Sea of Tranquility. Just after we witnessed it touch down, Cronkite took off his glasses, smiled at the camera and uttered, "Whew, boy." Though the words were simple and understated, the emotions were not.

Six hours later, people around the world heard Neil Armstrong's memorable and uniting words "This is one small step for man, one giant leap for mankind" as he took man's first tentative steps on a celestial body other than our own. It wasn't just an American moment; it was a triumph for all mankind. We watched Buzz Aldrin's ghostly image follow Armstrong's to the lunar surface. Together, they gathered moon rocks, their movements eased by working in gravity that is one-sixth of our own. That's how it felt inside the house; each day the mood got lighter, as if gravity was loosening its hold on us.

We gathered the next day for lunch. All the windows, blinds, and curtains were open, filling the house with light and fresh air. It was a breezy, sunny day. After lunch, as Mamma and I were clearing the dishes, Granddad announced he was walking up to Frankford Avenue and the auto parts store. "Would you like to join me on my errand, Buddy? I just have a few things to get."

"Yes, sir, I'd like to come with you. Wait a sec—I'll go get my shoes on."

"I'll wait for you out on the front porch." With that, Granddad headed for the door. My feelings were hurt yet again because he didn't think to invite me as well. As we washed the dishes, I told Mamma how I felt.

"Don't be too hard on your Granddad. He always wanted a son. He never asked me to go with him to the auto parts store either, if that's any consolation. I think he believes it's a guy thing. You must know he loves you." After we finished with the dishes, Mamma told me, "I'm heading outside to bring in the laundry off the clothes line. Why don't you go up to my old bedroom and take a gander at the books there? Pick out a few to take home. Granddad said you can have as many as you like. There are some good ones up there that I think you'll like."

I went up to the room where Buddy and I slept. To the right of the door stood a bookcase stuffed full of hardback books. I glanced across the titles. Many I had already read, like *Tom Sawyer*, *Swiss Family Robinson*, and *Black Beauty*. Though I'd already read it too, I took *Heidi* off the shelf to examine its cover. Its dust jacket was still intact. Printed on it was the image of a dark-haired girl with two goats standing before a mountain and a pine tree. When I opened it, a musty smell escaped and floated up. The pages had long since yellowed. A date and inscription were handwritten on the first page in blue ink: "December 25, 1932. For Martha, 'May peace and plenty be the first to lift the latch on your door, and happiness be guided to your home by the candle of Christmas.' With all my love, Ma." I closed the book and carefully returned it to its place upon the shelf. Then I took another to see if there was an inscription in that one too. I wasn't disappointed. There on the page above the title, *Call of the Wild*, my grandmother had written many years before, "To Margaret, 'May you have the hindsight to know where you've been, the foresight to know where you're going, and the insight to know when you're going too far.' Know that my love will follow you wherever you wander. Forever love, Ma."

I found that every book on the shelf had its own inscription and the date it was given to either my mother or my aunt. Finally,

I pulled out *The Secret Garden* by Frances Hodgson Burnett. On its green, worn, hard cover was a pasted print with a young blond-haired girl wearing a red coat and matching hat. The title's letters were embossed in gold. I flipped to the first page looking for the inscription. There on the first page was a note: "To Margaret, happy tenth birthday. 'Mothers hold their children's hands for just a little while and their hearts forever.' Never forget, you'll always be mo leanbh fairy órga—my golden fairy child, Love Ma." As I passed my finger slowly over the blue ink, I felt a connection with my long-deceased grandmother, and for the first time felt the loss of her passing. I took the book and curled up on the bed. Before long, I was transported by its pages to British-ruled India. I felt pity for the spoiled, lonely, and unwanted young girl named Mary.

Just as I was starting the third chapter, I heard the piano being played. It felt eerie, as if the ghost of another Mary, my unmet grandmother, was rising from below—her spirit released perhaps by the opening of these books and reading her long-ago words. *Who could be playing the piano?* I wondered. I dropped the book on the bed and tiptoed down the stairs to the point where the stairwell wall opened to the room below. From there I could investigate unnoticed as I peeked around the wall into the living room. I spied what appeared to be my mother's back and her bowed head sitting at the piano. Sheet music was spread out in front of her. I'd never witnessed my mother playing a piano. I had no idea she even knew how.

As silently as I could, I slid down and sat on a step to listen undetected. The music she was playing sounded like a Chopin piece, but I wasn't sure. At home, Mamma had two Chopin albums she'd played often on our phonograph. But this piece wasn't on either of them.

Light suddenly rushed in through the open Venetian blinds in the front window, as if a cloud outside had moved out of the path of the sun, freeing its shimmering rays. Bars of golden light illuminated dust particles that floated through the air like tiny fairies. The dissonant music was sweet yet sad, as if Mamma's soul was sinking beneath the weight of her memories.

When Mamma finished the piece, everything was still for a while. I waited, hoping she would play some more. Giving up, I was about to head back upstairs when I heard the rustling of paper. Mamma began another tune. This one was merrier than the first. She played it louder and more assuredly. As it was ending, the front door opened. In walked Granddad and Buddy. Startled, Mamma suddenly stopped playing. "You're home quicker than I thought. I hope you don't mind, Da. The piano kept calling to me. I didn't mean any harm," she said as she started to gather up the piano music.

"Mind? Sweetheart, I can't think of anything I'd like more than to hear music in this house again. I miss the sound of the piano. You have no idea how silent and empty this house is without it." Granddaddy put his bag down and went over and sat next to

Mamma on the piano bench. Buddy climbed the stairs and sat next to me wordlessly. Without any sheet music, Mamma began to play "I've Got You Under My Skin." At first, she was figuring out the melody, but within a short time she had it and played it quite well. I recognized it because I had heard her sing the song before. When she finished, she immediately launched into "Mary's a Grand Old Name" by George M. Cohan.

After that ended, Granddad asked, "Do you still know how to play "Red Is the Rose"? It was one of your ma's favorites. She loved the way you sang it."

"You know, Da, I haven't played a piano since I sat here with Ma. It feels like her spirit is coming up through the keys guiding my fingers. I don't know how else to explain how my fingers remember how to play. It's been so long. Walking through this house, I am constantly struck by a memory of her. I feel like if I were turn my head at the right moment, I might catch a glimpse of her smiling at me. This afternoon when I was walking through the living room, it was like her ghost was speaking to me. I could hear her voice so clearly. She said, 'Come, Margaret, play something for me.' Oh, Da, I miss her so."

"I know, Margaret. Me too, me too."

"Do I sound a bit touched?"

"Yes, but that's okay. I hear her sometimes too, and those are the good days."

Mamma rested her head on Granddaddy's shoulder. "I am so

surprised I can play anything at all." She then sat up and said, "I'll give it a go." After a few chords, she began to sing.

At the final verse, Granddad joined her to sing, "'Tis all for the loss of my bonny Irish lass that my heart is breaking forever." When she finished that one, Granddad asked her to play another. "How about playing 'Step It Out Mary' for me? I always liked that one." When Mamma finished performing that tune, Granddaddy put his arm around Mamma's waist and drew her toward him. She wrapped her arms around his neck. "No man ever wore a scarf as warm as his daughter's arm around his neck," he quoted. "I should have given you this old piano years ago. I want you to have it. I'll get it shipped."

"Thanks, Da, that means a lot to me. Truly it does. I know how much it means to you. However, shipping it would be far too expensive. And in any case, I think it should stay right here for as long as you're in this house. This is where it belongs."

"It belongs with you, Margaret, and don't worry about the expense. What am I going to do with the money? I can't take it with me when I go to meet my maker. But most importantly, it's what your mother would've wanted."

"That may be true, but if I had it in my home in Maryland, it would feel wrong—it would be out of place for me. It would just be a daily reminder of all that I've lost. No, Da, let's leave it here. It's here where I feel Ma's spirit. I feel her while playing her piano where she used to sit, surrounded by her things and sitting next to you. This feels right. This is where I'd like it to stay. When I come back, I will play for us again."

"If that's the way you want it, then." Grandad took a pause and then said, "I love you, Margaret."

"I love you too, Da." she said. Then her voice quivered as she struggled to add, "I've missed you terribly."

We were supposed to head home on Friday, but Mamma postponed our return until after the *Apollo* team returned safely to Earth eight days after they left it. The space mission united us as a family and a nation. While we were getting ready to leave, I overheard Granddad say to Mamma, "It's been nice to get to know some of your kids, Margaret. I particularly enjoyed having a son in the house. I must admit, I have a soft spot for that young Buddy. He's a good kid. He reminds me of you when you were small, not his looks so much but his charming, lighthearted character. That Charlotte is a smart one. You must be proud of her. She'll go far. She reminds me of Martha."

"But she looks like you."

"Yes, I can see that. Both were well behaved and a pleasure to have around. You've done a fine job with them. I've met Eugene and these two. Now I need to meet Jackson Junior and Emma. Before I die, I want to make peace with my family."

"Please, don't speak of dying, Da. I can't bear the notion. As Daideo used to say, 'May you live to be a hundred with one extra year to repent.'"

"Thank you, Margaret. I hope to be around for a long time to come, but I doubt I'll make it to a hundred. We'll have to trust in God and leave it in His hands."

When Grandad dropped us off at the train station, he gave Mamma a much longer and tighter hug than when we arrived. When we took our seats on the train, I saw that Mamma's eyes were moist, yet she seemed happy—her mood was light all the way home.

Fourteen days in Philadelphia reunited our family and gave us our only living grandparent. At least for a while, we enjoyed a new tranquility in our home. The photos sent back from *Apollo 11*, looking out over the moon's horizon at the splendid blue globe beyond, united us as citizens of the Earth and gave us a new vision of our world. Yes, we believed that anything was possible when we looked out together from the Sea of Tranquility toward our beautiful home planet. At least, that is, for one spectacular moment in time.

CHAPTER THIRTY

❧ ✦ ❧

EMMA

By the time I was twelve, my correspondence with Emma had grown in importance. Over time, we gained trust, and we shared our deepest thoughts. Her physical remoteness made it easier to be honest, her character made it easy to trust her, and her thoughtfulness made me respect her opinions. She had a gentle way of making me look at my issues and concerns from new perspectives. She didn't tell me what I should do but helped me figure it out for myself. Because of that, she helped me become more confident and secure. She trusted me as well with her hopes, her fears, her failures and triumphs. It's easier to share your secrets with someone when they've trusted you with theirs. Through our letters, I found an honest advisor, a steadfast advocate, and a lifelong companion: in short, I found my sister.

October 22, 1969
83900 Cloverdale Road,
Creswell, Oregon

Dear Charlie,

How are you? It's been a while since I last wrote. Sorry, I've been busy with moving.

We rented a new home that is about a forty-minute drive to Nate's job. It's an old white farmhouse with a wraparound front porch. Down the lane are our only neighbors within a mile of us. They're older but very nice. They're our landlords. The woman inherited the farm from her parents. Until recently, their son and grandkids lived here, but he got a job up in Seattle.

We've got nearly ten acres and even a big old red barn. It's beautiful but a bit lonely sometimes. We only have the one car, so when Nate's at work we're stuck out here. Still, there are lots of benefits. The kids only have each other, so they've become each other's best friends. They're loving all the space to run around in and explore. They have a lot of freedom. There's a big vegetable garden we've taken over. It's nice to go outside and pick our supper. We just got a puppy that we named O'Brien after Mamma's Irish family. It's a big-footed, clumsy mutt that's part Irish setter, part I-don't-know-what. Its fur is the same color as Sarah's and mine. That's why Nate chose him.

He said he looked as if he belonged in our house. We picked up four hens and a rooster from a local farmer to complete our country life transformation.

Paul's school is nine miles from here. The very first day of kindergarten, he somehow missed getting on the bus to come home. I wasn't happy with the driver, who is supposed to count heads before taking off, and I let him know it the next day. Fortunately, Paul's teacher drove him all the way out here. I can't depend on that sort of thing all the time. I'd feel better if we had the second car, or even a mule (just joking).

On days when I need the car, I take Nate to work, but it's a huge hassle getting all the kids in the car, and Paul on time for school, and it's a lot of driving. We're going to have to figure it out soon. I want to start nursing classes in January at Lane Community College in Eugene. I'm trying to get a head start by reading a biology book that's required in the first class. The rent is cheaper out here, but we'll need a second car to make it work. With the cost of a second car, I'm not sure if we're really saving any money by moving so far out. I dream of buying a home, but Nate is not all that happy with his job these days and is looking for a new one. So who knows where we'll end up.

Right now, I am sitting on our front porch. Paul and Sarah are playing with O'Brien and are a sight to be seen. It recently rained, and they've managed to find every mud puddle within a hundred yards of the place. Jacob, thankfully, is napping beside me on the porch. My plan is to take a hose to Sarah, Paul, and O'Brien before they're allowed back in the house.

I love your letters. They make me feel like I am there with you. I am always impressed by how mature you sound. You're a gifted and thoughtful writer. I hope you pursue your talent—though my best advice for you is to follow your passions and not just your talents. Tell me more about the house. I want to know every detail. I know Mamma is over the moon now that she has a home of her own.

Oh, there goes Jacob. He's awake and crying—gotta run.

Love as always,

Emma

November 11, 1969
4712 Cobb Road
Landover, Maryland

Dear Emma,

Thank you for your compliment about my writing in your last letter. Yes, you're right: I want to be some sort of writer someday. Aunt Martha gives me a new blank journal every Christmas with a command to fill up all its pages before year's end, and I usually oblige.

We all enjoyed your package of photos. Your kids are

really getting big. What happened to Paul's two front teeth? One looks busted in half and the other is totally missing. I'm so glad Sarah has your hair; it's beautiful. Is Jacob walking yet? I liked the description of your house, but it sounds too remote for me. How do you keep the kids occupied? More importantly, how do you keep your sanity with all those kids and no place nearby to go? I think I'd be certifiably crazy by now if I were in your shoes.

We just got another dog too. Daddy found him. He's huge. Daddy thinks he's a mix of Irish wolfhound, poodle, and Akita. Talk about clumsy, he's always knocking over stuff. Mamma says if he grows into his paws we can put a saddle on him. He's sweet and playful, and we named him Caesar. Daddy is talking about getting some chickens too, though Mamma hasn't agreed to it yet.

You asked about the house—well, as Mamma puts it, we bought a garage with a house attached to it. Ever since we moved in last December, it's been like living in a construction zone with one project after another. The place has been transformed since we moved in nearly a year ago. The first project we conquered was the kitchen. For weeks, Mamma cooked our meals on a Coleman camp stove and kept food cold in coolers and boxes on the back porch. Daddy bought a bunch of used cabinets off some folks in Silver Spring who were remodeling their kitchen. Buddy and I refinished them, and they look like new. Daddy installed Formica countertops and a linoleum floor. He and Chip installed a breakfast bar, and Mamma picked up some stools at Goodwill, which she reupholstered in easy-to-clean red vinyl. They look nice against the breakfast bar. It's the nicest kitchen we've ever had. Upstairs there is a large half bath (toilet and sink). Daddy says he'll put a shower up there before the year's out, but he's running out of time to get it done on time.

When we bought the house, Daddy said I could paint my room any color I wanted. So I painted it a deep, dark purple. Daddy's not crazy about the color; however, he's relieved I didn't paint it black as really I wanted to. Mamma said she thought the black would be depressing, so I switched to purple. Purple is cool too. I bought a blue fluorescent light that looks groovy with all my posters. Eugene just sent me a poster by Peter Max. It's called *Moon Tripping*, and it's a tribute to the *Apollo 11* mission. Have you seen it? The poster, I mean. It's of a guy floating in space. It reminds me of Eugene—not physically, but because he's always looking up at the stars.

Buddy, Mamma, and I watched the whole *Apollo 11* broadcast last summer up in Philadelphia with Granddad. That was cool. I enjoyed getting to know him finally. Mamma said he's flying out to Oregon to stay with you all for two whole weeks. Maybe one day I can come out to meet my niece and nephews. I'm glad Granddad and Mamma are on speaking terms again. I am grateful that he gave Mamma the money for the down payment. It's nice fixing up your own home. I never would have been able to paint my room purple if we were still renting. It makes it feel like my own place.

Daddy and the boys have been working on getting the garage in working order. I've never seen Daddy so happy. He has dreams of running his own business and retiring from the railroad. Even though he's not so old, he'll get a pension after he works there one more year.

The garage has two bays and one has a mechanic's well in the floor. If you pull a car over it, you can walk down some cement steps to get under a car. In the other bay, they use metal ramps to raise the cars up and use a creeper to slide under the cars. Do you know what I mean by a creeper? It's a large skateboard that you can lie down on to move beneath the cars. There's also an office and storage area in the garage. Daddy installed new fluorescent lights and built new bay doors so he can lock the place up at night. It still needs work, but they're using it already. Word is getting around quick, and Daddy, Chip, and Buddy have plenty of auto work in addition to fixing stuff up around the house. Everyone around here is working seven days a week.

Chip had to go to summer school to retake math and English to graduate, but he finally did, to Mamma's relief. A few weeks ago, he got his draft notice. The other day we learned that he's heading to Fort Carson in Colorado for basic training. He leaves in a week. I'll miss him, although I won't miss him and Daddy arguing. I think Chip's relieved to be leaving too. However, these last eight months, he's been a big help getting our home together and the garage up and running. A while back, Daddy took the keys to Chip's motorcycle away from him, but he's been such a big help around here that Daddy gave him the keys back. Daddy's been paying him and Buddy too when they work on cars for customers. I don't get paid anything for working in the house or garden, which I don't think is fair AT ALL!

I started junior high school this fall. I like the change of going to different classes. My favorite classes are English, art, and French. Instead of taking the bus, I ride my bike. It's faster, and I like the independence.

To get to our house, there's a driveway that goes past the left side of the garage (as you're facing it). There are two cement strips for the tires and gravel in between, though much of the gravel has worn away. You need to be careful when aiming the car (or bike) up the hill if you want to park in front of the house. Mostly we leave the cars down by the garage. When you turn the corner to our street, you can only see its rooftop and a bit of the second floor rising behind the garage. The house is on the very top of the hill. To the left of the house, the yard slopes down to a level area. There's a creek winding through this part. Daddy and I put the vegetable garden in near the creek. He said the soil was best there.

When Daddy's not working at the railyard, he spends every minute working on the house, the garage, or someone's car. I don't know how he does it. Buddy is learning to work on cars too and really seems to like it. Daddy says it takes him a bit longer than the other boys to learn something new but he more than makes up for it in enthusiasm. Plus, Daddy noticed he's really good with the customers. He told Mamma the other night, "That boy can charm the skin clean off a rattlesnake." Shoot, I could've told him that a long time ago. Buddy's always been a real good talker. He certainly knows how to get people to like him.

I can't remember Mamma and Daddy getting along so well and for so long a stretch. It feels good. Before, it was like we were always holding our breath waiting for their next argument to start. It was a constant roller-coaster of emotions in our house. It's different now. It feels more relaxed, steady, and hopeful. Aunt Martha came up for a bit. Together with Mamma, they did some reupholstering and made a bunch of curtains. Martha left yesterday. She's heading to Philadelphia to visit Granddad before he flies out to see you all.

Tomorrow Eugene is coming home for a few days, so he can spend some time with Chip before he takes off for the army. They're going up to Baltimore to see a Bullets game. Mamma is looking forward to having everyone home—everyone except you, of course. I wish you could come back for a bit, but I understand it would be hard with all the kids.

All my love to you, the kids, and Nate.

Your sister,
Charlotte

CHAPTER THIRTY-ONE

THUS SPOKE SPOCK

*E*arly back in '68, between basic and engineman training, Eugene came home for two weeks. His old friend Scottie was heading to Vietnam after some additional training. Both were home on leave at the same time. They went out to Ford's Theatre to see a performance of Eugene O'Neill's play *A Moon for the Misbegotten*. It would be the last time any of us would see Scottie, but we didn't know it yet.

Then in November of 1969, Eugene was home again on a weekend leave. Not long before, Mamma had found a used box set of *The Chronicles of Narnia* for 50 cents at the Goodwill thrift store. It was a Saturday morning. I had my nose in the fifth book of the series when Eugene came down the stairs. After basic training he returned to the Great Lakes naval station for engineman training before being assigned to the USS *New Jersey*. He did well, and his superiors recommended that he take the test for admission into the Naval Academy in Annapolis. He passed and got in with a recommendation from Congressman John Glenn Beall, Jr., winning Daddy's vote even though Beall was a Republican. Mamma had gone down personally to the congressman's office to ask for the recommendation. Daddy was prouder than a peacock and Mamma over-the-moon happy with his acceptance. It meant a longer commitment to the Navy for Eugene, but he'd come out with a college degree. The Naval Academy in Annapolis was only a forty-minute drive from our home.

The night before, Eugene and his new best friend, Martin, had gone to hear Roberta Flack at Mr. Henry's on Capitol Hill. He'd gotten in late. Martin is a midshipman at Annapolis too. That night Eugene was taking Chip to watch the Bullets and Wes Unseld play the Milwaukee Bucks. When he came downstairs, Mamma said, "You missed breakfast. I am cleaning up now. You'll have to take care of yourself. After I finish in the kitchen, I should get some things for dinner tonight at the store. We'll eat early so you can get to your game."

"No problem, Mamma. I'll grab something," Eugene said. He joined Mamma in the kitchen for a few minutes and then came out with a plate of toast, a banana, and a cup of coffee. He sat down next to me and asked, "What are you reading there, kiddo?"

I held up my copy of *The Horse and His Boy* and showed him. "Ah, the children's novel by the former atheist who rediscovered Christianity."

"What do you mean? It's by C. S. Lewis."

"I know, Charlie, but do you know each of his *Chronicles of Narnia* books has a Christian theme? Each one promotes Christian beliefs."

"How so?"

"Well, take the first one, *The Lion, The Witch, and the Wardrobe*. It's about the crucifixion and resurrection of Christ. Aslan is Jesus."

"Wow, I didn't see it until you mentioned it, but you're right. It makes total sense."

"If you want a little balance, try reading Nietzsche."

"Who's that?"

"He was a great German philosopher."

"She's too young to be reading that nonsense," came Mamma's voice from the kitchen.

"It's not nonsense, Mamma," Eugene argued. "It's just a different opinion from your own."

"Why don't you like him, Mamma?" Eugene asked. "He tried to tell people that God is dead and to convince them to be atheists. He made a lot of good points and observations."

Eugene turned his chair so that Mamma could hear him better over the sound of the faucet running as she finished up the dishes. "You don't have to agree with everything the man said to gain a lot of perspective from reading his books. Even if you have different beliefs, you can respect his thinking. For example, 'Without music, life would be a mistake.'"

"I don't have to read Nietzsche to know that," retorted Mamma.

"He also said, 'To live is to suffer, to survive is to find some meaning in the suffering.' What do you think about that one?" he asked us both.

"There's truth in that," Mamma said.

"I disagree, or maybe I am not sure exactly what he means," I responded.

"How so?" asked Eugene.

"To live is more than just to suffer. That's a part of life but so is joy. His statement is too limiting or maybe something is lost in translation. You said he's German. I do believe you must find meaning in suffering to prosper, to grow as a person, to be a person capable of happiness, but even without finding meaning to your suffering, you can survive. You continue to breathe in and out even if you don't find meaning."

"Hey, Mamma, did you hear that?" asked Eugene. "We have a budding philosopher in our midst. The point is his statement got you to think, and that makes him worth reading. I have a book up in my room called *The Story of Philosophy* by Will Durant, you're welcome to borrow it."

Mamma came out of the kitchen and said, "You stick to your C. S. Lewis, Charlie. You're doing just fine. In the meantime, I must run up to the convenience store and drop some checks off at the post office. I'll be back soon. I just have a couple of things to pick up."

"Do you want me to go for you, Mamma?" Eugene asked.

"No, it's all right, Eugene; you just finish your breakfast."

Mamma was looking for her keys when Eugene said, "You want to know a secret, Charlie?"

"What is it?"

"Mamma was the one who introduced me to Nietzsche."

"*Also Sprach Zarathustra*," said Mamma.

"What's that?" I asked.

"Richard Strauss's Opus number 30 is inspired by a book written by Nietzsche called *Thus Spoke Zarathustra*," Mamma said. "I have a copy of the recording if you want to hear it. When I first played it for Eugene, I told him about the book, and that's when he started reading Nietzsche."

"You've already heard some of it, Charlie. Remember the opening music in the movie I took you to see the last time I was home?" Eugene started to hum the tune.

"*2001: A Space Odyssey*? Yeah, I'd like to hear that record."

Before she left, Mamma took the album from the bookcase and placed it on the turntable. "Here you go," she said as she carefully lowered the needle. "Enjoy, kids. Eugene, don't go telling all my secrets while I'm out. See you two in a bit." With that she shut the door behind her.

I picked up my book and Eugene grabbed the Sunday *Post*. We sat there for a couple of minutes, both of us listening to the record and reading. I glanced over at the article that had Eugene's attention. It was about today's huge antiwar protest that was taking place down on the National Mall near the Washington Monument. Peter, Paul and Mary, Arlo Guthrie, and Pete Seeger were coming to perform and to lend their voices in protest of the war. We'd seen footage of thousands of people coming to town, of the stage being set up, and of other preparations on the news last night while Eugene was out.

"I'm surprised you aren't down there, Spock."

"Wouldn't be good for my naval career, little sis. I could ask the same of you."

"Mamma forbade me. I did ask."

"Too bad—it's history in the making."

"If you want to know a secret, I was planning on sneaking off and going anyway. But then I heard you were coming home, and I didn't want to miss spending time with you. Don't tell Mamma."

"I'm touched. I won't tell; it's our secret."

"Spock?"

"Yeah, honey."

"Talking of secrets, who's Birdie?"

"Wow! Where did that come from?"

"I've heard her name from time to time. It hasn't happened in a long time, but Mamma, Daddy, and even you have called me that in the past. But when I asked any of you, you all changed the subject. I just want to know."

"Shoot, I guess you should know about her. Probably should have told you a long while back. But if I tell you, you can't bring it up to Mamma or Daddy unless they want to talk about it. Okay, do we have a deal?"

"I won't mention it."

"Promise?"

"Promise."

"She was our sister."

"You mean Emma. She's still our sister, she's just far away."

"No, honey, I mean Mary Rose. We called her Birdie, but she died when she was only a bit more than four years old. That was before you were born."

"What?" I jumped from my seat. "What are you saying?" I walked over to the turntable and lifted the needle from the not-quite-finished record and then returned to my seat next to Eugene. My head was spinning. Suddenly, a ghost was taking form. "I can't believe this family!" I cried. "Why didn't anyone ever tell me?"

"It was too painful for Mamma after it happened. It was a really bad time. Daddy just wanted to protect her, I think. Or maybe it's too much for him too. It was obvious after it happened that they couldn't talk about losing her, and then it became habit. Mamma was eight months pregnant with Buddy when she died. Then the baby came, and you weren't far behind. We got in a habit of not talking about her." He shrugged his shoulders and added, "Sorry, honey. No one was trying to hurt you."

"Tell me about her."

"She was named after both of our grandmothers. You look a lot like her, or at least you did when you were little. Who knows what she'd have looked like if she'd gotten older? When you came along, it was like Birdie had come back but stronger. She was a premature baby and had to stay in the hospital for a while after her birth. When you were born, you looked like Birdie at two months of age. I don't remember how early she was, but Daddy said she looked like a five-pound fryer when she came home. You, on the other hand, were a good-sized baby and healthy. She never was. Mary Rose was sick all the time. We called her Birdie because when she was an infant, when she got hungry, she would make this funny chirping sound. When she got bigger, she was always singing or humming all day long. For Christmas one year, Aunt Charlotte gave her this hurdy-gurdy music box by Mattel. She'd walk around all day cranking that thing and humming along with it. Mamma threw the music box out. She couldn't look at it or see another child playing with it."

"No, she didn't," I said

"Didn't what?"

"Throw the toy out. I've seen it. It's in Mamma's bottom dresser drawer. I never asked about it because she'd be mad about me going in her drawers without permission. I was only looking for a scarf. That explains the toy. What killed Mary Rose?"

"The Asian influenza came around. We all got sick, but little Birdie got quiet and listless. Mamma and Daddy took her to

Children's Hospital, but there wasn't anything they could do. We buried her at Lincoln Cemetery over off Branch Avenue."

"Will you take me to see her grave someday?"

"If you want me to. After she died, Mamma and Daddy bought two more burial sites there. That's where they'll be laid to rest one day."

"I'm glad you told me, Spock. It explains a lot." Then I added, "I think secrets are like a cancer in a family. They eat away at what's good and what holds us together. They fester in our minds because we're left to wonder the worst. We're left feeling locked out. Promise me you won't keep secrets from me."

"Sorry, Charlie, no can do. Everyone has a secret or two. I'm sure you have a few, or you will, and that's okay. But I agree about the danger of keeping too many family secrets. I'll try to lock you out as little as I can." Just then we heard the car pull up in the driveway. Mamma was back.

She opened the door carrying a single bag. I could tell something was off by her expression. "I have some sad news, Eugene."

"What is it?" he asked, the concern in his voice.

"It's about your friend Scott. I ran into his mother at the convenience store. I asked after him, and she told me that a helicopter he was in was shot down by the Viet Cong, and he and the other men haven't been seen since. That was over two months ago. It was awful. I didn't know what to say to her. Officially, he's missing in action, or that is what the army calls it. I'm so sorry, Eugene. I know you two were close friends."

I heard Eugene take in a deep breath as he bowed his head down on his chest. Mamma and I waited anxiously. After a minute or so, he raised his head. His eyes were filled with tears. "I'm sorry, you'll have to excuse me," he choked out, and bolted up the stairs to his room. We heard his door shut behind him. There he remained for the rest of the day. I wanted to knock on his door but didn't, leaving him in silence and alone.

Part Eight

1970

CHAPTER THIRTY-TWO

୫✤ଓ

THIRTEEN

*T*he day Daddy finally qualified for a railroad pension, he quit. At first, money was tight. Some months were tighter than others, but gradually things got better. Mamma took care of the books and the taxes. Buddy helped with the cars and the customers. As the car repair business grew and with Chip off at boot camp, Daddy slowly became overwhelmed with work, and he made me join them in the garage. Daddy and Buddy taught me how to do oil changes, tire rotations, and tune-ups; they took care of the rest. I didn't mind learning about cars, but I hated the grease stains on my hands and whined enough that Daddy hired help just to get rid of me. I had never before scrubbed my hands so much or so hard. It was difficult enough in school. Going through puberty with grease-stained hands and enduring the taunts they attracted from fellow students was too much for me. I was enough of an outcast as it was; I didn't need to mark it on my hands.

Daddy hired Buddy's friend Danny, who was fourteen and a half—a year older than Buddy. Since becoming a teenager, Buddy had become girl crazy, which Danny encouraged. Whenever I brought a girlfriend home and they were together but out of earshot of Daddy, they'd make annoying remarks like "Are those real or is that tissue paper you got up there? I think it's tissue—come over here and prove me wrong." Or "Oh, shake it, don't break it, sexy mama." When Daddy was within hearing distance, they'd limit their remarks to "Why hello there, beautiful." I mostly tried to avoid them when they were together, but it wasn't easy. They worked after school two to three days a week and on Saturdays.

Other than paying the household bills, Mamma had never done bookkeeping before. She spent hours going over tax laws and payroll deduction instructions. Running a business together made for more than a few disagreements between our parents.

One Saturday, I was watching television waiting for the *Apollo 13* launch. It was scheduled to take off at 2:13 p.m. Daddy, Buddy, and Danny came up from the garage for lunch later than normal to watch the rocket launch. "Maggie, ain't lunch ready yet? You said two o'clock. It's two, we're here, and we're hungry. We've got three more cars to finish 'fore six."

Mamma lifted her head up from a pile of papers on the dining room table. "I must have lost track of the time," she said as she gathered the papers together. "It's these taxes. They're driving me crazy. I don't know if I can keep up with all of this, Jack. We may need to hire a bookkeeper. Taxes are due next week, and I am terrified I am missing something important. We should hire an accountant to do our taxes in case we're ever audited."

"You're doin' just fine there, old Maggie girl."

"How would you know, Jack? You simply sign whatever I put in front of you. That should scare you."

"I'm not worried none. I know you'll figure it out."

She went into the kitchen and turned the heat on under the soup that was on the stove. She called out, "Charlotte, come set the table and get the boys some milk." Sticking her head out of the kitchen, she added, "Jack, I never said I was good at math and accounting. Taxes are too important to get wrong, and I don't know what I am doing here. My head is spinning. I need help."

"Darlin', we can't afford to hire no bookkeeper," Daddy hollered toward the kitchen, "and accountants are too dang expensive. Someone gotta do it, and you're the one with the most book learnin' around here. You went to college. You're smart. You'll figure it out."

"I went to college for music and then nursing, not business and accounting. Besides, I never finished." I watched as she rapidly pulled stuff out of the refrigerator. Then she returned to the kitchen doorway and nodded toward Danny. In a voice filled with frustration, she added, "If we have enough to hire help in the garage, why not part-time help in the office as well?"

"I've got help. 'I got you, babe," sang Daddy, mimicking Sonny Bono's intonation. "Besides, the help in the garage brings in the money. Your job is paying the bills. You tell me which is more important, bringing it in or sending it out?" Turning toward the television, he asked, "Charlie, is that the countdown? Turn up the sound on that thing."

"My job is to keep us right with the IRS and out of jail," Mamma said in a louder voice to be heard over the TV. She plopped a ham sandwich in front of Daddy. "You won't be making any money if we end up in jail. I don't know if I am doing it right. I'm trying to tell you, I can't do it."

"You'll figure it out. Remember what the Good Book says: 'Blessed is the one who perseveres, havin' stood the test, you'll receive the crown of life.' I got faith in you, old gal," he said playfully as he put an arm around Mamma's waist and pulled her toward him.

"I wish you didn't have faith, and don't do that in front of guests." Mamma turned and headed back toward the kitchen. She returned with sandwiches for Buddy and Danny.

"You'll have to admit it, Maggie, bookkeepin' is a whole lot better than scrubbing other folk's laundry and lookin' after their kids. At least you don't have to do that no more."

"I don't know, Jack. Physically it's easier, but mentally it's much harder."

"Like most things, darlin', the more you do it, the easier it'll get," encouraged Daddy. "Just keep at it—perseverance, Maggie, perseverance."

"You're not listening to me, Jack. I've been persevering, and I am still not sure if I'm doing it right. If the IRS comes for us, you'll be going to jail with me," warned Mamma. "It's your signature too."

"As long as we get the same cell, I won't mind one bit."

"Augh! I'm going crazy here. It's no joking matter, Jack."

Just then the Saturn rocket took off. It was a perfect launch.

"Will ya look at that?" Daddy said, and we all turned toward the television. Mamma joined us to watch the launch, and momentarily their argument was forgotten. Across our television screen, the Saturn rocket sailed through a clear blue Florida sky and passed behind a fluttering US flag.

"It's a good one. It looks like a very good one," pronounced Walter Cronkite. It was the sixth manned Apollo launch we'd witnessed in the last sixteen months. It was still impressive, if a bit less magical. Once the rocket went out of sight, it soon went out of mind. The station switched to animation, and we moved on to our lives.

Unlike the previous moon missions, NASA feeds didn't dominate prime-time viewing. The following evening, the networks seemed to lose interest, along with the rest of America, and returned to their regular programming. Instead of listening to mission control that Sunday following the launch, we watched Florence Henderson on *The Ed Sullivan* Show sing, "What do you do when love dies?" We forgot, for a time, about the crew hurtling toward the moon. But on the following day, Monday, April 13, things would go horribly wrong for the *Apollo* crew, and all eyes and ears would return to the news of their flight through space.

On Monday morning, Mamma mailed off our taxes to the IRS. "Boy, it's a relief to have that done," she sighed when she got back from the post office. That evening as we watched *The Carol Burnett Show*, there was an explosion aboard *Apollo 13*, caused by a fault in the electrical system of one of the oxygen tanks. The spacecraft lost electrical power. The command module remained functional on its own batteries and oxygen tank, but these were usable only during the last few hours of flight. The crew had to shut down the command module and move into the lunar module, using it as a lifeboat for the return trip to Earth. But we did not learn about the crew's ongoing ordeal out among the stars until the next day.

At school they interrupted class so we could listen to the news. Back at home, we returned to our seats in front of the television screen, where we sat transfixed each evening for the next three nights. Despite abundant adversity caused by limited power, loss of heat, and a shortage of drinkable water, the crew returned to Earth safe, if dehydrated, thanks in no small measure to the efforts at NASA. Tragedy thwarted turned into triumph of epic proportions.

With all the talk about the unlucky number of the flight and the unlucky date of the accident, Mamma realized that she had mailed our taxes on an inauspicious day and feared she'd made an unfortunate mistake. Mamma was very superstitious: "How could I have done such a thing?" She worried for weeks. But despite her fears, the IRS never came knocking on our door.

Since turning thirteen, Buddy was spending more and more time locked in the bathroom. There were no locks on our bedroom doors, and the bathroom offered the only guarantee of solitude. Normally we shared the upstairs bathroom, but he would ignore my pounding on the door, stamping on the floor, and loud complaints. "Use the downstairs bathroom, why don't you," he'd bark. In frustration, I would. One day, while cleaning the bathroom and mopping its floor, I pulled the linen dresser away from the wall. There, stashed behind it, were three well-worn *Playboy* magazines, giving me some idea as to Buddy's bathroom activities, although I was too naïve to get the full picture. I sensed that my discovery could be used to my advantage: I used it to blackmail him.

Holding the magazines with my wet pink rubber gloves, I entered his bedroom without knocking and said, "Look what I found."

"Give them to me," he said as he leapt from his bed and snatched them from my fingers. "That's none of your business."

"Then don't leave them in our bathroom."

"Oh, shut up, freak."

"That will cost you."

"What?"

"My silence is going to cost you."

"What do you mean?"

"Well, I'll spell it out for you. I won't tell Mamma about these and what you just called me if you and Danny quit insulting me and my girlfriends."

"We haven't insulted you. We're just playing around."

"Well, quit playing around then. We don't like it."

"Ah, come on; you're making a mountain out of a molehill. Your girlfriends like it."

"Says who? They're my friends, and they certainly don't like it. It's insulting. If you want to impress girls, you're going about it in totally the wrong way."

"I'm doing just fine."

"Yeah, so where are all your girlfriends then?"

"You don't know everything."

"I know the only 'girlfriends' you have are the imaginary ones in those magazines. I am telling you to watch your mouth around my friends, and that goes for Danny too."

"I'll think about it."

"I warned you." Then I cried out, "Mamma." Intentionally, I wasn't loud enough for her to hear me but loud enough to worry Buddy about my intentions.

"Okay, okay, I'll lay off."

"And Danny too?"

"Danny too."

It didn't stop him from holing up in the locked bathroom nearly every afternoon, but at least he stopped heckling me and my girlfriends. After a short break, he started saying hello to my girlfriends as they passed, but he was never rude again. I could have just repeated to Mamma the insulting things he had said to get him into trouble, but the Ward kids frowned on squealing, and in any case, blackmailing was much more fun.

CHAPTER THIRTY-THREE

𝕰 ❖ 𝕮

THE EUCHARIST AND CONFESSION

*D*espite my best efforts to keep Buddy away from my friends, he stole my girlfriend. That is, my new best friend, Maureen Riley. She saw Buddy's winsome, wicked smile and that was it. He hardly had to say a word. After that first alluring look, she mostly forgot all about me.

It started when Maureen rode the bus home from school with me. We had to decide on an experiment for our joint science fair project. We had narrowed it down to two options. I was in favor of working out how astronauts living on a space station could grow some of their own quick-growing foods, like bean sprouts and radishes. That way their food would last longer, and they could have fresh vegetables in their diet. Alternatively, we were considering working out how to improve their drinking water supplies. As we were walking past the garage and turning the corner to head up the driveway, we heard Buddy call out to us from inside one of the bays.

"Why, good afternoon there, ladies." I was surprised to see Buddy grinning not only at Maureen, but, it seemed, at me too— Buddy usually greeted me with a scowl. In that moment, I first realized that my brother was a very attractive guy. With that realization, he suddenly looked older to me. When his face lit up with a smile, he was hard not to like. Maureen was immediately hooked. When we got to my room, instead of talking about our project, all Maureen wanted to do was to pump me for information about Buddy.

That year Maureen and I won the school's science fair competition and were preparing to take our project to the statewide competition, to be held at the University of Maryland. Maureen stopped by unannounced on a Saturday and rang the doorbell. Mamma answered the door, and Maureen asked to see me. Mamma told her I was up in my room and that she could go on up and get me.

She never made it to my room. Sometime later I came down and saw Mamma sitting at the dining table cutting off the tips of a batch of green beans.

"Mamma, is it okay if I go over to Carol's house?"

"What about Maureen?"

"Maureen, Maureen Riley? What about her?"

"Where is she?"

"How the heck should I know?" I asked as I shrugged my shoulders, confused by her question.

"Isn't she with you?"

"What gave you that idea?"

"She came by for you. I sent her up to your room more than an hour ago."

"Well, she never made it. I haven't seen her since yesterday."

"I haven't seen her come back down. I doubt she could've slipped out unseen."

"I don't know," I said.

"You sure?"

"Yes, of course, I'm sure."

"Well, she hasn't come back down. What do you suppose happened to her?"

Then it occurred to me where she might have gone. "I have a good idea."

"And what might that be?" Mamma asked, perplexed.

"She's infatuated with Buddy."

"Oh, is she now?" Mamma said, sounding a bit annoyed as she looked up the stairs.

Before Mamma could make a move, I ran up to Buddy's room and banged on his door.

"Yeah, who is it?" came Buddy's voice from behind the door.

"It's me, Charlie."

"Yeah, what do you want?" he snapped.

"Maureen," I responded and then opened his door without waiting for an invitation. Sitting on the bed next to Buddy was

Maureen. They both looked flustered, and Maureen's shirt was halfway unbuttoned. I looked them over. "Hi, Maureen. My mom says that you came by to see me. You get lost?"

Maureen's creamy white skin turned pink before my eyes. Her blush started across her cheeks and moved down her face to her neck. "Oh, I ran into your brother, and we got to talking."

"So, you done talking?"

"I guess so," she responded.

"In that case, why don't you button up your shirt and come with me? My mom's wondering what happened to you and what you two have been up to. I am heading out."

We didn't win the state competition; some guy named Lawrence won. Even with our project long over, Maureen kept finding reasons to stop by our house, and despite her pronouncements that she wanted to see me, I knew it was Buddy she really wanted. Still, we remained good friends. She had a dry sense of humor and an infectious laugh. She was upbeat and adventurous. She loved reading, was often irreverent, and liked to have fun. Her mom insisted that she attend Mass at least once every week. Being Catholic, she had lots of options. At Saint Mary's there was a Mass each day of the week, twice on Saturdays, and six times on Sunday. The Sunday after Halloween she invited me to go to church with her. They were having a special All Saint's Day Mass for teenagers.

"A friend of my sister Colleen is performing at the folk Mass," she informed me. "He has a real nice voice and plays guitar. His name is Michael, and he's kind of cute. You'll like him—he's a bookworm just like you. I'll introduce you after Mass," she promised.

Mamma was thrilled that I was going to my first ever Catholic Mass. Neither of us was surprised when Buddy decided to join us.

Saint Mary's was the largest church I'd ever been in. When we arrived, only one wing of it was filled with people. As we entered, Maureen dipped her fingers in some water that was in a vessel attached to the wall near the front door. "Do what I do," she commanded. So Buddy and I dipped our fingers and crossed ourselves as Maureen had done. We'd seen our mother cross herself often enough—it felt good, strange and yet somehow familiar. We followed Maureen, who sat down on a pew at the back of the crowd. Three golden-robed priests walked up between the aisles, followed by an altar boy. The priest in front swung a silver incense burner from side to side. I was mesmerized by the ritual ceremony, sensing its rich meaning even if I didn't understand all its symbolism. It was seductive in its sincerity and gravity. The sound of the priests' chanting was soothing.

During the service we sat, stood up, and went down on our knees several times. Each time, we followed Maureen's lead. I watched as a priest blessed some cloth, the wine, and the wafers. I couldn't hear everything the priest said, only words and phrases such as "lamb of God … confess … body … bread … blood. The priest spoke aloud, and the congregants replied in unison, including

Maureen. Then people started to line up before a platform in front of the priest.

"Do exactly as I do," instructed Maureen. "We're going up to take Holy Communion."

"We'd better not," I cautioned. "We don't know what to do."

"It looks pretty simple," Buddy whispered as he watched the congregants walk up and kneel in front of the priests. "I'm going. What do we have to do?" he asked.

"After you kneel, put your hands together in prayer. The priest will walk up to you and say a few words. When you hear him say, 'Christ,' you respond, 'Amen' and stick out your tongue. That's it. Then he'll put a wafer on your tongue, and you get up and come back here. Simple."

Because of where I sat on the pew, I was in front of Maureen and Buddy was behind her when we got up. We walked up and got in line. When it was my turn, I walked up to the priest and knelt. As he stood before me, he held a thin pale cracker. Then I heard him say, "… body of Christ." Body! Did he say body? My head was in a scramble. I panicked. Did I hear him say "blood" earlier? It sounded like cannibalism, even if it was symbolic. Without thinking, the words, "Ooh gross," poured out of my mouth. Holding the wafer in midair, the priest looked at me scornfully. I felt Maureen kick the back of my foot. That's when I remembered to say "Amen," and stuck out my tongue. The priest hesitated, but then he placed the wafer on my tongue. It tasted dry and bland. It made me think of

338

the ash in that urn we'd discovered in our basement.

I went back to our seats. When Maureen joined me, she looked angry. But when she sat down she couldn't help herself—her body began to shake as she struggled to stifle her giggles. She slipped down onto her knees as if she were praying, though few others were on their knees at that moment. She hid her face in her hands as she endeavored to gain control of her laughter. To make matters worse, when he joined us back in our seats, Buddy too began to giggle and slid down on his knees next to Maureen. It was contagious, making it impossible for me to resist. Soon we were all on our knees.

Walking home, Buddy made us laugh even more as he imitated the expression on the priest's face and his hesitation to place the wafer on my proffered tongue. When we got home, Mamma was anxious to hear how it went and peppered us with questions. Finally, Buddy blurted out what I had said to the priest during communion. Mamma was mortified and angry with all three of us, but mostly with Maureen and me.

"Maureen Riley, you should know better. The Eucharist is not a joke. It's sacred. You've all committed a mortal sin. You must repent and pray for God's forgiveness. I mean it," Mamma scolded. She continued, "Maureen, how could you have allowed them to take Holy Communion? You knew full well that Buddy and Charlie had no business receiving the sacrament. They've never been to confession; neither have they been baptized in the Catholic faith. Buddy, I can forgive you. You didn't know any better. But you, Charlotte, I am so ashamed of you. How could you say something so insulting, and to a priest, even if you've never been to a Mass before?"

"No one told me they call the wafers the body of Christ. What if you were dropped on the moon and someone said, 'Here, eat this. It comes from the body of a dead person'?"

"Charlotte, you knew full well it wasn't the actual body of Christ. You're supposed to be an intelligent girl. Now, how could that have been the actual body of Christ?" questioned Mamma.

"Even if it's merely symbolic, it sounded real creepy. I just wasn't prepared. It slipped out."

"It is not creepy—it's beautiful. And if you had been educated in the faith, you'd understand it. The Church is filled with symbolism and sacred traditions. When you take Holy Communion, you're taking the spirit of Christ into your very being. That is why you must go to confession before you receive communion, and to do that, you must be baptized Catholic." Mamma then gave Buddy and me a long lecture about the meaning of transubstantiation.

When she finished, I said, "I don't know, Mamma. It happened so fast. I didn't have a chance to reason it out. It was just a reflex reaction. I am sorry. I didn't mean to insult anyone. I will confess this. I don't think I'll ever make it as a Catholic, at least not a good one."

"That's okay, honey, there aren't many true 'good' Catholics. It's more of a goal than a destination. You can only keep trying to be your best self."

CHAPTER THIRTY-FOUR

℘ ❖ ℭ

TIN SOLDIER

PFC Jackson Ward
HS 56 322 945
Hq Co 5th Sup & Trans Bn
5th Inf. Div. (Mech)
Fort Carson, Colorado

Dear Charlie,

Thanks for your letter and the cookies. They didn't last long, but they sure made me popular while they did. Yesterday I had my first pass since arriving here. I had a whole day off base. I went for a hike up in the nearby mountains. My bunkmates think I was crazy to go for a hike after our daily marches here in full gear. But I wanted to get away and to be alone. Around here, you can't take a piss without someone over your shoulder. I hiked along a road up into the Rocky Mountains, then followed a trail to a peak to watch the sunset. Once the sun went over the horizon, I just lay down and stared at like a million stars. I've never seen so many. It's real peaceful, beautiful, and lonely up in the mountains here. Geez, I miss you guys.

In answer to your question, no, we don't get to listen to the radio. There are no televisions on our side of the base, no newspapers, and no pay phones. We're cut off but good. That's how the army wants us. The only news we get is from letters from back home, so keep them coming. When I was out yesterday, I stopped at a diner and I finally got to hear the Casey Kasem's Top 40 broadcast you wrote about. I liked the idea that you might be listening to the same broadcast as me. I heard Joe Cocker's version of "Cry Me a River." It sounded pretty good to me. What do you think? Though I'm a thousand miles away, it makes me feel closer to you imagining that we might be listening to the same program.

Boot camp is a lot like home—there's always some guy yelling, telling you what to do, and calling you an idiot. But the food is better back home, and you get a whole lot more time to eat it. Just like Daddy told me, I've been keeping my head down and doing as I'm told. We're all in the same boat. We're lowly foot soldiers counting the days until we get out of here; though, to be honest, we're afraid of what is waiting for us in Nam. We try not to think about that. Instead we think about the leave we're getting after basic. It's hard, but I am having an easier time adjusting than a lot of these goons. I guess all that time I spent with Daddy riding my ass is paying off. My hide is thicker than a lot of my bunkmates. When I left, I didn't think I'd miss home so much. I wish I was back there or, better yet, opening up the throttle on my bike down a long stretch of highway.

We get up every day before the sun at 0430. Each morning while it's still dark, we head out for a march in full gear. The drill sergeant makes us march double time, which is more like jogging than marching. If anyone doesn't do it right, the man shouts into our ears, "Charlie is going to get you and you are going to die, soldier!" He doesn't mean you, Charlie. He means the Viet Cong. Charlie is what they call them. But I can't help it—when he yells, "Charlie is going to get you," I think of you, and you don't scare me one bit. But the sergeant don't know that, and I ain't telling. After our march, we have breakfast at 0600, then we have training. Lunch is nothing but C rations— you don't want to know what those are. This week after lunch, I train as an MP—military police. I get extra weapons training for that. My biggest fear is not the gooks but ending up being sent to some college campus and being forced to point my gun at some cute chick like those guys at Kent State. Shit, I don't want any part of that.

Got to go. It's almost 2100 and lights out. One thing is for sure, I don't have any problems falling asleep. I am so tired at the end of each day, I'm snoring before my head hits my pillow. Soon I will be done with basic training. I am looking forward to getting a break before they send my ass to Nam.

Give Mamma a kiss from me.

Love,

Chip

Part Nine

1971

CHAPTER THIRTY-FIVE

ജ❖ൽ

GREETINGS FROM VINH LONG

*T*he first letters I ever received from overseas were postmarked from San Francisco, California, though these were actually sent from South Vietnam. I'd come home from school, and there on the table would be an envelope addressed to me.

> SP/4 Jackson Ward
> 7th Sqdn, 1st Air Cav
> APO SF 96357
> June 3, 1971

Dear Charlie,

A big thanks for your most recent care package. Yes, I did get the copy of the *New York Times* you sent with the article about the Pentagon Papers, and no, our letters aren't censored. The army doesn't have time to read all our letters, so write away. As far as the article, I don't know what all the fuss was about. You think the pilots didn't know they were bombing the shit out of Laos? We know when they fly over Cambodia too. It's war, baby. There are no rules but kill or be killed. You've got to survive any way you know how. If the gooks cross the border, then so do we. Otherwise they'd have a big advantage. If we don't chase them down when we got them in our snares, they'll live to kill us another day. We knew Johnson wasn't sharing stuff with the press and Congress. You don't tell your enemy your plans, now do you? Tell your hippie friends to get over it. I'm not saying we have any business being in this shithole, but as long as we are, we have to do whatever it takes to win. That's war.

On to sweeter stuff—the cookies you made went quick. My hut mates jumped at them as soon as I opened the box. I didn't mind; for the most part they share whatever they get from home too. Last time I didn't tell you much about my hooch companions. For your information, a hooch is where we sleep. It's part tent and part cabin. There are six of us in this one.

Calvin is from Baltimore. He's a brother, but I don't mind. He's real light skinned and from a distance he looks almost White. He is a bit shorter than me but stockier. Coming from the same area helps. I guess if he can put up with my shit, I can put up with his. We've got each other's backs and that's what matters down here. We arrived about the same time. He calls me Saltine as in the crackers. He doesn't say it mean like, so it's okay.

Sam's a hick from a place named Plano, Texas. It's somewhere near Dallas. He's been here the longest, by about a month, so he thinks he outranks us somehow. He's got thick lips and dark hair, and his skin looks naturally a bit tan. I'd think he had some darkie blood if it weren't for his light-blue eyes, though I guess he still could be, or maybe he's got some Mexican blood. I know better than to ask him, though, I doubt he'd take it too kindly. He's annoyingly polite when he's sober, but he can be a real asshole when he gets drunk. I don't know which is worse. He's a good mechanic though. He's got a Chink girlfriend, so he's out of here as much as he can be.

Rodney is from Cincinnati. We call him Professor on account of he went to college for almost three years studying mechanical engineering. When he dropped out (or flunked out, he won't say), the army got him. He looks a bit bookish too—a bit short, thin, and don't look like he's seen the sun much until he got here. He has a girl back home he writes to a lot. Problem is she's written to him but once since he arrived, and it has him weirded out. Good thing his parents send him lots of letters and packages, or I think he'd lose it.

Steel, that ain't his real name, it's Eustis, he's from outside of Raleigh, North Carolina, and he's another brother. Before

Nam he worked in a gas station fixing cars. We call him Steel on account of his biceps. Every morning, he does a bunch of pushups. It makes me tired just watching him. He reminds me a bit of Eugene, how he was always copying Jack LaLanne and doing those exercises. One day a few weeks back, I was late getting back on base, and Steel covered for me. He's cool. His grandparents farmed tobacco just like Daddy, so we got a bit to jaw about.

Last to join our hooch in Vinh Long is Matt. He's a Californian pretty boy from somewhere outside of LA. Before the army got ahold of him he had long hair below his shoulders. He listens to a lot of Jimi Hendrix. Matt's okay, but I think he fried some of his brain cells on acid or something. He says and does the strangest shit sometimes. Matt went to auto mechanic school back in the States and got some sort of certificate to prove it. That's why the brass put him in with us, but I wouldn't want him working on any bird I was going to take a flight in. Calvin and I are always checking on his work. If there are five steps to fixing something, he will do four of them right and totally forget about the fifth one. He'll close up an engine and be missing a wrench. Maybe he'll get better with time. He's only been here a couple of weeks.

Thanks for the bug repellent, music cassettes, paperbacks, magazines, and your letter. We all like that "American Pie" song. Does that dude have any more? Calvin liked the

Bill Withers tune you sent, "Lean on Me." He said he wouldn't mind some Isaac Hayes or Marvin Gaye the next time you put a cassette together. I wouldn't either. The Dylan stuff was okay but not big around here. We'd prefer more party music to get the heart pumping.

We're all helicopter mechanics, of course, working on mostly Hueys, but we repair Chinooks and anything else with a rotor. Hueys are the two-bladed main and tail rotor helicopters you see on the news transporting troops and gear around here. Chopper pilots are some tough sons-of-bitches. They fly in here at night with big red X's on their airmobiles. The X's tell us the bird needs fixing. By the time they come out of the mess after breakfast, we've put their eggbeaters back together. Often, it's the main or tail rotors, but we work on a lot of steering leakages, especially on the Hueys. One limped in here last night that was one rotation away from the rotor crashing. The Jesus nut was holding on by a single thread and ready to come off. That's the main rotor retaining nut. It holds the main rotor onto the helicopter. If that comes off when you're up, you'll be meeting Jesus real soon. We patched a bunch of holes on that one as well as the nut, and it's in the air again. You'd be amazed at what you can fix with a bit of duct tape. The tape is green here like everything else. I am glad I learned to work on motors. It's what keeps me out of the rice paddies and the bush; it's probably why I'm still alive.

351

Don't get me wrong, life on the Fort ain't no picnic, though some of those pilots might argue it. It's a different war than the one Daddy fought. Sometimes we don't know who our worst enemy is here: the gooks or the brass, though right now I'd say it's the mud. It's the rainy season.

Keep writing. I hope you don't mind; I let my hooch buddy, Steel, read your letters. He hasn't gotten a single letter from back home. The dude needs some, so I share yours. Maybe in your next letter you can say something directly to him. You two have some things in common. He always has his head in a book when he's not working. You both like to think too much. He's reading one of the ones you sent called *The Day of the Jackal*. He seems to be liking it. By the way, his favorite band is the Moody Blues, so if you could get some of their music, he'd appreciate it. I hope I've given you enough info on him for you to think of something to write.

You can't know how much your letters mean here. I am grateful for how often you write. Life in Nam can be crazy. Your letters are a piece of home that keeps me anchored. When I read them, your words push all the insanity aside for a few minutes. Keep them coming, baby sister. Give Mom a hug, say hi to Buddy and Dad too. Tell them all I miss them.

Love,
Chip

P.S. Send more cookies. Lots more.

P.S.P.S. Stay away from hippies. Matt just went off again. Steel rescued him before he could get into trouble. He was screaming at the rain in a torrential downpour, naked, and stoned out of his mind. Weed is plentiful here and cheaper than the water-downed beer.

CHAPTER THIRTY-SIX

80 ❖ 08

FIRST IN WAR, FIRST IN PEACE, AND LAST IN THE AMERICAN LEAGUE

Charlotte Ward

October 1, 1971

Dear Chip,

It's been a rough week and a half here. First let me say, I hate, hate, HATE Bob Short! I hope he gets sores where the sun don't shine and where it does too. May the harm he's done to this city come back and infect him. May it physically manifest into some awful, disfiguring disease. I don't want him to die, I just want him to suffer. I want justice. I guess you know why everyone in D.C. hates the man, but you missed all the drama. I was at the final game last night. Finally, let me tell you I resent anyone in or near Arlington, Texas. What kind of dinky town is Arlington anyway? Whoever heard of it before

355

they stole our team? Why should they have a team but not our nation's capital? It doesn't make sense.

My heart's been broken. For the last two years, I have been a devoted fan. Do you remember my friend Carol Wilson? She's even taller than me and has light-brown short hair. I started to go to a lot of Senators baseball games with her before you left for boot camp. Since then, we've gone to nearly every home game. Her dad gets us in for free. He's much older than the other dads in our school. He's retired from the government, tall and lanky with thin gray hair. During the baseball season, he works as an usher at RFK. He does it more for fun and the love of the game than for money.

Two months ago, Carol learned that her dad isn't really her dad. He's her granddad, and her sister, who's sixteen years older than her, is really her mother. Carol freaked out when she learned this. I would have too. Carol still isn't straight on how she feels about it, especially with her sister being her mom. They've never gotten along really. However, it does explain a lot. Her sister is trying to be more like a mom these days and wants to be called Mom. Her grandmother is real quiet and a bit distant. She's nice enough, always making cookies and stuff, but it's hard to know what she's thinking. Carol calls her Grandma sometimes but feels weird about it. It's easier with her grandfather. There's just one dad in the house. She still always calls him Dad.

One of the perks of his job at RFK is he can bring family members in for free. He tells the guys at the gate that we're both his daughters. I think they know I'm not related, but no one says anything. I enjoy riding with him to the park in his Mercury Comet. Not because it's a nice car—it's okay. Its suspension seems a bit mushy to me. I like the rides because he really loves the game and tells us all sorts of interesting facts. The amount of baseball trivia he has stored in his brain is amazing. He's a walking Major League encyclopedia. He likes it that we love the Senators nearly as much as he does. You can tell he enjoys our company on these rides. He gets animated. Because of his job, he has to get to the park early, so we always catch batting practice. I really like this because that is when you get a chance to talk to the players. There's rarely a sellout. Usually we get to grab a couple of seats behind the Senators dugout. During practice we sit on top of the dugout and chat with the players. Some of them know us by name. Carol and I both got Frank Howard to sign baseballs for us. We've spoken with the great Mr. Williams. He never says much to us other than "Hello, ladies" or "Enjoy the game, girls." Still, it's a thrill that Ted Williams addresses us.

Do you remember, at the end of 1968, Bob Short beat out Bob Hope in winning the right to purchase the then pitiful and perpetually losing Washington Senators? Carol's dad said it seemed as if Mr. Short had breathed life into the team. He

357

was thrilled when Mr. Short coaxed Mr. Teddy "Ballgame" Williams out of retirement to manage the team. After a rocky start to spring training down in Pompano Beach, it looked as if Mr. Williams had performed a miracle. He transformed our last-place bums into a competitive professional team. For me, hope grew up through the ruins of our riot-torn city and reunited us for a while. We had a team we all were proud to call our own. I, like other Washingtonians, fell in love with Mike Epstein, Paul Casanova, '69 ERA winner, Dick Bosman, and my favorite, Frank "Hondo" Howard. I don't remember, were you still here when they changed D.C. Stadium's name to Robert F. Kennedy Stadium? Boy, we were all so happy when the Senators finished with a winning record after such a long drought. It was a great time to be at RFK, a great time for Senators fans, and great to be a Washingtonian again. But that was before.

The honeymoon was short lived. Last year, Bob Short mortgaged the farm to try and get majority control. Short was short on cash, and he took it out on the fans by raising ticket prices to the highest in the league. An upper deck outfield seat at RFK cost $3.50. Shoot, you can get one of those up in Baltimore for 50 cents. Remember the Carsons down the street? Well, like many others, Mr. Carson started taking his three boys to Baltimore to see a ballgame. Even with the gas, it's a lot cheaper to take a family to Memorial Stadium than RFK. It takes a bit more than an hour to go up to Memorial Stadium and about twenty-five minutes to get to RFK from here. Now his kids are Oriole fans. I don't think his youngest, Pete, has taken off his O's cap since they won the World Series last year.

As bad as all that was, the worst was yet to come. The penny-pinching, egotistical, control freak Mr. Short named himself general manager. Can you believe the arrogance? If he bought a hospital, would he think himself qualified to perform heart surgery? He started making decisions going against Mr. Williams's strong protests. Why did he hire the great Mr. Williams if he wasn't going to listen to him? Short is short on brains, that's what I think. Just because you've got money, it doesn't mean you're smart. Boy, the man has made some disastrous trades. He began selling off the talent starting with Joe Coleman, a top young pitcher. Not surprisingly, with high ticket prices and diminishing performance, attendance fell off and the revenue followed. He killed the golden goose. Last year we ended with a losing record of 72 wins and 90 losses.

But the final death blow was yet to come. A few weeks ago, rumors started circulating about a possible trade. Short was sharpening his knife and stuck it into our collective hearts when he announced that the Senators were moving to Arlington, Texas. That was a little more than a week ago. Last night was the last Senators game to be played at RFK. It was against the arrogant New York Yankees.

It's a game I'll never forget. It had been raining during the day yesterday but was starting to clear up when Mr. Wilson picked Carol and me up from school. He did that because we wanted to get to the stadium extra early. By the time we got there, fans were already pouring into RFK. We went to our usual seats. We said goodbye to our favorite players, wishing them good luck. You could tell they were real beat up over it too. They didn't want to leave us.

Maybe fifteen minutes before the game started, two guys hauled out one of the biggest signs I've ever seen. It read how dare you sell us short in bold green paint. You could hear people shouting, "Give them room!" as the two guys carried their sign. Some folks helped them up on top of the dugout where Carol and I were. They told us their names: Dean and Ron. They're students at Northern Virginia Community College. A bunch of other kids joined us there too and started yelling, "Let's see your face. Why don't you show, chicken Short?" If he had dared to show up, he'd have been lynched from the upper deck for sure.

A bunch of fans gave a standing ovation when someone up in the stands draped a sign that read "Short stinks." There were a bunch of other signs too. A lot of these I can't repeat though because of the obscenities—Mamma wouldn't like it. We saw a boy about our age drag a Styrofoam dummy of Short through the stands. At one point I saw him crying. He wasn't the only one. Grown men were crying too.

Our own Dick Bosman was the starting pitcher. You could tell he was emotional out there on the mound. Carol's dad abandoned his post in the first inning and joined us behind the team's dugout. "I'm going to watch this game with my girls," he told us. I liked how he included me in that statement. Thousands of fans and neighborhood kids simply walked in without paying because the security guards left their posts early in the game as well. The park was rocking with all the noise coming from the fans.

By the sixth inning, Bosman had given up three home runs and the Yankees were up five to one. When Frank Howard came up to bat, the fans went wild. We were all praying for some of his magic, and he delivered big time by crushing a fastball into the left-field stands. We all leapt to our feet and started screaming. The applause lasted long after Hondo went back in the dugout. When he rounded the bags, Frank tipped his hat and threw it into the stands. Then he stood just outside of the dugout looking up at the fans. We saw tears in the big man's eyes. Before he went into the dugout, he blew a kiss up to us, his adoring fans. I will always love him for that. It was heartbreaking and heartwarming. By the end of the inning, the score was tied. In the eighth, we scored two more and were leading the stinking Yankees 7 to 5.

Everyone knew that we'd swarm the field once the game ended. With two outs in the top of the ninth, the Senators held the lead and side-arm pitcher Joe Grzenda was on the mound. But the fans couldn't wait and began pouring onto the field one out too soon. Carol's dad told us to stay in our seats, so we didn't end up on the field as we'd planned. I wish we had. A teenager scooped up first base and ran away with it. Next, some kids grabbed the ball boys' folding chairs and ran off with those. People were ripping up whatever they could, including the grass. With only a few security guards in sight and no home plate, the game was forfeited to the Yankees, who officially won the game 9 to nothing. Can you believe that?

That was the end of baseball in our nation's capital, maybe forever. I'm done with the Senators, and it's the end of my career as a sports fan. Obviously, I get far too caught up in it and become not just obsessed but possessed. It's just not mentally healthy. I may need professional help. I will try to let it go.

Driving the knife deeper into my wounds, at school today I saw a bunch of fair-weather fans jumping on the Orioles bandwagon. I'm sick of hearing them going on about how the O's are returning, yet again, to play for the American League championship. They're chanting, "World Series, here we come again." They're not in it yet. The ALC hasn't even started. I hope the Oakland A's pulverize them. It's official, O's fans are more annoying than even stuck-up Yankee ones.

God, enough about baseball and that snake Short. Let's

talk about something else. I want to say I think it is great that you are working on helicopters (and not riding in them). Remember Eugene's friend, Scott? He's still MIA. I bought a metal bracelet two weeks ago for $2.50. It has Scott's name, rank, and the date he went missing on it. I am wearing it now. We're supposed to wear it until he's found. So thank you for keeping those machines running safely. How is it on base for you and your friends these days? How's Sam? Perhaps your friend Sam is happy. Short took the Senators to Arlington, Texas, which, like Plano, is a suburb of Dallas. I looked it up. Tell him he's got our team and we want it back. Darn, letting go is harder than I thought.

I'm glad you've a local friend with you. Because your friend Calvin is from Baltimore, I bet he's an Orioles fan? Is that right? His O's are in ALC championship games AGAIN! This Monday the first game will be played in Baltimore against the Oakland A's. If I was a good sport, I'd wish him good luck, but I am not. Okay, okay, let's move on. I am done venting, I promise.

As requested, I am enclosing a letter and some books for your friend Steel. I've asked him to write to me about the books and whatever else he'd like to discuss with a teenage girl he's never met. I made a cassette copy of the Moody Blues's latest record. A friend at school loaned it to me. It's called *Every Good Boy Deserves Favour*. I really like it. Have you heard the new John Lennon album, *Imagine*? It's not the heart-pumping "party music" you said you like, but I like it. If I can get ahold of the album, I'll make you a copy.

Aunt Martha came up for a week and for a belated birthday present, took Mamma to the new Kennedy Center for the Performing Arts. The building looks a bit like a gigantic pizza box on the Potomac. They heard Leonard Bernstein's *Mass* and brought home the album. They both loved it. However, Mamma fell into one of her black moods after Martha left. The last couple of days, Mamma and Daddy have been at it again whenever Daddy's in the house. Fortunately, he's been spending a lot of time down in the garage.

Now that they've lowered the voting age, have you registered yet? Nixon will be the Republican nominee, but of the Democrats, whom do you prefer: McGovern, Humphrey, or Wallace? Elections must seem a million miles away from life in Vietnam, but it matters. McGovern promises to end the war and Nixon promises an all-volunteer army. I just want you home, and annoying as Buddy is, I don't want him going over there.

On a fun note, last January a new comedy came out called *All in the Family*. It's hysterical. I hope you're able to watch it over there. Have you seen any episodes? We started watching back in spring and haven't missed a show since. It first aired in January, but Buddy and I didn't hear about it until later and turned Mamma and Daddy on to it. It's the one thing we all do together these days. Mamma and I especially like Jean Stapleton. Despite being funny, it deals with some powerful stuff, which makes for some lively family discussions on Tuesday nights.

Buddy is playing a lot of basketball at the Boys Club. He's a point guard mostly and is quite good. He's hit a growing spurt and grew about two inches in a few months. So far, his team has played only four games, but they've won them ALL. This last summer he made a bunch of money mowing lawns and working with Daddy in the garage. We share a paper route. I do it one week, and he does it the next. That way we each get a chance to sleep. I make money babysitting and dog walking for a couple of families. That and school keep me busy. Buddy spends his money about as soon as he gets it. I save most of mine in the bank. I have plans. I'm saving for college. As soon as I turn fourteen, I am going to look for a regular job. I get up to a dollar an hour for babysitting. Dog walking pays less. I hear that the minimum wage is going up to a buck sixty soon. Tonight, I am babysitting the Murkowski kids down the street, so I have to get going.

I guess Eugene is doing fine. I haven't heard much from him lately. Emma wrote saying she's going to nursing school part time. That's all the news for now. So, big brother, keep your spirits up and your head down, and get your butt home.

365

Missing you,
Charlie

P.S. The cookies are for you, Steele, Matt, and Rodney. Tell Sam and Calvin they can get their own stinking cookies.

CHAPTER THIRTY-SEVEN

ഇ ❖ ൙

GREETINGS FROM KHE SANH

Hi Charlie,

Your care packages and letters are medicine for a lot of what aches. I can't express enough how much they mean to me and to my buddies. Sometimes here, home feels like a fantasy, and it becomes hard to imagine a world where losing a baseball team is some sort of tragedy. I'm not making less of your feelings; if I was there, I'm sure I'd be cursing that asshole Short too. It helps my sanity to imagine that such a world exists, and one day, if I'm lucky, I might be back there with you. Sorry, I didn't follow your instructions—I shared your goodies with Sam and Calvin. They need it too. They did read your letter, so they know how you feel, if that helps. Steel really loves getting those books and letters from you. You're a good egg. I am proud to have you as a sister.

Despite Daddy's warnings not to volunteer for anything, I

made a couple of nighttime runs with a pilot I liked. His name was Andy. A few weeks back, he wanted to deliver hot grub to some of our guys stuck in the bush. I went twice with him. Well, last night, his bird didn't make it back. I'm really bummed out about it; we all are. I won't be volunteering anymore, you can count on that.

The closer you get to getting out of here, the suckier the jobs get. Because I'm tall, I was chosen to head out to rescue some downed birds. For the last few weeks, when the siren goes off, I grab a duffel bag full of straps. By the third siren, we're up in the air because there are guys out there counting on us. We fly over to the wounded bird and I get to tie down the rotor blades and the tail rotor, then I get on top and put the slings on and hold them up in the air to hook on the other helicopter that lifts the wounded one. It helps to be tall to avoid touching the metal hook because you can get a bit of an electric shock if you do. Two nights ago, just after our pilot got our bird up, our tail rotor gave out, and we started to plummet toward the ground. My heart nearly gave out. Lucky for us, we had a real good pilot and he was able to use just the main rotor and landed us safely on the ground. Another group had to go out and help the other helicopter that night. I prefer to stay on base but there's been a lot of action around here lately and I keep getting sent out.

Back when we were in Vinh Long we complained about

the bad chow, weak beer, rain, and mud. We didn't know how good we had it. The rains are gone and now it's just hot with lots of red dust flying everywhere each time a bird takes off or lands, which is pretty much all the time around here.

I am counting the days until I can come home. Shit! There goes the siren—gotta go.

Love you Charlie,
Chip

Part Ten

1972

CHAPTER THIRTY-EIGHT

ℬ ❖ ℛ

VERY PERSONALLY YOURS

January 28, 1972

Dear Emma,

Last month was the worst one ever. I got my monthlies! Yuck! No wonder they call it "the curse." Do I really have this to look forward to for the next fifty years? God must be a man; a woman would have come up with a better system for procreation. Thank goodness I had a few cloaked cryptic classes about "our reproductive organs" in school or I'd have had absolutely no clue what was going on. I would have thought I was dying. If this happens to nearly every woman, every month, how come we're not supposed to speak about it? It's crazy. Thank the good Lord I have you to talk to or I'd be totally hysterical.

I need your help. Mamma's idea of the great "Mother-Daughter Talk About the Facts of Life" consisted of a blue pamphlet by Kotex titled "Very Personally Yours." The very title implies it's a secret, keep it to yourself, don't share, and absolutely *don't talk about it.* The booklet suddenly appeared on my bed one day. She didn't even hand it to me "personally."

The information inside was about as useful as what I learned in school, which was all about ovaries and eggs. Nothing prepared me for the day I woke up in my bed in a sea of blood or the cramps that made me double over in pain. Is that normal? It feels like some beast is inside me, pulling at my insides. The only good thing is it happened during Christmas break and there was no school. When the *curse* takes over my body again, I don't know how I'll manage when I need to leave my room. Really, Emma, you'd think Mamma could bring herself to tell me a few things. I could use a little help here. Just because she had to go it alone, does it mean I have to suffer equally? I have no way of knowing if that amount of blood is normal. How bad are the cramps supposed to be? What can you do about them? It's been more than 28 days (it's been 37), and it hasn't happened again. Is something horribly wrong with me?

After the flood, I scrubbed and scrubbed my sheets, but you could still tell. I thought, *Good, that way Mamma will know that I started, and she'll come talk to me.* Nope, I was sure wrong. All I got was a package of sanitary napkins and a box of tampons delivered in the same way as the pamphlet, only this time these were concealed in a brown paper bag. I got my first bra the same way. The napkins aren't enough. I leak all over the place in no time at all. How can I go to classes like this while using just the napkins? So I thought I'd try the tampons, but I used them wrong. It took me some time to figure out what I was doing wrong. Apparently when I slid the cotton plug up you-know-where, the paper tube went up there too. It was very uncomfortable, and I thought I should forget about using them. I tried sleeping with a towel under me, but it doesn't always stay in place. Finally, out of nightly desperation, I tried tampons again and got it right this time. Could I have damaged myself by using them wrong before? Could that be why I am so late this time? When and if this happens again, I am terrified of going out into the world, especially to school. How do you control it so that you don't leak? Obviously, white skirts and slacks are out.

I've tried to raise the subject with Mamma, but she is obviously embarrassed and distressed to speak of it. To sum up her response: just read the pamphlet and keep your legs crossed. The cherry on top (excuse my pun) was the other day I came home and found my friend Maureen in a deep conversation with Mamma at the dinner table.

"Hey there, Charlie. Your mom and I had a great talk while I waited for you to come home," Maureen told me as she stood up. Then she did a bizarre thing: she hugged Mamma. Get this, when we got upstairs to my room, Maureen informed me that I have the coolest mother ever, that she just had the most informative conversation about the birds and bees she'd ever had with anyone. "I sure wish I could talk to my mother like that. You're so lucky to have her, Charlie."

Really! Can you f------g believe that, Emma? I just wanted to scream. After Maureen left, I confronted Mamma about it. And you know what she said? "It's different when it's your own daughter." I ask you, who better to talk to than your own daughter, for crying out loud? Argh, you're my only hope. I'd call to talk to you, but the only phone we have is in the living room. It's impossible to have a private phone conversation in this house. I wish you lived closer. Help!

Give hugs to Paul, Sarah, Jacob, and Nate too.

Love,
Charlie

February 9, 1972

Dear Charlotte,

I hate to tell you, but my experience was no better. At least you had a "reproductive" class in school. We didn't. The only thing I got to prepare me for the inevitable was the same (or a similar) booklet. Mamma hasn't changed in that regard. Just before Nate and I got married, Mamma came into my bedroom and asked, "Is it too late to have that mother-daughter talk?"

I hadn't told her yet, but I was already pregnant with Paul at the time. So, I said, "I think it's a bit late for that, Mamma."

"Are you sure there isn't anything you want to ask me?" she prodded.

"No, Mamma, I think I'm okay," was my response. With her duty done, you could see the relief on her face. That's as close as we got to "the mother-daughter talk."

To answer some of your questions (I'm sure you'll have more): 1) Not all women are regular and not all women menstruate every 28 days. Normal is what is normal for you. Especially in the first year, it can vary a lot. It takes time for your body to get the hang of it. 2) It is highly unlikely that the hard paper tampon tube harmed you in any way. Keep using them. 3) For some woman a heavy flow is normal. It is for me too. 4) When you go to school, where dark, loose-fitting clothing, a thick pad, and use the tampons at the same time. Until you get used to it, for the first few days of each cycle, I recommend that you stop at the lavatory to change your tampon between each class for your peace of mind. If you end up late to class, find a female counselor or teacher and let them know that you're getting used to "being a woman" and need a bit more time in the bathroom. They'll understand and should arrange accommodation for you. 5) Cramping is worse for some than others. Take Midol. Just tell Mamma you need some. Also, a hot water bottle on your abdomen might help. 6) Place the towel under your sheet to protect the mattress; having it under the sheet will stop it from slipping around while you sleep. I hope this answers your initial questions. You're bound to have more as you grow into full womanhood. I am always here for you.

As you know, I've been taking a few nursing classes at night. My current class is all women, and I've formed some wonderful friendships with many of them. One woman brought to class a new book called *Our Bodies, Ourselves*. It's an incredible reference book full of useful information. Knowledge is liberating as well as empowering. We should have power over our own bodies. Our bodies have been shrouded in mystery for far too long. This book is revolutionary because of its honesty. I wish I'd had such a book years ago. Even today, I've learned a great deal from it. Some of it is very progressive and maybe too advanced for your age, so be warned. However, I think it is a Bible for women's reproductive and health issues, and every woman should own a copy.

As far as keeping your legs crossed. Mamma is one hundred percent right about that. I know you are an intelligent girl, and you have dreams for your future; however, I will say this anyway: *now you can become pregnant!* Sex is a deeply intimate act. It can bring you closer to the one you love, or it can leave you feeling empty if it's with the wrong man or even with the right guy but at the wrong time—so wait, wait as long as you can. I love my kids, but the dictionary term for parenthood should include the word slavery. Once you are a parent you must put another person's wants and needs ahead your own. You cannot eat if your child is hungry, sleep if they're awake, or go out the door if they are not cared for. When I met Nate, I thought I knew what love was, but there is no greater love than the love you have for your child, and there is no greater responsibility either. It is when you hold your own baby that you understand selflessness. You live for your child. But beware: squandered potential can leave us bitter. Achieving your potential is a million times harder when you are responsible for a child. That is especially true for women. So, my talented little sister, spread your wings, reach for your dreams, and keep those legs crossed!

Finally, I am not sure how Mamma would respond to your having the aforementioned women's health book, but I'm sure Dad wouldn't like it. They'd be uncomfortable at a minimum due to some graphic images as well as a lot of the information inside. I doubt they'll appreciate me giving it to you, but I am going to send it to you anyway. If they blow up at me for sending it without asking their permission first, well, at least I am way out here. I will mail you a package with several books inside, so when Mamma inevitably asks you, "What did Emma send you?" you can decide if you want to keep the women's book a secret, but that is up to you. It would not be fair of me to tell you to keep secrets from your parents.

We are all doing well here. It's a challenge to keep up with the kids and my studies, but I am sure it will pay off in time. Not much has changed since last we spoke. Both Paul and Sarah have been taking swimming lessons at the YMCA indoor pool in Eugene on Saturdays. I have the car on weekends. Little Sarah is a real fish and can outswim her older brother. His asthma hasn't helped. Paul won the second-grade spelling bee this week and likes to wear his medal around the house. I'm proud of him because he studied hard to win. Little Jacob is always trying to keep up with his siblings. At age three, he seems more hyper than I remember the older ones, or maybe I am just getting tired. Nate's a wonderful dad and works hard to support his family. I used to babysit a lot when we lived closer to town, but way out here it's been hard to pick up any steady at-home work. The rent's a lot cheaper, which helps make up for it. We're struggling, but somehow always manage to get by. Once I get my nursing degree and little Jacob starts school, it'll get a whole lot easier here financially. Give my love to everyone. I miss you guys.

Love,
Emma

CHAPTER THIRTY-NINE

❧❖☙

BAPTIST SWEEPSTAKES

*I*t was Halloween when I got a phone call from my friend Stacey. She invited me to an autumn teen party at her church. They weren't calling it a "Halloween" party because that would be heathenistic, but you were supposed to show up in a costume anyway. Daddy was happy to let me go because it was at a Baptist church. With only hours to prepare, I struggled to figure out a costume and searched the house for possibilities. In a closet I finally found a Nehru jacket that belonged to Eugene, and it gave me an idea. I borrowed a beaded necklace from Mamma and fashioned a headband from some embroidered ribbon. I wore it around my forehead and went as a hippie. Mamma applied some makeup, including eyeliner, mascara, lipstick, and a small flower painted on my cheek.

Stacey showed up with her hair in big curlers, a face covered in cold cream, and the puffiest bright pink bathrobe I'd ever seen. The effect was chilling. When the boys kept asking me to dance song after song but ignored her, she became angry with me. Thirsty from all the dancing, I headed over to the refreshment table. Stacey followed me.

"I never should have invited you. You're stealing all the boys."

"Stealing? It's not my fault they keep asking me to dance."

"You don't have to accept."

"You shouldn't have shown up here looking like your mother on a bad day. It's not an attractive look."

"Are you insulting my mother?"

"I didn't mean your mother. I meant any White, mush-faced, middle-aged woman with huge curlers wearing Liberace's robe. It hardly brings out your best features. You knew there'd be boys here. It's a 'teen dance,' remember? What were you thinking when you picked that getup? It's off-putting and more than a little frightening, to say the least."

"It's a Halloween party—you're supposed to look scary."

"Well, you've certainly succeeded in that. You scared off every boy in sight. Anyway, I thought it wasn't a Halloween party. I thought Halloween was too devilish and that this is a fall party. Shoot, it wasn't me who scared the boys. You did that all by yourself."

"I won't invite you ever again."

"You're just a poor sport. Excuse, me, I promised Carl the next dance. Enjoy the punch."

Stacey was angry and ignored me the next time I went roller skating. Then, out of the blue in May, she called me to invite me to a teen picnic her church was hosting. Glad to mend our friendship, I was happy to accept. This time she was dressed for success. She wore short shorts that showed off her long legs. I don't know if the minister approved, but the boys sure did. The next month, I received another invitation. Stacey asked if I would come to church with her one Sunday. I tried to beg off, but she kept saying that after church some of the kids would get together in Bible study, and it would be fun.

"Doesn't sound like a whole lot of fun to me."

"I promise. You'll have fun. It's important to me. Come as a favor to me."

"Why's it so important?" I asked.

"We're all supposed to bring a guest next week. It will make me look good. Come on—I'd do it for you."

"You would not. Your parents would skin you alive if they heard you went to some church that wasn't Baptist."

"That's beside the point. I'd do it if I could, and you can." She had me there, so I agreed.

Daddy was thrilled. I was bored at the service, and it seemed to go on forever. Contrary to her predictions, I didn't have fun in the teen "self-run Bible study group," though it was better than

383

the main service. A self-righteous boy named Owen proclaimed himself the leader and tried to take over the group, which caused some bickering. He tried to interrogate me and peppered me with questions.

"Have you accepted Jesus Christ as your immortal savior?"

"That's between me and God."

"Have you invited him into your heart?"

"No, but I've invited him to dinner."

"Your soul is no joking matter. In what faith were you baptized?"

"I haven't"

"Haven't what?"

"Been baptized," I said, knowing that would really get him going. I could see the light go on in his head; here was a golden opportunity to save a soul in peril.

"You know you're going to burn in hell if you don't accept Jesus Christ as your personal savior and get baptized. Only Baptists are welcome in heaven," he informed me.

"Will you be there?"

"Where do you mean?"

"In heaven."

"Why, definitely. I've been saved."

"Good." I said, thinking it was fine with me to be going in opposite directions, but I didn't say it, and I let him think what he wanted to think.

After church we went to Stacey's house to hang out. When we were in her room, she asked if I wanted to be saved.

"Saved from what?" I asked, just to see what she'd say.

"Saved from eternal hell. That's what."

"No thanks. I'm good."

"No, you're not. You're in danger. I'm offering you salvation. When you ask for the Lord to enter your heart and you get baptized, Jesus will wash away all your sins so that you can enter the gates of heaven and enjoy peace and everlasting life. Becoming a Baptist is your passport into heaven. You can't get in without it."

"Are you telling me that only Baptists get into heaven?"

"That's right."

"That doesn't make any sense. The Baptist Church, in the history of man, is a relatively new denomination of Christianity. Do you believe that God is the Father and that he created us all?"

"Well, yes, of course I do."

"Does a father love one child more than another?"

"No. But he can love them differently. Look how he has marked the Negroes as inferior."

"How do you suppose they're inferior or that they're marked?"

"Well, they're Black, aren't they?"

"And we're White. I have blond hair and blue eyes. Does that make me better than you because you have brown hair and brown eyes?"

"No, obviously not."

"Well, Hitler thought it did. Blacks aren't made inferior by God. Whites did that. Let me ask you a question. Do you believe that we are all God's children and that God loves us all?"

"Yes, of course I do. It's in the Bible."

"Well, the people who live deep in the Amazon rain forest, they've never had the opportunity to become Baptists. They've never met a Baptist minister or seen a Baptist church. How can you say that God would give them life just to damn them to hell without the chance of salvation?"

"God comes to everyone and whispers to them. If they haven't become a Baptist, it's because they've turned away from God."

"I'm sorry, Stacey, but that's just plain stupid. The majority of people around the globe are *not* Baptists. It's an American religion. If what you said was true and God is telling everyone they need to be baptized in your faith, there'd be a whole lot more Baptists all around the world."

"That just proves that God has blessed America above all nations."

"Come on, Stacey. Where do you get this stuff?"

"From my pastor."

"You should read more."

"Reading rots the mind and pollutes the soul."

"Wow, did your pastor tell you that too?"

"No, my stepdad did."

"I wouldn't start listening to him now. You never have before.

You'll end up just like him, ignorant as well as stupid. Aren't you the one who's always calling him the Great Moron?"

Annoyed, Stacey said, "I give up on you. If you want Satan to claim your soul, that's your business. Do this for me if you won't do it for yourself. Come on, Charlie, I am just asking you to say a few words and let the pastor dunk you in a pool. It don't hurt. They're doing a group baptism in two weeks. You can just pretend to be saved. It might even be fun. Please, do it for me."

"Pretend? Are you kidding me! Wouldn't that be a lie before God? I thought you said you wanted to save my soul. If anything, pretending won't secure my place in heaven but in hell."

"You won't be doing harm to anyone, and if you don't believe, it won't change anything."

"Level up with me, Stacey. What's really going on? Obviously, you're not worried about my eternal soul. What gives?"

"You want the truth?"

"Of course I do."

"Well, the pastor is having a sweepstakes. If you bring someone new to church, you get ten points. If you get them to come a second time, you get ten more. If you get them to accept Jesus as their personal savor and they get baptized you get a hundred points. At the end of July, whoever has the most points wins a brand-new color television set. You see, if you help me here and just get a little water over your head, you'd be helping me out big time."

"Stacey, you're my friend and I like you, but I could never

do that. If there is such a thing as sin, I am sure that would be included."

"Oh, come on, you're making way too much of this. I'd do it for you."

"I'd never ask."

CHAPTER FORTY

❧ ❖ ❧

VOICE

For my fourteenth birthday, I got a copy of Elton John's *Goodbye Yellow Brick Road* album and a work permit. From the day I landed my first real job, I've had one ever since. I started obsessively saving for a future I was determined to realize. With each paycheck, I allowed myself a small percentage for spending; the rest I put away in the bank. With babysitting money and from what I earned looking after people's pets, I had been buying my own clothes for some time. Now with a regular job, I felt I had grown another feather on my wings. When I had a bad day, I'd open my savings account book and dream of going to college and the new life that would bring. I wanted a life different from my parents'. What that was, I didn't know yet. Nevertheless, I knew I'd need money, good grades, and drive to make it happen.

I walked up to the local Peoples Drug Store. It was the first place I applied. There was a lunch counter off to one side, divided from the store by a partial wall. My timing was perfect; I walked in right after my predecessor had walked out. The manager said I had the job if I could start immediately. I took the apron from his extended hand, tied it around my waist, and got behind the counter. He pointed out a few things—how to use the soda machine, where to get more ice cream when I ran out, how the cash register worked—and introduced me to the short-order cook, Aaron.

Behind an opening in the wall was a small kitchen where Aaron flipped burgers and assembled club sandwiches. By trial and error, I learned to make ice cream floats and milkshakes in tall metal cups. Aaron and I would drink and eat up my mistakes. By looking at the picture on the menu, I learned how to make banana splits in long glass boats, and hot fudge sundaes topped with maraschino cherries that were stored in oversize gallon jars and floated in bright red syrup.

The earlier shift was far busier. Two waitresses, a cook, and a kitchen helper worked during the breakfast and lunch shift. At night, it was just the two of us. Aaron and I soon got into a groove and worked together well, without conflict or much comment. Often the last hour was very quiet, and we'd both sit and read, waiting for someone to come in or for closing time, whichever came first. After school started up, we would pull out our textbooks between customers and start on our homework. Often, it felt like it was our diner—our own private study hall. As long as the customers were happy and the register checked out, the manager didn't bother to come on our side of the half wall except to grab a soda or take the register drawer after we closed. Aaron and I didn't work together all the time. Sometimes a grumpy old man, George, worked the evening shift. Those were long nights.

The kitchen closed before the counter did. Aaron usually finished work about an hour earlier than I did, leaving me to stock up, clean up, and close out the register by myself. Some nights, I'd have a couple of closing-time customers who'd down an apple pie à la mode or some other dessert and a cup of burnt coffee, making me even later to get home. After we became friends, Aaron stayed and waited for me so he could walk me home. He didn't like the idea of me walking home after dark alone. He would sit quietly in the kitchen reading or working on his homework, waiting for me to finish up and clock out.

Aaron was two years older and a junior at Bladensburg High School, where I had just started attending as a sophomore. I didn't see him often at school. But when I did, we walked together. During those walks after work or at school, we talked, sang, laughed, and cried. We shared our dreams of college and a future filled with hope. Aaron was the oldest child and only son in his family. He had three half sisters and an alcoholic mother. He didn't even have a bed to himself. He slept on the sofa while his mom and sisters took the only bedroom. Despite his disadvantages, he had straight A's at school. Like me, he was determined to make something of himself and saw education as the key. He became my closest friend, confidant, role model, and first boyfriend.

We were both shy and innocent. Neither of us had ever had sex. I remembered my sister's warnings: "It only takes once, and you can say goodbye to your dreams." Sex was not in my immediate future, and Aaron respected that. We never did anything more than kiss or caress. Sometimes we'd sit on a bench with our heads together and talk away, trying to figure out the world and our place in it. Other times, we'd walk silently with our arms linked one over the other.

One crisp October night when leaves covered the sidewalks, we walked up the hill behind the shopping center where we worked. We were walking close to one another, but we weren't touching. We were lost in conversation when a sudden, short siren blast startled us into silence. We turned and were surprised to see a police officer charging out of his cruiser toward us. "Halt!" We heard him say, and we both froze.

Until that moment, I'd always seen the police as protectors. They were the ones who bravely patrolled our streets at night so we could walk unmolested or sleep safely in our beds. My parents taught me to obey and respect the police. So I couldn't fathom that he was coming for us.

He addressed me first. "What in the hell are you doing with that nigger?" he shouted in my face while pointing at Aaron. I was dumbfounded and didn't know how to respond. "Did you hear me ask you a question?"

"Yes sir. We're just walking. We just got off from work, and ..."

"Walking? At night with a nigger? Looks to me you've been doing a whole lot more than just walking, you little cunt," he said. I didn't know what that word meant, but instinctively I knew it was insulting and crude. He leaned in toward me; I could feel and smell his stale cigarette breath as he spoke. I'd never been more frightened. "How many times you spread your legs for that nigger? Well, I'm talking to you. What do you have to say for yourself?" I tried to reply, but I couldn't get my mind or tongue to work.

Just then, Aaron tried to say something, but the officer spun around and cut him off. "Did I say you could speak, boy?"

"No, sir."

"Then keep your fucking trap shut." He turned to me and commanded, "Don't you move." He grabbed Aaron's arm and marched him up the hill about fifteen feet or so and then slammed him hard into the chain-linked fence that separated the street from the backs of the stores. Its vibration moved down the fence and behind me. With his hand resting on his gun holster, he spoke to Aaron. I could only make out a few words of what the cop was saying here and there. I couldn't hear any of Aaron's replies. After a few minutes, the officer left Aaron standing against the fence and returned for me. As soon as he did, he stepped closer to me than he had been before. He placed his left hand on my breast, pushed me against the fence, and left his hand where it was, pinning me in place. I could feel the linked chains of the fence in my back. I looked up the hill toward Aaron, but he had turned his face away. Then the officer let loose a stream of vile accusations as to the sexual activities he imagined I did with Aaron. I didn't understand most of the terms he used, but I knew his words and his hand made me feel degraded, humiliated, and, most of all, terrified.

While I was silent and submissive, he continued his accusations, gropes, and threats. "Your own kind not good enough for you? You cheap piece of shit. I ought to take you somewhere and teach you a lesson." Unexpectedly, he asked the question that unleashed my tongue and gave me back my voice. "What would your parents say if they knew you were with that nigger?" Suddenly, without thinking, words started pouring out of my mouth like water from a broken dam.

"Aaron works for my dad," I lied. "My dad sent Aaron to escort me home—safely." I emphasized the last word. He pulled back from me just a bit. Feeling the power of my lies, I rambled on, "Do you know my daddy, Mr. Ward? Most people around here do." For once, I was glad of my father's reputation of being a quick-tempered and large man. "If you are around here much, you must know my daddy, Jack Ward. He is big, tall, got an awful temper."

The officer pulled further away, and his pinning hand dropped to his side. I found greater courage. "We live just around the corner at 5605." He stepped back still more and looked up the hill a moment. "Daddy gets crazy mad if I am late."

I could see the doubt flash for a moment in the cop's eyes;

so, in an instant, I decided to take a chance. "If we don't show up quick, my father will be out here looking for us." With real panic in my eyes and voice, I added, "He's going to kill me if we're late."

Gratefully, I heard a distant car approaching, and the cop pulled even further away from me. When the officer turned to look in the direction of the sound, I turned in the opposite direction toward Aaron. "I have to go!" I yelled over my shoulder at the cop and didn't wait for permission. I marched up the hill as the car was passing. I didn't recognize it, but I gave a silent thanks to the unknown driver.

When I reached Aaron, I whispered, "Let's go, now!" I didn't dare reach out to grab his arm as I wanted to, but he started moving without any further encouragement. Together we walked rapidly toward the top of the hill. We fully expected to hear "Halt!" once more but didn't.

Once we turned the corner to my street and were out of sight of the cop, we both took off running. We ran the entire block and a half home. Looking back, I shudder to think what might have happened that night if I hadn't found my voice.

I told another lie that night because I didn't want Aaron to walk home alone. When we got in the front door, Mamma and Daddy wanted to know why we were both out of breath and trembling. "You both look as if you've seen a ghost. What's going on?" Daddy asked suspiciously. I knew if I told my father the truth, he would go out looking for that police officer with murder in his eyes. He'd take me in tow to identify our tormentor. As much as I hated that police officer, I wasn't prepared for that kind of confrontation and possible aftermath. I was afraid of what my father might do and the consequences of those actions. Instead, I told him there had been a gang of racist boys who had chased us home. That was why we were out of breath and why it was too dangerous for Aaron to walk through our neighborhood alone. Thankfully, Daddy drove him home. After that, I was afraid for Aaron and wouldn't let him walk me home after work anymore. He protested, but not for long. We both dreamed of a world that would leave us be. It hurt his pride that he was unable to protect me when I walked home alone at night. It hurt us both that such gallant intentions would put us both in danger.

CHAPTER FORTY-ONE

୨୦ ❖ ଓ

LOOKING THROUGH CRACKS

*A*unt Charlotte had arrived for a weeklong visit. The next morning when I got up to go to school, she was still asleep. Daddy was late leaving for the yard and was still drinking his coffee at the table when I came down the stairs.

"Good God, girl. Is that getup what you think you're wearing to school? You look like you're ready to walk up to a soup kitchen. Lord, you look destitute in those patched-up dungarees. I won't have you shamin' us wearin' them rags."

"Daddy, it's the fashion. Everyone's wearing this style. These are my favorite jeans." I had sewn a peace symbol patch on my left thigh, another patch on my rear pocket, and wide embroidered ribbon along the bottom to make them longer so they would drag the ground. The ribbon was starting to fray. They were perfect and the coolest garment I owned.

"I don't care. You look pitiful."

"But everyone is dressing like this."

"If everyone jumps off a cliff are you gonna follow them?

"If I dress up to school like I am going to church everyone will make fun of me."

"Charlie, I won't have my daughter lookin' like some kinda bum. Do you hear me?"

"Daddy, please. 'The times they are a-changin," I quoted.

"Not in this house. Now get upstairs and put on somethin' decent. I want to see you wearing a skirt. You're a girl and can dress like one."

"Oh, Daddy." And with that I ran upstairs. After school when I got home, I was still angry. Aunt Charlotte and Daddy were talking at the dinner table and sipping iced teas. When I came in I greeted her warmly, gave her a hug, said I had some homework to do, and ran upstairs without saying a word to my father. A while later, there was a knock on my door.

"Who is it?" I asked through the door.

Aunt Charlotte opened the door and peeked in. "It's me, honey, may I come in?"

"Of course."

"Charlie, honey, I want to ask you something," she said as she took a seat on the side of my bed. "I want to know what in the world is going on with you two."

"What do you mean?" I shrugged.

"Now don't try to hide from your old Aunt Charlotte. I mean

you two used to be like two peas in a pod and now you hardly speak to one another."

"Who?"

"Don't play dumb. Now, who'd ya think?"

"Daddy?"

"Sweet child, don't you know that you can hide the fire, but the smoke still gonna show. Who else? Now you tell me what's goin' on between the two of you."

"There's nothing,"

Aunt Charlotte tilted her head and looked straight at me. "It don't look like a mess of nothin' to me, child."

"I don't know. It's just gotten difficult to talk to him. He flies off the handle at every little thing."

"Like what things."

"Like this morning. Like how I dress. Everyone is wearing blue jeans, miniskirts, and halter tops, but he wants me to dress like it is still the 1950s."

"Well, I'd have to agree with your daddy there. What I see girls wearin' these days leaves little to the imagination. A young lady shouldn't be wearin' the same outfit you'd find on a streetwalking hussy. It gives the boys the wrong idea. In my opinion, halter tops or miniskirts shouldn't be allowed in schools. It's cruel on the boys. Darlin', no matter what they tell you, men are the weaker sex. Show a young man a bit too much of your God-given womanly gifts and all the wires in their little brains combust. It's hard enough on the boys to concentrate on learnin' without a pretty young thing like yourself walking around in some skimpy outfit. Believe me, child. If you go to class wearin' one of them halter tops that show your midriff and frame your cleavage, the boys will think you're offerin' them jugs up like menu items. If you don't want to be treated like a hussy, then don't dress like one. Dressin' modest is a way to show the boys you respect yourself and that you won't let them disrespect you."

"Okay, I get it. No hot pants, miniskirts, and halter tops. Daddy won't let me wear a dress or skirt above my knees, but he'll let me wear shorts all summer long. They must be no shorter than mid-thigh, but that's shorter than my skirts. What's the sense in that? I was wearing blue jeans this morning, and he made me change them. Jeans cover more than a skirt. All the kids are wearing blue jeans, Aunt Charlotte. I am a freak at school. Kids make fun of the way I dress. I can't afford to wear all the latest fashions. I saved up for some jeans, and now he won't let me wear them. If I can't at least wear blue jeans, I'll be the laughing stock of the school. Please, Aunt Charlotte, he'll listen to you. At least get him to allow me to wear blue jeans and T-shirts too. They're not church clothes, but they're not indecent. Please, I am desperate."

"I don't know about sticking my nose into it."

"No disrespect, Aunt Charlotte, but haven't you already put your nose in by coming up here? Now I am asking for your help. He listens to you."

"I don't know," she shrugged. "If I feel the timing is right, I will try to get him to agree to blue jeans, but no miniskirts, okay?"

"Okay," I replied.

"Is that it then, between you two?"

"That's it. Well, no, there are other things too."

"Like what?"

"Why doesn't he want Mamma to work outside of the house? For a long time now, Mamma has wanted to get a job. There have been times we really could have used the extra cash, that's for sure. Here's Mamma with over two years of college taking in washing. Why is it better that she washes and irons other people's clothes rather than work in a hospital? Why's that? She could earn a lot more. Wouldn't he like a partner when it comes to earning money?"

"He's worked hard so that your mama could stay home with you young ones. I agree with that too. Children need their mama to look after them."

"But we are old enough now to look after ourselves."

"I don't know why, honey, other than he doesn't want his wife to have to work outside the home. He's got his own reasons. He's a proud man, your daddy."

"There's more to it. Sometimes everything is going great and then I say or do something that upsets him, and it sets him off, and I don't even know what it is I've done wrong. He won't say. For example, one time, Mamma sent me up to her room to get something from a drawer, but I opened the wrong one by mistake.

In the one I opened, I saw an old photograph of a lady. I brought it down and asked him who she was, and he blew up. Another time, Emma sent us a color photograph of herself and her family and that got me thinking, from whom in the family did she get her red hair? I asked him if someone in his family had red hair, and he got mad. Why, what made him the way he is? If I understood that, it would make it easier. At least I'd know where the land mines are and could avoid setting him off."

"Honey, now, don't try to rake up the family secrets of every sausage you eat."

"What's that supposed to mean? You and Daddy, always talking in Southern riddles."

"It means that you mustn't be digging in the past. Some things are better left buried."

"I don't agree with that notion. If we don't understand why, we are left to imagine, and that can be destructive. I don't understand him. Sometimes he talks about his childhood as a place of love, carefree days, and music. Other times, it's as if it's a dark nightmare that haunts his days.

"It can be both," my aunt mumbled.

"Aunt Charlotte, sometimes we'll be having a nice chat, getting along just fine, and suddenly he clams up and gets all sullen. Like when I ask him how his mama or his uncle, your daddy, died, he just says, 'It was the Depression,' like it was some fatal disease."

"It was a fatal disease for thousands of folks. Some died quick, others took longer."

"Like your daddy?"

"Yes, like my daddy."

"Tell me about him."

"Why you wanna know such stuff, child? Sometimes it's better to let them sleepin' hounds lie."

"No, Aunt Charlotte, the silence is poisoning the atmosphere around here. There are a lot of secrets lying around this house, and they fester. Without even meaning to, it feels like we knock into these secrets like stumbling on a hornet's nest. If I knew where they were, maybe I could avoid them. Or at least understand why Daddy reacts the way he does. I love my daddy, but I don't understand him, and it's driving us apart."

"Honey, it may be best to cut your own weeds and leave your daddy's alone."

"Why won't you tell me? It would help me understand."

"Some secrets aren't mine to tell. Oh, child, you don't know."

"That's just it—I don't know what, Aunt Charlotte?"

"You want to know what happened to my daddy?"

"Yes, I do."

"Well, he shot himself. Is that what you wanted to hear?"

"Oh, my God. I am sorry, Aunt Charlotte. Sweet Jesus, that must have been awful for you. I am so sorry. What made him do it?"

"Depression."

"Now you sound like Daddy. A lot of folks went through the Depression and they didn't all kill themselves."

"No, not *the* Depression, just plain ol' depression. It was many things that just wore him out."

"Was he always depressed?"

"No, even during much of the Depression, he was happy, or at least content. I guess you could say that all our sorrows started five years before my daddy killed hisself. It started when my brother, Rudy, died. Before that, we was poor like everyone else, but we were happy enough. We had each other, a roof over our heads, and for the most part, enough food. Our clothes were threadbare, but so too were the clothes of most of the folks we knew. The good thing about everyone around you being poor is it doesn't seem like any great tragedy—it's just life, and life's a struggle."

"What was Rudy like? Daddy always starts grinning when someone mentions his name."

"Rudy was perfect in every way. He was just too good for this Earth, and that's the truth. God called him home early. Do you know he was named after an old-time film star, Rudolph Valentino? Mamma loved them movie pictures, went ever' chance she got, which wasn't often enough for her tastes."

"In what ways was Rudy perfect?"

"To start with, he was the most beautiful boy you'd ever seen. If Michelangelo had met my brother, he'd of painted him on top of that Sixteenth Chapel over there in Italy. When God made him, he took the best bits from our family. Mamma was a beauty; everyone said so. But Rudy looked like an angel sent down from heaven. He had my mama's full lips, Granddad's thick, wavy hair, and Daddy's big blue eyes, only lighter. When he spoke to you it was like you were the most important person in the whole world to him. He made you better just knowing him. He could look inside you and see only your best parts, and you just didn't want to disappoint him.

"His were the lightest blue eyes I'd ever seen. They looked as though there were tiny lights shining from inside. His voice, oh, it was smooth as honey and just as sweet. His voice would pierce through the chorus at church like it was coming from an angel. Your brother Eugene reminds me of him a bit. It's not just his good looks, but it's the way he moves all graceful like a cat. It may be hard to believe, but Rudy was far more handsome than your brother. He'd take your breath away. Everyone loved Rudy.

"I should've been jealous of him. I'd hear folks say, 'It's a shame the girl didn't get more of her brother's good looks.' But Rudy was kind and generous. He seemed not to know folks thought he was special. When he was fourteen, he got a job over at the general store in Winton on Saturdays. I think old Mr. Thorton hired Rudy just so all the girls and ladies would come by to do their shoppin' with him instead of drivin' into Ahoskie to shop at Gerock's or some other store.

"Each week after gettin' paid, Rudy would bring me home

something. Sometimes it was a piece of candy, or a hair ribbon. Once he got me a Japanese fan. I loved that fan—still have it. I used to open and close it, over and over, to look at the pretty birds and flowers that are painted on it. Took it every Sunday in summer to church. Now I keep it safe in a drawer so nothin' will happen to it. He'd bring movie magazines home to Mamma and give her the rest of the money he earned. One time, he took us all out to go see a movie, *The Virginians*, with Gary Cooper. I fell in love with Gary Cooper watchin' that movie.

"I could go on and on. He ran as graceful as a deer, played basketball and baseball at school. When he died, it took all the light out of my parents. There was never any more laughter in that house once he was in that eternity box and six feet down. I still miss him. I miss him more than either of my folks, though I miss them too."

"What happened to your mom? I heard she ran off."

"Yeah. She went up to Winston-Salem to stay with her sister Coralee. She said she had to get away for a spell. She said everything at home reminded her of Rudy. While up there she met a man. Mamma always wanted to go to Hollywood in California, and this man promised to take her. So she up and left us. For years, we didn't know what happened to her for sure. Her sister got a couple of postcards from her. I never did. That hurt me real good. It was like she forgot she had another child. Like I didn't matter. If it hadn't been for my Aunt Sarah, your granny, and my Grandma

406

Rose, I don't know what I'd of done. They were real good to me. Like I was their own all along."

"When Daddy heard she run off, he took off after them. He was gone for close to three years. He worked odd jobs and sent back what he could. He never told me if he found them. He just showed up back home. I never moved back in with him. I stayed at the big house with Grandma Rose and your daddy's folks."

"How did Rudy die?"

"Meningitis what killed him, but it ain't how he died. One Saturday, he came home from work and said he had a headache and stiff neck. Mamma touched his forehead and said he had a bit of a fever. She sent him to bed thinking it was a touch of the influenza. The next morning, Mamma went in Rudy's room to check on him. When she opened the curtains letting in the sunlight, he started cryin' somethin' awful. When I came into the room, he was talking gibberish, his eyes were glazin' over. 'For long he started havin' trouble breathing. He was suckin' in big gasps of breath. I got so frightened. Mamma told me to go get Daddy. Daddy came in and lifted him up like he weighed nothin' and carried him to the truck. Mamma and him drove Rudy up to the hospital. They told me to go to your daddy's house and tell Aunt Sarah and the family what was goin' on and to stay with them.

"My folks didn't get back home until late the next mornin'. But they came home without Rudy. Just like that … Saturday morning he seemed fine, by Monday he was gone. You never know what's comin' for ya, that's for sure."

"Six months later, Mamma left, and right after that Daddy followed. We got envelopes from him from time to time with money and short notes. He never was a man of many words. Ma did most of the talkin' in our house. We got letters from places with strange names like Dubuque, Las Cruces, and Yorba Linda. But later we got envelopes with money but no letters at all from places like Spokane and Boise. By then I don't think he was lookin' for Mamma anymore. I thought I'd never see either of them again. One afternoon, it was early fall, Grandma and I were sittin' on the front stoop shuckin' peas for cannin' when way down yonder I seen a man walkin' down our road toward the house. I asked Grandma Rose if she was 'spectin' company. She looked up to see what I was lookin' at. Even with her old eyes she knew straight off who it was. 'Best set another plate for supper,' she told me, 'your pa's come home.'"

Aunt Charlotte took a breath, then sat silently for a bit. Anxious to keep her talking, I asked, "Then what happened?"

"I don't know. My daddy was just never the same. He had me stay over at Grandma Rose's place. I was glad of it. Cousin Ida was gone to Texas by then. I slept in her old room. It'd been so long since my daddy had been gone that livin' at the big house was home to me. He stayed alone in our old house. It was just 'cross the road that went through our farm. He'd come over for meals, bring his laundry over to get washed, but he wouldn't say much.

I couldn't get him to talk about all the places he'd seen, though I tried. Couldn't get him to talk about farmin' 'cept what needed sayin'. We tried, but he just wanted to be left alone. So, that's what he got."

Aunt Charlotte took another deep breath, then went on. "One day, your daddy and I were playing a game of hide-n-go seek. I was sixteen, almost seventeen and your daddy was about nine. We headed down toward the dryin' barns. There's an old pecan tree behind the barns about twenty feet away. Leaning against that tree, we'd cover our eyes and count to a hundred before we shouted, 'Ready or not, here I come.' It was my turn to hide. Jack started countin', and I took off for one of the old sharecroppers' cabins. No one had lived in them regular for years. Still, sometimes we'd hire some extra help during the harvestin' and tobacca dryin' season and the extra help would stay in one of the old cabins for a few weeks.

"The cabin, not much more than a shack, really, stood up on some posts and stones. You could crawl clear underneath it. The floorboards, more like planks, had gaps in between them so you could peek up through the floor. When the afternoon sun came pouring in, lighting up the room, you could spy on the folks inside. I crawled under that old shack knowing your daddy was scared to go under it, so I figured it'd be a good hidin' place." Aunt Charlotte sat quietly for a while until I thought she wasn't going to continue. But then she took a deep breath, let it go, and went on, her voice a bit softer.

"I wasn't under it long before I heard the door squeak open. I thought it was your daddy lookin' for me at first. It didn't take me long to figure it wasn't young Jackson's footsteps I was hearing. These were too heavy. I peered up and could just make out a pair of old clodhoppers."

"What's a clodhopper?"

"That's the kind of boot farmers wore back then." She let out a long sigh before continuing, "Anyway, I heard a chair drag across the floor, then a plop as he sat down. I was trying to figure out if it was my daddy, Uncle Wyatt, or some hobo lookin' for a place to sleep. Those boots were about all I could make out and they were real common. He just sat there all quiet. I don't know why, but I was afraid, so I waited real still like and watched. He was just sittin', not movin'. But all of a sudden, he let out a long sigh, dropped a shotgun butt to the floor right above me, and said, 'Lord, forgive me.' The words no more than left his lips when I heard the close report of a shotgun going off, followed by a thud as he fell to the floor. The sound was ringing in my ears—I just froze. It all happened so fast. I guess I was in shock or somethin'. I couldn't move a muscle. I don't know if I drew a breath. It weren't long 'fore I felt something warm drip through the floorboard gaps, but still I couldn't move.

"Gradually, I 'came aware of young Jackson crying out, 'What happened, Charlotte, you all right?' His voice got louder as he got closer. His voice is what woke me up. It woke me like an electric shock. I had to protect little Jackson. In an instant, I knew I had to stop him from goin' in that cabin. I crawled out fast and screamed at him to not come any closer.

"I frightened him—I had never yelled at him like that before. 'Don't move,' I shouted toward him. Quickly, I ran up the porch and took a look inside to confirm my fears. It was my daddy, all right. I'd thought it was when I heard him speak, but I needed to be sure. I knew straight off it was him from his clothes, though there weren't much left of his head."

"Oh, my God, Aunt Charlotte. How horrible for you." I went to her, wrapped my arms around her, and kissed her cheek. When I released her I asked, "Did Daddy see what was inside?"

"No, sweet pea, I made sure of it. I ran off that porch, grabbed his arm, and dragged him home. He saw the blood that had dripped onto my forehead, but I told him it weren't mine. Telling Uncle Wyatt was the hardest thing I'd ever had to do, 'cept burying Rudy maybe."

"I am so, so sorry, Aunt Charlotte. What a horrible thing for a young woman to go through. You're incredible and so strong. Despite what you've been through, you're a, kind, positive, and, well, normal person."

"I wouldn't go so far as callin' me normal," she joked. "Honey, you know that old sayin', 'If'n it don't break you, it'll make you stronger'?"

"Yes, it's from Friedrich Nietzsche. It's one of my favorites.

It goes, 'That which does not kill you will make you stronger,'" I informed her.

"Who said it?

"Friedrich Nietzsche. He was a German philosopher."

"You learn that in school?"

"I like to read a lot. Actually, it was Eugene who turned me on to reading Nietzsche."

"Well, there is a whole lot of truth in it. I did a lot of growin' up in that moment. Every day since that one has been a better day. If you live through somethin' like that, you know you can live through 'bout anythin'. But you gotta decide if it's going to make you or break you. Bad times like that don't make your heart stop tickin', but you gotta decide to go on livin'. And that's what I've tried to do. I am grateful every day I can get up and outta bed and my family can do the same. If you have that, you got nothin' to complain about and a whole lot to thank the good Lord for."

We sat there, each lost in thought for a few minutes until I broke the silence.

"Aunt Charlotte?"

"Yes, baby."

"What happened to Daddy's mama? Why won't Daddy talk of it?"

"Holy Baby Jesus, honey, sometimes recallin' bad times is just too hard. Maybe that's how it is for your pa. It done wore me out. When you bring up an old memory, it can be like you livin' it again.

Some wounds are harder to heal. There's no sense in scratchin' at an old wound and makin' it bleed all over again. Now, that's enough remembering for one day, and even so, that tale ain't mine to tell. You best let that one be."

"That's what you always say."

"Then why do ya keep askin'?"

CHAPTER FORTY-TWO

❧ ✦ ☙

LAWN MAIL

*A*t the start of the school year, there was a lot of talk about busing. Near the end of the semester there were rallies protesting busing. One Friday there were so few students left after lunch that we were told to go home or go to study hall to wait for the afternoon buses. Out on the football field, there were people with megaphones chanting, "Hell no, we won't go." The pro-busing or indifferent kids watched from the bleachers. Both on the field and in the bleachers, it felt more like a party atmosphere than a serious protest. That is, except for the loudest protesters, who had gathered around a table near the field's eastern exit. Over the table was a red, white, and black banner with the American and Confederate flags across it. Between the flags was a cross. Strewn over these symbols were the words KU KLUX KLAN in red lettering. Men stood around the table and handed out flyers. According to rumors they weren't local people; they'd come from out of state to try to halt busing in Prince George's County.

Early the following Monday when I left the house for school, our entire front yard was covered in white pamphlets. I picked one up to examine it. I didn't have to see or read much before I ripped it to shreds. I walked into the house to get a trash bag and came out and started to pick them all up. Just then, Mamma came out.

"What's this?" she asked, confused.

"Hate mail," I said. "Looks like we had a visit from the Ku Klux Klan."

"*What?*" With that she picked one up. "Oh, sweet Jesus. This is vile, sick. It's vulgar. We had better get them picked up before your father sees them. He'll blow a fuse."

On some of the pamphlets there were ink drawings that were supposed to be Black people. They looked more of a cross between a human and chimpanzee. One slogan read "Fight for your land and join the Klan." But it wasn't just Blacks they were attacking. There were cartoons of what were supposed to be Jews: short people with big noses. I even found one that warned about Roman Catholics. It had a drawing of what looked to be an inebriated leprechaun. "Jesus, Mary, Joseph, and all the saints," I said, imitating an Irish accent. "Look, Mamma, this one is addressed to you." I held it out and she took it. On the last page was the cartoon and a warning about Catholics' allegiance to Rome.

"May they all rot in hell," Mamma cursed. After we got every pamphlet picked up and in the trash bin, I said, "Mamma,

I want to thank you."

"It's my lawn too."

"No, not for helping me pick up the lawn, but for not being a bigot, and not raising me to hate anyone just because they're not like us. Most of all, thank you for being nice to Aaron."

"Charlie, Aaron is a real nice boy. He has a fine character, and I am glad you two are friends, but I hope that is what you remain, just friends."

"What if we are more than just friends?"

She took my hand and led me to the front porch.

"Sit," she commanded. After I sat down, she joined me on the stoop. "Honey, the world is not what we'd have it be, but we have to live in it. It's okay that you two keep company, but I don't want you to think I'd want you marrying a colored man. I have nothing against coloreds. They're the same as any of us. Some are good and some are bad. God made us all different, but we are all God's children. Do we love one child more than another? No! Like the coloreds, the Irish have known horrible suffering because of bigotry and ignorance. It's not because he's colored that I object. It's the world I fear, and I have good reasons. Marriage is hard enough without everyone around you trying to tear you apart. Even if you loved each other deeply, your marriage would be difficult. He wouldn't get jobs or promotions because his wife is White. People would not rent or sell a house to you because you're mixed. People who you thought were your friends will turn their back on you, and not just Whites but coloreds too. People from both races will despise you. People can be very ugly and even violent. It would be just the two of you against the entire world. But that is nothing compared to what your children would endure. Think about that. Maybe someday, honey, people will leave their bigotries behind, but that day is a very long way off."

"Mamma, I hear what you say, but things are changing now. If Dr. King, Medgar Evers, and Bobby Kennedy have been the generals in this war, then maybe interracial couples are the soldiers who will make the change happen. You once told me—and I still remember it to this day—that people fear what they don't understand and hate what they fear. Segregation has kept us apart from understanding each other's cultures. With busing, my generation will have the chance to get to know one another. Some will even fall in love. We are all Americans, but we are living as two separate peoples, and that can't continue. If there were more interracial families, then people who once hated Blacks or Whites would have a niece, nephew, or grandchild who's mixed. Some would turn them out, but others would learn to love them. Maybe that is how the change will come. By mixing families, we become one people."

"Charlie, dear, change may be coming, but it is not coming that fast. Let me point out that the generals you mentioned in your supposed revolution are all dead, murdered. You could never live in a small town or in the South, or you could easily share their fates. Whomever you choose, Charlie, I will try to love him for your sake. But think before you give your heart away. Be very careful, honey. It's a dangerous world."

"I don't want these evil-minded people who put these flyers on our yard to win, but I think you'd better cool it when it comes to Aaron. Just until this busing business is finished, and these hooligans move on. Your friendship with Aaron is probably why they've targeted our house. They're a murderously hateful lot. Don't doubt that they'll do more than drop flyers on our lawn. Don't think of just yourself either—think of Aaron. How would you feel if something horrible happened to him? Will you do that, Charlotte? Will you keep your distance for a while? You can talk all you want on the phone, but publicly, keep your distance. Okay?"

I hated it, but I saw her wisdom. It was true; I would feel horrible if something awful befell Aaron. I knew that although my danger was real, his was greater. "Yes, Mamma, until things die down, we'll cool it."

Relieved, Mamma added, "The times maybe changing, Charlie, but it takes time to travel such a wide distance, and it will take more than just one more generation, I fear."

"A generation? I don't think Blacks are willing to wait another lifetime for equality, or should. But in any case, Mamma, I don't have any intention of marrying young. I want a chance to find out who I am, and what I can do on my own. But I think at some point in my life I will want to marry or at least find a partner. When that happens, I hope to be guided by my heart and not by my fears.

I want to find someone who is a kindred spirit even if he is not from the same country, culture, race, or religion. The times may be changing faster than you might think."

Just then we heard Daddy calling from inside the house.

"Maggie, where are you, Maggie?"

"We're out front, Jack. We'll be right in," she called back to him. "Well, I am heartened to hear that you plan on waiting until you are much older. Let's hope by the time you're ready to find your, what did you call him, kindred spirit, that this is a new world. Let's hope you're right. But if it's not a new world, think before you act, and think about what I've said, my dear. Be careful. Be very careful."

"Maggie!" came Daddy's call from within the house.

"We best go in," I said.

Just then the front door swung open behind us. "What are you two doing out here?" Daddy asked.

"Just talking, mother-daughter stuff."

"If you're finished, I'm hungry. I'd like some breakfast if you can spare the time."

"Yes, Jack, I'm coming." With that we stood up and Daddy headed back inside. Spontaneously, we both reached out and hugged each other before reentering the house.

CHAPTER FORTY-THREE

AGNES AND THE RISE OF FEMINISM

*L*andover Mall opened with much fanfare and anticipation. It was the first enclosed shopping mall in Prince George's County and the largest in the region. Finally, we didn't have to leave the county to shop at a Hecht's or Garfinkel's. I heard the Woodward & Lothrop store jingle playing for weeks on the radio: "Make your world beautiful at Woodies."

For neighborhood kids like me, it meant a boom in employment opportunities. On the Saturday before the mall was scheduled to open, I, along with hundreds of others, spent a day filling out job applications. In the mall's basement, the area's first multiplex cinema house was getting ready to open. They had eight movie theaters. The day after I dropped off my application, I got a call offering me a job with AMC theaters. The biggest perk of the job was that family members got in to the movies for free, which thrilled Buddy. After I started working there, we had a weekly family night out at the movies. Afterward we often stopped off at Farrell's Ice Cream Parlour and shared a couple of 75-cent hot fudge sundaes. While it lasted, it brought us closer.

One evening I sat embarrassed as Mamma cried during *Fiddler on the Roof.* I first heard her sniffling when Hodel, the second daughter, boarded a train for Siberia. She looked sadly at her father, Tevye, and said, "Papa! God alone knows when we shall see each other again."

When Tevye responded, "Then we will leave it in His hands," that's when Mamma audibly lost it. On our way home that night, we teased her about it until she shared with us that the scene made her think about Emma.

While I worked there, Buddy watched *American Graffiti* five times. I bought him the album for his birthday, and he played it incessantly. Providing entertainment for my family was a perk, but the pay wasn't. Because movie theaters sold food like restaurants, they were permitted to pay less than the $1.60 per hour minimum wage. Counter help was paid $1.40 per hour; projectionists were paid $1.80. When I was hired, I was told that after a few months if I worked hard, I would be promoted to projectionist. Slowly I realized that only boys got to be projectionists, many of whom were hired after me. After one of the boys messed up loading the film into the projector for the third time, I confronted the assistant manager.

"Excuse me, Mr. Cowens. May we talk?"

"About what, Charlotte?"

"Remember when you hired me, you told me that if I worked hard, I could become a projectionist."

"Did I? I don't remember that."

"Well, you most definitely did. I told you then that the salary was too low and that's when you said after a few months I could be promoted. I've worked hard, a lot harder than some of the birdbrains you've made projectionists. The Saturday that Hurricane Agnes came through, I was the only one who showed up on time. Remember? I had to wait for you to open the doors."

"Now, that I remember."

"I've been on time for every shift, my cash register is always correct, and I leave the counters clean and well stocked. So what gives?"

"You have to wait your turn."

"I've waited. My turn has come and gone several times over. You made Andy and Mark projectionists, and they were hired long after me. You promised. It's only fair that you promote me."

"I can't do that."

"How come?"

"It's company policy. It comes from headquarters in Kansas City."

"Company policy about what?"

"Only boys can be in the projection rooms."

"That's not fair, and you never told me that."

"It's the unofficial policy. I couldn't tell you. I shouldn't have now, but I like you. What does it matter? I can't make you a projectionist. There's nothing I can do about it."

"So you lied to me."

"We were shorthanded then. I was under pressure to staff the theater."

"You admit it—you lied to me."

"I'm sorry."

"You're sorry? Well, I quit."

I got angrier and more indignant as I rode my bike home that afternoon. I thought about what Emma had told me about Gloria Steinem. She said Ms. Steinem had said that sex and race were easy, visible differences used to organize human beings into inferior groups for cheap labor. I didn't like being on the short end of that selection system. I was furious by the time I stormed through our front door. Buddy was in the living room watching TV. Furious, I told him what had happened. I was surprised and upset by his reaction. "That was no reason to quit. Can't you go back and apologize?"

"Apologize! For what?" I barked.

"Come on, Charlotte, I've got plans. I'm meeting Perry and Chuck tonight. They haven't seen *American Graffiti* yet. You and your temper just ruined my plans," he added bitterly.

"But my boss lied to me, Buddy."

"So what? People lie all the time. You can't go off half-cocked every time someone lies to you, especially when that person is your boss."

"But they pay the boys more than the girls even when we do a better job. That's not fair."

"Fair? Shoot, that's just life. Whoever told you life's fair? You best better get over that notion right quick. Not even God made us all equal. Some are healthier, smarter, better looking or born rich. Fair? Girl, life ain't never been fair. Get over it."

"I'm not getting over it, and I'm not going back there. I guess you'll have to pay for your own stinking ticket like everyone else then," came my retort.

From the kitchen, Mamma overheard our argument and butted in. "Charlotte, Buddy's got a point. You shouldn't let your temper get ahead of you. Next time you quit a job, make sure you have another one lined up first. Otherwise, you're only hurting yourself. You worked there for a while and now because of your temper you won't get a good reference. No employer will hire someone who quits without notice. And that theater will go on with or without you. They won't change their policies because you think them unfair. You've only hurt yourself."

"And me too," interjected Buddy.

"Quiet, Buddy. You're not helping now," Mamma said.

"But Mamma," I complained. Buddy's got a job at the Shell station paying a buck ninety-five an hour just for filling up gas tanks and washing windshields. All I want is to be paid the same. I work just as hard. His job doesn't require any special skills."

"Charlotte, honey, Buddy is right about one thing. You'll be much happier if you accept that life isn't always fair."

"Mamma, the world won't change unless we fight for it. I don't care what that old ninny Phyllis Schlafly and her kind says or does, the Equal Rights Amendment will get passed. One day women will get paid the same as men, and get the same job opportunities too."

"Oh, honey, that sounds grand, but with less than three percent of the Congress being women, men still rule the world. People don't let go of power without a fight."

"Yeah, I know. I read the paper same as you. I've been following the news about the Amendment."

"Why do you think so few women are in Congress? Tell me, if half of voters are women, how come there isn't a single female governor? You can forget about ever seeing a woman in the White House; a Black man has a better chance than a woman and a Black man's chance is about nil. The ERA won't get passed any time soon. Right or wrong, men feel that because we give birth, we can't do the same jobs as they can. That's just how the world works, and no matter how angry you get about it, it won't change. All you'll do is get yourself upset and depressed."

"Mamma, didn't you tell me that no one will respect me if I don't first respect myself? That's what I am trying to do here. We women have to respect ourselves and believe in our own abilities first before we can demand respect from men."

"Charlie, maybe if you live long enough you'll live to see

equality for all, but in the meantime, you have to get along. You're young; you want change right away. As you get older you'll realize that, despite our best efforts, the wheels of change move painstakingly slow and even move backward sometimes. If you don't accept the limits of our sex, you'll just drive yourself crazy. Trust me—I know. Tell me, if you were deaf, you'd accept your limitation and learn sign language, wouldn't you?"

"I'd have to, but this isn't quite the same, Mamma."

"Yes, it is. Women have limitations in this world. That's a fact. We must accept these limitations to get along. If you want to be happy, Charlotte, let it go."

"Mamma, sometimes the wheels of change need a push, and for us to believe that change is possible. Look at what we did in getting a man on the moon. That happened relatively fast once we believed it could happen."

"Yes, dear, but it was still a man who walked on the moon."

When Daddy got home, he said nearly the same thing, though he added that motherhood was the path to fulfillment for a woman. I responded, "I'm looking for a different path to fulfillment, Daddy."

"Honey child, women are needed more in the home than in the workforce. It's a dog-eat-dog world, and you're better off not having to be a part of it. Don't deny your womanly nature. In the Good Book it says, 'Her children rise up and call her blessed; her husband also, and he praises her.' You should be proud of your womanly role. You have the responsibility of raising the next generation. What's more important than that?"

"Daddy, cows can reproduce and raise their young. I want to do more than what a cow can do."

"Can a cow teach its calf to write? Don't be selling your gender short and don't be putting down motherhood. There's a lot more to raising children than just giving them nourishment and protection. You'll find in Proverbs, 'She opens her mouth with wisdom, and the teaching of kindness is on her tongue. She looks well to the ways of her household and does not eat the bread of idleness.' You're no cow, and your mama ain't one neither. You show some respect for the profession of motherhood. That's what your mama is."

"I respect her, Daddy. I know she works hard and makes lots of sacrifices for us. But I still just want to have a choice. I want to be treated equally. What is wrong with that?"

"Child, it's the nature of the world you've got to accept. Now, you can learn the easy way or the hard way. That's your choice. Fish ain't gonna start flyin' in the air just 'cause you want them to, and birds aren't gonna make their homes in the sea. Men can't bring forth babies. Girls become women, women become mothers. Children need raisin'."

"Why can't I do both?"

"'Cause your children would suffer."

"Maybe I don't even want children."

"Not now. But you won't be able to deny your nature. Someday you'll want kids of your own."

"Time will tell."

"So, I guess we'll have to wait. In the meantime, learn to get along in this world and accept your lot in life."

The next morning, I went out looking for work, determined to find something other than waitressing and something that paid a fair wage. I wanted to prove to my parents that the world was changing. While riding my bike, I spied a help wanted sign asking for a gas attendant, paying two bucks an hour. It was prominently displayed in the Mobil gas station window on Route 450. Behind the counter was a guy wearing blue overalls, and I asked him if I could speak to the manager. He went into the garage and came back a minute later with another man.

"Hi, I'm Eddie, the manager, what can I do for you, miss?"

"Good morning, sir. I'm looking for work. You have a help wanted sign in your window."

"Sorry, I don't need a cashier. Like the sign says, we're looking for a gas attendant."

"Exactly. I can pump gas. My dad's a mechanic. I've been around cars all my life. I can check people's oil and clean their windows, and I am dependable," I offered eagerly.

"Well, that position's been filled."

"But a moment ago you said—"

"I know what I said, young lady. Now, I don't have anything for you."

"But, but, I am confused. Don't you need a gas attendant? I can do the job and—"

"I've already told you. I don't have nothing for your kind."

"Excuse me, what kind is that?" I asked, genuinely perplexed.

"Are you deaf or something? I said that position's been filled."

"Filled? Then why do you still have the sign up?"

"I don't need a troublemaker. You best clear out."

"Right. Okay," I said and turned to leave, though I was still confused by his curt and rude behavior.

As I was walking out, I heard him say to the man in the blue overalls, "Do you believe that dyke bitch?"

Furious, I hopped on my bike and took off as my newfound feminist fury was finding another gear. I bought a paper and scanned the help wanted ads looking for jobs that said, "No Experience Required." I applied for a roofing assistant and then a painter's assistant position paying between two and three bucks an hour. The responses were much the same as Eddie's had been. I was even turned down as a bagger at the Super Giant store.

Out of frustration, I wrote Emma. In her, I found a comrade-in-arms and a mentor, which fueled a more conspiratorial relationship between us. Knowing I wasn't alone in my struggle to be treated fairly helped me feel stronger and less alone, but I still needed a job.

Defeated for the present, I applied for a waitress position and was hired right away. The Cheverly Howard Johnson Hotel had a restaurant adjacent to it. The hotel and restaurant sat on a hill overlooking the Baltimore-Washington Parkway.

The manager's surname was Dubourg de la Loubère, but we called him Mr. Dubourg for short. He was the best-looking man I'd ever seen and reminded me a bit of Gregory Peck. He had a charming New Orleans accent and patois. Mr. Dubourg towered over most people and stood at about six-feet-five. He was lean yet strongly built. Every day he came to work in sharply creased trousers and stiffly starched shirts. His shoes shined so they reflected the light. Even his belt glistened. This was obviously a man who spent time in front of the mirror, but he didn't come across as overly vain. On the contrary, he had playful, flirty eyes but was always courteous and kind. I wasn't the only female to notice his good looks and charisma. Once, two women diners asked me to deliver their hotel keys to him. They tipped well, so I was happy to comply.

One evening after the last customer had left, we were closing. I was filling the salt and pepper shakers out front. The other waitress had left early to go to a party. The chef, a Vietnamese woman, always left soon after the kitchen closed, leaving the sous chef, Marshall, to clean the kitchen. The manager, Marshall, and I were all who remained that night. Mr. Dubourg went through the vestibule to lock the front doors but came back quickly and yelled,

"Get away from the windows! Quick, get in the back, *now!*"

As he followed me into the kitchen, he explained. "When I locked the doors, I saw two men with shotguns coming up from the parking lot." He stopped next to his office and dialed the police while crying out, "Both of you, get in the refrigerator. I'll lock you in while we wait for the police!"

After he hung up the phone, I peeked out of the refrigerator before he could lock it. "Come in here with us," I said. "It's not safe."

"I can't. They saw me. If they get in, they won't stop looking until they find someone, and I can't lock the refrigerator from the inside. One of us must be out here to let the police in when they arrive. Now go! Get in there."

Frightened, Marshall and I went inside the refrigerator. I started pacing, more from the cold than fear. It seemed to take forever, but eventually a young police officer opened the door. The would-be thieves were long gone.

After I'd been working at HoJo's for about six months, two men sat in my station one evening. One ordered the Wednesday night special, Salisbury steak with mashed potatoes and gravy, while the other ordered the Italian spaghetti. As I was about to set the spaghetti plate down, its recipient reached up and grabbed one of my breasts. I was stunned and drew back, visibly upset.

432

"Oh, come on. You're a waitress," he said mockingly. "You must be used to it. Now give me a smile if you want a nice tip," he added while laughing and smirking at his friend. Without stopping to think, I dropped his plate of spaghetti on his chest and watched as it dripped onto his lap.

"Just because I work for a living doesn't make me a whore," I said indignantly. He stood up, cursing, and started to move out of the booth and threateningly toward me.

But before he could reach me, Mr. Dubourg came over and grabbed him by the arm and said, "I don't know what you said to upset my waitress, but I've never seen her rude or impolite to anyone. So I know full well, if she's angry, you did something mighty wrong. You better clear on out of here, and don't you ever think of coming back."

Still holding on to my customer's arm, Mr. Dubourg walked over to the front door, pushed it open with his left side, and shoved my customer out the door, spaghetti sauce and all. His friend was right behind and tried to speak.

"I'm sorry for my friend."

"I don't care. Out! I want you out of here." With that he held the door open, and the man left willingly. My manager then returned to me.

"You all right?"

"Now I am."

"Good." He never asked, and I never told him, what it was

that got me to drop the plate. But after that, I was loyal to him. If someone called in sick, he could count on me. Though I disliked waitressing, I liked my boss. It was right after he moved on that I quit. I learned that it's important to know that your boss has your back when you are a young female serving the public.

Part Eleven

1973

CHAPTER FORTY-FOUR

⁊❖ℭ

ALABASTER SKIN

During my brief tenure at Bladensburg High School, I never fully fit in, though it was much better than junior high, where my secondhand clothing labeled me "white trash" and my good grades tagged me as a "dork." While it lasted, I found a profitable activity during the fuel shortage. Long lines at the gas pumps created a lucrative market. I loaded an old wagon with thermoses of hot coffee, milk, sugar, donuts, pastry, sodas, and newspapers and walked along the gas lines selling everything at 100 to 200 percent markup. With the added money, I improved my wardrobe. Nevertheless, I couldn't shake the dork moniker once it was established in the minds of my classmates.

At Bladensburg High, I made some friends among the nerds and the hippies. I moved easily between them but never fully identified with either. One benefit at Bladensburg was that I reunited with my old friend Stacey. We hadn't been in the same school since fifth grade. She didn't care for any of my nerd or hippie friends, so I kept them apart. We were both good at sports and played basketball at the Boys Club. However, we feared our school reunification would be short lived.

As the probability of busing loomed, Stacey's parents threatened to take their kids out of school entirely rather than send them to a majority Black school in a Black neighborhood. They were not alone; many White families ended up doing the same. Money poured in from frightened parents for the construction of "private" Christian schools. Stacey's parents were going to keep her out of school until the nearby Baptist school opened, putting her a year behind for graduation.

One liberating improvement was that I stopped riding the school bus, which now, because of busing, would have taken me to a new school, Fairmont Heights High. For Christmas, Chip had given me a bright-yellow men's ten-speed bike he'd put together from scavenged parts. It rode well, and I loved riding around exploring new territories; my world expanded because of those wheels. Riding the school bus from my neighborhood had never been fun. I would hear "What a dork" when I passed a bully while seeking an unclaimed bench in the rear of the bus—the only space permitted me. My new bike released me from that daily ordeal.

Busing placed a burden on the number of available school buses. The county's solution was to have schools start earlier. High school began at 7:15 a.m., which meant I had to leave the house by 6:30. In the winter, I was in homeroom class as the sun came up. When I left the house each morning, I could hear Mamma getting dressed, but I was out the door before she emerged from the bath or bedroom. Early winter mornings were cold, but my exertion quickly warmed me. In the predawn blue-black light, everything was pleasantly still on the streets. On the side streets, my navigation was seldom impeded by the cars. I felt as if I owned the streets. It was peaceful, full of hope, and was my favorite time of day.

A one-lane bridge crossed over the John Hanson Highway and the B&O Railroad tracks that separated the White and Black areas. As I rode through the Black Fairmont Heights neighborhood, people were just starting their day. I waved to men and women as they came out of their red brick and white houses to pick up their *Washington Post.* I'd yell, "Good morning!" to them across their deep green and well-manicured lawns. I passed kids walking to school. I didn't know it then but going to school through the neighborhood and not on the bus with the other White kids was going to make a significant difference in my school life.

On my first day, I went to my homeroom class. Whites and Blacks were watching each other. Self-segregating, the White kids sat against the wall and the Black kids congregated by the windows. Only one White girl sat with the Black kids. I didn't know her. However, I knew a lot of the other White kids, and didn't like the ones I knew. I decided to sit in no-man's-land and took a seat in the middle. I wasn't trying to make a statement; it was just where I felt comfortable. But the other kids thought I did it to deliver a message: I wouldn't join the White side, nor would I suck up to the Blacks.

My second class that semester was driver's education. The first day we met in the cafeteria as they readied a room for us. Because of busing the school had its highest enrollment ever. They were cleaning out areas that had been storerooms for decades to accommodate the increased number of students. On the second day, we were to report to our now ready classroom. I had trouble finding it. To get to this classroom, I had to go outside and head toward the left-rear side of the building. There was no sign on the pair of red metal doors, but it looked like what had been described to us. I saw a couple of kids I recognized from the day before, so I guessed I was in the right place.

Maybe the teacher was having a hard time finding it too. He wasn't there yet. I grabbed a chair and a desk toward the back of the classroom near the entrance and waited. Coming in right behind me was a tall, thin young man who looked older than the rest of us. He took the desk behind mine. He didn't stop to chat with friends as many others were doing but kept to himself. On his head was a crocheted hat bearing the Afro-American flag colors of black, red, and green. His thick, wild, kinky hair poured out beneath it, creating a ring around his face. Soon after him, a tall, heavyset Black girl entered, scanned the room like a queen, and then walked up to me and said, "Hey you, honky bitch, you in my seat."

"Pardon me," I responded, genuinely confused.

"You heard me, bitch. Move yo' fuckin' White ass."

Having spent nearly nine years in school, I knew you couldn't give in to a bully or life would be hell on Earth from there on out. You'd spend your days at school with a big target on your back. It was better to get into a fight and lose than not stick up for yourself at all. I was scared to death but knew I couldn't show it. I had to do something. I stood up, and the girl smiled, thinking she had put me in my place. But then I did something that surprised her: I picked up the chair. She got ready to fight, but instead of hitting her with it, which I had considered but thought better of, I turned it over, made a show of examining it, and said, "Damn, girl, I can't find your name anywhere on it. If it was here, I'd definitely give it to you." I then turned the chair back over, set it on the floor, and waited for her to make the next move.

She was about to throw a punch when the guy behind me said, "Leave her be."

"Say what?" she asked, surprised and angry as she turned and cocked her head.

"You heard me. I don't want you messin' with her. You understand me?"

She was about to say something else, but just then the teacher came in. He was a middle-aged, balding Black man of average height and a bit thick in the middle. The boy and girl kept eye contact until she finally backed down and sat down.

The teacher immediately handed us our driver's education booklets and started reading from it. Occasionally, he'd stop reading and explain something. At the end of the class, he informed us that we'd have a written quiz in two weeks. Before we would be allowed to continue the class behind the wheel of a car, we needed to prove that we had memorized this booklet by passing the quiz. This gave us greater interest in reading the booklet.

When the teacher dismissed us, I was relieved to see my adversary already leaving. She was the first one up, knocking over a chair as she passed and not bothering to stop and right it. She was out the door before a crowd bottled up the exit. Standing in line waiting to leave was the guy who had rescued me. I went over to him to show my appreciation. "Hey, thanks for helping me out there. My name is Charlie. What's yours?" I asked.

"I don't talk to no White girls," he responded.

"What's that? I don't get it."

"You heard me, I don't talk to White girls."

"Why's that?" I asked.

"Don't you get it? I can't be seen talkin' to no White girl!" With that, he turned around and faced the door, giving me his back and ending any further discussion. Stunned and a little hurt, I stood there as kids passed by me and out the door.

My last class of the day was English Writing. I was looking forward to this course. I'd heard good things about the teacher,

Mr. Williams, from a few girls I'd met at lunch. In the cafeteria that day, I was sitting alone when a group of three popular-looking girls sat next to me. They were curious. My biking to school and my seating placement in homeroom had apparently made me a curiosity throughout Fairmont Heights. They were determined to learn more about this skinny White chick. The tallest girl was the lightest. She had creamy, coffee-colored skin and soft, curly, dark-brown hair, and was stylishly yet modestly dressed. She easily could have been a model. Her name was Deborah and she was the ringleader. Like me, she was a reader, and not just of fiction; she was well informed about current events. We would spend a lot of time that semester talking about the latest revelations regarding President "Tricky Dick" Nixon, as disclosed in the Senate Watergate hearings. We had long chats about the *Roe versus Wade* decision by the Supreme Court and about Billy Jean King playing Bobby Riggs and what that all meant for women. The other two girls were Channel and Anita. Over time, we became good friends. I, like the others, were caught under Deborah's spell. She was the most likely to succeed. Not only was she smart, poised, and beautiful, but she sang wonderfully and knew how to perform. Her mother had the same light creamy skin tone, but her father was the stunner. His skin was like dark chocolate, but his eyes were shockingly light blue-green. Those eyes could pin you to the wall. He'd gone to college, he spoke in a rich, deep voice, and he worked downtown for the federal government. He liked to engage us girls in political discussions or challenge us to games of chess.

Deborah sang in the school's highly touted and well-known gospel choir. She invited me to check it out. "I've heard you sing. You're not too bad. You should audition," she told me at lunch one afternoon. But I didn't want to sing like my mother and sister did; I wanted to be different.

The choir room was right next to the front entrance and next door to my homeroom. Especially when the doors opened, you could hear their infectious and enticing voices. The director was a no-nonsense, drill-sergeant-type, slim young woman who proudly sported a large Afro hairdo. She marshalled her students into a well-disciplined and rehearsed choir. Under her direction, they polished their collective talent until it shone like a gem. The one White girl who sat with the Blacks in my homeroom was the only White person in the choir. In class she was quiet, reserved, and shy, but in chorus you could see sheer joy light up her face. It was the one place she seemed animated. That school year, the Fairmont Heights High School choir won numerous competitions, was featured on local television, and earned a trip to perform in Europe. The choir was the school's crown, but Deborah was the jewel at its top.

On the first day, the girls at lunch explained that the year before the county desegregated the students, they had deseg-regated the teachers. Many of Fairmont Heights's best and most experienced teachers were strongly encouraged to move to White schools, making room for new White teachers. Mr. Williams, an

English teacher, and Miss Smith, the choral instructor, were some of the few excellent Black teachers who remained. The only White teachers they could entice to teach in Black neighborhoods were those recently out of college who had little or no real experience and were desperate for work. Half the school's teachers, the White half, were only a few years older than we were.

When I got to Mr. Williams's class, he said that our first assignment was to write a poem. We had a week to complete it in any style we liked. In the meantime, we would read examples of classic to modern poetry in the classroom and then discuss their styles. We were invited to find a poem or song lyrics to bring to class to share as extra credit. As the class was ending, a poem popped into my head, and I had to write it down before I forgot it. Because I had my own transportation and didn't have to catch the bus, I was in no rush to leave. When I told Mr. Williams what I was doing, he sat patiently working on papers as I finished up. Finally, I got up to leave.

"Well, did you finish it?" he asked.

"Yes."

"Are you going to let me see it?"

"I don't know if I should. It might be a bit too raw, too honest. It's kind of an emotional reaction to my first couple of days here. Maybe tomorrow I'll feel differently."

"The best poetry is honest. Truth is what makes it powerful. You might feel differently tomorrow, but that doesn't change what you felt today."

"Okay." I placed my backpack on a desk and fumbled through it to retrieve my poem. "Here it is," I said as I laid it in front of him. I grabbed my backpack without zipping it closed and headed for the door. "I'll see you tomorrow," I said as I left, not wishing to wait for his reaction to my poem.

Charlotte Ward

Mr. Williams/English Writing

January 8, 1973

Alabaster Skin

By Charlotte Ward

You stare at me

with your

dark

brown

accusing eyes

You think you can

label

size

categorize me

in just

one

glance

Alabaster Skin

You whisper
to no one
that I'm a
rich bitch
silver spooned
with thoroughbred thin ankles
and that
you know in an instant
this tall blond
speaking
in prep-school-type voices

So
you blame me
for all the injuries
and injustices
felt
(or imagined)

But, Sister
yes, sister
you don't know
where I've been
and sister
yes, My sister
you don't know
what's
beneath
this alabaster skin.

CHAPTER FORTY-FIVE

❧ ❖ ☙

FIRE

Our house is perched on the highest hill in the neighborhood. From my bedroom, I look out over our garage and down on all the surrounding houses like some goddess on Mount Olympus. I spy children playing in backyards and neighbors entering their homes as snippets of their daily lives pass my view. Our dead-end street has four houses all built in the 1920s, each with a large lot, a half acre or more. But to get to our street, you need to pass through a neighborhood where the homes are newer. These were all built in the late 1950s and are on quarter-acre lots or smaller.

It was a cool, crisp late autumn morning. I was looking out at an imposing old oak tree. A few stubborn orange and gold leaves clung to its branches and were made iridescent by the early morning light. On the corner, before you turn onto our street, is the Murkowskis' house. The oak tree stands just beyond their fence. Mr. Murkowski runs his own construction business, and his wife, Carmela, has a beauty parlor she runs from their basement. He calls her Mely. Mr. Murkowski is Polish, though born in New Jersey. His wife is from Puerto Rico. On the side of the house, Mr. Murkowski dug out a side entrance to the basement and poured a cement walkway from the street leading to his wife's business. There on the basement railing hangs a sign: MELY'S BEAUTY SALON.

I used to babysit the five Murkowski kids when their parents had a "date night." Their house seemed to be in a constant state of joyful chaos. I envied them. They weren't timid about showing affection and would cuddle together when they watched television. Whether they were coming or going from the house, they always kissed each other. Inside their house, shoes were flung into piles, towers of papers or other items stood by the sofa, toys were everywhere. The coffee table was always blanketed with a puzzle or a game. Counters were covered with cereal boxes, jars of jam, and empty coffee mugs. Evidence of their life was tossed about without care. But the house was clean if chaotic and usually filled with tempting culinary aromas. They preferred to talk all at once, their cacophony of voices filling the house. When Mr. Murkowski came home, all the kids leapt on him, trying to hang on as he crossed the living room like a coat tree for kids.

Carlos, whom we called Carl, was twelve when the accident happened. He was the only difficult one to babysit, though he was a good kid overall. Back then, he liked airplanes and wanted to become a pilot. He thought he was too old for babysitters and, because he watched the kids when his mother was in the basement working, he didn't think I was needed when they were both out of the house. My presence infringed on his authority. Still, he was another pair of eyes and made my job easier.

Next to him, there were the then ten-year-old twins, Izabela and Irena. They were more alike than just their features. The only way I could tell them apart was that Irena bit her nails. When I babysat, I paid most of my attention to the two little ones. Seven-year-old Teresa was bashful and looked up at me through the thickest pair of eyelashes I'd ever seen. Then there was six-year-old Antoni, whom we called Tony. They were just eleven months apart. Tony was curious and once took apart his father's watch to see how it worked. But as soon as he opened it, the spring jumped out and fell down a vent, where it was lost forever. His dad left the inoperable watch by the television to remind him not to mess with other people's things. Still, after that incident his father went out and got him a Remco crystal radio set.

Teresa and little Tony loved it when I read to them. I'd go to the library and pick up several children's books before I came over each week. After their baths, they'd snuggle against me, encouraging me to change my voice to match the characters in the stories. I read Beatrix Potter's tales in a British accent, except for Peter Rabbit, whom I made sound a bit like Tony. The two little ones showed me the same easy affection they showed one another. As they lay in their beds drifting off to sleep, I felt that I was in a small way a part of this loving, gentle family.

That Saturday morning, I sat gazing out my window as two ladies stepped out of their car and walked into Mely's Beauty Salon. I was about to go downstairs for breakfast when something caught my eye. Behind their house was a detached garage with a green roof. Smoke was rising from it. I looked to be sure that it was smoke and not steam coming from one of Mr. Murkowski's tools, but I glanced down the empty driveway to the curb. The absence of his truck indicated he wasn't home. The smoke plume grew steadily thicker. I ran downstairs yelling, "Fire! Fire!" Buddy came pouring out of his bedroom and followed me downstairs as Mamma came out of the kitchen. Daddy must have already been down at the garage. "Mamma, there's smoke rising up out of the Murkowskis' garage!"

"Are you sure?"

"Yes, I am."

"I'll call the fire department. You run to their house and make sure the family knows," she instructed, and I grabbed my boots by the front closet and ran out the door, not bothering to stop for a coat. As I sped down our steep hill on my bike, I passed our garage while yelling, "Fire! Fire!" hoping Daddy would hear. Just as I was closing in on the Murkowskis' house, there was an explosion, and a whirlwind of flames soared up over the garage. I rounded the corner and rode up their driveway as the garage was engulfed by fire. Neighbors started storming out into the streets. Carl ran out of their kitchen door, followed by the three girls. Then I saw Mrs. Murkowski race toward her kids as she shouted, "Where's Tony?"

"I don't know. I haven't seen him in a while," answered Carl.

"Come search the house," she commanded, and they took off inside, screaming Tony's name.

I threw my bike aside and went as close as I could to the garage side door, but the heat kept me at bay. I stood there and cried out Tony's name, thus giving way to my fears that he was inside. Within seconds, Mrs. Murkowski returned and rushed by me. She tried opening the garage's side door but burned her hand on the metal nob. She then kicked it open and was greeted by a tumbling wall of flames that scorched her hair and clothes as she stumbled back. Determined, she tried again to enter despite the blaze. I screamed at her to stop, but she wouldn't until Mr. Moffitt from across the street raced up and grabbed her and then threw her to the ground to snuff out her smoldering clothes. Pinning her to the ground, he refused to let her go, though she thrashed out at him desperately.

In the distance we heard the sirens of the rapidly approaching fire truck. Carl came back outside and started crying frantically, "Mamma, we can't find him." It was then that Mrs. Murkowski let loose the most heart-wrenching, animal scream I'd ever heard. Her cry, fueled by pain and unbelievable horror, pierced my soul and etched its sound indelibly in my mind. I fell to my knees and covered my eyes. Though the fire's heat grew stronger, I was unable to move. It was only when a fireman came to me that I was aware of their arrival. As he placed a hand under my arm, I heard him say above Mrs. Murkowski's screams, "Are you injured?"

"No, sir," I answered. "But, I believe her little boy is in there."

"Come, move away," he said in a commanding tone as he pulled me up. Soon I felt my mother's arms around me as she guided me out of their yard. When we hit the street, I turned my head into my mother's shoulders and began to weep uncontrollably. Cannons of water started hitting the burning garage.

The sound of Mrs. Murkowski's shrieks has stayed with me until this day. In day and night dreams and at odd moments, I hear her cry of pure agony inside my head. It catches me off guard—stops my breath. Is this what it means to be haunted? Is war like this but a thousand times greater? Do soldiers carry the burden of that sound magnified? Is this what Daddy means by shell-shocked or what Chip's army calls stress-response syndrome? Is this why they won't talk about what happened in their wars?

This thought brings me greater sympathy for my father and brother. I say sympathy and not empathy, for haunted though I may be, I cannot know what it is to be in a war and to be surrounded constantly by such sounds and by wounded souls.

After the accident, there were no more date nights at the Murkowski house. Later, we learned that Mr. Murkowski had been storing gasoline in his garage because of the Arab oil embargo and the subsequent gas shortages. I heard that horrible sound again the same day of the fire when Mr. Murkowski returned home. His screams rose up and across our neighborhood and reached all the way through my closed bedroom window. Other than in my dreams, it would be nearly two years before I'd hear that wrenching sound again. But this time it would emanate from within my own house.

Part Twelve

1974

CHAPTER FORTY-SIX

ଈ❖ଔ

THE LETTER C

Despite Daddy's excuse for not hiring part-time office help, we had more money than we'd ever had before. We weren't remotely well-to-do, but we weren't counting every penny anymore. Mamma no longer brought home overripe bananas and apples that were bagged, bruised, and marked down 75 percent off the regular price. She still mixed powered milk with whole milk to cut costs. However, for the first time, Daddy paid for us all to go to the movies and for dinner at Shakey's Pizza Parlor afterward. If we watched the sales, we could buy new clothes at Montgomery Ward instead of used ones from Goodwill. For helping around the house, sometimes Mamma would give me money to go to the roller rink out in Seabrook on Route 450. There, I'd see my old friend Stacey. We no longer went to the same school, so it was fun to catch up. Stacey was a regular at the rink. She dreamed of joining the New York Chiefs roller derby team after high school.

After some discussion, Daddy agreed to let Mamma fly out to Portland, Oregon, so she could see Emma and finally meet her grandchildren. Funded by our new relative affluence, Mamma called Emma every Saturday. Mamma's joy and anticipation of her reunion with her older daughter grew as the date of her departure approached. She had one suitcase filled with toys and clothes for Emma's kids. Adding to her happiness, Chip was due home in August. With the Naval Academy just down the road, Eugene would be home for the holidays and the occasional weekend. Mamma's anticipation and delight were infectious. I looked forward to having all my brothers back together again.

While doing her housework, Mamma sang lighthearted tunes like "Candy Man" by Sammy Davis, or my favorite, "Anticipation" by Carly Simon, that filled the house with contentment. She and Daddy were more affectionate. There was a warmth and tranquility in the house. I felt like we had finally arrived—that we had made it.

Then, three days before Mamma's scheduled flight to Oregon, the phone rang. Mamma picked it up. "Hello," she said. "Hi, how are you?" There was a minute or two of silence before she said, "Mon Dieu, tout comme notre mère." I knew then she was speaking with Aunt Martha. French was their secret language when they didn't want others to know what they were saying. They'd both learned it from the nuns at their school in Philadelphia. To break the code, I took French at school. Both Eugene and I excelled at it.

I turned to Buddy and whispered to him, "Mamma said, 'My

God, just like our mother.'" After she hung up, Mamma started crying. Unease crept back into our home.

After a few minutes, she composed herself and looked up into our frightened faces. "Your aunt has breast cancer." It felt as if all the oxygen was sucked out of the room with that pronouncement. I found myself holding my breath. I was unsure what to do. Finally I went over to her and put my arms around her as she broke down weeping. She struggled to gain control. Looking at me, but more through me, she said through her sobs, "Just like our Ma."

Buddy and I did our best to console her. When Daddy came home, she told him the news. He tried to comfort her, telling her they had a lot more medicine now to kill cancer than they had when her mother was diagnosed.

"I know, they have chemotherapy now but that's hard too. She'll be sick for months and months. I need to be there at least until Ben gets back—he's out at sea. One thing is for sure, I can't go out to visit Emma. After she heals from the surgery, she starts treatments. She needs someone to look after her. Cancer is no picnic, I know. I'll be leaving tomorrow."

"Why do you have to leave so soon?" Daddy asked.

"Jack, she's having surgery on Thursday. The doctor doesn't want to wait. She needs me. I've got to go. I'm going!"

"Honey, I know how you can help Martha and still go to see your daughter."

"How's that?"

"Call the airline and postpone your flight. When school lets out, I will send Charlie down to take over looking after Martha. You can still go see Emma's family. I think that is what would be best for everyone, and Charlotte will get to spend some time with her aunt."

"I don't know. Being a nurse, caring for the sick is hard work. It can be rough. Charlotte is still young."

"Hard work never killed nobody, darlin'. You know that. Charlotte can do it. It'll be good for her. What ya say there, Charlie-girl, you want ta pitch in so your ma can see her oldest child and finally meet her grandkids? Can we depend on you?"

"Yes, of course you can count on me. I love Aunt Martha. It'll be fine, Mamma. I want to do it," I said, feeling proud and mature for being asked. "I can do it, Mamma. I don't want you to miss out on seeing Emma either."

"Sweetheart, that's kind of you, but it will be harder than you think. Sickness is messy, and it strips the patient of all pretenses. It's not simply holding someone's hand. There's medicine to keep straight, vomit to clean, baths to give, tears to dry. You think you can handle all that?"

"I've babysat. That's messy too. I can do whatever Aunt Martha needs. She'd do the same for me."

"Yes, she certainly would. Well, if you think you can handle it, I think it's a wonderful idea. Thank you, Jack, for suggesting it."

Mamma gave me a hug and whispered, "I love you." Then she

gave Daddy a long embrace and whispered something in his ear that I couldn't make out.

By the time school let out, I was grateful to be heading down to Norfolk. In the five weeks since Mamma had left, Daddy expected me to run the house like Mamma, including cooking the meals. I did my best, but it took me several weeks and lots of phone calls to Mamma before he stopped getting angry at my efforts. "How can you mess up rice?" he complained when I burned it. "All you do is add water."

With Mamma's over-the-phone help, I prepared a bunch of meals and put them in the freezer so Daddy and Buddy could heat them up as needed during the two weeks Mamma would be in Oregon. Finally, school let out. Early the next day, Daddy took me down to the Greyhound bus station on New York Avenue in D.C. and waited with me until my bus came. From there the bus went to Richmond, where I had to wait for the Norfolk bus. After six hours of travel, my bus finally pulled up to a red brick building a little after 4:00 p.m. When I descended, Mamma was there waiting for me. She stood with me as the bags were unloaded along the platform. I grabbed my luggage. One piece was an old green canvas bag from Daddy's days in the army. The other was a suitcase I got at the Goodwill for the trip. Mamma picked up the army bag.

"Come, follow me. Your aunt is waiting in the car."

There in the station parking lot stood Martha's new four-door Thunderbird, white with a black top. The rear door's hinges were on the rear panel so that the door swung open opposite the front, like a pair of church doors. Martha was in the front, and I climbed in the rear after we got my things in the trunk. From what little I could see, she looked good. Her hair was lighter and looked surprisingly thicker than I remembered. But when we got home, she removed her wig and I got a jolt. I hadn't thought about a wig, and when it came off I could see her once proud head of hair had noticeably thinned. Her makeup was expertly applied, but it couldn't mask her sallow appearance and loss of weight. She seemed to have aged decades since we were last together at Christmas. I tried to hide my shock, but my tears betrayed me. Martha pretended not to see.

"It's hard to keep the wig on in this heat," she said, though it was much cooler in her house than it had been outside. "It makes my scalp itch after a while," she added. "I have a few of them. One advantage is I don't spend as much time at the beauty parlor."

"Come," said Mamma. "I will show you where you'll be sleeping." Together we hauled my luggage upstairs. Mamma showed me the room next to Martha and Ben's room. "You'll sleep in here."

"Where are you sleeping?" I asked.

"I've moved down the hall to the den. I take off in four days. I thought it best that you go ahead and get settled next to Martha in case she needs you in the middle of the night. Sleep with your door open so you can hear her. She is going through chemotherapy. Her next dose is tomorrow. She's usually okay the first day after, but then she progressively gets sicker and weaker for a few days. You'll have to help her through that. She'll need help in the bathroom, and she'll probably throw up a bit. You must keep her hydrated. I've kept a diary for the doctors. Write down all her medications, treatments, and reactions, like how many times she throws up and if she had diarrhea. It's important. It's there on your nightstand. You should familiarize yourself with it. There's a book about the treatments the doctor gave us there too. Please keep up with the diary and bring it to each doctor's appointment. It's been very useful."

Suddenly, I felt panicked. It was at that moment that I truly understood what was in front of me, and I was afraid I might not be up to the task despite my earlier bravado. For weeks, I had imagined I would be akin to Florence Nightingale without realizing what that meant. I had visualized spoon-feeding Martha chicken broth or walking her into the doctor's office. Despite Mamma's warnings, I hadn't thought about vomit and bowel movements until then.

Sensing my moment of panic, Mamma sat down and said, "Come, sit down next to me." When I sat, she pulled me beside her on the bed. "Listen, you don't need to worry, Charlotte. I know it sounds a bit overwhelming at first, but you can do this. I know you can. You're a stronger person than I was when I took over caring for my mother. You'll soon get used to it. Martha is an easy patient.

She'll tell you what she needs. You've taken care of babies—it's no worse than that."

"But it's different. Babies don't suffer from pride. They're not embarrassed by their nakedness."

"That's true, but you quickly lose such pride and modesty when you have an illness like cancer, or in childbirth for that matter. You'll find that out in due time."

"Mamma, I won't be as good as you, but I will do my best."

"Well, that's all I can ask. But don't sell yourself short. You may turn out to be a better nurse than I ever was."

"That I highly doubt."

"Charlotte, sweetheart, I know you will be the nurse Martha needs, and I am grateful and proud of you for it. Don't doubt yourself. Now let's get back downstairs. Martha will think she's been left out of the party. Time to start getting supper ready."

The next morning Mamma told me, "I should show you around town today. We'll take a tour after breakfast when we're on our way to the medical center." What I didn't know was that she wanted me to do the driving. Although I had passed my driving class and had my learner's permit, I didn't have my license yet.

"Don't worry. You shouldn't have to drive, but it's best to know just in case. When she can, Martha will drive, but you should be able to take over if needed. She can suddenly take ill. You'll take cabs when Martha's not up to driving to appointments. I've discussed it with her already."

First, she took me to an empty church parking lot to get accustomed to Martha's car. After a few practice moves, Mamma directed me out onto the city streets. I was nervous but thrilled as I drove first to the post office, then to the grocery store at Ward's Corner, then through the tunnel that crosses the Elizabeth River over to the doctor's office, then to the hospital, and finally to the cancer clinic for Martha's infusion.

Mamma stood back as I helped Martha with her bath. When the time came for Mamma to leave, I was feeling a little more confident. Those last few days had brought Mamma and me closer together. I was walking in her footsteps. I could feel her gratitude and newfound respect, and it made me feel good about myself; still, I cried when she pulled away. I was going to miss her in so many ways.

As Martha and I spent our days together, we grew close. Each morning we'd share the newspaper and talk about events. We discussed the kidnapping victim turned bank robber, heiress Patty Hearst. We debated about why President Nixon kept refusing to hand over the White House tapes to Congress. Under pressure, he eventually submitted a transcript of some of the tapes, which was incriminating enough. We talked about the possibility of impeachment and about Nixon's aides G. Gordon Liddy and John Ehrlichman, who were convicted of conspiracy and perjury in connection with the Watergate scandal. I read aloud John Dean's testimony from the newspaper. "Nixon got caught, and his problem is he broke a lot of laws covering it up. But other presidents lied to us too," I told Martha. "The Pentagon Papers prove our involvement in Vietnam goes all the way back to President Truman."

"Yes, I know. I still like Mr. Truman and think he was a decent man. But I am sorry I voted for Nixon," Martha admitted. "I feel betrayed."

"Yeah, my dad feels the same way. Mamma came close to voting for Nixon, but in the end she stuck with McGovern."

"So, she's the one."

"What do you mean by that?" I asked.

"Nearly the whole country voted for Nixon. It was a landslide. He fooled us all."

After we finished with the news, we'd end our morning ritual with the daily crossword puzzle. I picked up several 5,000-piece jigsaw puzzles at the Giant Open Air Market, and we put them together while joking and telling stories. With detailed instructions from her, I gave my aunt manicures and pedicures. It was the first time I'd ever done that for anyone. Patiently, she taught me to knit. Before the summer was over, I had made a wearable sweater and a few hats and scarves. When she had an appetite and felt up to it, she directed me in the fine art of cooking as she sat in a chair I'd placed in the kitchen.

On about the twelfth day since we were on our own, we were getting ready for her doctor's appointment. She opened her pocketbook, pulled out her keys, and said, "Here, take these. You drive." From then on, I did all the driving. I only called cabs when I went on my own to the grocery store. As the weeks passed, Martha grew weaker and her need for me increased. During the long hours at the clinic, I sat beside her as the chemotherapy's poison slowly dripped into her veins. As a frequent attendee, I was accepted by the other patients in the treatment room like a member of an exclusive tribe. We were all travelers on similar journeys. We talked about the latest Watergate news, remedies for diarrhea and nausea, foods to boost energy, and ideas for hats, wigs, or scarves. As they sat, I gave manicures, pedicures, and foot and shoulder massages. In turn, they gave me their stories; some funny, others enlightening, and often poignant.

On a particularly rough day when Martha had been sicker than normal, I gave her a bath and put her to bed. She finally fell off to sleep. I returned to the bathroom to clean the tub, and there in the tub's drain were clumps of Martha's once lustrous hair. It was then that I broke down and cried. That was when I realized how much I loved her. The intimacy of care had brought us closer together than I had ever imagined possible with anyone. She trusted me completely, and I trusted her with my secrets and dreams.

One day when she was too tired to do more than sit up in a chair, I asked her how she felt. "Like I've been spit out of a gigantic wave," she said. "Having chemotherapy is like getting caught in a tumultuous wave. It spins you around, drags you on the sea bottom

469

along sand, stones, shells, and debris, and just when you don't know which way is up and your lungs feel like they'll burst for lack of air, the wave spits you onto the shore. That's where I am now. In between infusions, you have a time when you're sick and then a time when you recover some. That's when the wave releases you from its grip. I feel as if I am lying on a beach exhausted. Slowly oxygen is returning to my lungs, brain, blood, and muscles. Soon I will feel a bit closer to being normal just in time for the next wave to drag me out again. With each round of waves, it gets harder to recover. The sand, stones, shells, and debris are all the physical nuisances like hair loss, nausea, ringing in my ears, rashes, and dry skin. One at a time, these are minor, but put them together and it's an ambush. Still, I have much to be thankful for. I have you."

When she felt too tired to sit up, we lay in bed together while I read to her, or we watched television. Neither of us cared for soap operas, so we'd tune in to *The Today Show, Hollywood Squares,* and *Jeopardy.* Sometimes we'd watch *Password,* which was on at the same time as *Jeopardy.* With the game shows, we'd try to be the first to yell out the answers.

Once when I was switching channels I stumbled on Lena Horne singing with Kermit the Frog on *Sesame Street.* After that, we watched *Sesame Street* often. One morning as the show began, a voice came over the television and announced, "The following program is brought to you by the letter C." Then we heard Cookie Monster's voice say, "Now what starts with the letter C?" Then he appeared on the screen.

"Look at me—watching children's shows with my niece and actually enjoying it. I never saw that coming," she commented. Together we laughed as Cookie Monster sang, "C is for cookie; that's good enough for me," and crumbled chocolate cookies over his face. After the show, I went down and made lunch. Cookie Monster's simple tune kept ringing in my ear. Standing in the kitchen, I started singing, "C is for cancer. I won't let it be. C is for chemo, kills the other C."

That afternoon, we called Mamma, who was back home from visiting Emma. She shared all the news about Emma: her kids, home, husband, life, and dreams. Then we made our weekly call to Granddad. When I spoke to him, holding the telephone cord was like holding his heart strings; I could feel him crying, though I couldn't hear him sob. There was no sniffle to give him away. His cry was in the tremor of his softened voice and the pauses between his words. Just before he hung up, he said, "I am grateful Martha has you to care for her. I will never forget what you've done for her. I love you, my dear Charlotte."

"I love you too, Granddad," I heard myself say. I meant it more than I ever had before.

CHAPTER FORTY-SEVEN

‹›

HERSTORY

Our days together were coming to an end. Ben was due back in a few weeks. He had managed to get assigned ashore for the time being. Soon I would have to return home and to school. Martha and I spent our last two weeks together looking for a potential nurse's aide who was willing to do maid work. The plan was to start her three days a week. After I left, she'd work five days a week, helping him with the shopping, cooking, and cleaning and taking care of Aunt Martha. We placed an ad in the local papers and the phone rang off the hook for a couple of days. We set up eight interviews. When Martha and I met our third applicant, Anna Johnson Pryne, we cancelled the other pending interviews. We were instantly charmed by Anna and happily fell under her spell. The moment I answered the door and saw her quick smile, I liked her. Martha approved of her appearance: her clothes were a bit demur for my tastes, but they were sharply pressed and well tailored, and the color suited her coffee complexion. She was warm, intelligent, and confident. Martha hired her on the spot.

When she began, I showed her around the kitchen and rest of the house. I did my best to fill her in on what else I thought she needed to know to care for Martha, especially on her bad days. Anna was quick to take charge of Martha, me, and the entire house. She seemed to know not only how to make my aunt comfortable—helping her with her toilette and coiffure—but how to make her laugh. We looked forward to the days when Anna was in the house. There was more energy in the air and light in the home. On her first day, I learned Anna's eldest son was a freshman at Howard University in D.C., while her younger son was still in high school. She was a native of the Tidewater region and Hampton Roads. Her father and brothers were oystermen, and her husband, Leo, worked at the naval base. She was proud of her Johnson family roots, which explained why she introduced herself with two last names. "My folks been free since before we became a nation," she told me. Knowing that she'd be there, not only to care for Martha but also to keep her company, made it easier to think about leaving.

When she arrived on her second day, she found me crying in the kitchen. Martha was still asleep upstairs. Anna asked what I was crying about, and I told her I was afraid that, once I returned home, I might not see my aunt again, and I was worried what her dying would do to my mama.

She dried my eyes, gave me a big hug, and then drew my face

toward hers. "Tears never cleaned no spilt milk. You're better off lookin' at all the gifts that God has given your aunt. For one, she can afford to hire help. There's a whole lotta sick folks can't do that. She has and can afford good doctors. But most importantly, she ain't alone in this fight. God gave her a family that loves her. Darlin', that's a whole lot of goodness.

"As sure as you're livin', you're bound to have your share of troubles. No one leaves this life untouched, unhurt, or unmarked. You'll have your own battles to come. I pray you have as much help as your aunt has right now. This here and now is Miss Martha's fight. The question is not how someone dies but how they choose to live. Now, let's get on with helping her do just that. Besides, your aunt is plenty tough—she's a fighter. So don't go burying her just yet.

"Come on, child, give me a smile. Don't you know that joy and laughter are the strongest medicine there is? Let's be sure to give your aunt some of that today, all righty?"

Anna managed to get twice as much done in a single hour as I could in three, though she never seemed in a hurry. With the cleaning, laundry, shopping, and much of the cooking done in her three days of work, I had less and less to do. All that was left for me was to keep Martha company.

One late Tuesday morning, Martha and I were lying in her bed watching television. *Sesame Street* had just ended. One of the show's characters, Maria, had helped Elmo deal with sadness. A friend had moved away, and he was feeling down. As I rose to turn off the TV set, I asked my aunt, "Was my mama a depressed, moody child? Did she have big mood swings when she was growing up?"

"Heavens, no. She was the happiest little girl I've ever known. What made you ask that?"

"Well, it was Maria and Elmo dealing with sadness, and well, it made me think about you and Mamma—that you were children once. At home, she has frequent mood swings. Sometimes she gets so depressed that we lose her for days and weeks on end. When she's depressed, she walks around the house like a zombie and no one can reach her. Well, Eugene used to be able to sometimes, but he's gone now."

"I'm sorry to hear that, though I am not surprised. Your mother had a hard time putting herself back together after Mary Rose died. She's had some rough times and a lot of shattered dreams."

"What were her dreams?"

"Oh, you know, to be a famous singer, to be an accomplished classical opera singer. She's talented and beautiful. Everyone expected great things from her. But none of it turned out like she'd hoped, like we all imagined."

"Then why did she get married and start a family so young? Why didn't she pursue her dreams?"

"Life just doesn't always happen the way you plan. It is what it is. I dreamed of having a big family. It's better to count your blessings than cry over what might have been."

"That's what Anna said."

"Anna is a wise woman. Your ma has been blessed with all of you. We all have childhood dreams, but then we become adults and have to accept what God gives us."

"Boy, you're sounding more and more like Anna."

"What can I say? Great minds think alike. What were you and Anna talking about—what was the context?"

"Oh, we were talking about a bunch of stuff. Tell me, what was my mother like as a child?"

"Well first, your mother was everyone's favorite. Margaret was a joyful, vivacious child, always singing and dancing. I did better in school, but she was the truly talented one. To tell you the truth, I was jealous of her. Our father's eyes would smile when she came dancing down the stairs each morning. It hurt to feel so dull next to her. She just lit up every room she entered—the golden child. Our neighbors would say that they looked forward to seeing her perform at Carnegie Hall. Everyone was sure she'd end up famous. Since she first sang at church, she was quite the celebrity in our little parish.

"Even though I was the older child, I knew I stood in her shadow. When I was about fourteen, I heard Da say to Ma, 'Isn't Martha a bit too morose?' Boy, that stung. What fourteen-year-old girl wants to be called morose, I ask you?"

"Well, if it's any consolation, I heard Granddad tell Mamma that I was a lot like you. I think he meant our personalities."

"Well, I'll take that as a compliment, but not morose."

"I know what you mean. I know I come across as more serious and less charming than Buddy. He's the charismatic one."

"But you're the clever one."

"We all have our talents."

"Your mother tells me you want to be a writer. That's a tough field to break into."

"I'm not going to be a writer. I've changed my mind. Don't get me wrong, I love writing, but I want a steady paycheck."

"Now, you do take after me. That's very practical, and I'm glad to hear it. Do you want to teach English or something? You could support yourself and still write."

"No, I want to be a lawyer."

"A lawyer! Wow, Charlotte, I'm fifty-seven years old, and I've never met a woman lawyer. Wouldn't it be more prudent to set your sights on something a bit more attainable?"

"There are woman lawyers out there, and there's no law against it."

"There aren't many. You'll encounter a lot of obstacles to becoming a lawyer. Even if you get into law school, it's expensive. Why not try for something a little more obtainable, like becoming a teacher or nurse?"

"I think we both can agree that I wouldn't make the best nurse."

"I disagree. You've been wonderful."

"Thanks, but I wouldn't like being a nurse. It's different when you're caring for someone you love."

"I love you too."

"I know that. I've always known that. Those sweaters you make for me each year, they make me feel cared for—loved."

"I'm glad and touched," Martha said as she leaned over to hug me.

"The thing is," I said as she released me, "I think I'd be good at law. I love reading and not simply fiction. I like reading about current events and history. I like the idea of researching and finding support for a good argument to fight injustice. I like the notion of using the law to set things right and make them fair."

"Sounds noble, my dear, but still—I don't know, Charlotte. You may be biting off more than you can chew. The world isn't fair, never has been."

"We don't have to accept injustice. Isn't it our responsibility to try to make the world a better place rather than to merely complain about it? I know it's impossible for one person, but if we each give a little, we can accomplish a lot. When I look at the big picture, it can seem overwhelming. But I will hate myself if I don't try. I'll face one obstacle at a time."

"Honey, it will take a lot of time, effort, support, unfaltering determination, and luck for you to accomplish what you seek."

"Every journey starts with a single step. Even if I fail, I will get further down the road than I am now. Don't worry, Aunt Martha, I am not totally naïve. I've been thinking about this for a while. I have many hurdles to climb. First, I need to pay for and then get a bachelor's degree. I'm thinking of majoring in journalism or English for my undergraduate. After all, writing will be a good skill for a lawyer. Or perhaps philosophy might be good preparation—you study ideas and arguments to defend them. But I'll need to work for a few years after I graduate with a bachelor's so I can save money for law school. A teaching degree might be wise so I can teach while I pursue law school."

"You'll have to be twice as good as the men applying just to be considered. Have you thought about that?"

"Yes, of course. I know there are a lot of prejudices and obstacles for women trying to get into law schools. Not just my grades, but my test scores must be superior. A counselor at the University of Pennsylvania told me that although I have a 4.0 GPA, they weigh it as a 3.5 GPA because of my school system. That's seems unfair because no one at my school can get higher than a four-point-o. How can we compete with schools that are not weighted?"

"Like I said, la vie n'est pas juste. There's no law of nature requiring life to be fair."

"I'm aware of that. To compensate for the weighted grade averages, I needed great SAT scores, so I studied extra hard. It paid off—I got a perfect sixteen hundred on it. I'm a good test taker. I've spoken to several college counselors. I know the LSAT exam is much harder. I was told that even if I get into law school and graduate with honors, I will still face prejudice in getting hired. Many firms are unwilling to hire a female lawyer. The obstacles may feel infinite, but it has been done."

"You'll need endless perseverance and determination."

480

"I'd like to work for an organization like the American Civil Liberties Union. They've hired female attorneys before. My goal is to help further rights for women and minorities. I'm guessing it'll take a decade to achieve a law degree, because I'll have to take time off from school so I can earn money to pay for it. I hope to be a lawyer by the time I'm thirty."

"Shoot, that's a daunting but lofty goal. Have you told your parents about your plans?"

"Nope, you're the first. Whenever I bring up college, Daddy says it'd be a waste of money on a girl. He thinks I should study typing, shorthand, cooking, and sewing. Mamma will think I'm setting myself up to fail. She thinks I should become a teacher and keeps talking like it's a fait accompli."

"I am honored that you shared your dreams with me. I hope to live long enough to see you achieve them. But I think you're wrong about your ma. I think she'd be proud of you for at least trying. But don't you want to have a family and kids?"

"Not now."

"Well, of course not now, but eventually?"

"Maybe, I don't know. I don't think it's necessary to be married with kids to have a good life. I don't want marriage and kids to define me. Yes, I'd like to be loved by a good man. But a good man to me would be someone who supports me in achieving my own successes. I'd do the same for him. I want someone who respects me and sees me as his equal. If I can't find a man like that, I'd rather be alone."

"You could end up successful but lonely. You may have to give up an awful lot to achieve your dreams. Are you sure it'll be worth it?"

"Worth it, yes. Aunt Martha, women are always expected to be supportive of their spouses. Shouldn't we expect the same from them? If you love someone, don't you want to help them be their best self? Shouldn't that be a two-way street? I don't want to be stuck in a relationship where I'm disrespected and unfulfilled and unhappy. In any case, that will have to come after law school. It's a long way off."

"By that time, it might be too late to have children. You may not think it now, but you could regret that."

"It's a chance I am willing to take."

"Men have had it their own way since the world began. To them, being in control and being the boss is normal and right, and that includes the 'good' ones. I know, I married one. Where would Ben's career be if he had to follow me around to support my career instead of the other way around? No, he'd never make it in the navy with an unsupportive wife. Someone has to bend, and that someone is almost always the woman in the relationship."

"But why must that be? Why can't a man follow a woman for once?"

"Honey, there are bills to pay and men get paid more. It makes financial sense for the woman to sacrifice her career in support of her husband's. That's just the way it works."

"Women should get paid the same as men for the same job. That's what I want to fight for: equality."

"You're smart and gifted, Charlotte. I believe you can achieve whatever you set your mind to, but it will be very difficult. There are more obstacles than you can see now. Look how long it took us to get the vote. Equal pay? I won't live to see that. You might have to be content to simply lay the groundwork so the next generation might have a chance at equal pay."

"Even if we can close the gap some, that would change women's lives."

"It sounds exhausting. Life can get in the way of dreams. You might meet a young man who seems perfect. Such scenarios are all too frequent in this world. Passion can strike even the most determined person. It just takes once to get pregnant. You do know what I mean?"

"Yes, of course, no sexual intercourse, at least none without contraception."

"Wow, you kids are rather direct these days. I suppose it's good you can talk openly about such things. But as I said, it can take just once to get pregnant, and contraceptive devices aren't always foolproof."

"Yeah, I know about the different types of contraception, and abstinence is the only foolproof method. I'll be careful."

"Charlotte, may I ask you a very personal question?"

"Sure."

"Are you a virgin?"

"Yes, Aunt Martha, I'm a virgin. I took sex education in school.

We went over the different types of birth control and their effectiveness."

"Oooh, that's a relief. The way you were talking, I was worried. Just remember—you might be able to walk away from romance, but you can't walk away from a child. Once you have a child, you can't make one decision that doesn't put its welfare first. It's easier to get sidetracked than you may think. Sparks can fly in the heat of the moment, and then you end up doing something you regret. Before you know it, you're walking down the aisle and your belly is swelling. It can be hard to stay on track."

"I know. I'm not looking for a fairy tale."

"No? It does sound like a nice dream, though."

"Well, Aunt Martha, remember in *South Pacific* when Bloody Mary sings, 'If you don't have a dream, how you gonna have a dream come true?'"

"Don't forget, Charlotte, in *South Pacific*, Bloody Mary was singing to a sailor who was falling in love with her daughter. The song is about falling in love. If you want your dream to come true, you had better stay away from boys altogether. Remember, boys are a dangerous distraction if you are to attain your goal. Most of all, if you want to succeed, you'll have to stay focused."

"I intend to."

"Charlotte, I believe you." Then Martha paused before she added, "But I believed in your ma too."

CHAPTER FORTY-EIGHT

THE LONG RIDE HOME

Mamma was coming on Saturday. In anticipation of her arrival, Martha and I got all dolled up. I styled one of her wigs and applied some makeup. When I finished and was admiring my handiwork, Martha said, "It's your turn, dear." She then proceeded to give me my first manicure and pedicure. She didn't stop there. Pulling out a pair of tweezers, she commanded, "Come over here and let's do something with those brows. After that, we'll conquer your hair."

Mamma arrived in a good mood, and after she unloaded her suitcase from the car, she examined the two of us. "Wow, you two look gorgeous. What a sight for sore eyes. Give me a half an hour to scrub this road dust off, and I'll get fixed up too. What do you say we go out for dinner tonight and celebrate being together?"

"That's a fantastic idea," Martha replied. "I feel like getting out and having a bit of fun with my two best girls. I'll find a dress for

Charlotte to wear while you get ready, Margaret. We'll be three fashionable ladies out on the town—my treat. I insist."

We went to a restaurant that had white tablecloths, and Mamma let me have a bit of wine. I was unaccustomed to alcohol and felt its warmth seep into my head, making me giddy if a bit slow tongued. I was happy listening to Mamma and Aunt Martha sharing memories and jokes. Our waiter was a handsome, thirty-something Italian-looking man. As he walked away from our table, both Mamma and Aunt Martha looked him over and then simultaneously burst out laughing. They were acting like a pair of twenty-somethings. It was hilarious to watch. I ordered a dessert and they ordered coffee.

When dinner was finally finished, Martha lamented, "This has been wonderful. I hate for this evening to end."

"Why don't we keep it going then? Do you feel like going to a night club to hear some music?" asked Mamma.

"Absolutely," snapped Martha and me in unison, which made us all laugh out loud. "I know just the spot," said Martha.

It was dark out by then as Mamma drove, following Martha's instructions. I wasn't sure where we were. When we got out of the car, I could smell the ocean, so it had to be near but not near enough to hear it. In the parking lot, Mamma switched shoes with me and applied heavier makeup on me than she'd normally permit. With her high heels on, I was at least six-foot-three. Mamma stood back and pronounced, "You look at least twenty.

Besides no one will card you at that height."

She was right. The man at the door was only about six foot, though muscular. He looked up at me and never asked for I.D.

There was a live band playing music and a dance floor in front of a low stage. We found a table close to the dance floor, and before we could order any drinks, Mamma grabbed my arm and pulled me out onto the floor. She proceeded to give me a swing lesson. We both laughed constantly through my entire lesson. While we were dancing, a man came over and asked Martha to dance, but she declined. She was happy just watching. After two songs, we finally sat down and joined Martha for a drink. I ordered a rum and coke, and Mamma ordered a plain coke. When our drinks arrived, Mamma swapped our drinks. "Let's not get carried away there, Charlotte," she said, putting limits on my little foray into the adult world. Still, I had a wonderful time.

A gentleman came over and asked Mamma to dance, and she accepted, just once. They were both good dancers, and Martha and I enjoyed watching them. When she returned to her seat, I asked, "How come no one asks me? I'm the only single lady here."

"Honey, in those heels and at that height, few men will have the nerve. It's intimidating," Mamma explained.

"It's empowering. You should wear high heels more often. It'll save you a lot of trouble," advised Aunt Martha.

Mamma and I returned to the dance floor. She tried to teach me a few more intricate swing moves. I got confused and ad-libbed a few moves of my own. Both sisters busted out with laughter, but I didn't mind. I was having fun. In the dance floor's flickering mirror ball light, I could envision the carefree, vivacious young woman who was once my mother.

The next morning, we packed up our things and loaded the car, and each of us gave Aunt Martha a long hug goodbye. As Mamma headed out the driveway and down the road, I turned and waved to Aunt Martha. I found myself with tears in my eyes. I was going to miss her.

Mamma and I were both quite lost in our own thoughts all the way across the bridge crossing the York River. Somewhere on Route 17, I broke the silence. "Why did you marry Daddy?"

"Wow, what a thing to ask. Where did that come from?"

"Well, you're so different. I'm curious. What was it about him that attracted you to him?

"His constancy, loyalty, and honesty."

"Really, that's it?"

"Why, what did you think?"

"I thought perhaps it was his irresistible good looks, Southern charm, or smooth voice—certainly something magnetic. Constancy, loyalty, and honesty. Really, Mamma, those sound like characteristics you look for in a dog, not a lover. What about kindred spirit, or the sparks just flew whenever I saw him, that sort of thing? What about passion?"

"Passion? You better watch out there, my girl. Passion burns away, but before it does it can burn you and leave you with nothing but ashes."

"Or it can grow. It can be a light."

"I never thought I'd say this, but maybe you do read too much. That kind of love is for novels, not the real world. You're still young and inexperienced. What do you know of passion? You're only sixteen."

"Certainly, I know about desire. The desire to be loved passionately. I'm not saying I'm looking for it now, but when I do, I want it to be, among other things, passionate. Yes, I read a lot. But surely, if literature is filled with such ideas, then the desire for a passionate love is universal and a common human desire. Didn't you desire it?"

"Yes, I did once. I wanted the whole fairy tale. Of course I did."

"What happened?"

"What happened? I kissed a frog, and no, he didn't turn into a prince. What are we talking about? I thought, according to Martha, we were staying clear of boys. She said you wanted to go to law school. Law school, really, Charlotte. You do dream big."

"I'll wait on looking for love until I finish with school. But when and if I ever fall in love, I want something more than 'he's acceptable.' What do you mean, you kissed a frog? Are you saying Daddy's a frog and not the prince you thought he'd be?"

"I wasn't referring to your father."

"You weren't! Whoa, who then?"

"I got burned once, and my desire for a passionate love affair . . . was extinguished."

"How so?"

Mamma just stared out the window and was silent for a while. I wasn't willing to let it slide; my curiosity was piqued. After a couple of miles, I pleaded, "Mamma, tell me. Aunt Martha said you were the happiest of children, positive and carefree. What happened? I want to understand."

"You're young."

"I am old enough."

"I shouldn't be telling you any of this."

"You know I won't tell a living soul if that's what you're worried about."

"I know I can trust you. I suppose this could be a cautionary tale. You need to be cautious with your heart and not let passion lead you into making a monumental mistake. The truth is, I loved a man once, before your father. As you said, the sparks flew. I thought he was the sun, the moon, and the stars. I was a fool, and he was a fraud. More than my heart was broken."

"Contrary to what you might think, I don't find it shocking that you loved someone before Daddy. So you had a life before Daddy. What happened to the other guy?"

"He suddenly remembered he had a wife."

"Ouch, and you didn't know? He didn't tell you?"

"I would never knowingly go out with a married man. Yes, of course, I was clueless. That is why I am telling you. I was protected, inexperienced, and naïve. You can learn from my mistakes."

"How long did you date him?"

"Nearly a year."

"In all that time, you didn't have a clue? I mean, didn't you wonder when he went home at night?"

"His wife and kids lived in Chicago. As I said, I was naïve. He was an army doctor stationed in Washington. He had a difficult schedule and had to travel occasionally, or so he told me. What can I say—I was stupid and couldn't put two and two together. There were signs, plenty of them, but the truth is, I chose to ignore them. Like I said, I wanted the fairy story."

"What signs did you ignore?"

"Well, I wanted to meet his parents, but they were in Chicago, of course. I tried to get him to go to Philly to meet my dad. He never seemed to have two days off when we could take the train. But even closer to home, I wanted him to meet Martha and Ben. I tried a bunch of times to arrange for us to have dinner together, but he kept having excuses and putting it off.

"Martha smelled a rat, but I wouldn't doubt him. One day, she stopped by Walter Reed Hospital, where he and I worked. She knew my schedule and found us having lunch in the cafeteria. We had just sat down when Martha showed up. As soon as she joined us, she started peppering him with questions. I was embarrassed by how she was drilling him. He hadn't finished much of his lunch when he suddenly remembered he had to get back to his ward. When he left, she said straight off, 'He's hiding something. I bet he's married.'

"That made me mad. We had a big ruckus over it. The truth is, Martha figured out in ten minutes what I couldn't see in ten months. Well that's my sister for you; she's shrewd. As they say, love is blind, or at least passionate love is. It can leave you sightless."

"Did you get suspicious after that?"

"I guess she managed to plant a seed of doubt, though I tried hard to ignore it at first. I told him what she'd said, just to see his reaction. He made me feel so guilty for mentioning it. The truth is, I wanted to believe him."

"How soon after you broke up with him did you meet Daddy?"

"I had already known your father for some time by then. He had been a patient in my ward. The war was ending when he cleared for duty. They made him a driver at the hospital for the duration. Your father rescued me. He was a life raft."

"What do you mean, a life raft?" Mamma got silent again, and we drove on for maybe five miles, passing endless rows of tobacco and corn plants before I asked the question again. "What do you mean that Daddy rescued you?

"From myself. I was a real mess when David broke up with me. There, I've said his name. I haven't uttered it in decades. Don't ever mention any of this to your father. Do you understand me? It would only hurt him, and he doesn't deserve that."

"Yes, of course, I promise. I never would; you know that. Give me some credit. I have better sense than that. Just tell me, how did Daddy rescue you?"

"Like many of my patients, your father had been asking me out. But because of his job, he stuck around longer, and he never gave up. He was persistent. Then one day I came to work and David was gone—transferred, I was told by another doctor. He never said a word to me. One day he was just gone."

"He didn't even leave you a note?" I asked, surprised.

"I did get a rather threatening letter in the mail at work from him a few days later."

"Threatening, how?"

"It was a very carefully composed letter. There was nothing in it to reveal that he had ever had any extramarital affair with me. In the letter, he said that he was telling me for the last time to give up my fantasy about him. He said he did all that he could to dissuade me. He even said in the letter that he was aware of my wild ways, hanging out at night clubs and running around with numerous men. That was a lie. He was careful to write a letter that I could never show to anyone. He cautioned me to mend my ways. He said that if I ever tried to contact him or his family, he would go to my superiors and inform them of my low character. God, I was such a fool to think that he ever loved me.

"Your father found me crying in one of the storage rooms just after I read David's parting letter. I guess I was sobbing a bit too loud, and he heard me and opened the closet door. I was sitting on a pile of bags of dirty laundry when I looked up and saw his kind, sympathetic face. He dried my eyes and asked if I wanted to talk about it. I wasn't ready. He was so patient. He took me out to a diner on Georgia Avenue that night, and we had a long talk. He told me all about himself, and I told him about growing up in Philly. I told him about my mother dying. How David had led me to believe we would get married. I cried a lot. Your father told me I wasn't alone. That he was there for me. He said he fell in love with me at first sight. Before the night was done, he asked me to marry him. I fell into his arms. He was my white knight."

"And just like that you said yes? That doesn't make any sense. You hardly knew Daddy and you agreed to get married after one date! That sounds insane."

"I didn't say yes immediately, but it wasn't long after."

"How long after?"

"Maybe two weeks later."

"What was the rush? Wow, that's a whirlwind romance. It seems rather impetuous."

"I had lost my mother a couple of years before. If I ever had a kindred spirit, she was it. She was my anchor and my compass. I was adrift. I'd known your father for months at work. I knew he was a good, hardworking, and honest man. He'd provide for me. He seemed a good catch. He is a good catch. Other nurses liked him a lot. He could have had his pick. Your father can be quite charming."

"I hate that term 'catch.' It makes one sound desperate."

"Maybe I was desperate. I was desperate to feel worthy of

494

being loved, and I did love your father for his gallantry, and he was charismatic. He swept me off my feet and into his caring, strong, capable arms. It was a safe pair of arms. We may be mismatched in many ways, but it doesn't mean we don't love each other."

"I don't know, Mamma. You don't make love sound too alluring."

"Alluring? Don't be allured. Relationships take a lot of work. Learn from my mistakes. That is the point in my telling you. For the most part, you're pretty level-headed, but sometimes your passionate viewpoints cloud your reasoning. You often see things as starkly black or white. That is because of your youth. But life will teach you there are many shades of gray to the truth."

CHAPTER FORTY-NINE

LABOR DAY

Mamma and I got back from Norfolk late on Sunday, two days before the start of school. I was anxious to get back to applying to colleges and for scholarships. I was taking another class from my freshman English teacher, Mr. Williams, who was also my mentor. To help with college applications, he encouraged me to continue writing during the summer.

"Every college, university, and scholarship organization requires writing samples," he advised.

"But I don't know what topic they're going give me. Shouldn't I wait to find out?"

"Whatever the topic, they're going to want to learn about you. Write about yourself, your experiences, your dreams, and then you'll have a library of material to pull from. Whatever the topic, you can reshape what you've already written." Following his advice, I spent many hours writing stories from my past and was anxious to have his input.

The next morning was Labor Day. Mamma sent me down to the garage to deliver more coffee to Daddy and the boys. I was just heading back up the hill when a car pulled up. Through the car's open window, I heard a voice call out, "Hi there, Charlie. When did you get back?"

I turned around and there was Stacey in the driver's seat. Another girl I didn't know was sitting next to her.

"Hey, Stacey. I got home yesterday. Whose car is that?"

"Mine," she said, grinning as she turned the engine off and got out of the car. "Well, at least it's mine to drive. My mom and stepdad got it. They're tired of getting up early to take me to school." She bent her head toward the window and spoke to her passenger. "Hey, May. Get on out of the car and come and meet my best friend."

I was surprised to hear her call me her best friend. When the girl got out and started to walk around the car to join us, Stacey introduced her. "Charlie, meet my sister, May."

"Sister! How's that? Where've you been hiding her?"

"She's not my real sister. Well, kind of. We're stepsisters. She's been living down in Nashville, Tennessee, and now she's come to stay with us. She just got here last week."

"Hi there, May. Pleased to meet you. I'm Charlotte, but most folks call me Charlie," I said as I offered my hand to shake.

"Hi Charlie, my name is Maybelle, but folks just call me May

498

for short. I'm pleased to meet ya."

"So, May, what brings you to Maryland?"

"My ma died."

"Wow. I am very sorry. How'd she die?"

"She got drunk and wrapped her car 'round a tree. So now I get to live with my dad."

"God. I'm sorry. I feel awful for asking."

May shrugged her shoulders but said nothing. Uncomfortable with the silence, I fidgeted and asked, "So you're not just visiting. This is permanent."

"For the time being, I guess." Just then, Buddy came out of the garage and started taking a long and all too obvious look at May. May was shorter than Stacey and me but had much fuller breasts than we had. Her tight shirt was buttoned low and showed off her ample cleavage. Her pants were tight as well and accentuated the curve of her hips. While Buddy looked her over, she was taking her own long, appreciative look at Buddy. Then he let loose one of his famous Buddy smiles. This one said *you're-the-best-thing-I've-ever-seen*, and she was hooked.

"Good morning, loooovely ladies," he oozed. "Is there anything I can do for you?"

Though he was looking at May, Stacey answered, "Well, yes, there is, Buddy. My radiator keeps overheating. I gotta carry a jug of water with me everywhere. It's a pain. How much would you charge just to check it out?"

"Checking it out is free. Once I figure out the problem, I'll let you know how much it costs to fix it. Here, give me the keys." Stacey tossed them to him.

"We'll head up to the house," I told him. "Come get us when you've got it figured out."

At the house, we went up to my room. Stacey asked about what I'd done over the summer while May thumbed through my record collection. I had about a dozen albums, and a whole lot of forty-fives. Looking over my collection, May asked, "Got any Elvis or Tammy Wynette, or how about some Dolly Parton?"

"Elvis? Isn't he a bit old hat? He's, like, popular with middle-aged folks who go to Las Vegas, isn't he?"

"Old hat? He's the greatest recording artist who ever lived."

"That's subjective."

"No, it ain't. He's sold more records than anyone. With music, people vote with their pocketbooks. He's the greatest—that's just a fact."

"The Beatles have sold more," I corrected her.

"That's four guys. He sold more if you divide what they did by four. He's the greatest single recording artist."

"Okay, I'll give you that. But he's not putting them out like he used to. All I am saying is he is no longer all that current. In any case, no, I don't have any Elvis or Tammy whatever her name is."

"Wynette."

"Yeah, Wynette. Next time you come over, bring some records and we'll play them. Okay?"

"Okay. You might even like 'em."

"I might. Hey, do you like Creedence Clearwater Revival?"

"I've heard 'em on the radio," she admitted. "They're okay."

"They're a bit country, or at least they play a swamp, bayou kind of rock. This one might appeal to you," I said as I put the B side of a 45 on my turntable. "It's called 'Who'll Stop the Rain.'"

As the music played, we caught up. "I worked all summer in the shoe department at Montgomery Ward," said Stacey. "Once school starts, I'll only work on Saturdays. My stepdad is making me give him half of each paycheck to help pay for school. He wanted to take all of it, but I threatened to quit. After all, it wasn't my idea to go to private school. It was his."

"I just got a job working Friday and Saturday nights at the Italian Inn up on Annapolis Road," interjected May. "Last Saturday was my first day. Most of my money comes in tips. My dad gets the paycheck and I keep the tips. I'm going to public school, so he can't say it's for the tuition. I'm saving up to get my own place."

"You in a hurry to move out?"

"Somethin' like that."

"You don't like it there?"

"I only met my dad once before Ma died, that I can remember. He left us when I was three. I've spoken with him a few times on the phone, usually around Christmas. It's weird living there. Stacey's nice, but I'm used to having my own room and so is she, right?" Stacey nodded in agreement. May added, "I'll be eighteen in December and can do what I want after that."

"Why aren't you going to Baptist school like Stacey and her brother?" I asked.

"Dad says he can't swing it, my arriving all sudden like, and that's just fine by me."

The record ended, and I got up to flip it over. When "Travelin' Band" started to play, I asked, "So, Stacey, what do you think—will President Ford pardon Nixon?"

"Shoot, it doesn't mean a hill of beans to me what Ford does."

"But don't you believe in justice?"

"Justice? That's just for folks like us. Those rich suits never pay up. He'll let him off. You mark my words. That's why Nixon chose him. Sure as God made little green apples, they've already made a deal. It won't change my life one bit. If it ain't one crook in the White House, it's another. I hate politics. Let's talk about somethin' that matters, like who do you think is better looking, Robby Benson or David Cassidy? May likes Robby, but I prefer David. What's your vote?"

"I'll go with May on that one. I like his eyes. But it doesn't matter. We'll never meet either of them."

"Perhaps it doesn't matter, but it sure is more fun to think about them than Tricky Dick and his cronies."

As the record was ending, May chimed in, "Your brother has eyes like Robby Benson's, don't you think?" I got up to turn off the record player. "Both them songs were all right, but I liked the second one best. You got any more like that?" she asked.

Before I could answer, we were interrupted by the sound of Buddy climbing the stairs.

"Hey there, Buddy," Stacey said. "What'd ya find out?"

"Good news! Your radiator is okay. You just had a couple of dried-out hoses. I'll only charge you for materials. No charge for labor. It'll be two bucks."

"That sounds good. How long will it take?"

"It's done."

"Done? What if I said I'd take it home and get my stepdad to fix it?"

"Then I'd be out two bucks. You gals hungry? Want some lunch? Mamma's making up some ham sandwiches."

"I'm hungry," answered May as she jumped off my bed.

"Great. Come and tell me all about yourself," he said as he led May out the door and down the stairs.

"So what's that all about?" asked Stacey.

"Buddy's been bit by the love bug, that's what. And by the look on her face, I'd say May's been bit too. She's a bit coquettish, don't you think?"

"What's that mean?"

"Flirtatious."

"Yeah, I suppose so."

"Well, so is Buddy. You want to make any bets on how long their flirtations last?"

"Gamblin' is a sin. I'm a Baptist. We don't gamble."

"Shoot. Life's a gamble. Every time you drive your car, it's a gamble. I give 'em 'til Thanksgiving. May's got what boys like, in a Marilyn Monroe sort of way, if you know what I mean. She keeps dressing like that, she'll get a lot of attention from the guys at school. She'll have her pick."

"I don't know. Buddy's awfully cute."

"Oh, God, not you too! I thought you liked Chip."

"Chip? Whatever gave you that idea?"

"You did."

"You're crazy."

CHAPTER FIFTY

⮟❖⮞

APPLE PICKING TIME

September was flying by. I was waitressing once more and saving every penny for college. Each time I got a college acceptance letter, grant, or scholarship response, I called Aunt Martha to share the news. With Aunt Charlotte's help tracing our Ward family tree, I was able to qualify for a $1,000 scholarship from the Daughters of the American Revolution.

One late September day, I came home to find May and Mamma working together in the kitchen. When I opened the door, the aromas of garlic, onions, and tomatoes assailed me. They were singing, and their voices harmonized well together. It was evident that they were having fun as they worked, singing, "When the moon hits your eye like a big pizza pie, that's amore." Quietly, I set my books down and stood in the kitchen doorway; they were unaware that they were being spied upon. Mamma was washing dishes and May was at the cutting board.

"… Hearts will play tippy-tippy-tay, tippy-tippy-tay like a gay tarantella." Watching them, I was jealous of their easy camaraderie, and I felt as if I was being replaced in my mother's affection. I knew I was wrong to feel that way, but I couldn't help it.

"You two sound like you're having fun," I said, interrupting their performance.

"There you are, honey," Mamma said when she turned around. "You're home late. Did you have a good day at school?"

"It was fine. I had to stay late. Mr. Williams helped me fine-tune a couple of my college applications. What have you two been up to?"

"We're making Italian sauce from your Pa's tomatoes," answered May. "We're having spaghetti tonight."

"We're? You sound like you're moving in."

"After all her hard work, she is joining us for dinner," interjected Mamma. "Come sit down. We were about to take a break. May was telling me about her mother. Did you know she recorded a record and had it played on radio stations? Her mother was a singer."

"No, I didn't. I thought you said she was a bookkeeper for some doctors."

"That was just her day job. The reason we moved to Nashville was so she could pursue a singing career. She nearly made it a couple of times. A few years back, she sang backup for Dolly Parton at the Grand Ole Opry. Miss Parton asked her to come out on tour, but Ma couldn't go on account of me. Then last year she got a limited record deal and she cut a forty-five. But just getting a record produced ain't enough. You gotta get the radio stations to play it. The summer 'fore last, we spent two weeks and then every weekend going to as many radio stations as we could across Tennessee, Kentucky, Mississippi, and Alabama. She'd walk into those stations dressed to the hilt and ask them to play her forty-five. Some of them interviewed her on the air too. We slept in an old tent in campgrounds. I had the best time of my life."

"Working in nightclubs, is that where your mother learned to drink?"

"Charlie!" snapped Mamma. "What's gotten into you? That was rude."

"I didn't mean anything by it. But I was under the impression that your mother drank from what you said and from how Stacey's mom carries on about her when I'm over there."

"She hardly ever did. I never saw her take a drink, and I never saw her drunk neither."

"But isn't that how you said she died?"

"I just said that because Stacey was standing there. Yeah, she had a couple of drinks that night. That's what the autopsy said, anyway. She went to a Fourth of July party with her boyfriend, Roger. They'd been dating for about two years, but I think he was cheating on her. The other guests said they got into a big fight and broke up. She was upset, and it was raining heavily. I wasn't with her, so I don't know why she lost control of that car. But my mother wasn't no alcoholic. Stacey's mom likes to make it sound like she was, but it ain't true. My dad's the one who had a drinking problem when he walked out on us back in Cherokee Hills where we're from. He never cared whether I had enough to eat or if there was enough money to keep the lights on. Now he acts like he's all worried about my eternal soul. We have Bible readings every night after supper and spend all day in church on Sunday. He thinks that makes him a 'Good Christian.'"

"I am sure he loves you in his own way," Mamma said, trying to comfort her.

"Loves me? Back when Mamma was putting herself through bookkeeping school and working as a waitress, her car died and she needed another one. For three months, we didn't have electricity. At first, it wasn't so bad. We used kerosene lamps at night and read a lot. But come November there wasn't any heat neither. Ma kept calling my dad demanding he pay up his child support. He kept promising he would, but the checks never came. She kept threatening to have him put in jail, but she never did. She said having him in jail would be revenge but it wouldn't help us none.

"After she finished school and got a good job, life got better, but we still had to live in a double-wide. When I came up here and saw Stacey's fancy bedroom furniture that he bought her, I 'bout split a gut. My ma was responsible, smart, beautiful, kind, and talented. My stepmom puts her down for her clothes—and yes, she wore sexy clothes, but that was for the stage. That don't make her a tramp, I don't care what anyone says. Stacey's mom is not real happy to have me around. She makes that very clear. But she doesn't have to keep trash talkin' my ma, who was a thousand times better person than either of those two.

"I'm sorry I'm rattling on. It's been hard living there."

"May, I'm so sorry I said that about your mom. I don't know what got into me. You and your mom were obviously very close. I'm sorry I didn't get a chance to meet her."

"I wish you could have met her. You would have liked her. Everyone did. She wasn't just my mom, she was my best friend. She was my whole world."

Mamma reached over and placed her hand on top of May's. "I know exactly how you feel. It's been almost thirty years since I lost my mother, and I still miss her."

"May, I am so sorry. Please forgive me," I pleaded, genuinely regretful for my coldness toward her.

"You're forgiven, Charlie. I know you didn't mean no harm. Next time I come over, I will bring you a copy of her forty-five. She wrote the song on the B side. It's called 'Second Chance Man.'"

A few weeks later as I climbed our hill, coming home on a cool October Sunday afternoon, I saw May on the top of a ladder with a sack tied around her waist. "Hey there, May," I yelled. "What are you doing up that tree."

"Picking apples. Wanna help?"

"Naw. It looks like you're managing just fine. You know those are too sour to eat?"

"Those are the best ones for making pies and sauce. Your Ma and I are fixin' to do some canning."

"No pies tonight? One of your pies sounds good to me right now."

"Yeah, I was going to make a pie for supper too. Don't worry."

"How come you're here today? I thought your dad insisted on you going to church on Sundays."

"Lucky for me, he's given up on my eternal soul. He's letting me work at the restaurant on Sundays too."

"Wow, glad to have you in the sinners' club. Careful you don't start growing horns, fraternizing with us liberals."

"He's more worried about me going to school with Blacks than you liberals. He thinks they're all perverts and criminals. Back in Nashville, I went to school with a few Blacks and never had a lick of trouble. Dad says I still gotta be home for Bible study on Wednesday nights. That was our deal. Plus, I gotta go to church with them on Sundays, but I can leave right after the service."

May was no longer wearing her mother's wardrobe. Her clothes were much looser. I guessed that was because of her parents. She was a better student than I had expected and did exceptionally well in math. She liked to bake, and Mamma let her use our kitchen. While Buddy was down in the garage, she'd bake brownies, cookies, pies, and cakes. We all started to gain a few pounds. Sometimes she'd make us all dinner too, and she'd leave the kitchen scrubbed top to bottom when she finished.

One evening after dinner, May, Mamma, and I lingered at the table together. "I used to cook for my ma and me back home," May told us. "I had dinner ready when she got home each night from work. I helped her with her tax work too."

"Tax work?" I asked.

"Yeah. She did a few folks' taxes in the trailer park and word got out quick. 'Fore we knew it, she had more people askin' her to do their taxes than she could keep up with. She taught me how to do 'em, and I did the easier ones. She'd check them, though. I got half the money from each one I prepared. I took a class in bookkeeping at school, and she helped me learn how to do that too. There was a veterinarian near our place, and I'd help his wife with the bookkeeping and got paid under the table. I liked that job."

"Lord, how I hate doing the bookkeeping. I don't have a head for it," complained Mamma.

"I can take over for you, Mrs. Ward. I like working with numbers.

"That would be a dream come true if you could do that."

"It'd be my pleasure. You've been so nice to me."

511

It wasn't just into Mamma's and Buddy's heart that May moved, but Daddy's too. Sometimes she'd join Buddy, Chip, and Daddy down in the garage, making herself useful, helping out with the customers and tidying up around the garage as well. She was becoming indispensable and a part of the family. We all got used to having her around. Still, Mamma made Buddy keep his door open when they were up in his room. The first couple of times he took May to the movies, Mamma gave me some money and told him to take me too. We all knew she was hoping I would be some sort of a chaperone, but I sat in the back of the theater rather than next to them while they necked. The second time we went to the theater together, I told them as we were leaving, "You know you won't fool Mamma when we get home."

"What are you talking about?" Buddy asked.

"I'm talking about that ring of hickeys around your necks. What are you, a pair of vampires? Yuck, you're gross."

"Really," responded May, concerned. "Are they that noticeable?"

"Well, yeah, you can't miss them," I answered.

"What am I going to do?" she said in a panic. "My dad is going to have a fit if he sees me with hickeys. God only knows what my stepmother will do. She's likely to throw me out."

"Relax," I said, trying to console her. "We'll stop by our house before Buddy takes you home. We'll try some of my mom's makeup to cover them up. If that doesn't work, you can borrow a scarf to tie around your neck. Do you have any turtleneck shirts at home?"

"I have a couple."

"You better wear them for the next few days. Next time take it easy."

CHAPTER FIFTY-ONE

LIARS' FEAST

*I*t was a few days before Thanksgiving, and Mamma was happy with anticipation and yet apprehensive too. She wanted everything to go perfectly, and she let me know it. For days, we cleaned the house, ironed tablecloths, and polished silverware. Around noon the day before our big feast, I came home from shopping and found her cleaning the already spotless living room. I hung up my raincoat and went to the kitchen to give May the bag of groceries Mamma wanted. Then I returned to the living room. An old Andrew Sisters album was playing on the stereo, and Mamma was singing along with the record. As she sang the lyrics, "… when he plays with the bass and guitar," she grabbed my arm and twirled me around and continued singing. "They holler out, beat me Daddy, eight to the bar."

I did my best to keep up and joined in singing the chorus. When the song ended and she released me, I said, "Boy, you're in a good mood."

"I've got a lot to be happy about."

"So, when's Eugene arriving?" I asked. He had a four-day holiday leave, and we were all looking forward to having him home. Our whole family would be together, accept for Emma, of course. Aunt Martha, Uncle Ben, and even Granddad were coming. Mamma's father had never been to any of our houses before. His coming made it feel as if he was at long last giving his blessing on Mamma and Daddy's marriage. He, Aunt Martha, and Uncle Ben would be staying at a nearby hotel, but we'd have the entire day together.

Answering my question, she said, "He said he'd be here sometime around nine or ten o'clock."

I returned to the kitchen, where May was pulling the last of her pies out of the oven. The aroma was intoxicating. She'd made two each of apple, pumpkin, and pecan. "Goodness, that's a lot of pies."

"I'm taking two of 'em to my house."

"Still, that leaves four pies. Is there any chance of getting a slice now?" I asked her.

"That's up to your ma."

"Forget about it," came Mamma's prompt reply. "Those are for our feast tomorrow. Why don't you focus on getting the table ready, Charlotte?"

I poked my head in the dining room. Daddy and Buddy had enlarged our table by placing a long piece of plywood on top of it, securing it with duct tape. Their handiwork was hidden under a long white, starched tablecloth. "What needs to be done? It looks pretty ready to me."

"Decorations. It needs to be festive."

"Decorations? Like what?"

"Use your imagination. You could make colorful leaves. Upstairs in the hall dresser, in the crafts drawer, you'll find some colored paper. Go outside and find some big leaves to use as a template. Then just trace and cut. Use up all the autumn colors."

"Outside? But it's rainy and cold."

"You won't melt. Take an umbrella. When you're done, sprinkle your leaves on the table."

"Okay, I can do that."

"And make those napkin turkeys for everyone like you did a few years back."

"You mean the ones with pine cones and napkins folded like a fan for the tail?"

"Yes, they were cute. Maybe you can make some place names too. Be creative."

I grabbed my raincoat again and pulled on some boots and went outside. Fortunately, there was a break in the rain, but it felt cold enough for snow. I wandered our yard and found leaves, pine cones, and some pussy willow branches at the bottom of our hill. I filled a vase with the pussy willows and put it in the center of our credenza. For place names, I made little pilgrim hats and wrote each person's name on them. When I finished, Mamma placed her mother's freshly polished silver candle holders in the center of the table. Standing back to admire the table, she said, "It's *un chef-d'œuvre* (a masterpiece), Charlotte. You did a fantastic job. You put your heart into it, and it shows. I love it."

"*Ce fut un plaisir.* It was a pleasure."

"We're about ready. Do you have much homework you need to get to?"

"Not much. Just one English assignment. I have to write a poem, short story, or essay about Thanksgiving, but I haven't come up with an idea yet."

"Well, while you're waiting on your muse, how about cleaning the upstairs bathroom? There's a bucket, mop, and cleaning supplies already up there." Before I could answer, Eugene walked through the front door.

"Well, isn't this a pleasant surprise. I didn't expect you until much later," greeted Mamma as she rushed over to hug Eugene. He dropped two heavy bags to embrace her. "What's this, your laundry?"

"Yes, it's my laundry, plus I've got a bit more time than I originally planned."

"You do? That's wonderful. How much time?"

"Well, a few weeks. I'll explain later."

"Is everything all right?"

"Yes, of course. Everything is great."

Just then May came out of the kitchen, wiping her hands on a dish towel.

"Hello," said Eugene. "We haven't met."

"I'm May."

"May, this is our oldest brother, Eugene. Eugene, this is May, Buddy's girlfriend," I added.

"Nice to meet you, May. Mamma's told me some nice things about you. I'll just stow these bags upstairs. I'll see you all in a bit."

"I'll go clean the bathroom," I said and followed Eugene upstairs. I had just started wiping down the sink when Eugene popped into the bathroom

"So, where's Chip? I saw Daddy and Buddy down at the garage when I came up, but I didn't see Chip."

"He's walking Caesar. Or so that's what he tells Mamma and Daddy."

"What's that supposed to mean?"

"Well, when he gets back, his eyes will be red. He takes the dog for a walk whenever he wants to get stoned."

"Does he do that a lot?"

"Let's just say the dog gets a lot of daily walks. It drives Daddy crazy."

"Are he and Daddy still going at it?"

"No, they've had a *détente*, or at least they're *entr'acte*. They get along well enough for now. But it's like we're sitting on a time bomb. Mostly, they stay out of each other's way. Chip has been trying to find a job, but the market is not so good right now. There's a lot of competition. He wants desperately to move out. He has a friend from Nam named Sam who lives in Texas. He recently got a job as a helicopter mechanic. The helicopters fly men out to the oil rigs in the Gulf of Mexico. Sam said he'd let him know if a job opens up. So far, nothing has. Buddy's frustrated. He calls Sam a lot."

"So, what do you think of May? Do you like her? Is she good for Buddy?"

"She's nice. She's grown on me. She's become kind of indispensable around here. She not only helps in the kitchen but with the bookkeeping. That's been a big help, especially to Mamma. She's my friend Stacey's stepsister.

"Yes, I know."

"Well, May's mother died, and now she has to live with her dad. He wasn't much more than a stranger to her until she moved up here. Stacey's mom hasn't been very welcoming. In fact, she's been downright hostile. I don't blame May for hanging out here as much as she can. She and Buddy hit it off straightaway. Now Buddy wants to marry her, but you're not to mention it to Mamma and Daddy. He's waiting until after Thanksgiving to spring it on them, and I think that's for the best. Mamma is on cloud nine right now in anticipation of having everyone here, especially Granddad. I don't want to spoil it for her with any drama. So please keep it quiet, okay?"

"Yeah, sure, I won't say a thing. It's not for me to tell anyway."

"Is everything okay with you? I asked.

"Yep, sure is. Couldn't be better. I best go down and help Mamma and get out of your way. Thanks for the update."

As he left the room, I thought there was something he wasn't telling me. He wasn't himself.

Thanksgiving Day was warmer than the day before, but it was still drizzling on and off. When Granddad, Aunt Martha, and Uncle Ben arrived around midday, Mamma had hot-spiced cider waiting for them. Granddad came in wearing a tweed suit and hat, looking a lot like Rex Harrison or perhaps a much older Christopher Plummer. Aunt Martha came in wearing a new wig and a beautiful blue-green dress I'd not seen before. She seemed even thinner than before, but her smile lit up her face when she greeted me. Uncle Ben handed me a bag with several bottles of wine in it. "Here, Charlie, take this into the kitchen."

Mamma joined us and took Martha in her arms and gave her a long hug. "Goodness, you're a bag of bones. How are you feeling?"

"Great, absolutely great. I'm getting better every day and looking forward to this feast." Mamma then turned and greeted Granddad.

We all sat in the living room while Mamma served us hot cider. "I've got a good joke," said Buddy.

"Yeah," said Daddy. "Let's hear it."

"Well, see, Nixon, Kissinger, Billy Graham, and some hippie guy are on this airplane when the pilot has a heart attack and dies. The four passengers have to jump to safety, but there's only three parachutes. Nixon immediately grabs, one saying, 'I'm the most important man here. I am the president of the United States, the leader of the free world. The world needs me to survive,' and he jumps out.

"Next, Kissinger grabs one, saying, 'I'm the world's smartest man and the advisor to the president. I must survive too,' and he jumps out.

"Then Billy Graham says to the hippie, 'Go ahead, son, I've made my peace with God. I'm ready. You take the last parachute. You have your whole life in front of you.'

"But then the hippie says, "Don't worry, reverend, there's two left. The world's smartest man just grabbed my knapsack.""

Buddy started laughing at his own joke, and we joined him.

"So, Buddy," Granddad said, "your ma says you've got a girlfriend. Is it serious? Should I be getting an invitation soon?"

Buddy squirmed and blushed, saying, "She's a real nice girl. We've been dating a couple of months. There's no need to rush us."

"No one's rushing you, son. You've got time. It's just your ma has mentioned her a couple of times, and seemed the two of you were getting serious."

Wanting to help him out, I told a joke. "Hey, Granddad, can you tell me the difference between an Irish wake and an Irish wedding?"

"One less drunk. That's an old one, Charlotte. You'd better stick with your studies."

Coming to my aid, Daddy told a couple of jokes of his own. His went over better than mine did. Then Mamma got us all to sing a few songs before she gathered our empty cider cups and we headed to the dining room.

Mamma had cooked up a storm. The turkey was golden brown and the mashed potatoes smooth. There were baked sweet potatoes, stuffing, green beans, fresh rolls, gravy, cranberry sauce, and all of May's pies. The table was festive. Aunt Martha seemed in good spirits, laughing often. However, I caught her and Ben exchanging furtive glances—there was something they weren't sharing. Sipping his wine, Granddad told a couple of funny stories about growing up in Philadelphia. Several times he asked Eugene how things were going at the Naval Academy. But Eugene deftly changed the topic each time. Glancing around the table, an idea for my English assignment started to form. As our conversation moved across the table, a poem's couplets began pouring into my head:

This holiday table is set for yet another pilgrims' feast.

There is wine for our spirits, but souls are in retreat.

Daddy opened another bottle and refilled the wine glasses. I had more cider. We were all on our best behavior. Even Daddy and Ben were swapping anecdotes.

Although we joke and laugh as our familiar conversation dances.

We never stop for the truth, thus endangering our chances.

Despite all the good cheer, I couldn't help but feel that we were all holding our breaths, hoping for the best but fearful of hidden booby traps and land mines.

So we perform the old rituals, each character carefully cast.

These were a lifetime in the making and were surely meant to last.

Toward the end of the dinner, Daddy made a remark that I feared would spark an explosion. "Thank you, Chip, for showing up clear-eyed. I hope you're not thinking of taking the dog on any walks tonight."

You could see Chip was offended by the remark, but he kept his peace. "No, Dad, I was thinking of helping clear the dishes so that we could get to those pies."

"Great," added Mamma, "I'll put the kettle on. Who wants tea or coffee?"

"You sit, Mamma," I said. "You've worked hard enough. Chip and I will get started with the desserts and the cleaning up." As I cleared the plates, I thought how similar exchanges were probably occurring at other tables. Families gathering to perform old rituals was my poem's topic.

For now, we depart and forget until next year and the next pilgrims' table.

As I washed the dishes, I kept repeating my poem in my

head, adding and editing lines and trying to remember them long enough to go upstairs and write them down. Chip remained in the kitchen with me, silently working at my side. By the time the coffees, teas, and pies were finished and the evening came to an end, we had the kitchen spotless, and Mamma's approval.

The Friday after Thanksgiving, I headed over to Stacey's house. I didn't want to be home when Buddy informed my parents about his wedding plans, in case there was any drama. When I arrived, Stacey's parents were nowhere to be seen. We headed straight up to her room. Last year she had gotten all new bedroom furniture and bedding. Standing in the center of the room was a double-sized white canopy bed with a curved, arching top. Over it was a pale-pink eyelet drape with ruffles along the side that matched the cover and mattress skirt. On either side of the bed were matching white end tables; each held a lamp with a pale-pink shade. Stacey had called her room a princess sanctuary. Now she shared it with May.

"Where's May?" I asked.

"She said she was walking up to the store. She was in a real mood this morning. May and my mom got into a fight."

"That's not news."

"This one was a really, really bad one. I like May, but it's been a war zone here since she moved in. I'll be glad when she's gone. No offense to May. Let's play something. Do you want to play Clue?"

"Yeah, sure."

"I call Miss Scarlett," she announced as she went over to her closet and pulled out the board game.

"You're always Miss Scarlett."

"Well, if you wanted it, you should have called it." We set up the board game in the center of her bed. We had to sit carefully so we didn't tip the board. "Who do you want to be this time?"

"I'll be Professor Plum."

"Professor Plum? Why not Mrs. Peacock or Mrs. White?"

"It hardly matters. Just deal the cards."

Once we had it all set up, Stacey rolled the dice because Miss Scarlett always goes first. She rolled a nine and moved her piece to the lounge. She moved several tokens to the lounge. "I suggest that the colonel did it with the gun in the lounge."

I looked through my cards and had all three. I showed her the card for Colonel Mustard to disprove her guess. Then I picked up the dice. "Back in September, you should have taken my bet about May and Buddy," I commented.

"What bet was that?"

"The bet that they wouldn't last until Thanksgiving. I was totally wrong. They're still going strong. Buddy is really into her. She seems nice enough. What does your mom have against her?"

"She's got her reasons."

"What reasons?"

"It's just they're different, is all, and May's not her own."

"That's not all that nice of your mother. Isn't that what you call not being very Christian?"

"Why do you say that?" Stacey asked, a bit defensively. "She's taken her in and given her a roof over her head. That's Christian, ain't it?"

"But she sure lets her know she's not wanted here. Your stepdad has been the real saint in comparison. He treats you like his own. Why can't your mom do the same?"

"He ain't no saint, I can tell you that. He don't treat me like I was his own. The reason he prays so much is to try and wash away his own sins."

"Doesn't he provide for you?"

"Yeah, and he's taken what he wants too."

"What do you mean?"

"I mean he's a pervert. He don't do it anymore, but he used to play with me when my mom wasn't home."

"What do you mean, 'play with you'?"

"I mean he used to put his hands on me and make me play with his thing."

"What thing?"

"The thing that men got between their legs and we don't, you moron."

"Shit! Stacey, that's sick. It's gross. Did you tell your mom?"

"Not at first. He said she'd be angry at me if she knew. But she got suspicious and started asking me questions. Finally, I told her. I just wanted it to stop."

"What did she say when you told her?"

"She told me to tell him no, and if that didn't work, I was to hit him and hit him hard. So, I did. But that didn't stop him. Finally, I threatened to call the cops. That got his attention quick. He hasn't touched me in that way since. I wish I'd known that 'I'll call the police' were the magic words. I would have said 'em a whole lot sooner."

"And your mom is still with him. Why didn't she leave him then?"

"She said we'd be a lot worse off without his paycheck. That's all right, he don't touch me now, and he gets me stuff. That's why he bought me this bedroom set last year, to keep me quiet. He don't know that my mom knows."

"Shoot, it's still creepy having to live with the guy."

"It's okay, now I know how to handle him. I tell you what's creepy—having to sleep in the same bed with May. She tosses and turns all night long."

"Why don't you get bunk beds then?"

"I'm not giving up my bedroom set. No way."

"I guess you'll have to sleep with May, then." I rolled the dice and moved my piece into the conservatory. "Okay, I think Mrs. White did it with the candlestick in the conservatory."

"Nope, I got Mrs. White."

"I got to go use the bathroom," I said as I gently got off the bed so as not to disturb the board game. "Don't cheat while I am gone."

"I don't cheat. I'll find something on the radio."

"Just in case, I'll take my cards with me, and please, no country and western."

"My house, my music. Hurry up and go."

Their house was much smaller than ours. It had three bedrooms, no basement, and only one bathroom. Stacey's room was upstairs across the hall from her brother's room. The bath was on the ground floor next to her parents' bedroom. As I reached the bottom of the stairs, I could hear Stacey's parents arguing. Their voices grew louder as I passed their closed bedroom door and went into the bathroom. When I came out, I heard her mother say, "She's a slut and a liar. I don't trust her."

I know it was wrong of me, but I hovered in the hall and brought my ear close to their door. "You know it's true. When Maybelle showed up here dressed like some hooker, what was the first thing I asked her? Come on, Bobbie, you remember."

"You asked if she was a virgin."

"That's right. And what did she say?"

"She said she was."

"Not only that, she got up on her high horse and told me she was insulted by the question. You got on my case too, for asking. Well, that apple didn't fall far from the tree. Her mother had a shotgun wedding. Those clothes she wore when she got here were from her mother's closet. How could a mother walk around wearing such trashy clothes? She was already knocked up when we took her in. She kept that bit of information to herself, the deceitful tramp."

"She didn't know yet she was pregnant. It happened just before she left."

"That's what she told you. In any case, she knew she'd been screwing around. She lied, plain and simple. Bobbie, I am not raising her bastard child, I can tell you that."

"It's my grandchild."

"You sure about that?"

"What do you mean?"

"You sure that May's yours? Her mother was a slut."

"You never met the woman."

"I don't have to. I've seen her clothes."

"It'll be all right. Don't worry. May tells me she and that Ward boy are talking about getting married. With any luck, she won't be our problem much longer."

"They're talking. With any luck. Listen to you. You think that boy's stupid? You think he can't count? Once that baby comes earlier than he's expecting, he'll know it ain't his. What then? When he throws her out, what then?"

Standing there listening, my anger grew. I wanted to scream that they were both lying hypocrites. Here she was calling May a liar, but none of them was telling the truth to Buddy. I'd had enough. I dropped my cards on their coffee table and left without telling Stacey why. I hopped on my bike and raced home, my fury propelling me.

When I got in our front door, I was out of breath. I had ridden home as fast as I could. There sitting on the sofa were my parents, and across from them sat Buddy. It was obvious that they had been in deep conversation when I blasted through the door.

"Hi, honey, you're home early. Did you have a change of plans?" asked Mamma. "Why don't you head on up to your room. We're having a private conversation with your brother."

"I know what you're talking about," I said between gasps of breath, then blurted out, "It's not yours, Buddy. You don't have to marry her."

"I know that," responded Buddy.

"What!" shouted Mamma. Then she sank back into the sofa, her face turning an ashen color.

"What did you say?" asked Daddy as he rose up off the sofa. He stared at Buddy, but he remained silent. "It's not yours? Is that true, Buddy? Talk, boy."

"Daddy, I love her. It doesn't change a thing. I'll be the only dad the baby will ever know. I want her to be mine and that includes the baby. I don't want to lose her. I'll never find a better woman for me. We want to marry before the baby comes, so it can have my name."

"It's not just your name, it's my name too," Daddy said.

Mamma started crying. "You lied to us," she said through her sobs.

"No, Mamma, I didn't. I said that she was pregnant and that we wanted to get married soon."

"God is punishing me, Jack."

"No, Maggie, he's testing you."

Noticing me again, Mamma said, "Go to your room, Charlie. This doesn't concern you."

I went up to my room, opened and closed my door, and then headed to the top of the stairs to eavesdrop on their conversation.

"Oh, dear Jesus, haven't I been punished enough?"

"No one's punishing you, Mamma. Don't you want me to get married someday? You like her. You both said how you've come to depend on her, how she's already a part of this family. Why does it make any difference who fathered her baby? I'll be its dad from the day it's born."

"You're too young," said Daddy. "You don't know what you're talking about. Marriage under the best of circumstances is hard. Raising someone else's child can make it harder."

"Is that what you think, Jack? That he'll end up resenting the baby? Is that how it is?"

"No, Maggie. I am just saying marriage and raising a family is hard, a lot harder than he knows. The boy's too young."

"I agree with that," said Mamma as she turned to Buddy. "Honey, you're too young to know what you're getting yourself into."

"Before Charlie barged in here, you were ready to consent. I love her, Mamma, and whether you approve or not, we're getting married."

"Don't you threaten us, boy! How the hell do you think you'll support her, the baby, and yourself? You're a damn fool," Daddy said.

"I don't mean any disrespect. I want your consent. We both do. We want your blessing. Daddy, I love her. I want her near me. What's more, she loves me."

"Loves you? How can you be sure? How do you know she's not just looking for a lifeboat? She's in a difficult situation. It's only natural that she's looking for an escape."

"Jack!" answered Mamma. "She loves him. I know she does."

"Yeah, how come you're so sure?"

"Come on, Jack. You know it too."

"Daddy, there's no question that she loves me. She makes me feel better about myself than I ever have. When I look into her eyes, I see the man I want to be. I see myself through her eyes. May believes in me. She's everything I've ever dreamed about. I'll never find a better woman willing to marry me. I know it will be hard, Daddy, but you weren't much older than me, and you've made it through."

"It was damn hard, son."

"Yes, you've struggled, but you made it. Lots of folks struggle. But if I have her with me, it will make it all worthwhile."

"Buddy," Mamma added, "perhaps we survived, but barely. We were hoping you'd have it easier than we had it. Think about what you're doing."

"I *have* thought about it, and not much else. Mamma, Daddy, I love her. She's more than what I deserve. She's beautiful, smart, talented, and a hard worker. She isn't some princess, but a real partner. We're good together. We want your blessing."

"You want our support. Isn't that what you were asking for before Charlie dropped the bomb?"

"Yes, Daddy. I want to go on working in the garage. May is helpful around the house and the garage. You've said so. We've been saving money in case we need to move out on our own, but we'd rather live here with you. May's never had a big family. She loves you both. You know that."

"What about the child's real father?" asked Daddy. "How does she feel about him? Does he know? What if he shows up?"

"He won't. Look, May can't remember when her mom and dad lived together. It's always been just her and her mom. They were real close. When her mom died, she went a bit crazy. She felt lost. A friend was having a party and she went. There was a guy. She was crying, and he held her, and before she knew it … well it was a one-night stand. She's never seen him since.

"She truly loves you guys. You said yourself that you're fond of her and that she already feels a part of this family."

"God help her," said Mamma.

"What I am asking, Mamma, is will you help us?"

"This breaks my heart, Buddy. More than you can understand."

"I'm sorry, Mamma. We don't want to hurt anyone. But she needs me. Will you help us, or are we on our own?"

"Jack, we have to help them."

"I know, Maggie. I know."

CHAPTER FIFTY-TWO

ℰ❖ℛ

ON SUCH A WINTER'S DAY

*I*t was decided that May and Buddy would marry quietly. Two weeks after Thanksgiving, they went to the county courthouse in Upper Marlboro to tie the knot. They spent their honeymoon in Buddy and Chip's old bedroom. Chip moved in with Eugene, and they took apart Chip and Buddy's old bunk bed and made two twin beds that they then pushed together for the newlyweds. The only celebration was a single bottle of champagne poured equally into six glasses. The next day, everything returned to normal; the only change was that May slept in our house.

A customer dropped off an old crib and playpen. Daddy got to work refinishing them, which made May exceedingly happy. It wasn't the crib and playpen that made her joyful; it was Daddy's acceptance. May seemed to work even harder around the place. I have to admit she was grateful and showed it. In all the pandemonium, Eugene seemed temporarily forgotten, though we all asked him what was going on with him. With each question, he deftly deflected our inquiries.

One evening, I was playing Joni Mitchell's latest album, *Court and Spark*, and he came in to listen. We sat together on my bed in silence. After the song "Car on a Hill" ended, I got up and turned down the music and said, "Eugene, something is going on with you. Why won't you tell me?"

"Because, little sis, I don't know if you'll understand."

I was hurt by that, and he could tell. "I know you love me, Charlie. I don't doubt that."

"Then why can't you trust me? You know I'd never betray you. I love all of my family, but I feel closest to you. If I had a problem, you're the person I'd trust and seek out for advice. I hope you can trust me as well."

"I trust you, Charlie. But this might be hard for you to accept. You may judge me harshly, and that would hurt."

"I'd never judge you harshly. I know you are a good person. What could you have possibly done?"

"The navy and I have a difference of opinion."

"How so?"

"Babydoll, let me put it this way. They would give me a medal if I kill men in battle."

"Are you a conscientious objector?" I interrupted. "I'd respect that."

"That's not it. The navy is kicking me out because I love a man.

538

I can kill one, but I can't love one."

"Love a man? Love who, how? I don't understand."

"You remember my friend Martin who came here?"

"Yes, he was nice. What about him?"

"Well, I love him."

"Love him. Like how."

"Like Daddy loves Mamma."

I sat quietly and took it in.

"I admit, I've never thought about it, but I should have. Did you love Scottie?"

"Yes, very much. He was my first love."

"Wow, I am so naïve."

"You've been protected. This goes against Daddy's and Mamma's beliefs, but that's because it was how they were raised. Do you still love me, Charlie?"

"Love you? I adore you. I admit the idea is foreign to me. It will take me time. But I will never not support you."

"That means to world to me. God, I love you, little sis."

Eventually, it was the mail that caused the explosion. It was the first official day of winter, a cold and cloudy Saturday. Daddy was in the garage when the mailman dropped off the letters. Among the envelopes was something from the Department of the Navy sent to Eugene. Daddy demanded to see it. That's when the arguing began. I was upstairs getting ready to go out when I heard Daddy screaming. I crept to the top of the stairs to listen. May was down at the garage with Buddy. Chip was walking Caesar.

"What's this letter all about? Why is the navy kicking you out? What in the hell do they mean, 'behavior unbecoming an officer?' What's this incident they're referring to? What did you do?"

"Someone claimed they saw me with another man."

"Yeah, so?"

"Saw us making out."

"You mean like making love?"

"Yes."

"And were you?"

"Yes."

"Good God—was this a onetime thing?"

"No, Daddy. I'm gay."

I heard Mamma's voice say, "I admit it. I am not totally surprised."

"What are you saying, Maggie, that you knew?"

"No, Jack, I am saying that hindsight is clearer. The clues where all there, but no, I didn't know. Perhaps I didn't want to admit it. Regardless, he's still our son. He's our wonderful, generous, intelligent son."

"He's a godforsaken homo. Maggie, that's a damnable sin."

"Daddy, I'm the same person I've always been, and I'm also a homosexual. It's the way God made me."

"No, son, it's ungodly and unholy. It's an illness, and with God's help you can be cured."

"There's no cure, Daddy. It's not something I've chosen or contracted like the flu. It's just who I am. It's who I've always been."

"It's an abomination. It's a sin. No, no son of mine is a damn faggot. You need to get help."

"Don't you see that it's not something I chose? Don't you think I've struggled with this? I am asking you to accept me for who I am. I am the same as I've always been. I am your son."

"I can't accept this. Don't *you* see? Your immortal soul is in peril, son. This is for eternity. 'The unrighteous shall not inherit the kingdom of God.' It says so in the Bible. Repent, son. Save your soul. Turn away from these unnatural inclinations."

"I can't change this part of me any more than I can change my skin or eye color. It's natural to me, the way I feel. I've never been attracted to women. God made me male, White, and gay."

"The scriptures tell us, 'You shall not lie with a male as one lies with a female.' It's immoral. As the Bible says, it's an abomination!"

"I am not an abomination. I am your son. I am the same man who entered the Naval Academy. You were proud of me then. If I killed a bunch of men in a war, the navy would give me a medal. But if I love just one man in peace, they want to kick me out."

"No son of mine is a faggot. It's against the laws of man and the laws of God. You won't bring that sin into this house. If you won't seek a cure, you're not welcome in this house. I won't have you corrupting your brothers and sister. It's despicable, disgusting—it's a sin as great as murder. You can't ask me to sanction it. It's against the Holy Book."

"That book was written by men. It was their interpretation of God's words."

"Now you're questioning the Bible! You're a heretic and a sinner."

"Jack, please don't cast him out. I implore you. Think—the Bible says that only God can judge. He's our son. Show some mercy. 'Let him who is without sin be the first to throw a stone.'"

"I won't claim him as my own flesh and blood if he won't give this up. It's his choice, Maggie. Think about Buddy, May, Charlotte, and now the baby. Do you want them exposed to Sodom and Gomorrah? Eugene, think of your soul. No, son, you need to seek a cure."

"I have no choice. There is no cure for me."

"You can't, or you won't?"

"Both."

There was a pause. Then Eugene continued. "Daddy, can't you or won't you accept me for who I am?"

"I won't allow you to contaminate this house. I guess both. I can't see a way to accept this."

"Then that's it, Daddy. I'm sorry."

"Eugene, son, we'll find you help. Churches have programs for this."

"No, Daddy. I know you mean well. I've struggled with this for a long time. But I now know that I am who I am and that's it. There's no changing it. There's no exorcism for this."

"Please, Eugene, give it up. If you don't, I can't abide by that disgusting behavior. I love you, but I can't condone this. I just can't. It's too repugnant."

"There it is. I can't change, and neither can you. Daddy, I never meant to hurt you. I'm moving to California. I've been thinking about it for a long time."

"California?" Mamma cried. "Why so far away?"

"I have a place to stay in San Francisco. And I want to finish my education at Berkeley. They have a good program for me."

"A place? What kind of place are you talking about?" asked Daddy.

"I have a friend who recently moved out there. He said I can stay with him until I get settled."

"I won't ask you if this friend is your lover. I don't wanna know."

Two days later, Chip drove Eugene and his two bags to National Airport. Daddy tried to comfort Mamma by saying, "All baby chicks leave the nest sometime or another," but I don't think that helped in the least.

Before he left, Eugene promised Mamma he'd get a place with

a guest room. When the time came to part, he added, "When I get a job and a place, I'll buy you a plane ticket so you can come out for a visit." She hugged him but couldn't keep her tears from falling. She held him close and buried her head in his shoulder as he tried to comfort her.

"I'm sorry," Chip said, "But we gotta go if you want to make your flight." Gently, Eugene pulled himself out of Mamma's embrace. His shoulder was wet through from Mamma's tears.

After he left, Mamma spent a day and a half locked in her bedroom. When she finally emerged, she moved through the house in her somnolent way: she spoke when spoken to, she cleaned and cooked, but her eyes were empty. May, unschooled and unaccustomed to Mamma's down moods, tried valiantly to pull her out of her malaise. I tried to tell her that it was no use and that what she needed was time, but she wouldn't be persuaded. "I won't give up on her," she told me a bit accusingly.

"Suit yourself, May," was all I said. The rest of us held our breath, were extra kind to each other, and waited for Mamma to find her own way back.

Part Thirteen

1975

CHAPTER FIFTY-THREE

FAST ENOUGH

After Chip spent a year in Vietnam, his contract with the US Army expired. He returned home, supposedly to figure out what to do next with his life, but it was taking him more time than we'd thought. From Nam, he brought back a liking for pot smoking. He obtained an entire pound of Colombian Red and had no intention of selling any of it. He wasn't smoking all of it, though. He shared a lot of it with Buddy, me, and his friend from Nam, Calvin.

Whenever Daddy got mad about Chip smoking so much pot, Mamma would say, "Just give him time, Jack. He's been through a lot. We have to give him time."

Chip continued to work in the garage, but he and Daddy didn't work together; they would each fix separate vehicles. Often, Chip would leave the finishing work to Buddy and take off for a hike in the woods or a long drive on his motorcycle.

On New Year's Eve when Chip left the house, he said he was heading to a party. He was gone for two days. When he got home, Daddy was in one of his moods. Buddy and May were spending the holiday with some friends in Ocean City and hadn't gotten back yet. That day, Daddy had a couple of hard-to-please customers, putting him in a sour mood. To top it off, he and Mamma had been arguing off and on for weeks.

It was best to stay out of Daddy's way and not antagonize him, but when Chip returned, he walked right into it. His eyes were blood red. I guess he was too stoned to register the dangers. Daddy growled when he saw him: "Where in the hell have you been, boy?"

"Out."

"I can see you've been out. Do ya think I'm an idiot? Out where?"

"Just out."

"Goddamn it, Chip. I asked you a question—out the hell where?"

"For Chrissakes, Dad, it was New Year's. I was out with some friends. They invited me to stay and the party just kept goin.'"

"For two days! What've y'all been doin'? Smokin' that dope, I expect. Hell, boy, I can't rely on you in the garage. You just take off or you're too stoned to do any real work. You can't even pick up a damn phone and call your mother to let her know you're not dead in some ditch somewhere. What's gotten into you? You've no business being out all night long."

"Why not? I'm a grown man."

"Don't you sass your old man! You hear me, boy? And if you're so damn grown, why the hell are you still living with your mommy and daddy? I'll tell you why, because you're too stoned to take responsibility and get out on your own two feet. A man takes responsibility for himself. You're goin' nowhere, and fast."

"For God's sake, Dad, lighten up, won't you? You've been to war, you should know. Nam was hell. War is hell. Have you forgotten? Pot helps me from going crazy inside my head. Back off and leave me the shit alone, man."

"You think I don't know what the hell war is? I fought longer than you did. I didn't use war as an excuse to dump my responsibilities or to start drinkin'. While you live in this house you will do as I say. It's my way or the highway. There will be no more pot and no more staying out all night."

"I've been paying rent. I'm an adult. I can stay out however long I want. You can't be ordering me around anymore."

When I heard Chip say that, I knew he'd he stepped on a land mine. Could pot and Nam make him forget where all the booby traps were in this house? This one was about to explode.

"The hell you can. This is still my house, you worthless bum."

"Worthless bum? My money isn't worthless. You have no trouble taking it. I pay on time each month."

"We don't need your paltry little rent money, and we don't need your mouth either."

"Great. You don't want me around? I'll move out, then."

And with that, Chip started marching up the stairs. But Daddy was right behind him, step for step.

"You want to move out?" He pushed past Chip and entered his room. He opened the window and started throwing out whatever he could grab. Chip's new stereo equipment went sailing out the window, followed by his books, clothes, and records. They all flew through the air before crashing onto the lawn below. "You want to move out? Yeah, well, is this fast enough for you?"

I went into my room, grabbed an old duffel bag that was kept in the dormer closet, and ran downstairs. I stuffed a heavy coat, gloves, and scarf into the bag. Then I went to the laundry and grabbed some of Chip's clothes. Next, I went to the kitchen and packed what food I could snag quickly. While Chip was gathering what he could from the lawn, I snuck out the door and went down the driveway toward the garage—out of sight of our house but within sight of his motorcycle. When Chip emerged from the side of the house, angry and upset, I yelled to him. He came down the hill toward me. "What is it, Charlie?"

"Here, I grabbed some stuff for you. What you don't take I will hide in the shed out back. You can pick it up when Daddy's at work. Come through the woods and he won't see you." Then I reached into my pocket and pulled out all the money I had in the house. "Here, it's all that I have on me. Meet me after school tomorrow and we can go to my bank and I can get you more."

He grabbed me and gave me a long hug. He packed what he could, then mounted his motorcycle. "I'll pay you back as soon as I can," he promised. I watched as he disappeared around the corner.

I told Mamma what I'd done that evening and how we'd said goodbye. "It's bad luck to watch someone go out of sight," she told me. "You might never see them again if you do."

Her prophecy didn't come completely true, but it was a long time before I saw him again. He didn't meet me after school. Instead he rode down to Houston, Texas. His army buddy, Sam, helped him get a job there. I got an envelope containing the money he'd borrowed from me, and we got a postcard telling us he had landed a good-paying job as a helicopter mechanic for the oil industry.

He sent me another postcard with a picture of the Alamo on it. He wrote, "I know Buddy won't write. He doesn't like to. You're the writer in the family. So I expect you to write and often."

And so I gained another pen pal. He called on my birthday, but Daddy answered the phone. Their conversation was brief. I was thankful for May and Buddy. The house would have been far too empty without them.

CHAPTER FIFTY-FOUR

BEWARE THE IDES OF MARCH

*I*t was early on a Saturday morning in mid-March. I was washing dishes, and Buddy, May, and the baby were down in the garage opening up the shop. Down the short hallway, Mom and Dad were sleeping in. The phone rang, and I thought it was a customer. Buddy frequently forgot to switch the business phone on in the garage, which left it to ring in the house. I sprang up to answer it so as not to disturb my parents.

"Good morning, Ward and Sons Auto Repair, how may I help you?" I answered.

"Hello, Margaret, this is Ben."

I was surprised to hear my uncle's voice on the other end. Usually, it was Martha who called. Instinctively I knew it must be something bad, and fear rose up in my voice. "Uncle Ben, this is Charlotte."

"Charlotte? You sound just like your mom."

"What's wrong, Uncle Ben? Is Aunt Martha all right?"

"That's why I am calling. I need to speak with your mother." I could hear his voice crack slightly as he spoke.

"Hold on, I'll get her." I placed the phone on the table and ran to wake Mamma. I knocked on their door harder than I intended and called out, "Mamma, Uncle Ben's on the phone. I think it's important. You better come quickly." Before I could pull away from the door, she swung it open dressed only in a thin nightgown, giving little protection from the morning chill in the house.

It wasn't long after she started talking to Uncle Ben that she began to cry. I ran up to my bedroom and grabbed a blanket and returned to wrap Mamma in it. "I'll pack a quick bag and will be down today," I heard her tell Uncle Ben before she hung up. It was at least ten minutes before she could tell me what was wrong. I waited in silence as she gained control of her sobbing.

"They've found cancer in your Aunt Martha's lungs. It's in her bones too. It's not good. They're not giving her much hope, or time. She's weakening."

"I want to come with you."

"You stay here and help out. You've got school, besides. I will send for you if it gets bad. We'll hope and pray she gets better. The doctors aren't always right. We must hang on to hope and prayer."

"This is my senior year. We're not doing much academically. I can talk to my teachers and do any work from Norfolk. I've got straight A's anyway. Even if I don't hand in anything, I will still graduate."

"You can be more useful here. You'll join me later. That will have to do. Now, I must tell your daddy. Can you tell Buddy and May, and then call the others?"

"Of course."

I joined Mamma in mid-May. I missed my prom, and graduation, though I was supposed to give the valedictorian speech. My teacher and mentor, Mr. Williams, read it in my absence and sent me a cassette tape of his reading along with a few pictures of the graduation and a condolences card. It seemed a strange way to end my high school career, without a formal celebration marking its passing. There were so many goodbyes left unsaid.

When I first saw Aunt Martha, I was stunned. Her transformation was shocking. She couldn't have weighed more than eighty pounds. Her skin was dry and sallow and her eyes nearly vacant. She'd rally from time to time but slept a lot too. There wasn't much left of the woman I loved and admired. I didn't cry during those pain-filled two weeks as we watched her slowly slip away. "You gotta be strong for your Mamma and Mr. Ben," Anna reminded me. So I sucked in my breath and held back my tears and focused on whatever task I could do that day to be useful.

Martha died on my birthday, the same day Robert Kennedy died. There was no cake or balloons for me that year. Instead, I helped Mamma, Uncle Ben, and Anna plan the funeral and wake. I was grateful for Eugene, knowing he'd look after Mamma. Chip arrived the same afternoon. Emma arrived with Granddad, who looked decades older than the last time I had seen him. Emma had flown to Philadelphia to drive down with him.

For so many years I had imagined being reunited with my only living sister. In each imagining, we had heartfelt, joyful, and honest conversations. And yet when I finally saw her, I had no words. Emma was beautiful with still-long wavy red hair shining like new copper pennies. She was tall and thin like me, though I was taller. Her eyes were green, and her complexion milky white. Like our mother, she was stunningly beautiful. When she saw me coming out of the house to welcome them, she flung open her arms. As I was held in her embrace, a floodgate of tears flew open. All the tears I'd been holding back gushed out as I fell into her protective arms like I was five years old once more. I sobbed until my body and soul had nothing left. I poured all of my grief into her caring arms.

The services were held at the Basilica of Saint Mary of the Immaculate Conception in Norfolk. I wrote a eulogy, but I was too emotional to read it. So Eugene read it, plus he added some words of his own. A few rows back sat the church members who had worked with Martha volunteering for church charities. In front of them were her colleagues from work, and then finally our family was up front. I sat between Granddad and Uncle Ben. Buddy and

May sat on the other side of Granddad. Eugene and Daddy were on either side of Mamma and Emma, and Chip sat next to them. I was struck by a sad irony. Mamma's wish had finally been granted: her whole family was under one roof.

Uncle Ben was resplendent in his naval uniform laden with a chest full of military medals attesting to his many acts of bravery, yet he seemed as defenseless as a small child as he wept quietly. The priest was somewhat new to the parish. He began his well-rehearsed burial sermon spoken over a woman whom he'd hardly known. Uncle Ben's cries began to rise as if in response to each of the priest's words. His body began to shudder uncontrollably as he sobbed—his devastation made painful to witness because we were powerless to rescue him from his crippling despair. This strong, commanding man was broken. No words, no matter how eloquently spoken, could have given comfort in that hour. Yet the priest persevered, pausing at times between Ben's heart-wrenching cries.

In contrast to Ben, Mamma stood eerily erect and silent as she stared vacantly and dry eyed down upon Martha's coffin. It seemed as if her deep reservoir of tears had been emptied long before. Daddy kept his arm around her shoulder, but she gave no indication that she was aware of his touch. Granddad appeared frail as he leaned on his cane and then on my arm for support. Buddy stood on his other side, ready to catch him should he stumble. I looked at Buddy and signaled to him. He immediately understood my silent communication and took Granddad's arm. Relieved of that responsibility, I turned to Uncle Ben and wrapped my arms around him. What little strength he had remaining evaporated at my touch, and he collapsed fully into my arms—I had to quickly spread my feet apart to keep us both from toppling over. The feel of his trembling heart broke open the dam of my own grief once more. We clung to each other in our unfathomable grief, drowning out the poor priest's final words.

There was no solace in them anyway.

Four days later, Aunt Martha was laid to rest at Arlington National Cemetery. It was a chilly day for June and a bit windy. Granddad had spent the night with us, and we picked Uncle Ben up from his hotel in D.C. and drove to the cemetery. In a caravan of three cars, we drove over the Arlington Memorial Bridge crossing the Potomac and into Virginia. Robert E. Lee's memorial rose up like some antebellum mansion staring judgingly down upon us.

We all gathered at the cemetery's administration building as the family and a few friends from Martha's time in D.C. gathered and spoke. Uncle Ben went over to meet with a cemetery director for instructions and to sign some papers. Eventually it was time, and we all stood at the curb as we waited for the hearse. We piled into our cars and followed the hearse to the grave site. Once seated near the open grave, silent and solemn pallbearers in starched uniforms marched in unison and removed the casket from the rear of the hearse. They carried the coffin to the grave site and placed it on a stand perched over the grave. In unison, they turned and marched off. Then a priest began the services. I was oblivious to his words and stared off into the distance.

Across a road were more rows of uniform white tombstones. In a neighboring field of the dead, another burial was taking place. This must have been a military person and not a spouse, for the casket arrived at their grave site in a caisson. The flag was neatly folded and handed to a woman sitting in the front row. Soon after that, there was a twenty-one-gun salute, indicating a decorated fallen hero was being laid to rest.

Our services were brief, and before I knew it, it was time to leave Martha down in the cold dark ground. I shuddered to think of her down there alone. Emma already had Mamma's hand. Eugene walked behind them. I took Uncle Ben's hand, and we walked to the car together.

Afterward we all met at a restaurant—and suddenly it was all over. It was time for Eugene and Chip to head to National Airport to catch their planes. As we stood in the parking lot saying our farewells, Uncle Ben turned to me. "I have something I have to tell you and your mother before I head home. I'd like to take you two out to dinner tomorrow. I must go to the Navy Yard in the morning. Will that work for you?"

"Yes, of course," I answered. "I'll let Mamma know."

Granddad and Emma stayed with us one more night. After breakfast they, too, took off for Philadelphia. Immediately after they departed, Mamma headed to bed, leaving Daddy, Buddy, May, the baby, and me behind. When Uncle Ben arrived, I couldn't get Mamma to respond. She just stayed curled up and mute in her bed.

"I'm sorry, Uncle Ben, Mamma's not up to going out. She's not feeling well."

"That's okay, Charlotte. She's been through a lot. We'll let her rest. What I have to share concerns you most of all."

Uncle Ben drove us over to Silver Spring, and we ate at Crisfield's Seafood Restaurant. "Martha liked this restaurant," he said as we got out of the car, explaining his choice. The restaurant didn't look fancy. There weren't any tablecloths on the booth tables but rather paper placemats with sketches and descriptions of a variety of fish. At Uncle Ben's recommendation, I ordered the crab-stuffed shrimp. "That's Martha's favorite," he said, as if she was just around the corner.

Uncle Ben asked me a lot about my studies, interests, and plans for college. Still, I wasn't sure why we were there, and I nervously rambled through a variety of topics as he patiently listened.

Then he told me how important my coming to care for Martha had been to her and to him. "The time you spent with Martha meant a great deal to her. She got to know you. I am grateful she had someone who loved her watching over her while I was away. You know, Martha and I both wanted kids, but it never happened for us. When I met her, she told me she wanted a big family. But life doesn't always work out as we plan. She's loved all of Margaret's children, but she was closest to you. During the summer you took care of her, she told me she finally knew what it was like to have a daughter's love. You gave her a precious gift. Now we want to give you one." He took a breath, reached for my hand, and said, "Martha and I want to pay for your college education."

I was stunned, and I wasn't sure if I'd heard right. "What? What did you say?"

"We want to send you to college. We know what a wonderful student you are and how hard you've worked. We've discussed it at length. We've decided to pay for all four years of your under-graduate tuition. However, if you can get some scholarships, we'll help with graduate school too."

"Uncle Ben, I . . . I don't know what to say except thanks. Shoot, thanks isn't near enough. I don't know what to say. I can't find the words. Are you sure? This is unbelievable."

"Yes, Martha was adamant, and I am happy to see her wishes performed."

"Oh, my God. This can't be real. Am I dreaming?"

"Your aunt had some ideas about colleges she'd like you to consider. For example, if you went to William and Mary you could live at our house. I am away a lot and I'll probably be transferred in two years. Still, it would be nice to have you in the house when I'm home. It's a bit of a drive to campus. She also mentioned Phila-delphia. There are many fine schools to choose from there and lots of public transportation. You could live with your grandfather and that would help us all, as he's getting on in years. Or you could go to University of Maryland or a D.C. school and stay at home. I know you're late applying for this year, but maybe you can sort something out. This gives you a lot to think about. I can help some with room and board, but if you could stay with family, that would sure help make the money go further. Keep me abreast of your college applications, will you?"

"Of course. I still can't believe this is real." I stood up and went to the other side of the table and slid in on the bench next to Uncle Ben. I wrapped my arms over his shoulders and kissed him. "I love you, Uncle Ben. Thank you. Thank you both."

CHAPTER FIFTY-FIVE

§○❖○℞

EXTENSION CORD

I don't know what made me follow her. The memory of events from earlier that morning are hazy, obscured by what came after. Conceivably, it was a sixth sense developed by years of living with the Zombie. Possibly it was something unconsciously seen in my mother's movements as she passed me on her way upstairs. In any case, something jarred a signal in my brain. As I sat in the living room, a fuse steadily smoldered, and unease began to grow as she ascended the attic stairs. Something impelled me to follow, I know not what. At first my steps were slow, as I doubted the need for action.

I was climbing the first few attic steps when I heard the chair toppled over. That's when the fuse was struck, igniting an explosive alarm in my head.

"Mamma!"

❖

Back in the fall, Mamma had been the happiest she'd ever been. She was filled with hope and anticipation of the holidays ahead. She was queen of her own home, and her mood was infectious. We were lulled into letting our guard down, thinking the Zombie had finally been defeated. But the Zombie wasn't gone; she was lurking in the shadows.

Since Thanksgiving, Mamma had suffered a series of separations, disappointments, and heartaches. Her palisades were breached by the steady departure of her children, and the final blow was Martha's death. It left Mamma utterly defenseless.

It was a Sunday morning in early August. Although I wasn't due to leave until the coming Saturday, I was packed and ready to move in with Granddaddy. I'd been accepted and given a generous scholarship at Saint Joseph's College. Both Mamma and Granddaddy were thrilled I was attending a Catholic school and would be living with him. I could hardly contain my excitement. I told them I wanted to get up there a bit early to find a job, but in reality I was eager to set out on my new adventure.

Buddy, May, and the baby were at a friend's place in Ocean City for the weekend. Daddy was stretched out on the couch. The television was on. I don't remember what we were watching, but it must have been on channel 9. A preview aired about that night's 60 Minutes broadcast. Daddy tried to interest Mamma. "Hey, Maggie, look. They're interviewing Judy Garland's kids tonight about their mama." Mamma was a big fan of Garland. "You want to watch it?"

But Mamma gave no reply. Daddy turned to me and warned, "Your Mamma had a hard night. She didn't get much sleep. Why don't you help her out and make dinner and clean up? Will you, my girl? She needs a bit of extra space, but she'll find her way back. She always does," he said comfortingly.

When I heard the falling chair, I raced up the final steps. There before my eyes, Mamma's feet were twitching a few feet above the attic floor. I rushed and grabbed her around her thighs, lifting her to get my shoulders under her bottom to support her weight. I must have screamed because Daddy came racing up yelling, "What's wrong? Charlotte, what's going on?"

I glanced up and saw one end of a brown electrical cord looped over the rafters and secured with a knot. The other end was tied into a rough slipknot. It appeared to have snagged along its rubber surface and thankfully didn't completely close, as a rope might have smoothly done around my mother's neck. Though her body was limp, I could feel subtle tremors that gave me hope I had arrived in time.

Silently, I thanked God that Daddy was here. But I wasn't prepared for my father's reaction—he froze when he hit the landing. Then a horrible sound filled the room. It was the same dreadful, wrenching sound I'd heard when the Murkowskis' garage burned down along with their youngest son. Daddy's screams made Mamma shudder and my knees buckle. I struggled to keep her aloft.

"Daddy, please, I need help." I twisted to see him better. "Please, Daddy, help!" Still, he stood transfixed as his screaming melted into sobs. His shoulders slumped. The blood rushed out of his face, leaving it looking like an ashen-gray death mask. My big, strong Daddy was broken.

"Daddy, please. Please, help me. Daddy, help!" I begged until he finally responded.

He sucked in his breath and grabbed my mother from me. "Quick, get the chair and untie your mother," he commanded. A nightmarish struggle ensued as I tried to untie the cord, but it was tight. My fingers felt like claws. The rubber had a grip. I could see red marks around Mamma's neck. I felt trapped and helpless.

Finally, I freed her. Mamma was coughing as Daddy carried her down to an empty spot on the floor. Before she curled up into a ball, we heard her say, "I'm so sorry, Jack. I'm sorry. I wasn't thinking. I didn't think about you."

I was shocked by what my Daddy said next. "Damn you to hell, Maggie. How could you do this to me?"

"Daddy, please, what are you saying? How can you make this about you?"

Staring down at her, he replied, "Your mama has put a knife through my heart."

"For Chrissake, Daddy, she just tried to kill herself, not you!"

He looked in my direction. His face was twisted with pain as he barked, "Your mama knows what the hell she's doing. God is my witness, I've tried. Damn it to hell, I can't do this no more. Goddamn it, Charlotte, she hung herself."

Turning toward Mamma, he said in a lower voice, "To hell with you, Maggie. You're too damn hard to love. I kept my end of the bargain and then some. I gave you my name. I broke my back for you and the kids. What have you done 'cept broken my heart? You took everything I got to give. But what about you, Maggie? You promised to keep your heart open to me. Seems I've been tryin' to knock that door open most of our married life. Well, Maggie, get yourself another patsy—I'm done. You just took the last piece of me I've got to give."

With that, he turned to leave. I was terrified. Daddy never made empty threats.

Mamma stirred, and cried, "Jack, I'm sorry. I just wanted to end it. Forgive me, Jack."

But it was too late. Daddy was halfway down the stairs. I called after him, but he ignored my pleas. I slumped to the floor and listened for sounds below. As he moved from room to room, I called out to him again and again, but he gave no reply. Mamma pulled herself into a tighter ball and started to cry. Fear welled up in me as hundreds of thoughts battled inside my head. What did Daddy mean? I was afraid to leave Mamma, afraid of what she might do. I was afraid of being abandoned and left to deal with her alone. Then I heard the front door slam. Daddy was gone. Where to, I didn't know.

Mamma and I remained as we were for what seemed an hour, though it may have been a handful of minutes. Her back was turned from me. Finally, I lay next to her, wrapping my arm around her shoulder as I whispered, "Mamma, you got to talk to me." But except for a few dwindling sobs, she remained silent.

As the minutes added up, I grew incensed at her silence. I tallied up all the years of living with the Zombie. Finally, I erupted: "Damn it Mamma, you don't get to hide out in Zombie land this time. How can you guys lay this shit on me?" I yelled. "Don't give me the silent treatment. I don't deserve this. I've had enough!"

I could feel myself losing control as my anger toward her silence mounted. "Damn it! Why aren't we enough? If you killed yourself, it would rip us apart. Think about us. I know you miss your sister, but you're not the only one. What about Granddaddy? Think about him. He couldn't live through another daughter dying. What about Uncle Ben? She was his whole world. Is he off hanging himself? No. And he doesn't have a family like you to keep him going. You have us. People die. Everyone dies. You're not the first to lose someone close. And you're not the first to have a dream implode. Martha said that most people end up living lives they didn't plan on. Damn it, Mamma. Why do you think you're so special? You've been given a lot, but you're too miserable to see it."

In frustration I screamed, "Either you talk to me, or I'll call for an ambulance. You need a shrink! I can't handle this on my own. Either you help me or I'll call the police. You should be committed. I swear, I mean it, Mamma. Either you talk to me, or I'll call an ambulance."

Still she didn't stir.

"Okay, Mamma. It's on you." Hoping the threat was enough, I started down the stairs, but she didn't make a move. Her silence ripped me apart and unhinged me. I should have called the police or an ambulance, but I was still a Ward. Wards don't ask for help, and we keep our dirty laundry well hidden. Instead I grabbed my bags, my purse, and my car keys. I was nearly to Baltimore before I thought about what I was doing. As I drove, I raged against my crazy family and cried. I felt terribly alone. But then I started to think about walking through Granddaddy's front door. He'd want to know why I was six days early. It was then that I knew I had to turn the car back around. How could I abandon his daughter and expect him to open his home to me?

Two hours after leaving, I pulled up to our house again. As I turned the doorknob, I was terrified of what I might find. But when I entered the door, Mamma came rushing from the dining room and flung herself into my arms. "Dear God, I thought I'd lost you too," she cried. "I'm so very sorry for what I did to you. Thank you for coming back to me."

"Come, Mamma, I'll make us some tea and we'll talk." I led her to the dining table, then went into the kitchen. I returned with a teapot, cups, and saucers and set them on the table. While pouring, I apologized: "Mamma, I am sorry I took off. It was just too much for me to handle. But this can't be swept under the rug this time. We must make some decisions. Things must change, starting with you talking. You should see a shrink."

"No, no shrink."

"Then you have to talk to me, and we have to make some changes. Things can't go on as before." She drank some tea but made no response. "I know you think your life has been a failure, but that just isn't true. You raised five kids and created a lovely home. No, it wasn't the success that you imagined as a child, but you've had many successes."

"Thank you. I suppose you're right. You're all good and capable people."

"You know, Mamma, I'm mad with Daddy. I don't understand his reaction. It's not fair he left me to deal with this. I expected more from him."

"Don't blame him. It's not his fault. Your father's a good man."

"I'm not blaming him for your actions. I blame him for his. How could he make this about him? How is walking out on your wife who just tried to kill herself, and leaving your teenage daughter alone to deal with it, being a good man?"

"I pushed him too far. I should have known that hanging myself was the worst way I could do it. It's because of his mother."

570

"His mother? Why?"

"She killed herself."

"Killed herself! Why, when, how?"

"She hung herself. What's worse, it was Jack who found her. It was a gruesome sight. She'd been dead for days. Your father has never gotten the image out of his head. I should have known he would think I wanted to hurt him cruelly."

"Why did she kill herself?"

"She was probably in pain and she was alone. It was after everyone she loved had either died or moved away. She'd taken a fall and injured her leg about six months before she died. When it didn't heal right, she went to a doctor. That's when she found out she had cancer. She didn't tell a soul. Your dad found out about it at her funeral."

"When was this?"

"Your daddy was at Walter Reed. The war was nearly over. After he was discharged as a patient and before he had to report for work, he got a bit of leave. He thought he'd surprise his mother and just show up. He regrets it to this day that he didn't call ahead. He thinks he could have saved her, but I doubt it. What difference would it have made, anyway? At best he would have only postponed it. When he got to Ashokie, he stopped at the local market to buy a few things to bring to the house. It was a Monday. The store owner said he was going to pay her a call after closing. He hadn't seen her at church on Sunday, which wasn't normally like her. But she'd missed a couple of Sunday services recently, so he wasn't too worried.

"When Daddy got out to the farm, the house was empty. He went out into the yard to look for her. It was then that he caught a smell. It got stronger as he approached the drying sheds. She was hanging from one of the rafters.

"He stayed in Ashokie for a bit to bury her and sell what was left of the farm and tools. When he got back to D.C., a letter from his mother was waiting for him. She must have mailed it just before she hung herself. Soon after that, he asked me to marry him, and I said yes."

"Is that partly why you married him, you felt sorry for him?"

"No, it was more the other way around."

"Stop speaking in code. Mamma, it's time to tell the truth. Family secrets are like cancer, they kill what's good inside. Now that I understand why Daddy acted the way he did, I'm not angry with him anymore. The truth lets me understand him. But why did you marry him? More importantly, why can't you love him?"

"That's not true. I do love him."

"You never look at him the way he looks at you."

"What do you mean?"

"When Daddy looks at you, you can tell he's proud you're his wife. I can't say the same for you."

"I love your father in my own way."

"Maybe we have a different understanding of love. Maybe it's language that's limited. We should have a different word for each variety of love. There's the love of a pet, love of music, or even chocolate. But then there is a love that means you put the other person first."

"Sweetheart, that's what a mother does—she puts her children first. Your spouse is your partner."

"Okay, what about a soul mate or best friend as well as lover?"

"You can't learn about love in novels, Charlotte. You must live it. What do you know about love? Soul mate? Honey, you can share an entire lifetime with someone, but you're still two very separate beings. Love is showing up even when it's hard."

"And maybe it's not killing yourself. I believe that if you love someone, when you look into their eyes you see your better self reflecting back at you because that's the way they see you. Do you do that for Daddy? Have you ever?"

"You're rather hard sometimes, Charlotte."

"I am just telling you what I see."

"That's the way you see it. Truth without charity is cruelty."

"How do you think Daddy sees it? I know why he married you, but why did you marry him?"

"That's personal."

"You're my parents. This involves me too. You just tried to kill yourself. We need to get this in the open. What made you choose him?"

"He was gallant, and he wanted me so. I knew he was a good

man."

"But you didn't love him."

"I wanted to."

We sat there together for a while, each consumed by our own thoughts as we sipped our now lukewarm tea. Finally, I broke the silence. "Mamma, what did Daddy mean when he said that he kept his side of the bargain? What bargain?"

"To marry me and . . . and . . ." she stuttered, "care for my child."

"Who, Emma? She's his child too."

"No. Emma's is not your father's daughter. That is my sin."

"Holy Christ Almighty. Now I'm getting the picture. No wonder you reacted the way you did when you learned about May's baby. Is Emma's father that man named David, the one who dumped you?"

"Yes. When I told him, he disappeared and sent me that awful letter."

"God, I can be so slow. I should have figured this out a long time ago. All the clues were there. I should've known Eugene was gay a long time ago, but I just never put two and two together. For someone who is supposed to be smart, I sure can be dim. Daddy really did his best, Mamma. It must really hurt when your best isn't good enough."

"I tried too. I really did, but we're just too different."

"Opposites can work."

"I don't know. But you're wrong about one thing, Charlotte. I do love and respect him, even if I've been lousy about showing it."

"What are we going to do now? I don't know where Daddy went."

"Only one place he'd go."

"Where's that?" I asked

"Cousin Charlotte's."

"So what are you going to do now?"

"I don't know. Your father meant what he said."

"Well, let's look at your options."

"What options?"

"That's just it, Mamma, you've got lots of options. You're always looking at what you don't have, and that has blinded you to all the good stuff you do have. You've had lots of successes too. You created a family, a home. We all love and support you. You have options. For one, you can stay here with Buddy and May. What do you think about that?"

"I'd be in my own home, but I'd end up taking care of the baby. Kind of right back where I started, don't you think? May has skills. She'd get a job quicker than I could, and that would leave me taking care of the baby to earn my keep."

"Okay," I said, "what about moving in with Emma?"

"Same thing but worse. They live in the middle of nowhere. I'd end up watching the kids, and it wouldn't be my own home. I love my grandkids, but I don't want to be a full-time nanny. No, that's out."

"What about living with Eugene? He has an extra bedroom and lives in San Francisco. There are lots of clubs there where you could pursue your music."

"No, honey, that music scene is not for me. I'm too old now, and I don't know how I feel about his living arrangements. He's living with Martin like man and wife."

"What about Chip in Dallas? It's a big city with lots of opportunities. You could go back to school and finish your nursing degree. You could do that in San Francisco too. You'd get used to Martin. Eugene is still Eugene. You are lucky—you have options."

"You're right about some things and wrong about others."

"Like what?"

"That all takes money, Charlotte."

"I've got money. I've been saving since my first dog walking job. I've got thousands, and it's all yours. I don't need it now that Uncle Ben and Aunt Martha are paying for my college expenses."

"I can't take your money."

"Then think of it as a loan. I won't need the money until graduate school, and that's four years away. I can't leave things in limbo, Mamma, and go off to college. I need this settled. In any case, just getting away for a while might do you a whole lot of good. You could go visit each of your kids while you figure out what your next step should be. What do you say? Wouldn't you like seeing Chip, Eugene, and maybe Emma and the kids again?

Wouldn't that be good for you?"

"I suppose that would be grand."

"Great. I will go and withdraw my money," I said. I grabbed my keys before she could put up another roadblock. "I'll be back in half an hour."

When I returned, I got scared. Mamma's car was gone. When I went inside, there on the dining table was a note waiting for me.

"Dear Charlotte," it said, "I've gone to bring your father home. Love, Mamma."

ABOUT THE AUTHOR

Irene Liebensfeld was a poet, writer, painter, ceramicist, gardner, volunteer, caretaker, and world traveler. She was fiercely generous and an inspiration to those who knew her. She was passionate about reading, photography, dance, languages, cultures, the Boston Red Sox, riding her bike, working in her garden, and, above all, her family. Irene's American family lineage goes back to the Mayflower and Cape Cod. Irene, known to her friends as Reeny, died of cancer on April 1, 2020. She left behind a husband, two sons, and a cat who live in Maryland. She lived her life with grace, kindness, and a generous heart.

Made in the USA
Middletown, DE
22 October 2021

50802388R00347